The Force of Such Beauty

no? . . . Barbara Bourland is skilled at finding the noir in the every day, and illustrating the mechanisms of control that keep us in our place."

—Molly Odintz, senior editor for CrimeReads

"This is not your grandma's fairy tale. . . . Influenced by the struggles of real-life princesses, Bourland's brilliant satire skewers the theatrics of power, excessive materialism, and economic corruption."

—*The Washington Post*

"Sharp, witty, and intellectually intense, Bourland's prose is a force to be reckoned with." —*Chicago Review of Books*

"Riveting . . . opens with the breathless escape attempt of a modern-day princess named Caroline as she endeavors to leave her marble prison once and for all. In the pages that follow, Bourland traces the path that plunged Caroline into such visceral desperation, revealing how swiftly 'happily ever after' can morph into a cage. What unfurls is a darkly relevant depiction of the ways in which societal power structures hinge upon the subjugation of the female body. Caroline's story submerges the reader in the depths of contemporary royal womanhood and only allows you to surface in those final pages as the tension builds relentlessly to a shocking conclusion."

—*The Millions*

" 'Happy ever after' is not all that it's cracked up to be. Barbara Bourland dismantles the conventional princess story in *The Force of Such Beauty* to explosively examine the real-life notions of fame, power, and womanhood."

—*Veranda*

"Engaging and powerful, telling an exciting and wrenching tale that is both timeless and of the moment." —*Baltimore Fishbowl*

"Knocked me out . . . This one is so imaginative and beautiful and had me gasping at the end." —*Montecito Journal*

"Fractures the familiar tale of 'happily ever after' and reimagines it with spectacular style, vision, and substance . . . Thoughtfully interrogates the trappings of marriage, status, womanhood, and power, while reading as vividly and compulsively as a thriller."

—Jung Yun, author of *Shelter* and *O Beautiful*

"*The Force of Such Beauty* is a dazzling spiderweb, a richly imagined, chilling spin on the girl-meets-prince fairy tale that scrambles notions of power and femininity. With a sense of spellbound dread, we're seduced along with its complicated heroine into a magnetic world of startling beauty and tragic costs."　　—Lauren Acampora, author of *The Paper Wasp*

"A fierce spin on the fantasy of marriage that is pacey, propulsive, and fun."　　—Ros Anderson, author of *The Hierarchies*

"A wayward girl is made a princess, and then? Luxury turns to boredom, fascination to fear, fame to thralldom, and love to betrayal. . . . Caro is no passive princess in a tower; she is smart, incisive, and achingly real. I couldn't put this book down until its explosive, heartrending, thoroughly satisfying ending."　　—Jennie Melamed, author of *Gather the Daughters*

Fake Like Me
One of *Cosmopolitan*'s
"Books You Need in Your Life This Summer"

"Bourland has an astonishing ability to write viscerally about art, culture, class, and landscape, for a work that's bound to be one of the summer's biggest crime/literary crossovers."　　—*Literary Hub*

"Layered, complicated, big, bold, and disturbing, like the large-scale oil paintings that are the unnamed protagonist's medium, Bourland has written a one-of-a-kind, modern-day Künstlerroman that deserves a place among the genre's all-time best."　　—*The Millions*

"Barbara Bourland's art-world thriller is both elegant and visceral . . . [and] imbued with the intensity of artistic struggle in a manner that resonates with the high stakes and sharp precipices of classic crime writing."
　　—CrimeReads

"In an art world where we're all supposed to be cool and ironic and cynical, it feels good to love a book so fiercely and personally, the way our narrator loves her paintings."　　—BmoreArt

"An impressively intelligent thriller . . . Expect insightful paragraphs about the creative process sprinkled among the propulsive mystery."
　　—Refinery29, "Best Books of June 2019"

"Meet 'art satire thriller,' your new favorite genre."
—HelloGiggles, "10 Best Books of June 2019"

"Roars with creative impulse . . . Part thriller, part performance art, and wholly revolutionary, *Fake Like Me* confronts American art culture with female bravado." —*BookPage*

"A satirical take on the contemporary art scene—smart, witty, and eye-opening. This gripping tale throws back the curtain on a world of secrets and intrigue." —Liv Constantine, bestselling author of *The Last Mrs. Parrish* and *The Stranger in the Mirror*

"Bourland expertly shines a light on the nature of female ambition and desire and the often-dark heart of inspiration. Readers fascinated with the blood, sweat, and tears of creating art will be especially rewarded."
—*Publishers Weekly* (starred review), a Best Book of Summer 2019

"Menacing, swirling, hypnotic . . . A haunting, dizzying meditation on identity and the blurred lines between life and art."
—*Kirkus Reviews* (starred review)

"Bourland has an uncanny knack for spatial description and relates artwork and every last thing in Pine City—half *Dirty Dancing*, half *Twin Peaks*—with pristinely observed color and feeling. . . . The deck stacked against her, the narrator tells the glitteringly compelling tale of her fevered summer and wisely reveals meaningful intersections of class, gender, and making art." —*Booklist* (starred review)

"The creative process confronts reality in this compelling literary thriller centering on art, identity, and deception, as told in Bourland's sharp prose. A must for those with an artistic bent, a sheer reading pleasure for all."
—*Library Journal* (starred review)

I'll Eat When I'm Dead

"Delectable." —*People*, May Picks

"A smart, satirical take on fashion and media that will have readers snorting with laughter." —*New York Post*

The Force of Such Beauty

A NOVEL

BARBARA BOURLAND

DUTTON

DUTTON

An imprint of Penguin Random House LLC
penguinrandomhouse.com

Previously published as a Dutton hardcover in July 2022
First Dutton trade paperback printing: May 2023

THE LIBRARY OF CONGRESS HAS CATALOGED
THE HARDCOVER EDITION OF THIS BOOK AS FOLLOWS:

Names: Bourland, Barbara, author.
Title: The force of such beauty: a novel / Barbara Bourland.
Description: [New York] : Dutton, [2022] |
Identifiers: LCCN 2021031434 (print) | LCCN 2021031435 (ebook) |
ISBN 9780593329344 (hardcover) | ISBN 9780593329368 (ebook)
Subjects: LCGFT: Novels.
Classification: LCC PS3602.O89272 F67 2022 (print) |
LCC PS3602.O89272 (ebook) | DDC 813/.6—dc23
LC record available at https://lccn.loc.gov/2021031434
LC ebook record available at https://lccn.loc.gov/2021031435

Dutton trade paperback ISBN: 9780593329351

Printed in the United States of America

1st Printing

In memory of

my grandmother Pearl

Now

THE LAST TIME they caught me at the airport, I panicked.

The decision I'd made an hour earlier, to drive straight there like any regular woman and buy a ticket, was more than reckless; it was unequivocally selfish. In my defense it happened in a moment so opportune that I can still taste it on the sides of my tongue. How was I supposed to resist?

The service were drinking, their collars loose, cigarettes and playing cards between their fingers. I knew where Marie kept the keys to her rusted Peugeot. She was vacuuming upstairs. Everybody thought I was passed out for the night. It was so easy. Really—I almost did it just to see if I could. Is that a good enough explanation? As I was tying my scarf, a gift from his mother, the one with the interlocking Fs, over my prickling scalp—and the plastic of my sunglasses was cold against the tops of my ears—the hem of my car coat scratched my legs—sweat dripped into my underwear—it was a moment of, there's no other word for it, *possession*. I was *possessed*. I was Sleeping Beauty moving toward the spinning wheel, eyes dilated, holding my breath; I was Linda Blair in a nightgown screaming on the M Street steps. I was every woman who had ever seen a way out, and I grabbed at the moment so desperately that I left my children behind.

I wedged a manila folder into the bottom of my handbag and made it through four courtyards to Marie's car, parked on gravel, near the stables. I shifted it into gear, feet working the pedals from memory, left hand skimming the door until I found the plastic handle, rolling the window down. I pulled out of the inner driveway, punched in the code at the iron gate—it was agony, watching it open, so slowly, on its own time, doing what its motor always did—and with an inch to spare, I ripped out onto the road, barreling hard on first gear until the engine whined. I found the sweet spot in the clutch and shifted again. The little Peugeot jerked into second, and then third.

A grin stretched across my face.

Fifteen minutes later I was on the coast road, cutting a diesel streak to the commercial airport. Or rather, I hoped I was, because I hadn't driven a car in years. It was west, I thought, and so I drove west. When I spotted a sign reading *Aeroporto,* I jerked the wheel and followed it.

It took forty-five minutes to get there. I kept the window down the whole time.

Wind blew against my veneers; wet beads of mascara dripped into the hollows below my eyes. My bare legs splayed out beneath my coat. The four remaining hairs on my knee, the ones that refused to submit to the laser, were long, from weeks of growth. I yanked one out—I remember that. But mostly I remember the air: sputtering diesel; the sweet-sour scent of Marie's car from her gardenia perfume and menthol cigarettes, fat Italian ones that she hoarded (how long had it been since I had discovered the smell of something as personal as someone's else's uncleaned house or car? years! *years!*); and the damp, salty smack of the ocean.

I don't recall much else, besides a vague awareness of the fact that as I drove the sun went down and the headlights had to be turned on. I don't know if there was traffic; I don't think there was. I simply drove along the road with everyone else, another animal in the pack, heading northwest. And then I was turning into the parking lot, taking a ticket; pulling onto the ramp; nosing the dirty bumper into a space. I do remember wanting the parking job to look really nice and even. I didn't want Marie to be worried about her car, or to feel mistreated.

I tucked her keys into the visor and headed for the terminal, passing through the airlock of automatic doors into the cold embrace of the airport. It was the physical embodiment of white noise, a place designed to move you along. In bejeweled lilac mules, I fell into step behind a family. My coat was a blue cotton rimmed with white piping, lined in pine-colored silk. The scarf was still knotted very tightly around my head, though my wig was falling off in the back. My sunglasses, cream with olive lenses, took up half my face. Naturally, no one else was dressed like this. They had on zip-away cargo pants and money belts and leggings.

I made it halfway to the counter before they shouted my name.

"Caroline!" a girl's voice sang. Phone out, eyes wide. "Caroline!"

Me. My name.

Other people turned. I saw it forming on their lips. My name, my name, my name.

With that, my caper was over. The world went from black-and-white—an adventure of my own making—right back to smooth-motion, full-color, high-definition hell.

I died inside.

Caroline, Caroline.

The sound of my name, my name.

I turned right and walked my corpse to the nearest desk. Stared blankly at the logo, a tinny noise ringing in my ears, like there had been an explosion—and there had, I had died, it was the sound of my death—while the desk agent, a polite young woman with thick eyeliner and a patterned hijab, stared back at me.

"Your Serene Highness," she said, "it is a pleasure to serve you today."

She did not look me up and down as I would have done if our roles were reversed. Now I realized she must have spotted me long before we spoke, when people called my name as I loped across the cold tile floors, tan legs stretching for miles beneath the short coat, a head taller than everyone else. I opened my mouth to reply and paused instead to breathe. The desk agent said nothing. In this moment, I was supposed to say something, obviously. To explain why I was there, make a plan, move forward. On the departure board Riyadh was the only word I saw.

"Riyadh?" I said, almost a question, asking her permission: *Can I go there, now?*

"That flight departs in seventy-five minutes. It's possible. I will try?"

I nodded. "One first-class ticket to Riyadh, please," I said, hiding my shaking hands by rooting around in my bag for my credit card and old South African passport. I noticed, as I handed it to her, that the passport would expire in three weeks.

To her eternal credit, she didn't question the dates and began typing furiously, polished nails pummeling the plastic keyboard in front of her. *Etihad*, read the sign behind her.

In retrospect, it wasn't a *terrible* idea. Saudi Arabia, like everybody else, invested in our real estate; Finn was away with our airplane. Taking a trip to Riyadh on the national airline of the UAE could be a political act, if you squinted. And if I could get on a flight—any flight—I could make it to London, where Zola might help me.

I kept looking around, thinking the service would emerge from the cracks in the walls. They'd corral me like a bull, spear me with knives wrapped in ribbons as I roared in pain. And like a bullfight, everyone would watch and nobody would do a thing about it.

Days before our wedding, they caught me here. I didn't see it coming that time. I thought I could go home. But they cornered me, swallowed me up. It wasn't a scene. Things were different then; easy to destroy the security footage, pay off the gate agents. Sure, there was a nasty rumor, but nobody had proof and that was all that mattered.

Today, the service were nowhere to be seen.

"Mmm," the desk agent uttered, peering at the screen. "You are confirmed on Flight Fifty-Six. The plane will have a layover in Doha and continue on to Riyadh. It will be most convenient. You do not need to exit the airplane at the layover. I have a very nice suite for you." I thought she might pick up the phone, but no. She looked at me with expectant satisfaction; she had done something for me, and I was supposed to say yes.

Yes. I nodded and said thank you. I think I did, anyway. If I didn't: *Thank you. Thank you, wherever you are. You were the first person to help me in so long.*

She swiped my card; I signed the slip. She did not ask about baggage—another polite gift. The ticket stuttered out of the printer and she handed it to me. I took off my sunglasses and stared up at the security camera. *Hello,* I mouthed, knowing it would be watched, again and again. *Goodbye.*

Off I went through security, hands shaking, waiting with every step to be taken aside—but nobody stopped me. Alone for the first time in years, I walked to the gate. After my ticket was scanned, I walked directly onto the plane and was cocooned in a private room. A butler wearing white gloves brought a glass of champagne. He offered to take my coat. As I wasn't wearing anything beneath it, I shook my head. He opened a compartment and pointed to a pair of silk pajamas folded inside. I nodded, thanked him, and curled up into a ball.

Six hours later, Doha. Another hour, in the air again. Soon we landed in Riyadh. By then the pajamas were beneath my coat, covering my legs. The cashmere blanket from my chair was wrapped around my head, doubled and pinned in place with safety pins from the travel kit. The butler's white gloves covered my bleeding cuticles.

The round door of the 747 popped open with a depressurizing sigh, and as was customary, I was the first to exit the plane. Three steps into the Jetway and I found myself in the waiting arms of the service. Of course. I knew they would be there. *When had they left me alone, ever? Never. They would never.* Roland took my passport from my hand, and then my purse, with its folder of purloined paperwork. He held my arm as I walked up the Jetway. Otto and Dix—they were always together and looked so haunted, so *Germanic*—flanked us from the rear. I followed Roland automatically.

It was a relief, in a way. Before that day, I hadn't been alone in public for seven years. The service were as normal as being dressed. I was, at my core, truly convinced that I'd be harmed if they left my side— security will do that to a person, persuade you of their necessity. Especially if you cannot be incognito, which I was clearly incapable of being. I still cannot believe I went to the airport in underpants and a cotton car coat and a goddamned silk scarf with my husband's family name on it. It was so foolish.

I am such a fool.

◆   ◆   ◆

Seventy-two hours later, toting a new suitcase stuffed with overpriced luxury goods, a syringe of Ativan coursing through my veins, I returned to the marble prison that held my children, my husband, and me—and then I cried for two days. Jane and Henry (Jeanne and Henri to everyone else) came to my bedside. Their seashell fingernails pressed into my arms, their plump fists wrapped around hanks of my hair, but I did not look up or stop crying. I pushed them away. *Go to nanny Lola,* I told them. *Maman is having a bad day. Maman is sick. You mustn't see Maman like this.*

They went. They always did what they were told.

I was ashamed, and I was heartbroken.

It was the closest I'd come to freedom since before we were married. The mere proximity to the knife-edge atoms of independence sliced open my scars, remaking me into a seeping wound.

I lay in bed for two days. I grew infected with sorrow and regret and hatred.

For two days my children cried, and I did not go to them. I was destroyed. I was destruction itself, a specter of their mother, a rotten wraith left in her place.

Yet, I was—*finally*—on my way to becoming something else.

◆ ◆ ◆

Three mornings after my botched escape, the curtains were drawn. I opened my eyes to the sea, winking and foaming like it always did, under a bright blue sky and a thoughtless yellow sun. Puffy clouds floated across the horizon like nothing was wrong. I yanked the curtains shut.

I started the bath, turning the gold taps to scalding, easing under the shower's thundering spray. I stayed there, water drumming on my skull until scrubby nubs of dead skin began to flake off, a snake shedding herself. I wrapped myself in yards of towels, then coated every inch of reddened skin in coconut oil, scooping it from a porcelain bowl. I removed the chipped polish from my nails with a linen napkin. Wasteful, of course, but I hated how cotton crumbled in acetone, found it viscerally disgusting. I was accommodated in so many ways, you see; I was precious, I was to be accommodated. When my nails were clean, the stained napkin went into the trash; when my skin was dry to the touch, I abandoned the towels in a heap on the floor. I strolled naked to the red lacquered room where they kept my clothes.

It was more holding area than closet. Thousands of dresses passed through there, encased in thick plastic, to be worn exactly once before being shipped to the archive with a sheaf of notes about what my body had done and said and who it had stood next to while wearing that dress. A pretense at accountability. The clothing that stuck around was more day-to-day but still absurdly impractical, appropriate only for a life of luxury in this seaside nation. I tucked a white shirt into seersucker shorts, laced up white cotton tennis shoes. Then I drew a net skullcap over the damp remains of my thinning hair and looked for a wig.

I chose a blond ponytail with heavy bangs. I ran a brush through the ends, my other hand gripping its foam skull, and walked to the window. I pictured myself opening the casement and falling out of it—past the blue cliffs and into the sea, the ponytail still clutched in my fingers. I saw the golden locks washing ashore, tangled, the lacy scalp catching on a rock, coated in blood.

Then I remembered my children.

The foam neck broke in half. I looked down to find it was my own hands that had strangled it into cracking. My own hands that chose everything.

I pinned the wig in place. Blinked mascara, dusted a garish swirl of blush over sunken cheekbones, then opened the door and stepped out into the hall.

The service waited there for me, but they are shadows; they have no depth, I don't acknowledge them. I swept down the hallway, gliding across the silk carpets, past the floor-to-ceiling windows dating from 1355 and their heavy draperies, past paintings of other dead women and children, turning to the right and the left and then up some stairs to the playroom where my Jane and Henry spent their days.

The playroom had everything. There was a dollhouse version of the Talon, the prison we lived in, constructed out of the very same marbles, silks, now-extinct woods, and so on, with lifelike figurines of the families who'd lived there, including us. There was a zoo-quality habitat for a family of bunnies. There were two iguanas, both named Jerome. There was a wall of bookshelves with every children's series on the market—*Five Children and It* and *Narnia* and *Redwall* and *Boxcar Children* and *Ramona* and *Fudge* and *Harry Potter* and so on—and a textured globe, mountains raised in relief and rivers glassed in with blue water, that spanned three feet across, dotted with tiny flags to mark the places that Jane and Henry wanted to go. There was a miniature drum kit and a babies' baby grand piano, and a costume corner where the children could "shop" for Jane- and Henry-sized commissions from the costumers for the West End production of *Wicked*.

The playroom had absolutely everything, but at the moment, it didn't have my children. I texted the nanny: *Where are they?* She did not reply. I texted Marie, the housekeeper whose car I'd stolen. She did not reply, either. I wondered if she had been fired. I returned to the hallway and asked the service about my children.

"They are not here, *signora*," said Otto uncomfortably.

"Where did they go?"

"They are with *signore*," he replied. "You must contact him."

It was no use fighting with Otto. He was made of stone. I pulled out my phone and called Finn, who answered with a chilly "*Pronto.*"

"Where are my children?" I asked, trying to sound reasonable, and failing.

"We took a trip," he said simply, choosing not to tell me where. "They'll be with my mother until you are well again." He paused, let out a long sigh. "You upset them very much. Henri especially."

I felt pure shame, a hot burst of it, exactly as he intended. "There's really no reason to take the children," I said, but it wasn't convincing. "Everything is perfectly fine."

"You're so selfish," he whispered. I closed my eyes. "How could you leave them? To go to Saudi Arabia, of all places?"

Because I feel that much hate, I did not say. "What difference does it make?"

"Why do you talk like that?" he asked, painfully—a rhetorical question I refused to answer.

"You're so comfortable with the conclusion that our life doesn't belong to us," I muttered, the words thick, my tongue numb. Dr. Sun had told us that it was possible to transition into a near-vegetative state as a result of depression. *Watch her speech patterns,* she'd said to my husband, like I wasn't in the room. *Make sure she is awake at least twelve hours a day. Measure her cognitive abilities at least once a week. You don't want her to atrophy.*

Atrophy.

My favorite word: the destruction of a trophy.

"You don't get to resent this life," he sighed. "This is how it has always been. It is a gift."

I tried pleading. "Please don't take my children."

"We're giving you time to get well," he told me.

"I am well. I'm fine," I said, but it didn't sound right. I wasn't fine and we both knew it.

"I love you, Caro." It was the first time he'd said he loved me in months—no, years. "I'll be home tomorrow. I'll spend tonight with them."

"I love you, too," I replied automatically, and then I hung up.

A moment later he sent me a text: *Please eat some lunch.*

I don't doubt for a moment that Finn once loved me very much. I'd loved him, too—and I loved my children. I think about the days after Henry stopped crying, when we lay in bed with him and read aloud, Jane sleeping between us in her blue jumper. We drank black coffee and listened to the birds. The room smelled like baby shampoo and sweat, like sour milk and coffee. Is there a greater love available to us? Does God give us more?

The problem is not how much I loved them.

The problem is that I loved them at all.

There were days when I, too, thought all of this was a gift. When he gave me a yellow diamond ring and sailed me into this port; when I crossed a green velvet carpet toward a decrepit priest, ready to wrap us in the bounding lines of matrimony; when he locked a collar of pearls around my neck, led me down a balustrade like a dog on a leash, and we waved to ten thousand people; even when he shut the door on me for the first time; still, throughout all of it, this had looked like a gift. This life had looked so special. I would have done *anything* to keep it.

Now?

Now I would do anything—*anything*—to leave.

1

Then

ONCE UPON A TIME I was the fastest woman on earth. I was extraordinary: a rising mountain and the tiger who jumped over it like it was nothing. I ate when I was hungry and slept when I was tired, and in the hours between, I ran. My body was a vessel for my willpower; my body put other people to shame; my body proved what was possible.

When I think about that body, I'm homesick in the pit of my stomach. There is no word special enough to describe its singularity. It was carved from volcanic rock and brought to life with the force of a thousand goddesses. It carried me to the top of the highest wooden box and placed a golden weight around my neck, and it did all of that by the time I was twenty-one years old.

◆　◆　◆

Two hours, twelve minutes, eight seconds. 2:12:08. The record for the women's marathon, set at the Sydney Olympics in 2000.

❖   ❖   ❖

Then my body failed.

Eighteen months later, as I trained for Athens, home of the marathon.

❖   ❖   ❖

Of course it failed.

No body could stay that perfect, so exhilarating in its function, not for long—definitely not a woman's body—and so nobody, except me, was surprised when my hips grew another half inch, spreading overnight, changing the rhythm of my legs while I slept. The next day, running faster than I had ever run before, I was *flying*. There was a rocket attached to me, wind at my back and wings on my shoes. My body reached its apex, nearly. I was so close to ecstasy.

It would have been a two-hour, ten-minute marathon.

Would.

Because of my hips, the traitors that spilled out in the night—because of them my gait was newly wrong, incorrect, and because of that, I stumbled.

❖   ❖   ❖

I didn't know what was happening because I'd never been incorrect in my life. My gait had long been the very definition of the word. But what goes up must come down, and so at long last the mechanics failed me—one loose joint—my leg extended—I didn't lift it high enough—it didn't leave the ground—so I tripped, I stumbled—and as I put my weight on it again, the femoral head of my left leg, the ball that sits atop the thighbone, rotated forward and out of the socket of the hip, separating itself from the wall of my iliac bone.

Yet I was still in motion. I stepped again, right then left. I landed with all my force and speed, on this extended series of bones that had moved out of their home, and with that pressure the femoral ball ripped from the hip socket completely. My leg couldn't hold the weight. It crumpled along all the joints, limp and ragged. It folded like a piece of paper in your hands.

My cheekbone hit the ground first. It shattered in what they later called a spiderweb fracture, a beautiful name for what it was, which was the particular, craterlike demolition of the left side of my face. The rest of me followed, and with that, my running career was over.

◆   ◆   ◆

The reason for my fall, the diagnosis: osteoarthritis, a degenerative condition that wears away the cartilage between the joints. Arthritis. It's banal. The very word *arthritis* conjures visions of the elderly eating muesli with gnarled hands, struggling to open plastic bottles. A disease for the frail, not the strong. It can be inherited, or in my case, acquired as a result of severe overuse.

I remember the doctor telling me that the spread of my hips was minor, normal even. It wouldn't have been a problem for a regular woman. But my athleticism itself had made me fragile. In a cruel twist, the degradation of my legs was what in turn had helped them, over the past several years, fly so fast. The joints of my body wore out, became loose enough to respond to my muscles first—stronger and more powerful than my tendons—and so the tendons absorbed nothing, and the padding around my bones wore away, like frosting being scraped from the side of a bowl by a spatula. The pummeling force of eleven years and thousands of miles had rounded out brittle hollows that could separate and break with that one wrong step.

Combined with a sharply decreased rate of bone accretion throughout my adolescence—resulting from hormonal deficiencies caused by low weight and excessive exercise—I'd been decaying invisibly, and inevitably, for years.

I was in pain, of course. I was in pain all the time. But how was I to know that pain was *too much* pain? I thought everyone was in pain. I thought everyone's joints felt like they were on fire, because running is hard. I thought every muscle cramp was supposed to be agony. I thought it was normal—because of what it paid! I could go anywhere; I could do anything. Wasn't that supposed to cost you something?

I never knew what the cost would be until I paid it, because I was never examined deeply enough; I never had an MRI or even an ultrasound, because I never complained. All I did was run.

2

I MET HIM in the American hospital where they rebuilt my face. Scoria Vale was a yellow stone mansion on a rolling green hill with private rooms and one staff member for every patient. It had a movie theater with velvet seats; espresso machines and baristas; a sit-down restaurant with white tablecloths; and heated saltwater pools. The towels, made especially for healing skin, were the softest things I'd ever touched. My sponsor, a large athletic wear company, paid for it. I could not have afforded it on my own, but we'd signed a contract. Two years remained. I had to reappear, unbroken, to sell hats and shoes, moisture-wicking underpants. *Not right now,* they said, *of course, it takes time. Your hip will take time. But the way your face is, it's fixable, we know that it is, so let's fix it, let's move on. You'll be glad. We can do extraordinary things in America.*

There had been an emergency surgery in Johannesburg, where my fall happened, to remove the largest shards of bone from my shattered face and to deposit my hip back in its useless socket. Forty-eight hours after I arrived at Scoria Vale, this work was undone.

The leg was first. They scraped away the powdery excuse for bone that made up my left hip socket and exchanged it for a brand-new ceramic version, drilling it deep into the wide smile of the remaining ilium. Then the surgeons lopped off the pointed femoral head that sat atop my thigh-bone like a spike and fastened a smooth metal ball in its place. The socket and ball were joined with a plastic spacer. I was sewn up and placed in traction to await my next operation—the one on my face.

The spiderweb fracture was a mess. Scoria Vale's plastic surgeon, with her wall full of credentials, warned that it might take multiple in-terventions to repair. The spider had already begun to build a web of scar tissue inside the cheek, she explained, and would likely form a se-ries of lumps and depressions that she thought I would not want to keep.

She recommended a metal implant to stabilize the bone, then a later procedure to smooth it all out.

Fine, I told her. Turn my brain off again. Cut me up and put me to rights.

That was surgery number three.

Over the following month, my body knit around the implants. As predicted, the lumps began to appear in my cheek, as fragments of bone lodged beneath the muscle began to find their way to the surface. During that time my face looked as if it had cellulite—two square inches of fatty clefts and deep red pockmarks that ran from beneath my left eye and sagged to the jawbone.

I grew fond of that glorious, dented patch. I held my hand to it every waking hour, palpating the surface like it was braille. My *shatter*. In addition to the mere bizarre fact of its physical existence, the shatter was proof, absolute proof, of how my body had failed me. Everything else was the invisible shadow, the ghost of my arthritis. No one could see the degrading interiors of my bones, or the smooth new materials of my hip socket, but this—my teammates could see it, my government could see it. I could see it in the mirror and feel it under my fingertips whenever I needed a reminder. The shatter was right there, all the time. There was no denying it. The shatter *proved* that something had hap-pened to me.

I should have kept it. Fought for it. But I didn't fight anyone then. I did what I was told.

◆　◆　◆

He was just another resident at first: a clean-shaven man in silk pajamas and a waffle-weave cashmere robe. They all looked the same, the other patients at Scoria Vale, as though money incubated within them naturally, like a virus, and released from their pores. Cleanliness and comfort perfumed their sweat and atomized into their personal stratospheres. The patients of Scoria Vale—they were dewy with it.

He was easy to notice. Tall and broad, brutish even in a wheelchair, with a nose and jawline hewn from a tree. Handsome, but oversized. I assumed from his body that he, too, was an athlete. Hockey or discus or some other big-man sport. He was always reading, a book or sheaf of papers fanning from a folder, a pen held between his teeth. I don't remember the first time we made eye contact, though we must have exchanged a greeting or two. There were only thirty or so of us at a time. But we didn't speak at all until he graduated from the wheelchair to the cane.

I had a cane, too, which I resented and relied on constantly. It was a slow recovery to get there; months in traction, my leg up in a series of pulleys and supports, a catheter holding me in place, until an X-ray finally proved that leg and hip were back in functional alignment, and I was given the cane. (This was early, still, when I thought that the worst thing that would ever happen to me was being unable to run.) Mine was hospital-issue steel and rubber. His was made of carved wood so delicate that it looked like it would snap under his weight.

"Is that for show?" I asked one day when he passed by, hobbling down the paved path toward the rose garden with a pink newspaper tucked under his arm.

He paused. "The newspaper?"

"Your delicate cane, eh," I said. "It's a real twig. *Shame.* Couldn't they give you something *lekker*?" (*Shame*, a catch-all word for displeasure; *lekker*, meaning good, or better; my Johannesburg words, now long gone.)

"It's plenty strong," he said, looking me squarely in the eye. He sounded American.

"You're a big guy." I shrugged. "It's not stylish but the hospital one is safer." I raised my cane and handed it to him. He took it, gave it a hard lean, and nodded.

"You're the girl who fell," he said suddenly. "The athlete."

It took a moment to recognize myself in that description. "Yes," I agreed. "I'm the girl who fell."

"Something happened. Hip dysplasia?"

"No. Dogs and babies have that. Not women."

"I'm sorry. Painkillers," he explained. "I'm not at my best."

"Me neither. I'm on them, too." I tapped my bandages. Then I pointed to his right leg, encased in a complicated brace. "Bad break?"

"The leg is healed—it's the knee. I have to walk on it. It's—it's awful," he admitted, grimacing. "Makes me want to quit."

"You can't quit your own body," I said automatically, the rote recitation of an athletic mantra.

"Don't I know it."

"Hockey?" I asked.

"What?"

"Your sport."

He had a very brief look of shock before answering. "I'm in business. I'll go back to it."

"Oh," I said, realizing. I tapped the bench. "*Chair.* A game, not a sport."

After a beat his eyes brightened. "Yes. Chair. *Cher,*" he punned, French for "expensive," rubbing his fingers together.

I sang a few bars of Cher—*If I could turn back time!*—until he laughed.

"You're quick."

I raised my eyebrows. "I'm the fastest woman on earth."

"I'm Ferdinand," he introduced himself, holding out his hand. "Call me Finn."

I shook it. "I'm Caroline Muller," I said. "Don't call me Muller. I'll take off running. Then we'll both be in trouble."

It was supposed to be funny, a joke, but he looked sad.

"Let me buy you a coffee," he said. A real joke, because coffee was included. He took a step—and faltered. I held out my arm for him. Even with months of stillness my body was more powerful than his, than the orderlies', than anyone else's there. He hesitated.

"It's okay," I encouraged him. "I'm strong."

He leaned on me, a little at first, until it was clear that I could hold his weight. He was extremely heavy. Nonetheless—I was happy to be able to help someone besides myself. We shuffled to the coffee counter and ordered the same drink: double espresso with a glass of water and a lemon rind.

"They don't care about caffeine," I said, dropping the rind into the coffee, along with a teaspoon of water. I still spoke in shorthand, then, as though everyone knew who and what I was talking about: *They* were the Olympic Committee. "It's my most important addiction."

"Mine's near-death experiences," he joked, doing the same with his water and lemon.

"It's good we know ourselves."

He put his glass of water on the counter, downed his coffee, then reached his arm out for mine again and I took it. He pointed to a bench and I walked us there in our five-legged gait: cane, leg, legs, leg, cane.

"You *are* strong," he marveled.

I snorted. "This is weak."

"Will you run again?"

"No," I said. "Not like that."

"Because of your hip?"

"The hip will heal. It's the joints. I ran for so long and so hard that I developed something called osteoarthritis. I lost bone density, too, but that'll come back. For the joints to heal—I'm not allowed to run. Not if I want to get better."

"What will you do?"

"I don't know. I've never thought about anything else."

"University? You look the right age."

"I'm twenty-two," I said. "But—I'm like a plant. I've been repotted. I can't fit in the old container. I left school in year nine. Sitting still, memorizing facts . . . I couldn't."

"Education is carceral," he agreed. "I couldn't be in school again, either."

I didn't know what *carceral* meant. Bereft of a reply, I stared out at the lawn, where more of us, these ghosts in our fuzzy robes, were dotted across the emerald grass like bits of lint. My hip throbbed—a low burn—and I shifted position, tensing and releasing my legs and rear. But there was no comfort to be found.

"What does everyone else want? For you, I mean," he asked. An interesting question. I wondered how he knew to ask.

"For me to coach. To find the next great South African Olympian. But it's not like running was something I engineered. What do I say? 'Be as fast as I was'?" I shook my head, imagining it: walking the trails behind the next generation, red dirt building up in my orthopedic sneakers, working its way into the mesh, between the laces, under the grommets, over days, months, years. I would never forget how Johannesburg's red dirt felt as it broke my face. I'd found it in the cracked stumps of my teeth when I came to, licking it away as they loaded me onto the stretcher. "It's not for me." I shifted again. The pain persisted.

"Is that the whole of it? Being fast?"

His interest was a welcome distraction. "Yes. Speed is physical, but mental, too. You've got to"—I searched for the right word—"*eradicate* any self-consciousness, to find your best. But you can't teach that, either."

"The ability to extinguish the inner voice."

"Right," I agreed, surprised. "Exactly right." I wondered what happened to make him understand that, how important it was to compress the part of you that second-guessed, again and again, until it was small as any other cell.

"Where do your friends live? Cape Town? Johannesburg?"

"I'm from Johannesburg. Most of my teammates are away, training. My friends from school mostly moved up north, to Europe. One of them has a spare room in her flat in Lisbon. She invited me to come visit. I might go stay there for a bit. I'm supposed to walk it off," I said, rubbing my hip. "Walk it off for a whole year. I've seen the whole of Johannesburg. I think I've run every street. I'd like to go somewhere new."

"You should. Have you been to Portugal before?"

"I have, but I only saw the track, and the airport."

"What was it like?" he asked.

"The Lisbon airport?"

He blinked those hazel eyes—liquid gold and honey brown, flecked with green, big and almond, a cat's—and smiled. It was a sunbeam, his smile. Under its warmth the pain in my hip dissolved like an aspirin in water. "What was it like to run? Like you did."

"Animal," I replied. "I didn't know 'existential dread,'" I deadpanned, making air quotes around the phrase, "until I got here. That's what the therapist calls it. I didn't know time like I know time now. Running kept everything at bay."

"To win, then. What did that feel like?"

"Which time?" I asked.

"The big time," he said, nudging me with his elbow.

"Oh, *that* time." I returned the nudge. Our upper bodies, caught in the net of each other, waved back and forth. "I did the route a couple weeks before. Five miles in there was a hill I was absolutely dreading, because on my practice run I lost speed. But then six, seven miles went by and I realized that I hadn't even noticed it. The power of perception," I said. "I knew what was happening from that moment on. It was my purpose."

"You make it sound so simple," he observed gently. "Very blasé."

"I don't mean to be. It meant a lot." That record-setting run paled in comparison to the one that had caused my fall. Both runs meant everything to me. Neither would ever happen again.

"You're being a little bit evasive, I think." He pushed, refusing to let me avoid the true meaning of his question. "I know *you* know what I'm asking. I'm sure everyone asks it."

"People ask a lot of different things."

He snorted. A flutter of irritation evaporated off him. "What is it truly like," he asked, "to be the unequivocal best at something? To receive hard proof that you deserve a gold medal?" He managed to ask this in a way that came across as empathetic instead of combative.

But I loved to spar. "Why should I tell you?" I avoided his eyes and focused instead on his wavy hair, cut close at the sides by the Scoria Vale barber.

He solidified a bit, sat up taller, anchoring himself to the bench. "Because you want to." One part command. Two parts flirt.

"You won't like it," I flirted back. "People never do."

"Then I guess we'll never speak to each other again," he said slyly, another sunbeam shining from his great big face. I laughed.

"Fine. Okay," I said, throwing up my hands. "The truth is: It's disappointing."

"That cannot be true."

"It is."

"I don't believe you. It's the record. The most explicit form of competition. You're better than everyone else in the world."

"That's the trouble. *It's not about being better than other people.* Running is about the feeling of your body executing everything perfectly, an edge up on other people, yes, but on *yourself* above all. It's touching God, when you do it right. Someone felt it before me, and they'll feel it after me. That was—it was—I don't know. There's not even a word for it."

"A link in a divine chain," he offered. "Not one word, exactly, but . . ."

"Yes." I looked at him curiously. His broad face was open and understanding in a way that no stranger's had ever been. "That's . . . exactly right. I wanted to have—and to *be*—as many links as I could. What I found was that one was . . . not enough."

"Is there a new record?"

"Not yet, but . . ." I trailed off, swallowing two or three times, until I got hold of myself. "I was supposed to run next year in Greece. On *the* route. The first route. It's the anticipation that drives you. It's a tragedy when it's over." I frowned. "I wanted that run."

He turned to face me, and as he rotated, something hurt. A tear fell down his face, but he didn't bother to wipe it away; he let it be, dripping down his chin, onto his robe. I liked that. I liked that he was unembarrassed.

"It must be hard to accept," he said.

"Probably," I snorted. "I haven't done it yet. I don't even believe it, I don't think. I'm angry, I'm bargaining, I'm depressed, but I'm definitely not accepting."

"I know what you mean." He rubbed his leg brace.

"How did you hurt your knee?" I asked.

He didn't answer at first. I wondered, for a moment, if he was the type of person who expected a lot from others but gave nothing in return. In my brief experience, people routinely expected me to give. They were interested in me. I was an object of attention and had to live up to their interest—but they in turn had no experience in being objects, and so if I expected the same from them, they invariably failed to deliver.

"I drove a car into the side of a tunnel," he said in a scratchy voice that came from the back of his throat. "The woman I was with. She died. The police report said the brakes failed, but . . . I'm sure I . . . it was my fault." His face lost all color as he looked to the ground. I watched his tears fall directly onto the asphalt.

"Did the police blame you?" I asked.

"No. They were certain it was the brakes." His face contorted in distress—lips parting, breath ragged—and I wanted it to stop.

"Was she important to you?"

"I barely knew her," he admitted after a moment. "Somehow that makes it worse."

I found myself reaching for his hand and grasping it. He squeezed back, raised his head, and we gazed into each other's eyes. Rimmed with red, lashes matted and wet, pupils dilated, his golden eyes betrayed a depth that was experientially new for me. I knew exactly what was happening to him—the intensity of the suffering, the scale of it—as though I were feeling it myself. It was the strangest thing. In him I saw reflected all the disappointment and hurt I'd carried since the moment I first tasted the red dirt of the track in my broken teeth. It was so comforting to find him, another person who truly understood how powerful I was before, and how weak I was then, and it must have felt the same to him, too.

He needed help. All I could give was the one thing I reminded myself of all the time. "One of the most important lessons that I learned from running," I offered, "was to expect pain. I *expected* it. If you try to get rid of it, you'll lose your mind. When it happens, like it's happening now, you have to coexist with it."

"Coexist," he repeated, using his right hand to brush the wet from his cheeks. "Then what?"

"Move on," I said with a shrug, gesturing toward the forest that stretched out in front of us, the leaves a wild tapestry of yellow, orange, and red, that famous American fall. "I've never stopped moving long enough to think about whether or not I'm happy. This is the first time I've been still. It's unbearable . . . to live like this, doing nothing but reflecting. I don't want to accept this. I want to do something else. I want to forget about it. Even if I can't run anymore—I won't sit still, not ever again," I said firmly. "That's the honest truth. This sitting still business is killing me. I think it's killing you, too."

His left hand was still in my right, my narrow, girlish fingers clamped tightly around his heavy palm. Surprise shaded his face. "I never tell anyone the truth," he said suddenly.

"Why not?"

"I guess . . . I don't have anybody to talk to."

We stared at each other, falling down a rabbit hole, dizzy with it.

I can't believe that we said those things to each other—but we did. There I was with bandages over half my face and a brace around my hips, and he was this enormous man—not fat, *enormous,* a wall of meat—leaning on a spindly theatrical prop cane, tears running down his rugged face. We were a mess, together; telling the truth, together.

At that moment, a woman walked by, another patient in silk pajamas and a waffle-weave robe. She was hidden: eyes behind sunglasses, hair under a turban, neck wrapped in bandages. Yet even so bundled, she billowed with glamour, softening the air. She nodded to my friend and he nodded back. I felt their nod, anticipated it before it even happened, because, I think, it was more than acknowledgment, actually. It was knowing. They knew each other from somewhere else.

And so it was that we were pulled from the intimacy of our confessions by this stranger's passing by. Though he did not remove his hand from the claw of my grip, we were cut away from each other in that moment, our rabbit hole turned upside down and opened to the sky.

"Do you know a lot of other people here?" I asked as she drifted away.

"I've met some before. Yes. She's an actress," he said, uttering her name below his breath. I shrugged. "No?"

"I don't know things like that—films and things. Or I haven't. I guess I will now."

"What did you do in your off time?"

"Oh gosh," I said, sounding young. "I read, but it's not part-time, being an athlete. I ran and worked out and got stretched and ate and slept. Pretty boring. What do other people do?"

"People your age? I have no idea."

"How old are you?" I asked. "You don't seem old enough to say that."

"Thirty-two," he admitted, "but I feel old. And there's a big differ-ence between twenty-two and thirty-two."

"For some people, perhaps. I'll be twenty-three in a few weeks."

"What are you reading?" he asked, indicating the book in the pocket of my robe.

As I reached for the cover to show it to him, I let go of his hand. A perfectly natural end to our moment of closeness, though I regretted it as soon as it happened. "It's about a spy named Modesty Blaise."

"Is it good?"

"Good enough," I said wryly. "We're all junkies here, anyway. I've read the same chapter three times. You? You always have books, and papers."

"I read the papers for work. For pleasure I've been reading a biogra-phy of Frida Kahlo."

"Who's that?"

He gave me a searching look—apparently again it was something I should know—and again I shrugged. I'd left school at fourteen to train full-time, completing my diploma with the help of a lenient tutor, and was unembarrassed about how little I knew about the intellectual world because my success could only come at the cost of one or the other.

"I told you. I'm a dropout."

"Frida Kahlo was a painter," he explained. "She had an accident, like you. She looks like you, sort of, in the way she stands. Bent steel. I'll lend it to you when I'm through."

I didn't think of my fall as an accident, and it was strange to hear it described that way. The doctors never called it that, either; only "your fall."

He winced. "Speaking of pain," he said, waving at a nurse. She came by and handed out pills. We took them, grateful for the relief.

Silence descended after that; neither of us seemed to be able to speak. Our hands were apart, and I didn't know how to put them back together again. I read my book, and he read his pink newspaper. When I felt my eyelids grow heavy, I excused myself to my room for a nap.

He was not at dinner. I sat alone that night with my plate of chicken and vegetables. I thought about asking where his room was and stopping by with the Modesty Blaise book—I was nearly finished with it—but my after-dinner dose of pills made me drowsy, and so I did not seek him out.

In the morning he was nowhere to be found. Nor the next day, or the day after that.

He was gone.

The remaining period of my recovery was a blur, but the memory of that extraordinary conversation did not fade. It was so sharp that, if it hadn't been for the letter, I might have thought I dreamed it.

3

THREE WEEKS after my friend disappeared, an orderly brought me a large envelope. It held a sheet of linen paper thick as a tablecloth. In exquisite handwriting—heavy but controlled, like him—he'd written:

> *Dear Caroline, You might be the strongest person I've ever met. I hope your recovery will be swift. I look forward to whatever you do next—it will surely be as singular as you are—and hope to see you again someday. Stay in touch. Sincerely yours, the man with the silly cane, whom you inspired to keep moving when no one else could (Finn).*

In lieu of a return address, the envelope bore a stamp of three medieval towers, tiny pennants fluttering on their spires in an imaginary wind. Circling them were the words *Pax—Fortuna—Fiducia*. I struggled to define them through the painkiller fog. *Pax* was . . . "peace," *fortuna* was . . . "fortune," and *fiducia*, I assumed, meant "fidelity." I'd never seen the symbol before, and I couldn't figure it out. *A company, perhaps. Whatever his business was, his* chair? *He sounded American,* I thought, recalling the tilts of his vowels. I meant to ask someone, but then my pills kicked in fully, knocked me back. I set the letter at the bottom of my suitcase for safekeeping. *Stay in touch,* he'd written. I wanted to. I would figure out how once I was lucid.

The next day, surgery number four extracted, liquefied, and blurred the shatter into a round, high cheekbone, something I'd not had before, and replaced my broken teeth with implants, veneering the others to match. Before, my face had been innocent and flat—small mouth, big eyes, oval shape—but now the left half belonged to a stranger who was mature beyond belief.

To make it even they added an implant to the right side—the fifth and final surgery—and then I was another person. Two dimples lingered in the hollow of my left cheek when I smiled, the shatter's only evidence.

◆　◆　◆

I spent my final month at Scoria Vale in physical therapy. The exercises were horrible; tiny repetitive movements to try to build up muscles used for standing and supporting, not for running. The bulk of my body evaporated further still, the armature of my self dissolving entirely. I was left inside someone long and lean, a watercolor of a person in place of a photograph. My hair—which had always been pulled back tightly into gelled ponytails and buns—was allowed to hang straight. I cut a fringe on it for the first time. I wrote a letter to my parents, expressing that I didn't really want to take a coaching job at home, and included a Polaroid photo from the doctors. I expected them to be disappointed, but my father said he was glad to see me looking so carefree, and then he signed off with a big X and told me to do something useless for once. My mother said I looked like Jane Birkin. She said that I didn't have to come home, not if I didn't want to. She reminded me of Johanna Van Niekerk's offer of an open room in Lisbon and encouraged me to write her.

Hanna, as we called her, the daughter of my mother's friend, was someone I was close to but didn't know very well, rather like a cousin. Our mothers met in the early eighties through the United Women's Organization (a local faction of the FEDSAW, the Federation of South African Women), a group that worked in opposition to the apartheid government.

To be clear, my parents were not extremist, aristocratic, or even eccentric. Born of immigrants who paid a violent price for the sins of their fathers and grandfathers—my father came to Joburg from Namibia, my mother from Rhodesia, and their families from Germany and England generations before that—we were the tail end of a fraying braid of colonial middle managers and hardscrabble smallholders. My father, Rainer, uneducated but strong, worked in the Johannesburg gold mines. My mother stayed home and took care of me. We lived modestly. All their extra money went to my athletic career. In theory we could have stayed focused on our own lives, and our own lives only. But in practice, under apartheid one was either a revolutionary or a fascist. There was no middle ground. It was normal, even in our small life, to be affiliated with revolution. And so—the UWO.

My mother, Harriet, worked for them as a volunteer secretary, doing endless typing, her single office skill. Other work was mostly hosting gatherings, talking over coffee and cigarettes, trying to persuade the other white people they knew of one thing or another. Hanna's parents had done the same. As children we'd spent hours together during those meetings, playing pretend in parking lots, in strangers' gardens, helping domestics fold someone else's laundry. She was a sunny child, creative and slightly weird; whatever she was doing in Lisbon was probably interesting. I hadn't seen Hanna since the year I dropped out of St. Margaret's. I suspected my mother had intervened and generated the invitation, but I didn't mind. I was just happy to have somewhere to go. Somewhere to go and, as my father put it, be useless.

For Johannesburg was not a comfortable place to be at loose ends. My athletic colleagues were away, training up in the mountains of places like Colorado and Nepal to build up their red blood cells in the months before the Olympic trials. School and family friends like Hanna had taken full advantage of our generation's opportunity to leave South Africa and see the cultures kept from us for so long. My teenage running partner, a girl called Zola Mbatha, had relocated to London the day she graduated from Wits, enrolled in law school, and claimed she would never go back. South Africa was dead, Zola insisted. I called her a pessimist when she said it—I had so long romanticized our revolution, was so *proud* of my post-apartheid government as I ran in Mandela's name—but Zola was right. Apartheid ended, but the money didn't change hands and neither did the land. All the same people were still rich, and all the rest still poor. The laws were fresh, but the circumstances remained, in so many ways, the same stale, airless oppression.

And there was the question of our home itself. For eleven years, since my first race, my body had been the most important thing in my parents' house. I was an animal, a machine, that body, that prize, that winning streak, and then suddenly I wasn't. How could we live the same life—in the same house, it was still three of us—without our North Star? I couldn't bear it. Johannesburg would always be there, I told myself.

I decided to take Hanna up on her offer and purchased a one-way ticket to Lisbon.

◆ ◆ ◆

Scoria Vale lived up to its reputation. When I left after five months, I was beautiful—beautiful like the yellow stone mansion, like the velvet seats in the movie theater, like the other patients. The bulk of my muscles had faded away. Whoever I was before was gone, and she'd been replaced by big cheekbones. My eyes, once so feral and driven, turned hollow. When one of the orderlies put mascara on my lashes and lipstick on my mouth, I looked like a movie star, haunted and delicate. It was so different from how things were before, when I had my body.

The day before my departure, an orderly had tucked a glossy

magazine beneath my bedspread and said with a wink, "Someone left that this morning. Saved it for you."

I thanked her for what I thought was a general kindness. Maybe it was simple as, I was a young woman and the orderly thought I would want a gossip magazine. But maybe it was specific. Looking back, sometimes I wonder if he mailed it there.

I wonder about everything. I don't know anything.

As I waited for the airport taxi, I thumbed through the pages, my mind half turned off by the content, until I discovered a photo of my friend from the lawn.

Prince Ferdinand Fieschi of Lucomo (Finn to friends) was seen strolling the Riviera last week with his family, after a six-month recovery following a fatal crash in Genoa. His signature vintage Fiat, gifted to Finn on his sixteenth birthday, slammed into a tunnel this April after the brakes failed in a freak accident. Finn's left leg was broken in multiple places, including his knee. His fiancée, Lidia Antonelli, the 28-year-old kid-leather heiress of Firenze, was killed instantly.

I read it over twice. The stamp was not a company. It was a country: Lucomo. I realized, too, that he'd shared a secret with me: The woman they called his fiancée was in fact someone he barely knew. I meant to request his forwarding address from the desk, but before I could, the taxi arrived. In a flurry of activity, I was bundled into it and sent out into the world, to make my own way.

◆　◆　◆

The airport was overwhelming. Bursts of noise and smell, colors and shapes, were disorienting to senses that had for so many months known only the green lawns of Scoria Vale, the smooth white of its linens.

My period had recently reappeared—I'd only had it a few times before I started clocking real mileage—and I could feel it lurking now, ready to push its way out, my swollen flesh clutching every ounce of water it could find in a hapless defense. I felt skinless, certain that everyone could see how fragile I'd become. There was evidence all around to confirm this paranoia: People—men, mostly—stared openly as I checked in for the flight.

I walked to a sundries shop. Several men trailed behind, hovering as I bought a bottle of water. I made eye contact with the nearest one. He licked his lips, yellow eyes running over my skin, my hair, my legs. I lowered my head and walked off, trying for the first time in my life to make myself small.

In the security line, the officers pulled me aside. In a corner, where no one could see, under the guise of scanning the metal of my implants, one cupped the edge of my bottom as he searched my leggings and the other let his hands linger on the line where my breasts met my ribs. I endured it out of shock. Men had never done such things before— not to my other body. When my body was a vessel for my willpower, men watched but never dared to follow, never dared to speak, never dared to let me see them leer. They never touched me. Not with my piercing eyes tracking them, not with my neck rippling, teeth bared. My body once made men ashamed of their own weakness. Now—I was the one who was weak.

On the other side of Scoria Vale, the heads of men no longer lowered. Instead, they raised, they turned, lifted a foot, kept pace, and touched me without my permission.

They treated me like everyone else.

4

FRECKLES, GREEN EYES, Chiclet teeth, blond hair sticking every which way: I knew Hanna immediately. She leaned against a metal railing, filterless cigarette in one hand, colorful paperback in the other, scanning the faces but not registering mine. My face, once oval and flat, had been overtaken by two doorknobs, practically. I was told they were raised four-tenths of a centimeter but it felt like inches; I could see my cheekbones when I looked down.

I poked the book's cover by way of hello. A Mills & Boon romance.

She did the tiniest of double takes, the same thing I did every morning when I brushed my teeth in front of the mirror. I touched the left side, a nervous tic, and ran my fingers down the scar that lined my hair and jawline, where they'd pulled the dimpled skin away.

"They did a nice job, eh." Hanna winked, giving me a hug. "You're a stunner."

"It's weird." I blushed.

"You're beautiful," she replied firmly. "Like fairies came in the night and blessed you with a gift." She pulled on her own straw hair, plainly wishing someone would do the same to her.

No, you don't, I thought, thinking of the men in the airport. I nearly said something but didn't want to sound like I was complaining, so I swallowed it and said instead, "It hurts, getting redone. How do all those WAGs tolerate it?"

"Morphine and the promise of a nice house," Hanna cracked. In a tumble of knees and elbows, she looped my backpack around her pointed shoulders and barreled toward a taxi. "Caro, scoot. We'll barely make lunch."

"You're in school here, is that right?" I asked as we piled into the stuffy backseat. "Studying buildings?"

"Technically I'm at Magdalen, doing a DPhil in architectural history."

I had no idea what "maudlin" or a "dee-fil" was but assumed the latter was some type of diploma, so I nodded.

"Ergo"—she waved the Mills & Boon—"cathedral-based pornography. I've taken this term and the next to research my thesis, on the rebuilding after the earthquake. I practically *live* in libraries. Every time I check out a new stack of books I think my hymen grows back another layer. But there's lots to do here. Don't worry. *You'll* keep *plenty* busy."

She kept on, pointing out this building and that building and *oh there's a good Mozambican place by the gardens, you'll love it, it's like home.* I kept on bobbing my head in agreement as the fearless breeze of Hanna's verve blew through me, taking with it the sour creep of my travels.

Fifteen minutes later, the taxi crunched to a stop at a grand building. The exterior façade was disintegrating, the limestone streaking at the corners, but it was nonetheless very imposing. I followed Hanna up several floors of slippery marble steps to the apartment, a sprawling set of rooms that hadn't been renovated since the seventies. It had a kitchen, a dining room, a formal living room with a long terrace, and three bedrooms, the smallest of which was now mine.

"Technically it's Rally's apartment—well, Rally's grandmother's apartment, not that *she*, the grandmother I mean, lives here," Hanna was saying, opening windows to let the air in. "She ought to be home. RALLY!"

A slight girl, with fluffy brown curls and a wide smile, emerged a few moments later. "Hanna, *don't* yell. It's tough on a sensitive flower like me." Her accent was British, the wispy country type, made from teacups and rosebushes and ease. "You must be Caro," she said.

"Yes. Hallo."

"I'm Raleigh Griggs. We're perfectly late to lunch, if you're hungry. Drop your things, I'll be just a sec."

I stepped into my new room. A narrow bed, a nightstand, a dresser, and a crooked lamp, all scratched and dented, all marvelous to me. Abuzz with the promise of this new city and new life, I rooted through my bag for deodorant and a clean shirt, then stood by the door, toes tapping.

"Troops out!" Rally bellowed, and then the three of us were bounding down the stairs. We made it just in time to a café on the square, where a limp waiter droopingly informed us that we had but two minutes to order. Rally and Hanna then blasted a whole string of poorly pronounced Portuguese in his direction. The waiter scribbled it all down and disappeared.

"I think you asked him for an Easter ham," I joked.

"It'll be food, at least," Hanna said, satisfied.

"Caro," Rally said, lighting a cigarette. "What are you in for?"

"A job. Any kind will do. I'm a hatched egg, sans nest. Let me know if you have one."

"You've got a visa?"

"From my sponsor. Another eighteen months or so left on it."

"Fabulous. Loads of time. Statistically, most athletes don't quit until it's too late to start again. You're twenty-two. Easy."

"Twenty-three now."

"Pish. I won't hear any whinging," she said playfully. "It's no tragedy to medal at an Olympics. I barely got a first in history."

"I set the world record." I smiled. "A bit more than a medal."

"All right, enough bragging." She waved her cigarette in dismissal. "So. First thing is that you've simply got to meet everyone. There's a group of us going to the beach this weekend. Simon—I think he's from your way, right, Hanna?—anyway, he's got a house up there. We mostly play cards and bad croquet and wander into the sea and try not to drown."

"Cards I can play. Croquet, never."

"Peachy." Hanna and Rally grinned. "We'll tell the gang."

"I really do need a job, though."

"Jobs are horrible," they said dismissively, before bursting into laughter.

"Jinx," Rally said, pressing her finger to the tip of Hanna's nose.

"You've had a *trauma*," Hanna insisted, swatting Rally's hand away. "You absolutely must have fun."

"Hard agree," Rally chimed in. "Look, rent is one hundred euro a month and due a maximum of two weeks late. Does that work?"

"It works."

That first weekend was a thrill. Seven of us holed up in a dilapidated stone house, five minutes' walk over the wild dunes from the Atlantic Ocean. Six of us played a poker tournament, while Pieter, the seventh, sat around drawing in a rather graphomaniacal way. Rally, Hanna, Simon, Beni, Duarte, and Lenore had all met through university; together they'd traveled on gap years and Interrail passes, done Indonesia and Thailand, New York, San Francisco. Every city I'd run in, past all the bars and restaurants, shuttered against the daylight, they'd been through at nighttime.

At the beach, we swam in a line out past the breakers. I got ahead and had to be called back by the lifeguard. On the hot sand, coated in sunblock, the group chattered about other beaches they'd all been to, in Spain, Greece, Morocco, France. Moonlit parties at Ammoudi, cliff diving at Oia, surfing in Martil, getting kissed in Banyuls-sur-Mer. Just *hearing* the names made me feel cosmopolitan.

After that weekend, I didn't start drinking or anything, but I did start going out, staying up late, looking at the sky, meeting people. I spent my days walking. It wasn't running—nothing would ever be running—but it was forward motion. I walked a minimum of fifteen miles a day, gaining and descending a hundred stories in a few hours. I marched through every neighborhood in Lisbon, past the airport, even. When I ran out of suburbs, I walked across the massive bridge over the river and started in on the other side. I stopped in every place I was allowed, drinking in museums and palaces and castles because I had only ever seen the outsides of such things, passing them as I ticked off my daily mileage. At night, I went wherever I was asked.

That was how I fell in—I made it easy for them to collect me, to have me around. *Caroline Muller, she's in our set,* they said chummily to people they wanted to impress at parties. *She's all right. She's a good sport.*

◆ ◆ ◆

Though I managed to join up with Hanna and Rally's crowd without doing much of anything—initially I simply stood around, and they let me—over time I realized that I did a lot by simply *being different*. I was markedly different from them. They—*they*—*them*—which is to say, everyone my age who *hadn't* been an Olympic athlete—*they* had all begun going out as teens, taking weekend trips, seeing the world, while I went to bed by sunset and managed my protein intake. *They* went away for school and university. *They* had jobs and apartments and lovers. *They* knew politics and quoted poetry and philosophy, and to me *they* seemed very worldly.

I know now that I must have glowed for them. I was a flower in a greenhouse, unsullied by the air that everyone else was forced to choke on. Worldliness has its price—cynicism—which I lacked, almost wholly.

As to my obvious scarcity of general knowledge, I wasn't dumb.

Merely specific. I knew what it was like to play in the Mediterranean with my fellow track-and-fielders, our hard bodies colliding with each other like we were seals, before we were challenged by the swimmers to a footrace in the sand. I knew what it was like to get naked on a top bunk in the Olympic Village with a man who looked like an actual Greek god—then to do it again and again and again until you were separated three days later, tugging at the sleeve of your tracksuit at the airport, medal around your neck. I knew all kinds of things. But they were private and impossible to explain.

So—I didn't. I listened, instead, to what everyone else had to say; I asked questions; I was curious. I laughed easily because their jokes were new to me. I fell into their world the same way I'd been falling into every crowd since I'd met Hanna that day at the airport: effortlessly, and without apparent consequence. In that state of weightless listening, months flew by.

◆　◆　◆

Soon I had my first real heartbreak. It happened in the Alfama, that neighborhood on the river where the minuscule streets turn into stair-cases and back again with the rounding of a corner. It was my favorite part of the city, the place where all the buildings, frescoed plasterwork pastels, looked like frosted cakes. All the streets were patterned in white and black cobblestones that turned frictionless in the rain. I'd fallen in love with Lisbon by then, and I was also suddenly, desperately in love.

It's funny now, though it was awful at the time. Christian had floppy hair and wore flat useless sandals and his father did something in ship-ping. A minor British aristocrat whose family owned, among other properties, a deteriorating castle up in Sintra, he never picked up the check. Several years ago I saw him at a state dinner. He'd become red-nosed and fat-bellied. His wife lactated through her dress while he put his hand up the skirt of a defenseless waitress. I winced to think of those nights in Portugal when I would sit across a barrel from him in a dark bar, watching him order an extra-dry white port in fluent Portuguese before cracking a joke in Spanish, with my heart stopped because I thought he was so glamorous. I really did—I sat there at twenty-three and bit my lip and prayed for Christian to look my way.

He was my first prince, I suppose, but he was a shabby prince, his castle crumbling, his flock made of sheep and a few elderly villagers. I could never have predicted when I met him that I would become a real princess of a real castle someday—that I would be sitting in a tower, brushing my golden hair and praying for escape.

I'd been there for six and a half months at that point, though it could have been a day, or a year; time was a bowl of milk. Every night was some six-string variation on a bohemian melody. The night of my heartbreak was a late dinner on three long tables pulled together. Candles were stuck in empty bottles of Porto and wine rings overlapped on mismatched tablecloths. There was a narrow balcony everyone gathered on to smoke cigarettes. Christian was out there, looking over the city, flirting with someone who wasn't me like he'd done every night for the past ten days.

The girl sat across from Christian at dinner. I knew right away that he would leave with her. She was younger than me, nineteen or twenty. Portuguese and beautiful—the thick eyebrows an asset on her. She was elegant, too, far more grown-up than I, in a silk blouse, pale blue trousers, and a delicate gold cross. Her clean fingernails, filed into perfect half-moons, drummed onto the table over and over while Christian flirted with her shamelessly.

The Christian of Lisbon, young, lithe, magnetic Christian, before his belly popped and his nose went red, was a sight to behold. He could tune his entire body in to other people. It was like he was a radio and you were the frequency. This focused him into a beam of light, and so whatever life lurked beneath, thin or shallow as it may have been, became suddenly dynamic. He touched you like he was invited, finding places to graze with ease, the inside of an elbow or the top of a hand, lingering on you until you lingered back.

The first night I'd met Christian, at a very similar dinner over in Bairro Alto, he'd flirted with me that way. I did not understand how insincere it was. It hit me like a ton of bricks, a ton of those little square white cobblestones, burying me beneath him, beneath Lisbon. He insisted on walking me home. He held my hand. I let him come up to the apartment, let him pull the straps from my shoulders—let him see the impression left behind by my once-extraordinary body. The look on his face made me feel powerful again—he was so slightly afraid of me— and so buoyed I kissed him and devoured him and ran my hands along his legs and arms as he fell asleep.

In the morning, I honestly thought that we were in love.

Christian snored gently on his back, floppy hair splayed out over the linens. Quivering—a heartbeat with legs—I snuck out to the market and bought an armful of fresh oranges. I cut them open and juiced them by hand, scraping away the meat and squeezing out the pulp with my fingers.

When I returned to the bedroom with two glasses of juice, my Christian was gone. Christian was physically there, pulling on his trousers, but the Christian who had tuned himself in to my frequency had disappeared.

"Orange, cheers," he said, downing his in a single gulp. He buttoned his pants and kissed me on the cheek. "See you this weekend, yeah?"

He walked out the door without another word. From then on, I was a checked box. I was a channel that he'd changed.

For some reason I kept thinking that he would turn back to me. I really did. I thought every day that he was going to look me in the eyes and put his arm up against the wall and say, *So. What did* you *do today, Caro?* Then I'd tilt my body toward his, and he'd touch the inside of my elbow, and we would stare into each other and I'd make jokes and he'd laugh that roguish laugh, and we would live happily ever after. But

instead I spent the next two weeks watching him touch the inner elbows of five, ten other women, and every time it made me clutch my
stomach and want to vomit.

◆ ◆ ◆

The night of my heartbreak, when I heard the droll melody of Christian's particular laugh cease abruptly, I knew he and the beautiful girl
were kissing. I was humiliated. *Didn't he care that I was sitting right
there?* No. He did not. My heart broke into chunks, the aorta separating
from the valves with squishes and snaps.

Hanna, sat across from me, twisting the cage from a champagne
bottle into a doll's chair, raised an eyebrow.

"Are you dying?" she asked. "You're practically purple."

"I'm going home," I said, before it could get any worse. "I've got PT
early."

"You've *always* got PT," Rally said, popping in from the balcony
with a frown. "How *did* you find physios in a ragged hole like this?"

"It's not that hard." I rolled my eyes. "Anyway, my mum set it up."

Rally pulled on my hand. "Boo."

"I have to," I told her. "Don't forget. You promised to walk with me
after lunch." Hanna flashed the peace sign. Rally blew a raspberry. I
headed for the door.

"Wait! Caro needs a rental husband. Duarte! Walk her?" Hanna
yelled out. Duarte, a dark-haired man who wore sweaters against his
bare skin, was part of Rally's quasi-patrician social circle. Though I
never remembered anyone's inviting him anywhere, he always seemed
to appear. He nodded agreeably. Girls never walked alone in those
days. Lisbon was different then—not dangerous, exactly, but it was
seedy, rife with men drunk enough to decide every woman was a prostitute who wanted to be stalked through the empty streets to her door.
With an escort they left you alone, assuming you were paid for and
occupied.

Duarte and I walked down the darkened staircases toward the Rossio, the square where Rally's grand, crumbling apartment looked out over moldering hotels and a permanent scattering of pigeons. His legs danced down the grade easily, matching me. He made no mention of the purple I'd gone over Christian. Instead he asked if I would live here permanently. I said I was planning to stay in Lisbon for a few more months, at least through the end of July. Duarte thought that was crazy; he'd grown up spending his summers on a private island in the Baltic Sea, where the weather was even, the days never-ending. But I couldn't get enough of what I thought was an ideal level of heat and humidity. We don't heat our houses in South Africa, I told him—we suffer through the driest of summers and live damp through the winters. He nodded gently, trying to imagine it, and then he laughed. "Your people love to create suffering," he observed.

I snorted. "The Portuguese *pioneered* the slave trade."

"Nothing to be done about it now." He shrugged.

"How European."

"If you don't like it," he quipped stiffly, imitating EU leadership, "leave."

The Rossio was tinted orange from the gaslights, the edges dotted with metal tables and wicker chairs. At the last open café, a group of young Portuguese people our age drank coffee and port. Duarte knew them, and soon we were kissing cheeks and sitting down, and everyone was jousting drunkenly—snaps and cracks, insults and compliments.

An hour later I checked my watch. It wouldn't do to meet my PT with less than five hours' sleep. I patted Duarte's shoulder goodbye and slipped through the stately doors of Rally's building. Climbed the stairs; turned the skeleton key in the lock. I fell into bed, dreaming like I had every night of a life with Christian, sailing from port city to port city between holidays at home in his castle in Sintra, surfing the world on the crest of his family's money. I imagined myself pulling open dusty draperies and folding drop cloths while he shaved, tapping the razor against the porcelain. I pictured him heaving suitcases on the end of the bed while I hung coats in the armoire. I was sick to my stomach over him. I knew he would never love me. It was my first time ever as a young person.

◆　◆　◆

The next morning was neurotic agony. I woke up at dawn, soaked in self-recrimination—*When will these feelings subside, they have to, he'll never love me back*—then busied myself, shoving it away. My physical therapist arrived at seven in her usual robin's-egg scrubs, and we moved through the exercises: pre-Pilates movements, yoga, then painful manual release (what you might call massage, if you were a masochist) and dry-needling of the scar tissue in my left hip. After ninety excruciating minutes, she left. I mixed the dough for an almond torte, popped it in the oven, and began my laundry.

The almond smell wafted from the oven. The washer began its shush-shush-shush cycle. Bright ribbons of daylight sliced through the heavy drapes. By the time Rally emerged from the master bedroom in an old pair of men's pajamas, some of my humiliation from the night before had begun to burn off.

"Oof, last night was a smacker," she said, looking into the peeling mirror slung precariously above the fireplace. She wiped the mascara from her eyes and yawned, flipping on the kettle before dropping to the ground. "Caro, precious darling, would you please, please finish the coffee? I can't be vertical."

I rolled my eyes and found the tin of Nescafé. "Fine, but it'll be instant. What happened after I left?" I asked, scooping the powder into our cups, trying to be nonchalant.

"Hanna got terribly drunk and tried to steal a car. She disappeared with that German fellow. I don't expect we'll see her for a week." She crawled over to the freezer, liberated a cluster of grapes, and then, in one quick move, threw herself over the sofa. "Ugh," she said, holding the frozen bunch to her forehead. "*Porto*."

"What kind of car?"

"A little knobby one. She almost succeeded. We stopped her before it got too out of hand. She doesn't know how to drive, anyway."

"What happened to everyone from the party?"

"Christian left with that girl. I don't know how in the world you find him attractive. I think he's atrocious. He told us a story last night about falling asleep on the toilet."

"What?" Even in my rejected lover's haze, I found the idea grotesque.

"Honestly. He's a dog," Rally insisted, plucking a grape from above her eyebrow and pressing it into my palm. "You're far too good for him. Eat this fruit and banish him from your thoughts."

After a moment's pause, I swallowed it.

Though it didn't happen right away, eventually I stopped caring whether Christian would be somewhere or not, or who he left with. But I didn't get over the feeling of having played the game badly. That stayed with me like a scar.

5

IT MAY SEEM SMALL and inconsequential, this history of my time in Lisbon, but now I realize it was the only time in my life that ever truly belonged to me. Even though, or perhaps precisely because, I wasn't anyone important.

I refused to allow myself to fall into any other romances, though Hanna fell in and out of love so often that we barely saw her. Rally was around more consistently; she worked, but not in an office. As an employee of her family's real estate business, she was meant to spend the summer looking for a building (or two or three) to buy. This was only slightly more difficult than it seems. The records at the time were in paper and they had to be examined to ensure there were no liens on the property or easements from the government or city. Rally looked at about two places each week, big ones, the kind with eight or more apartments, and then went to the city's archive and rooted around in the dust until she emerged irritated and red-eyed and ready for a lavish dinner. I tried to help, but I was more liability than benefit, as I had a tendency to get lost in the records. I'd never been in an archive of anything before. It blew my mind that you could see bathroom renovations and births and deaths in the same yellowing documents. And I loved

the names, those Portuguese names—Cerqueira, Caetano, Mascar-
enhas, Peixoto—ran them over my tongue. *Zuzsh, shush, zchou, sou.*

I asked Rally if she thought there might be a place for me at her family's company. Shock rippled across her perfect face. "To do what?"

"To keep helping."

An absurd smile rose and sank, as though her family dog had asked
if he could use the dishwasher. "Caro darling, they barely keep me on,"
she said lightly, tousling my hair. "But you're an ace to offer." Two weeks
later, when she hired an assistant—another girl she'd gone to university with—I tried not to feel hurt. "She speaks Portuguese," Rally
explained.

I understood. I never was very good with languages.

I worked three events on behalf of the sponsor to keep up my end of
the contract: an IAAF qualifying race at the stadium, the opening of a
private specialty hospital, and a photo shoot with a soft drink company.
At each event I was one of a dozen athletes. But my body was now so
different from everyone else's that I was mistaken for a handler more
often than talent. I was treated differently. Little things, a hand on my
waist or the small of my back, motions that were meant to be friendly
but made me uncomfortable. I wormed out of sweaty palms and hairy
forearms, retreated stiffly from too-close-to-my-mouth cheek kisses—
but no matter how I reacted, the little things persisted. It became clear
there would be no renewal of my contract, and frankly, I didn't want
one. It was obvious to me that I'd lost everyone's respect. I could feel it
with every warm glance at my legs, my shoulders, my chest, my rear. It
made me want to hide under a blanket.

The once-bright novelty of my aimless bohemianism was beginning
to tarnish. I wrote my parents and told them I was worried about
money. Did they think I ought to come back to Johannesburg and take
the coaching job? They wrote back with an unequivocal no. *You should
have new experiences. Coaching is not for the young. You must promise
to go interesting places,* they wrote. *You must find out what else interests
you, Caroline. You've never had the chance. Take it—take it by the reins.*

And send postcards. Their letter beamed at me with the same pride they'd always had in me. My mother had sat in the stands during every warm-up, pointing: *That's my daughter. That one right there.*

It will all work out, they ended their letter. I held it to my heart and hoped they were right. Their attitude was a gift, but they sent money, too, in the form of access to a checking account. Leftover prize money, they said, about one hundred seventy-five thousand rand, that I ought to change over as soon as possible, while it was still the equivalent of twenty thousand euro. I would earn another hundred thousand rand on my sponsorship contract, but the rand fluctuated wildly and the contract would end in twelve months, along with the EU visa it provided. After that I'd need to change to a three-month tourist visa. Once that expired, I would have to go home. If I wanted to stay, I needed to get a job in the EU, both to earn in euro and to benefit from the healthcare systems that eclipsed what was available in my home country.

I applied everywhere: office jobs and museum jobs, even taking tickets at the football arena. The interviews consisted of curious inquiries about my athletic career, followed by three important questions: Could I sit for long periods of time? (No.) Could I stand for long periods of time? (No.) Was I eligible to work in the EU beyond the length of my current visa? (No.) The first two questions disqualified me outright for any cash jobs, and the third disqualified me for anything legal.

The rejections terrified me, but I pushed them into the back of my mind, certain that something would happen, that I would find an open door and walk through it.

❖　❖　❖

On my twenty-fourth birthday I was descending a hill when the rain came. It appeared immediately, and in sheets. It was impossible to balance on those black and white cobblestones when they were wet; they were murder in the rain. Worried the ground would be pulled out from beneath me, I picked up the pace, almost running. But before I could find safe harbor, I slipped and landed on my rear end in the rushing water.

The impact rang me like a bell. I panicked. My new hip—*had it cracked?* I tried to sense it, squeezing my muscles, but couldn't feel a thing. *If it was broken, would the sponsor get me another one? Could I even afford to have it removed, or would it have to sit there, a broken dish slatted through the tenderloin of my hip—a knife cutting into me with every step until it cut itself out again?*

I rolled on my side and felt the edge of it. It arced beneath my palm, solid, whole. *Nothing bad happened. Nothing was broken.*

I stood up and resumed walking.

I didn't know at all where I was going. My clothing was soon soaked through. I kept on, a spooked pony, darting quickly in any open direction. I passed from one street to another, drenched in rain, until finally I found a bench under an awning and collapsed on it, limbs trembling, cheeks hot, everything else frozen.

Perversely it felt good to be cold—to be animal again, to be in my body. The adrenaline from my slip onto the cobblestones, I realized, was no different from the adrenaline of a run. No matter where it came from, adrenaline was home. My muscles contracted and shuddered in little drum solos, trying to stay warm. Blood pulsed under my wrist. *This* was it, I thought. This was the thing that I had always, and still, wanted.

To live in my body.

6

I DISCOVERED MY BODY in April of 1990, when I ran my first race in Maboneng, a suburb of Johannesburg. I was eleven years old.

Two months earlier, Nelson Mandela had been released after twenty-seven years of imprisonment. Democracy had begun to rise in the sky like a bright moon. Beneath its silver light the fabric of apartheid was shredding. We could feel it everywhere—ripping and tearing into pieces. Every day was a new landscape, foreign and full of possibility. It was a strange time, even for children, for whom everything is extraordinary and inexplicable. People became emboldened, especially religious people. Most of all Sister Beatrice, the renegade Episcopalian nun who was headmistress of St. Margaret's, the small parochial school I attended.

I've met many other nuns since then, with their beatific faces, their spotless habits, their soft hands and polished rosary beads. While they seemed like fine servants of God, they did not even belong to the same species as Sister Beatrice, who was carved out of wood and lashed together with rubber straps and iron spikes. She was routinely arrested, detained, beaten, and jailed for protesting the apartheid government; bloodstains spotted the edges of her wimple, and she smoked hand-rolled cigarettes even while hiking. Her face was drawn, lips barely there, the eye sockets sunken beneath skin so leathery it was said that someone who had once attempted to stab her drew back their hand to find a broken knife. I'm certain she wore a reinforced vest under the habit, but we shall let the rumor stand.

Sister Beatrice greeted every student with a hearty HOWZIT and a smack across the shoulders that always knocked the breath from your lungs. She approached life the same way, taking Mandela's release as a smack from God: It was time to begin living as though we were no longer under apartheid. She organized a track-and-field day with the head teachers of three home schools in Alexandra, a nearby township, one of the segregated "neighborhoods"—designated plots of land without electricity or running water—where indigenous South Africans were forced to live.

Sister Beatrice chose the events carefully. Long jump was fine, but discus and shot put, which required special equipment, were not, and so on. It was decided there would be one long run through the woods that surrounded the school, three whole kilometers. Teachers and parents from all four schools promised to stand along the route to cheer us on. We spent the whole week leading up to it decorating the course with paper streamers.

On the day of the race, I made friends right away with a girl from one of the home schools. We met first near the tumbler in the school playground—it was a kind of barrel within a barrel that went round and round like a hamster wheel. Zola Mbatha was part Zulu, part Xhosa, and spoke both languages fluently, along with English. More than half her family were murdered under apartheid, though I wouldn't know that until many years later, and with little clarity. Zola was uninterested in reliving those traumas; she was unable to, as the national campaign went, become reconciled. When we met she was nearly two feet taller than me and three years older, but we had the same color shoelaces—bright green—and she had a big horking laugh, frequently punctuated by incredibly infectious snorts. After a solemn discussion about the day's events, we decided to run together in the big race. We stood nervously at the back of the pack while all the boys vied to be in the front line.

Sister Beatrice counted down from three through her dented megaphone, and then we were off. I had run, of course, before, playing tag and football, but I'd never taken part in a race. It didn't take long for me to get into the spirit of the thing. I ran forward. It was easy—it felt natural.

Zola ran a few feet ahead. She was so much taller that I believed she was intentionally keeping back, but no—we had the same stride. We picked up the pace, giggling at how fast we could go. We maneuvered around one group, and then another, jumping over roots and piles of leaves, and then we were at the backs of those boys who had jostled and shoved their way to the front.

The boys were already losing breath, straining to keep their speed. Zola and I glanced at them, and then at each other, puzzled, and then she let out that big horking laugh and we split, passing them like a pair of birds dodging an inconvenient lamppost.

We stayed as a pair for the next five hundred meters, and then—once we realized, from the parents' faces and cheers, that there was no one else to pass—she and I began to compete, lengthening our strides, gaining and then losing on each other step by step, and the endorphins hit and we sprinted to the finish. My legs had never been so long; my arms had never moved so well; the wind had never felt so good. Motion was the answer to every question.

Zola beat me by twenty seconds. But we beat the rest of the children by nearly six minutes.

From that day on, every time I closed my eyes, I imagined running in those woods.

◆　◆　◆

Zola was fourteen to my eleven, and already a runner. She trained, she said proudly, with a group called the Alex Elephants, a running crew in her township of women aged ten to fifty-five who ran together for safety and camaraderie, though it was safer than you might expect. Running was the only sport that could not be segregated by the government, could not be kept down by oppression, could not be bought out from under the feet of my peers. They could not, you see—they could not segregate the roads. Not during the day, anyway.

Our parents met after the race. Zola graciously invited me to join the Elephants on a run the following week. I was thrilled. It seemed completely natural to me that she should extend such an invitation, that we could run together. I was still a child, growing up in a time when everything was changing, so it felt normal that the world would open up this way, but now I know how special it was, to be included.

I began to run with the Alex Elephants, my mother driving me to the gates of the township each weekend. At first I couldn't get farther than a few kilometers, but that soon changed. The women of the Elephants transformed my life. They didn't run fast—they ran *far*. The elite runners in the pack were training for the Comrades, a fifty-five-mile race run every year from Pietermaritzburg to Durban, a seaside town below Johannesburg famous as the place where Mahatma Gandhi began his law career. The Comrades is what is now called an ultramarathon. It has been unofficially integrated for a hundred years, officially since 1971, a rare circumstance under apartheid. The leaders of the Elephants aimed for that big race, while the rest of us shadowed them, peeling off in age groups, more or less, as the distance wore us out.

At twelve I joined a regional team and began to compete nationally in the ten-thousand-meter junior events, which grew more mixed with each broken ribbon. This was not true for other sports; swimming, skiing, pole-vaulting, horseback riding—all these things required training facilities, which nonwhite athletes did not have access to. But when it came to running, there were thousands of people, of every color and age, who were immediately ready to compete. There was a sense of hope in everything as the government's cruelty was abolished, step by precious step. You could see it—colors were brighter.

I've never felt anything that rivaled South Africa's presence in the Olympic Games at Barcelona. We hadn't been permitted to participate since 1960. I was fourteen then and watched the opening ceremonies with our whole school, every single student sitting on the floor of the school gymnasium while Jan Tau ran with the flag. I looked at my own feet, in their own worn-out sneakers, and willed them to take me all the way there—to make me as strong as everyone on the screen.

For the rest of the games, Sister Beatrice left the TV in the gym. We could leave class whenever we wanted to watch. On the marathon day, for two hours, forty minutes, I was glued to Colleen De Reuck's every move, smacking the wood-paneled set every time the cameramen had the audacity to cut to the pack leaders. When Elana Meyer took the silver in the ten thousand meters, I remember jumping up and down and shrieking with such abandon that I nearly peed my pants.

I decided to try to meet eligibility for the next World Junior Championships. Powered by the jet fuel of hope, I dropped out of school and trained full-time. I qualified for the WJC marathon when I turned sixteen, the same year that Zola's parents stood in a ten-hour line to vote in our new government. I ran all around the world for Mandela, medaling in his name at over two dozen qualifying international competitions, including the European Marathon Cup, the Commonwealth Games, and twice at the All-Africa Games. In between races I always returned home to Johannesburg, no matter how inconvenient or long the flight, to run across the iron-soaked dirt of what we called my home track at Wits, the University of the Witwatersrand, where Zola had enrolled as an undergraduate. I loved running there, pitting myself against the varsity team for sport and cheap victories against everybody but her. When I was nineteen Zola and I took the night bus to Pietermaritzburg to run the Comrades. After, Zola graduated and moved to London, to attend law school. I turned twenty, the minimum age to marathon, the year before the 2000 Olympics. Zola passed her licensing exams and became a solicitor. I went to Sydney, set the record, then trained for Athens. Eighteen months later, on the track at Wits, I fell.

Running opened up our world in the way that my parents, and Sister Beatrice, and Zola, and the Alex Elephants, and everyone else we knew, had always longed for. In the early days of democracy in South Africa, running was how so many of us found each other, and it was how I found myself. I was at home on the track like nowhere else.

7

IN LISBON I DISCOVERED, completely by chance, an exhibition of Frida Kahlo. Like my friend from Scoria Vale had predicted, I saw my reflection—a line of bent steel—in Frida. Not in the paintings, but in the way she stood in every photograph.

The wall text described a life that had also changed in a single afternoon. Eighteen years old, riding the bus to Coyoacán, a collision with a streetcar. Pierced by an iron handrail "the way a sword pierces a bull." Spine broken in three places and so were her collarbone, her ribs, her legs, her pelvis. The handrail entered through her hip and exited through her genitals. She was demolished.

It said that in Mexico they call her *la heroína del dolor,* "the heroine of pain." I wandered through the exhibition twice. I liked best her self-portraits, made with a mirror set at the top of her bed. The captions throughout enraptured me; I loved the description from her friend André Breton that she was a "ribbon tied around a bomb," and the exhibition's insistence that she wouldn't have been a painter if it hadn't been for her accident.

I began to wonder what there was to make of my own pain. What I would become *because* of the accident. And—finally—began to truly call it, in my mind, an *accident*, as my friend from Scoria Vale had. Less and less *the time I fell*, with the attendant responsibility of *I*, and more and more an accident.

I held my hands to my face, palpating the place where my shatter had been, letting the ache in my joints fill me up. As hard as I tried to ignore the pain, it wanted to be acknowledged. It wanted to be known.

◆ ◆ ◆

There are 206 bones in the adult human body and approximately 300 joints, 24 of which are considered major. Number 24, my left hip, was entirely prosthetic, and the other 23 largest joints, in my feet and knees, were lacking between 30 percent and 41 percent of their articular cartilage. My right hip had lost about 10 percent; my spine and upper torso, 5 percent. Synovial fluid, the articulating lubricant material stored in the tiny accessory pouches of bursa, ought to be soaked up by the cartilage and squeezed out like a kitchen sponge each time the joint is in motion. But there wasn't enough cartilage in me anymore, especially down below, and not enough fluid, so my insides were rusty. They creaked and scraped and grated against each other, and those twenty-four largest joints in my legs and feet were all, at the ripe old age of twenty-four, in a state of chronic decay. I'd been told upon leaving Scoria Vale that if I didn't take care of myself, I could be wheelchair-bound by fifty. At the time it seemed absurd; now I was beginning to understand that might well be possible. The pain was persistent, splitting me open day and night with little abatement.

How to express it? Frequently: an ache so dull and low that you wonder if you're being pulled into hell. Sometimes the opposite: purple-colored lightning bolts dropping embers on your nerve endings. Swelling, of course—fat fingers and toes and knees—the heart forcing your blood into a thrumming, toxic mass of heavy discomfort. The sound of ripping paper, or a baby screaming, or a body hitting the pavement, but a feeling.

Frida painted her pain as lava, nails, a jagged hole down the center of her body. First her right foot turned into a claw. They cut off her toes. Later, the entire foot. "Feet, what do I need them for if I have wings to fly," she wrote in 1953. One year later she died and flew away.

I didn't have wings, metaphorical or otherwise. I only had my feet, and I would have done anything to keep them.

◆ ◆ ◆

My life as a bourgeois hanger-on continued without evolution. Stylish young people talking and drinking until the sun came up. We gathered on wicker chairs in stone courtyards, around serene fountains, across skinny balconies, at wobbly tables where everyone rolled their own cigarettes. Always like that, until the night I saw Finn again.

I was standing at a bar, picking up a Fanta for myself and Vino Verdhes for Duarte and Rally, when something ruffled the crowd. The room transformed. People spoke louder and laughed excitedly, as though they'd been hit with dental gas. Couples all through the bar leaned into each other as I returned to the table with the drinks in my hand.

"It's that singer," said a girl to Duarte's left. "The one from Australia." I craned my neck to look. She was right. It was *that singer*. Honey blond, wrapped in a tiny silver dress, she was the liquid candy center of some glossy universe—and she gripped the angled biceps of an enormous meat slab of a man.

It was him.

My friend from Scoria Vale.

◆ ◆ ◆

Too-sweet orange bubbles of Fanta exploded over the edge of my glass as I wondered whether or not to approach him. On the one hand: *No*. In a T-shirt, bike shorts, and orthopedic clogs, I still resembled a hospital patient. He wore a tailored blue suit, the color of the ocean depths, holding an amber glass of liquor in one paw and a shimmering star with the other. On the other hand: If I could walk up with a guileless grin, then it would be fine. We were bonded. He would remember me. Our conversation had been so extraordinary. Hadn't it?

Perched on my stool, chewing the straw of my childish drink, I watched them from behind my shaggy mop of hair. Flanked by a coterie of men in green military uniforms, Finn appeared rested, his rugged face lighter. He was kind to his date, to the staff. He possessed an ease of self, the certainty that he belonged not only everywhere but also specifically in this room. A room that was now centered around the two of them, iron filings repositioned by a magnet. I felt stabs of envy. Rooms had changed for me like this, once—locker rooms and stadia. But I wasn't a magnet anymore. I was a piece of iron like everybody else.

The singer laughed at all his jokes. Not in a fake way—she really, truly laughed—and he gave her his warm beam of a smile in return.

I slipped away to the bathroom, tugging at my shirt self-consciously. I dug around my bag for a lipstick Rally had lent back when I was chasing Christian and dabbed it on. It was dark, dark red. On my small lips it looked okay. Dramatic, but low in volume, so it was all right, not too much. I flashed back to when I left the hospital, when the orderly first put makeup on me. I rarely looked at this face, but it was beautiful—it really was.

When I returned to the table, Finn and the singer were gone. I was gutted.

"What's the occasion, painted lady?" Duarte teased.

"All that starlight." I said. "Sunburn." He leaned in to give me a friendly peck on the lips, but I turned so his lips landed on my cheek—it wasn't for Duarte, the color. I didn't want him to touch it. I didn't want anyone to touch it except Finn.

"Where'd they go?" I couldn't stop myself from asking.

"*Hustled* out," Rally whispered. "As if there was a bomb threat. It took all of two seconds."

"The security!" Duarte swirled his drink. "Oof, they were *bulging*."

"I spent a weekend in Lucomo once," Rally offered, as though it was a memory she would have otherwise completely forgotten. "I lost a thousand euro."

"I've only ever gambled in Ljubljana," Duarte said. "An attaché we met on the beach brought me to a mansion where people checked their guns at the door. There were peacocks inside and someone was waxing a Honda Civic in the driveway as though it was a Maserati. It was *terrifying*," he purred happily.

"I didn't gamble it. I *lost* it. It flew out of the car and into the street."

"You didn't go after it?" I asked.

"No. It's bad luck to chase money."

I smacked her on the arm. "That's the worst thing I've ever heard you say."

"It's how people *do* there," she insisted. "A cup of coffee is twenty euro."

"How does *that* work?"

"Lucomo is the *idle idyllllll*." Rally drew it out, clicking her teeth. "The main city, Le Chappe, is all skyscrapers and shopping. It's like, European Singapore, except you can't get arrested for spitting or whatever. I don't think, anyway. But it also has this teeny-weeny old town called Cap-Griffe that sits underneath the castle. No cars. Not even bicycles. It's so precious. The Alps behind it, and everything."

"Where does all their money come from?" I asked.

"Real estate," Duarte and Rally said simultaneously. "It's the most expensive land on the planet," Rally explained, while he nodded knowingly. "That long strip between France and Italy, and up into the mountains a little bit. The same family has ruled it forever. Like, seven hundred years or something. He was going to marry that girl? The one who died?"

"Lidia. My elder brother boarded with her in Geneva. He said she was a *nightmare*."

"They make bags for Fendi. Her family."

"*He's* so much more handsome in person." Duarte was chewing handfuls of peanuts and tossing the shells onto the floor. "Caroline sure thought so. You should've gone for it."

I tried not to blush.

"Caroline *should* marry a prince," Rally agreed. "You'd be ever so good at it. You have wonderful posture and very nice calves. And you're from, like, a fucked-up place."

"Plus, then you won't have to keep looking for a job," Duarte pointed out.

"You'll have to learn boat words. *Regatta. Jib.* You should probably get your tits done."

"I already had my face done," I protested. "Isn't that enough?"

"Sometimes *I* want to give up and get married," Rally sighed, lighting a cigarette. "It seems so much easier than, you know, *trying.*"

"Don't worry, you will," Duarte teased.

I was about to say I *knew* Finn, *thankyouverymuch*—when Rally, in a drunken attempt at a chastising slap across the back of Duarte's head, knocked over half the table. A ribbon of wine flung itself across my shirt; shards of liquor-coated glass scattered across the floor. Rally and Duarte howled with laughter—then changed tables as though nothing had happened. As the staff sopped up the puddles, their conversation became an escalating series of previous destructions of property: Trashed beach houses and ski chalets. Fractured train doors, dented cars, resentful cleaners. Rally and Duarte's assumed superiority, once so entertaining to me, struck me that night as immature and dull. I decided to keep my story about Finn to myself.

At the apartment, I shut myself in my room and scanned the bookshelves. Rally had stashed her grandmother's leather-bound set of encyclopedias in here. They were at least a decade old. Still, I opened the volume labeled *K–L,* licked my forefinger, and peeled back the onionskin pages until I found it.

❖ ❖ ❖

Lucomo, one of the oldest nation-states in Europe, was striking even from the pages of a book. Shaped like a dagger laid flat upon the coast, it totaled 122 square miles lodged firmly between the Mediterranean Sea and the Maritime Alps. The westernmost point, the dagger's handle, was a claw-shaped cliff that hooked into the sea. To the east, the dagger's serrated blade cut across forty miles of rocky beaches as it narrowed to a point.

It had been ruled by the Fieschi family for nearly seven hundred years. A picture of its monarch, Queen Amelie, showed a diminutive sprite who looked nothing like my friend. But her husband, Prince Armand, was massive, the obvious source of Finn's heavy brow and hard jaw. He was their only child, described in the out-of-date encyclopedia as a college student. It said they lived in a castle called the Talon, a thousand-year-old fortress carved atop the claw-shaped cliff for which it was named, and governed a population of approximately one hundred thousand.

Lucomo's most famous cities were Cap-Griffe, a historic gem nestled below the castle, whose late medieval streets were so small that single-horse-drawn carts collected the recycling, and Le Chappe, a Lamborghini-infested city known for its luxurious casino, film festival, and yacht club. Beyond Le Chappe extended the dagger blade of rocky beaches, lethargic harbors, and an inland stripe of orchards. Lucomo's residents were called by two names: Piétons, or pedestrians, in the west; and Marins, or sailors, in the east. It was a primarily tourist economy, with some agriculture; Lucomo's refreshing climate, strong winds, and three hundred days of sunshine nurtured people and plants alike. On its loamy hills, orange groves and cassia farms flourished alongside oleanders, mulberries, and palm trees; on its beaches, the rich revived themselves in the sun.

Called the golden oyster of the Mediterranean, the encyclopedia said, and politically neutral, Lucomo was the wealthiest and safest nation in the world. *Pax—Fortuna—Fiducia,* the words from Finn's stamp, its motto. *Peace, Fortune, Trust.* Trust. I noticed the translation—not exactly the same as fidelity, or loyalty, as I had previously guessed. The stamp's three towers were the oldest part of its castle.

I fell asleep next to the open encyclopedia. Soon I was jogging through Lucomo, my heart pumping strong and even, the sea breeze warm against the goose bumps rising on my arms. After an easy mile, I merged with a pack of runners and together we stopped, waiting for a race to begin.

We wrapped our arms around ourselves, fingers touching ribs, palms grabbing sneakers, quads bending backward in an inverse chorus line. Slaps of petroleum jelly landed on armpits and nipples to cut the chafe. Shoelaces tied themselves in lucky knots, hair bound itself up in ponytails tight enough to raise the eyebrows, as our muscles quivered in rapid-fire bursts. The wind ruffled the sleek nylon of my shorts and broke through the compression of my bra, like a cool cloth on a hot forehead.

Finn was there, suddenly appearing on the sideline, leaning on his embellished cane. The crowd behind him fell silent as we waited for the gun. I felt the world's doors opening all around me, my perspective shift, as the thing I missed most—anticipation—burned in my belly.

Time stopped. At the crack, I bolted. And then—I was running. I was free.

It was exactly as it had been in real life.

❖   ❖   ❖

I opened my eyes in the morning to a world where the memory of running and the memory of Finn had become permanently entangled. My scalp prickled with the dream's peculiar flavor for hours. The moment it faded, I felt its absence and wanted more of it.

I would have to find a way to see him again.

8

TWO WEEKS LATER Finn was on the cover of a cheap newspaper with an actress (not the singer). The actress, asked if she would be attending the upcoming Special Olympics games with him, a cause very dear to his heart and pocketbook, said that she was of course making a donation but was unsure of her schedule. Finn was tired of her, the newspaper wrote, as he'd tired of the singer, the businesswoman, the philosopher, the model. None compared to the kid-leather-heiress fiancée of Firenze who died in the car accident that brought him to Scoria Vale, they insisted. Lidia haunted him. Would there ever be a woman who would be his equal?

I scowled. *Equal? From where?* As an athlete I wasn't allowed to compete against men. We accelerated—but so did they. The performance gap between the sexes stood in most sports. The wage gap stood in every industry. The gaps were everywhere. Why did everyone insist on pretending, all the time, that anything was fair? Fairness only existed if you started in the same place, with the same tools and the same resources.

I ran my finger over his picture, pressing so hard the ink came away.

Unlike the actress, my schedule was quite certain. I could be there, in Shanghai, at the Special Olympics. I'd been invited by the committee to give a speech to the track-and-field competitors—ten minutes at their opening banquet. I could see him again. All I had to do was accept. And, of course, write a speech.

I holed up in my room and got to work.

◆ ◆ ◆

GOOD AFTERNOON. My name is Caroline Muller. I've medaled at the European Cup, the Commonwealth Games, the World Championships, the All-Africa Games, the World Junior Championships, and the Olympic Games. I hold the world record for the women's marathon. All of this bragging is to say, I'm one of you. I'm an athlete. And I'm here today to talk about what it means to me, after more than a thousand races, to win, but more important, what it means to compete.

When I was young, like all of you, I lived in a country that was segregated under an oppressive totalitarian regime. No one who was Black, or what we call colored, or Indian, or any shade that wasn't white, was allowed to use the same restrooms, live in the same neighborhoods, compete in the same sports, go to school together, or apply for the same jobs. The law keeping us apart was called apartheid, an Afrikaans word that means "apartness," and it was enforced with devastating violence.

We were, however, allowed to walk on the same streets. That was the one thing that was too hard to separate. For that reason, South African distance running has always been the most diverse sport we have. There is a long history of men and women, white and Black, colored and Indian, Xhosa and Zulu, running together on the road, for fun and friendship and competition. We have an annual race called the Comrades that's been unofficially integrated for a hundred years, officially since 1971. It's fifty-five miles long, and it takes eleven hours. [*pause for laughter*] I know. It's a big goal. But you have to dream big. You know that. That's how you got here.

I ran in my first race against a girl called Zola, who lived in what is known as a township, called Alexandra. Houses in Alexandra didn't have city electricity or running water; they had to get their own. We had very different home lives. Zola beat me, in that first race, and in hundreds thereafter, because running is something you earn. It's not something you can be given.

Through Zola, I joined up with a group of women road runners. We didn't go fast, but we went far—we did six-, ten-, fifteen-milers, around the townships. We were the Alex Elephants, because elephants can hear through their feet, and they're determined, and that's what we were.

We ranged in age from ten to fifty-five, and those runs were some of the best of my life. Together we trained for the Comrades, that fifty-five-mile race, and together, Zola and I ran it when I was nineteen years old and she was twenty-two. It is because of the Elephants that I discovered what kind of athlete I was—not a sixty-meter athlete, but a distance runner. Over six years Zola and I ran over twelve thousand miles together, the distance from Johannesburg to the top of Tunisia and back again. The Alex Elephants taught me how to dream.

And it is because of the dream we stand under today—an Olympic medal—that I spent the rest of my adolescence chasing the air on top of those wooden boxes. [*point to boxes*]

Let me tell you: the air up there tastes sweet. It tastes as good as an orange slice after practice—you know how it's always the best orange you've ever had? But—it's funny—I learned something after getting on top of all those boxes. There's better air. [*pause*]

Really! The air up there is *not* the best. I'm certain of it. I'm here to tell you, from experience, that *nothing, absolutely nothing,* tastes as good as the air at the *start* of the race, when you're at your marks, and the playing field is equal, and you're each of you athletes, side by side. The beginning is always the best part. It's pure potential—to find your personal best. All your old races are gone, and the only thing in front of you is this one. It is the only perfect moment of fairness in the whole world.

As I think you all know, and your families know, we must fight for such a moment. Without the revolution that brought about the end of apartheid, as a South African, I would never have been able to stand on the starting line at the Sydney Olympics. I would never have known fairness. I cherish that more than anything else in the world. And without the support of [these generous sponsors], we couldn't be here, either, celebrating your achievements, and the opportunities you have fought for, and earned.

I am so proud to be here with you today, to witness your beginnings, and to cheer you on. When you stand on your mark, I want you to take a moment to really feel how special it is—how rare the air is in here—and to remember that you are a link in a divine chain. Win or lose, you are an Olympian. Let's cherish our beginnings together.

❖ ❖ ❖

I think the committee had expected me to give a speech about my disability but I didn't want to, and it felt hollow, anyway, to discuss something that impacted me *after* I had accomplished the very thing that put me in front of the podium. More important, it didn't compare to many of the disabilities that the Special Olympians faced. I felt that it didn't. And while perhaps a brief summary of apartheid in South Africa was difficult for some to comprehend, it was nonetheless part of my life, and the world we lived in, and for me it could not go unmentioned.

Afterward I was seated with the contingent from Southern

Africa—athletes from South Africa, Zimbabwe, Namibia, Mozambique, and Botswana, and their families. Parents asked politely about what I'd been doing since my fall. I was able to say that since the *accident,* I'd been healing, and doing a lot of exploring; that I was living in Portugal and that it was my first time living away from my parents. It was not easy to stop running, I told them, but I was determined to make a new life for myself. I felt like a child, then, with all these lovely people beaming at me, proud that I was picking myself up and moving on.

I bonded with a family from Harare, the capital of Zimbabwe and three hours from where my mother grew up. Their daughter Anoona was a fifteen-year-old distance runner who planned to compete in the 1,000-meter. She was talkative, inquisitive. What was my favorite color uniform? Which color was the luckiest? Did ribbons in the hair slow you down? Did different colors have different weights? And so on. I told her I thought green was the best color, because it represented spring, and the opportunity to become ourselves anew. She burst into laughter and said I'd got it wrong. The best color was the one exactly between yellow and orange. The color of sunlight. The color of a gold medal.

The banquet ended around four in the afternoon. Already the sun was hidden behind the city's vertiginous skyline. I was awfully jet-lagged—it'd taken nearly twenty-four hours to get there, three flights where I stretched awkwardly in the cramped restrooms to keep my pain at bay—and I was scheduled to leave the next day. I would have loved to stay longer, but the flights were so expensive, and my turn-around had been the cheapest by a few thousand euro. It was what the sponsor was willing to cover.

My friend from Scoria Vale was nowhere to be seen. I loitered in the main entry hall for ten minutes, but he did not appear. Sagging with disappointment, I caught a lift back to my hotel on one of the athlete coaches. So familiar—the gray velour seats with their bright chevrons of color, the black rubber bumps on the floors, tracksuits shining as young people pressed their faces to the tinted windows, drinking up the bright clutter of the neon city.

I departed the bus last, craned my neck for him in the lobby, but my friend wasn't there, either. With a heavy heart, I rode the elevator up to my room.

The message light blinked on the phone next to the bed. I bit my lip and smiled.

"This is Finn Fieschi. We met nearly two years ago. I hope you remember me. I heard your lovely speech today. I was wondering if I might take you out to dinner. If you are even remotely hungry, please give me a call at your earliest convenience."

I listened to it three times, the low growl of his voice humming through the handset, but there was no phone number. Frustrated, I dressed up anyway, hoping he might realize his mistake and call again. I put on a green dress that I'd bought a week earlier, a mossy knit that had long sleeves and went down below my knees—modest, comfortable— and plain black sneakers with hidden orthopedic inserts. I lingered in front of the mirror, brushing my hair, changing my mind again and again about Rally's dark red lipstick until the phone rang.

I relished the sound of it so deeply that I nearly failed to pick up. "Hello?" I finally answered, breathlessly.

"Caro, sweetheart." My mother. "How did it go?"

"It was lovely," I reported, let down but happy to hear her voice. We settled into a long catch-up. When I mentioned how stressed I often felt walking to and from the Rossio apartment, always trying to find a spare man to walk me home, my mother sighed.

"I've been wondering about that. The world isn't made for young women to live alone. To be independent. I wish it was different, Caro. I really do. Perhaps you ought to order some pepper spray."

When we said our goodbyes, it was nearly seven. No new messages, no missed calls. I decided to be proactive. I put on the lipstick, locked my room, and went downstairs.

A woman with a severe haircut, heavy makeup, and a phone glued to her ear stood guard behind the front desk. She gave me the "one-minute finger." I waited impatiently.

"Yes, how may I help you?"

"I received a message earlier, but I don't know how to return the call," I said.

"Your room number?"

Two minutes later, she said, "From the Presidential Suite. I will ring it for you," and before I could stop her, she was dialing. "This is the front desk. I have a guest from four fifteen returning your call . . . Yes." She handed me the phone.

"I had to get the number from the desk," I squeaked, stretching the cord, turning away from the receptionist like a shy teenager.

"I'm an idiot," he said. "I'd nearly given up."

"I remember you," I blurted out gracelessly. "And yes, I'm starving."

"I've ordered dinner. Would you come up?"

"Oh no," I said. "No, I don't think so. I don't think I could do that."

"Understood. Hand me back? I'll come down."

The receptionist canceled his dinner with a trained blankness. The lobby was crowded with families in tracksuits, every chair taken. I stood to the side and pushed back my cuticles for minutes that felt like hours until a shadow fell across my sneakers.

"Do you recognize me out of my pajamas?" he asked, holding out his rib eye of a hand. I broke into a smile and went to shake it. He pulled me in, kissed my cheek, hovering a moment too long—as I did the same. A sharp bite of cedar melted from his neck. Our hands lingered, fingertips still joined, until I shyly looked to the ground and stepped back.

"Cane-free, even. We've evolved," I said.

Finn grinned—and let out a breath. His eyes dropped, a nervous, boyish sort of glance. I was relieved; he was excited to see me, too. "So," he asked, "where should we go?"

"I've never been here before. Could we ask the hotel?"

"Do you eat meat?"

"I'm from South Africa."

"Car's out front."

An armored black SUV waited patiently among the honking throngs of the busy streets, young Otto at the wheel, Dix holding the rear passenger door. I had to climb into it, ascending the sideboard like it was a stair, using the roof handle to hoist myself onto the seat.

"You look horrified," Finn said, amused, as he slid in next to me.

"This isn't a car. It's a bus."

"What do you drive?" More retort than question.

"I don't. I mean, I know how, but I'm not very good at it."

Otto hit the gas and dove into the single fast-moving lane.

"Look at his face. You're missing a true experience."

"I'd be too nervous. Maybe some people are born passengers."

He looked straight at me. "Not you."

❖   ❖   ❖

I don't remember what else we discussed on the way to dinner. I know the conversation was easy—it always was between us—but this was my first time being enclosed with him, and so the closeness is what I recall. Our throats uttered sounds—our ears received them—our breaths intermixed in the air—our hearts circulated blood from toes to eyeballs and back again. I recall no words, only the exquisite feeling of being near.

When traffic slowed, we stopped in front of a gigantic electronic billboard pulsing with lights so bright they flooded the car, tinting the air itself a neon orange. Bathed in this mist of color, we stared at each other. As we connected, a seed, a kind of pulsing anchor, sprouted beneath my stomach. I felt it as strongly as if it were a hot stone. I clutched at my waist in shock—only to feel the seed root, its tendrils burrow into my flesh. *Scratch all you want,* I heard it whisper. *I'm not going anywhere.* Finn blinked, concerned, and reached for me instinctively. As I watched my own hand rise to meet his, I realized that I was alive again with this man—*in my body again*—in a way that had been unavailable, prohibited to me, since my accident. "Jet lag," I explained, pulling my hand back with a shy smile. He waited a moment before retracting his.

I didn't let myself touch him, not just then, because I was trying to be what I thought of as strategic. Christian had been an influential lesson. Men—rich men, handsome men, powerful men; poor men, hideous men, weak men—men *do not want* women they can simply *have*. Men are socialized to chase and dominate, to win, to esteem combativeness. History as it is written is the history of men conquering, men pillaging, men owning, men commanding. Everything around us, from the faces on our money to the statues in the streets, reiterates that we value men who conquer—men who take something from others. And women are property. We have been property forever. It is so rare for a woman to belong to herself. Even now, as I write these words, grasping for order and truth, I wonder if I am yet possessed of myself.

For it was not a fair playing field; we were not evenly matched as I saw it—not even close. Finn was ten years older, educated by the world's most educated people, at boarding school, university, business school. He was heir apparent to the world's richest country. I was a twenty-four-year-old, handicapped, thus-far-unemployable former athlete with a grade-nine education on an extended faux gap year who gave the occasional motivational speech. My biggest hobby was *walking*.

But—I was beautiful.

9

IT'S NARCISSISTIC to sit here and wax on about how beautiful I was at twenty-four. I'll do it anyway because I want you to know how it felt.

Here is what I looked like: My implanted cheekbones made everything else about my face more precisely heart shaped. I hadn't cut my hair since the accident, and so it tumbled down my back in thick, healthy waves. My skin was a dream—elastic with youth and tinted with rose petals. And my body was no longer the rippling musculature that it had been since puberty. I had gone soft and weak and narrow, which is, of course, far more appealing to men.

To be that beautiful was both terrifying and edifying. Eyes found me when I entered a room, no matter what. I had two walks: One of confidence, which I already knew by heart, a walk that says *I will step on you if you get in my way*. The other one, I'd had to learn: the one of pleading shame, which says *Please don't—please, please leave me alone.* Not that it works, per se.

I wanted to find a purpose for the body that caused me so much pain. I wanted to be in control. When you are that beautiful, other people are arrested by your every move. You affect them simply by *being*. The average twenty-four-year-old will cede this power quickly—they are so . . . unsure of how to keep it.

But I was not. Transformed from hulking threat to delicate object, I had become, in the year since my accident, *hugely* aware of other people's sexuality. What had been invisible and unavailable to me before— the perfumed honey that could fill a room like a bouquet of lilies—was now something I generated everywhere I went. People bloomed right in front of me, coughing up clouds of vermillion pollen, their skin streaking orange and pink like a sunrise, pupils vibrating like tuning forks. In those moments it felt as though I could reach out and gently rearrange their features with my fingertips; that I was a painter and they were a painting.

But it wasn't a reliable power. After Christian drank me like a glass of water and pissed me out just as fast, no smile could bring him back. If I used it on strangers, it worked too well; they followed me down the street, made me afraid. So I hid myself, behind Hanna, and Rally, and Duarte; I learned that second walk and turned myself at angles, to stay out of the light.

With Finn I could not hide. He was something else, right from the start. The way he leaned on me at Scoria Vale and marveled at my strength; the way he looked at me, in one moment like I was a bird and he was a cat; in the next, I the cat, he the bird. He didn't cede power to anyone. He played with it.

In those first shocking months after the end of my athletic career, when I could not find a job, when my body did nothing but ache, when Christian rejected me because he could, when every man I met made me feel small and ripe for their plucking, I learned that the world was made from men—*for men*—that men controlled the world, and further—that their desire for my attention was the only leverage I possessed.

I could have learned other things, I suppose, but that would have required an education.

◆ ◆ ◆

That night in Shanghai, Finn took me to a steakhouse frozen in a cari-
cature of mobster films called Mancini's Chicago Cocktail. The walls
were covered in signed headshots of Chinese film stars, and the stage
held a pimply boy, his hair a platinum swoop, adeptly playing jazz stan-
dards on a scratched-up baby grand. Otto followed us inside, then sat
at the bar as though he weren't with us. Finn and I were escorted to a
circular booth done in vertical stripes of red and orange leathers and
given menus the size of laminated newspapers. I didn't bother to open
mine. Steakhouses were the same everywhere. "Aren't you hungry?"
Finn asked.

"I know what I want."

He put his menu down. "I'll have the same." He picked up the wine
list. "White or red?"

"I don't drink."

He moved back slightly, in surprise. "Really?"

"I take anti-inflammatory medicine that goes through my liver. Alcohol would stress it."

"I always thought that was a myth," he floated playfully.

"No."

"Have you *ever* had a drink?"

"Sure . . ." I had to think about it. "Champagne, a few times. Though
it was minerals—the carbonation—that I used to avoid. I didn't have a
Coca-Cola until I was at Scoria Vale. But I don't mind what anyone else
does."

"I'll skip it, too."

The waiter came. I asked what cuts were on for two, then ordered a
bone-in sirloin, rare, with béarnaise sauce, greens on the side, and
whatever else the waiter thought was best, and mineral water, the kind
with gas. He scribbled this all down, took our menus, and vanished.

"I liked your speech today," Finn said. He looked down, unfolded the blank square of his napkin, and hesitated a moment. Then: "'A link in a divine chain.'"

I'd put it in the speech cut on purpose. "You said that to me when we met."

"You remember." He turned toward me; in the circular booth, he was at eight o'clock, I was at five o'clock. The space between us narrowed as he took up the seven o'clock slice.

"I remember every word we said," I dared to admit. "Our conversation that day was so sharp and clear, when everything else was a fog. I wanted to see you again but . . . you disappeared. Sometimes"—I shook my head—"I thought I dreamed you up. That I made you up inside my head."

"My knee was infected. They took me to a trauma hospital that same night."

"Did you go back?" I knew the answer, but it seemed polite to pretend otherwise.

"No. I recovered at home."

"Home at your castle," I spun, testing the waters.

A crimson flush streaked down the trunk of his neck, to the hollow between his clavicles, visible in the opening of his crisp white shirt.

The waiter arrived with two comically petite bottles of imported club soda. Finn cracked them open with hands so large the bottles briefly disappeared as he twisted off their caps.

"My castle, you were saying," he said, regarding me with comic distance. "Tell me more."

"I had to look it up. At first I thought the stamp on your letter was a logo. For a company. I didn't realize it was a place."

"It's not only a place," he clarified, "it's a mailing address. I was surprised you never wrote."

"You didn't tell me." I frowned. "When I asked. What you did before."

"It would have changed our conversation," he admitted, the

dark fringe of his lashes fluttering almost shyly against his cheek. Almost.

"Because you're a prince and I'm a peasant?"

He unhinged that stone jaw—and laughed. "We don't have peasants."

"How do you hold on to it?" I could not contain my curiosity. "A monarchy. It's so . . . I think the word is *anachronistic*. Out of time?" He nodded. "Don't the"—I wrinkled my forehead—"*Lucomans* . . . want democracy?"

"The Lugesque," he named them, his native accent a sweet melody of sea and forest, French and Italian. "Not if they have safety and security. Lucomo has the smallest level of income inequality in the world. We have excellent public resources, healthcare, education. It is as perfect a nation as has ever existed." He lit up with pride, lowering his eyes again before lifting them to mine, the action like an archer's pulling back the string of his bow. "You should come and see it," he said plainly. An arrow, launched.

"I *would* have to see it, to buy that."

"You don't believe me." His smile was wide as the table.

"I grew up in a country dying for democracy. It's precious."

"How's that working out?" He raised one brow, sipped his drink.

"That's not democracy's fault. The money and power never moved, so people still live like they did before, but much of the violence, anyway, has been . . ." I searched for the right word. "Dampened. The state-sponsored kind, at least."

"It's corrupt. It's a democracy that only works for the rich."

"You're never corrupted?" I teased.

"I didn't say *that*." He tilted his head against the booth. "My grandfather was a Nazi." It came out like the kind of joke that Rally would make.

"Really?"

"I shouldn't jest," he corrected himself, in a way Rally never would have done. "It's an awful story. My grandfather Arturo was young, impressionable, when we hosted a man called Philippe Pétain during the First World War." His upper lip twitched in disgust. "Arturo thought Pétain very sophisticated. They maintained a long friendship. Pétain later influenced Arturo to ally with Hitler. We were occupied by the Vichy government from 1940 through the end of the war. It destroyed us—physically and economically. We had to pay reparations. It's been a lot to make up for."

"It's on you?"

"Technically I work for my mother," he said with a particular smile, sly and comic and humble all at once. "But I have a lot of autonomy." He pushed his hands against the air, a sardonic reassurance. "I've got my own plane and everything."

"Who buys the petrol?"

"It's not petrol. It's called avtur, aviation turbine fuel. She does. I've never been razzed this hard in my life." He grew serious then, observing me. "You don't approve."

I blushed. "I'm not qualified to criticize."

"Say anything." He meant it.

I took him up on it. "You inherited a country. You don't need my critique or my approval." It came out much meaner than I meant it to.

Yet he brightened at the jab; he seemed to relish my honesty. "I want it. Your approval. Let me try." He paused and folded the conversation into a fresh shape. "Do you believe in yourself?"

I shook my head. "I used to."

"I'll rephrase. Do you believe that what you did on the track was special?"

"Of course." I was unembarrassed. "I *was* special. My body was special. It was a gift. I'm trying to figure out if I'll ever be that special again. Maybe not." I shrugged.

"Not past tense. You are. Everything you said today was extraordinary. Not that you care what I think, but you're very smart."

"Thank you." I burned with pleasure. No one, not even my parents, had ever told me that they thought my mind and body were equal. A smart *runner,* yes. A creative *runner.* An economical *runner,* but not a smart *person.* I tucked the compliment into a pocket of my heart, where it stayed forever.

"No one trained to run those races except you. No one else sacrificed their education or any semblance of a normal life except you. *You* did all of it," he insisted. "I sacrificed my freedom and my independence, as did my mother, and her father, and so on, and because of that, my life is special. Not me, the person, but the life. My family has seven hundred years of born duty to peace and fairness and prosperity. History shows us that someone always rises to power. I wouldn't trust another soul on earth to take my place." He was solid in his sincerity, his body a tree, rooted to the world.

"I understand that," I agreed. "I *do* feel like my life is important. I—I don't know how yet"—I pulled my sleeves over my fingers as I stammered, balling my hands into fists—"but—but—I *will* find the answer." My throat lumped up. I looked away.

"What *else* do you know about me?" Finn asked, dialing the tenor of our conversation back to playful repartee. We'd come too close to honesty; it was easier as a game.

"You're not a very hot topic in Portugal," I said with a nonchalance that I hoped sounded legitimate. "The papers there are mostly concerned with footballers, local politics. I know you date a lot. Once I saw you in the *Trib.* But I forget why."

"I'm forgettable?" He seemed very lightly insulted, precisely as I intended. Competition was my specialty.

"I didn't think I'd ever see you again. It's like . . . you're a character in a soap opera that I used to watch but haven't kept up with."

"A soap opera." He took a long sip of water. Condensation ran down the glass and over his fingers. "Beware my evil twin."

"What's he been up to?"

"Guns and assorted arms. Light human trafficking, but that's incidental. His real passion is money laundering."

"How exciting."

"Once you've been a prince . . . the bar for entertainment gets set quite high."

"I can imagine." I smiled—he grinned—and then we were the only two people on the planet.

"I've followed you," he said.

"What's my story line?"

He ticked it off on two fingers. "You're sponsored by the sneaker company, and you're an official ambassador for the Special Olympics."

"Where do I live?"

"Portugal, you said?"

"Lisbon," I said, leaning my head against the banquette. "Near the Rossio square."

"I was there a few weeks ago. The city is starting to come back—I was impressed. Is it a permanent move?"

"It's a base, for now . . . *we* won't stay." I let *we* fall from my mouth like a stone.

"We?" Finn tugged at his collar, an unconscious gesture of dissatisfaction.

"I live with someone. Rally," I said, a lie in implication. I picked up my glass and eyed Finn over the top of it. "How does one become Lugesque, exactly?"

"You can be born there," he said, "or you can immigrate."

"What qualifies a person to immigrate?"

"Their connection to Lucomo."

"If they have a relative who lives there?"

"No. It's an investment question."

"You can *buy* your way in?" I raised an eyebrow. "That's not very sporting."

"It's a reality. Lucomo's unemployment rate is zero percent."

"How on earth is that possible?" I felt my eyes rolling.

"It's a choice any nation can make. If someone wants to move to Lucomo and build a business there—hire our citizens, contribute to our economy, learn our languages—we think that's worthy of consideration for our very beneficial citizenship. In that balance, we keep everything upright."

"What's beneficial about it?"

"Ah," he sighed. "We do not have an income tax." Before I could open my mouth to say THAT'S ABSURD, he reached out and touched me. My interior warmed, turned liquid—and I paused. He noticed the effect, then continued. "Our property taxes and VAT are sufficient revenue. We don't miss it."

The heat of his fingertips against mine. "Doesn't that bother your neighbors?"

"Not really, no," he said, his smile wide. "It raises all ships."

"I don't believe you."

"Look. Ask yourself. Who does income tax affect? It doesn't affect the rich. They get around paying it no matter what," he said, tapping my fingernails, one by one, as I scowled, incredulous. "But regular people can't do that. Most people can't lose thirty percent of their paycheck. We get it back from the rich in property fees. The balance is the same. Income tax is a regressive tax," he insisted. The tapping stopped and he rested his fingers over mine.

I supposed he was right, if you took the most cynical position, that the rich would abuse their power no matter what. I softened. "What if I'm a regular person, with a skill—say, I'm a nurse. I want to live in Lucomo but I can't afford your income-tax-replacing property fees. What then?"

"For that"—he raised his free hand in an agreeable defense—"there's a process. But you'd need fluency in our languages—French, Italian, and English."

"Why?"

"Why does *language* matter?" His grin was now big enough to swallow the table.

"Yeah."

"It reflects who you are? Gives you a sense of culture and belonging? Establishes the boundaries of nation-states?"

Eyes wide, I mimed, *I don't understand*. He laughed. "What I mean," I explained, "is do you really care about *France*?"

"Don't let them hear you say that."

"They'll go on strike. I'll get over it."

"France is a resilient country," he replied, admiration in his expression. "We became nations, relatively, anyway, at the *same time*—"

"*We*," I interrupted. "What a word."

He bit his lip, shook his head, and flipped my hand over like it was a turtle. Caging my palm between his thumb and little finger, pressing his index finger ever so slightly against my wrist, he couldn't stop smiling. Neither could I. "I'm sorry," I pretended to apologize. "Please go on."

He let his palm drop entirely onto mine. "Don't think I won't. Italy didn't unify until 1861. By then France had already had three revolutions. The French love a strike because they're good at centralizing power. In that sense, they're much harder to deal with than the Italians," he said as my heart raced, "who are so busy infighting that we work better with their business interests than with their government. As for English, it's the language of the global economy. It's an unfortunate necessity."

"What if one doesn't want to learn French or Italian or English?"

"Well," he said, looking down at our intertwined hands, "*one* could always get citizenship a third way."

"How's that?"

"By marriage," he said, gazing at me so intently that everything around us stopped moving. The waiter froze behind his tray. The bartender held still, vodka bottle in hand. The music stopped and so did my breath.

Our eyes locked, I let myself ask, in a quiet voice: "Why aren't you married?"

"I haven't met the right person." His knee touched mine.

"I'd think a lot of people would want to marry a prince."

"A lot of people want to be rich," he said, sounding cynical but nonetheless a little bit sad. "That's not the same as being the head of a government. It's rare, in this day and age, to want to live in service to others." Forehead twitching, *what can you do.* "People see it as a burden."

I thought about the attentive faces in the crowd during my speech. How happy it made them to hear my story, to feel unified. How good it felt to me, to say things that I believed to be true, and to have people listen. "I don't understand that," I told him.

"Not everybody is like you," he said, so sincerely, our pulses matching.

I felt a nervous fugue hit me outright. In an attempt to control it, I kept at our teasing. "If you fall asleep while wearing your crown," I asked, "and your head jerks down? Like on a plane? Does the crown fall off?"

"It most certainly does." He didn't miss a beat. "It weighs three pounds, like a bag of flour."

"Has it ever? Fallen off?"

"I'll never tell." This he said in a low growl that I felt beneath my skin. "How am I such a curiosity to you? Haven't you met dozens of heads of state?"

"Not dozens." I shook my head. "A few. But *they* were *quite* intimidating."

"I'm not intimidating?" he said, really fake offended now.

"No," I lied. "Though, to be fair, at *our* dinner date in Shanghai, the queen of England got *hideously* drunk and I couldn't get a thing out of her. Senseless, she was. Off her crown." For a moment he stared blankly. I kept going. "The corgis went to the toilet on the floor next to the table," I whispered dramatically, "and nobody did a thing about it. We *stepped* in it as we left," I said reverently. "*What. A. Thrill.*"

Then he erupted into a gale of laughter. A tear squeezed out of one eye, like it had back at Scoria Vale, but for different reasons. I reached up and brushed it away. "Tears always at the ready," I said, licking the drop from my finger. "Emotional. I like that."

"I'm never emotional," he said, serious now, watching me, blooming, that lily smell mixing with the cedar of his sweat. We were inches apart, glued to each other, our bodies composed in mirrored poses. And me thinking I was the lion, while he played the lamb.

◆ ◆ ◆

We tore the dinner apart in symphony, inching closer. Knives slicing, animal blood pooling. When we met I'd first assumed he played some big-man sport like hockey, because like those men he was comfortable with his bulk, moving with a total elegance that to this day I still haven't acquired. Even the way he chewed was somehow more than human: Ares sprung from the side of a vase. He set down his shield and slid into the booth, covered in blood and dirt, then ripped a steak to pieces because that's how gods behave.

As we lingered over dessert, the waitstaff gathered at the bar and turned down the lights, eager to leave. We didn't even notice. It wasn't until Otto—who had stayed at the bar nursing a glass of water this entire time—had a slightly pressured exchange with a group of men that I looked up.

They were gesturing urgently at Finn. "Somebody wants to talk to you," I said softly, flicking my eyes toward the group.

Finn didn't acknowledge them—didn't even bother to look. "Someone always wants something. If it's important, someone will tell me." As I watched Otto manage to dispatch the men out to the street, I realized that the restaurant was basically closed.

"I think we have to leave," I laughed, gesturing to the waitstaff.

"I don't want to go to bed. Nightcap?"

I touched the lapel of his suit. "Sure, but we have to stay out."

"What do you suggest?"

"Lose the jacket, and let's find a bar," I ordered, and he complied—
then I turned and walked to the exit. I felt Finn watching me, the whole
way. I beamed so brightly that even Otto smiled as he held open the
door.

❖   ❖   ❖

We found a dive bar near the hotel, covered in fairy lights and punk
stickers. The crowd of cool kids in their twenties, with dyed hair and lip
rings, barely gave us a second glance as we squeezed onto the only two
open stools in the place. I had to press my knees alongside Finn's. He
took my hand—a touch now defined, permitted—and ordered club
sodas for us, tipping outrageously. We leaned in and whispered to each
other. Or rather, he whispered questions and I whispered answers. He
wanted to know about Johannesburg, about running, about my team,
about my parents, and I answered steadily, willing to tell him anything
as long as we did not have to leave. As long as our bodies did not have
to split apart.

I tried my own questions, but he was deft—he always managed to
turn it back to me. There was nothing I could say about myself that was,
in his view, even the slightest bit boring. He behaved as though everything I said was worth writing down. I don't even know what I said.
What remains of that conversation are the amber pools of his eyes.

Around four I began to feel dizzying waves of jet lag, worse than the
ones I'd felt in the cab after my speech. It must have shown on my face
because he held his hand to my cheek. "You're tired," he said.

I pushed my face into his palm. "I have an early flight."

"Commercial? No. I'll take you," he said, like it was already decided.
He meant in his own plane. But I had to keep something of myself from
this man. I couldn't fall in with him so easily, like I'd done with everyone else. There were consequences with Finn. It was clear as the water
in my glass.

I shook my head. "No, thank you."

He looked confused. "Most women—in my experience—prefer to fly private."

At that I drew myself away, set my palms flat on the bar top. "I'm not like most people, and I'm certainly not like most of the women you go on dates with."

"I don't want this evening to be over," he replied, understanding me now.

"I don't, either," I said, my anger cooling as quickly as it had appeared, fatigue dragging me down. My eyelids were heavy, begging to close, to shut out the light. I was exhausted. "But it has to be, for tonight."

We rode back to the hotel in silence. There was so much I wanted. I wanted to go to his room, get on that plane, stay by his side. But I knew—I knew in my gut—that it was neither the time nor the place. I'd had one power for my whole life: my physical self. My enduring goal was to satisfy and maintain that self, and in that pursuit, I was determined to play the most strategic hand. I wasn't thinking about what a romance between us might mean; I was focused on the seed below my stomach, that hard knot of want, and the tender walls of my beating heart. I thought with my skin. I told myself that I had to wait him out.

In the elevator to our rooms, we stood close enough to kiss, but neither of us dared. In a way it was more intimate. We arrived at my floor too soon.

"It was wonderful to be with you," I told him.

He replied, with the tenderest note of sadness, that it was a true pleasure. I stepped into the hall, still facing him. Neither of us broke eye contact until the elevator was shut between us and there was nothing to see but its polished doors.

That is how it was for us, at Scoria Vale and then again in Shanghai—we began to talk and then the conversation became one long river, rushing to a waterfall. I can still *feel* the feelings from that night: becoming aware of his presence in the dark of the backseat—gazing at him across the steakhouse table—sitting in a dive bar so petite that we both looked like uninvited giants—parting at that bronze elevator. Those moments are burned into me. I feel them like an exhale. I dream about them every so often, still, and wake up grasping at the sense of them.

In the morning, when I looked for the hall newspaper—a habit my mother and I'd always had, to look up my coverage—I found a bouquet of spiky lavender dahlias outside my room. The card read, in the same exquisite penmanship from his letter to me at Scoria Vale: *Until another night; in another city; until another dawn.*

I pocketed the card and deposited the flowers at the front desk.

"I'm on my way to the airport," I told the receptionist. "I hope you can find a home for these. One of the athletes? Track and field, if you can look that up. Whoever comes in last at the final. If they're not staying here, can you please find out and messenger this over, and charge it to me? Thank you."

I scribbled a new note—*You ran a beautiful race today. Welcome to the Olympic club. Sincerely, your colleague, Caroline Muller*—and requested a cab. An hour later, I was standing in line at the airport, heading through security. I held my breath as I passed through. Thankfully no one pulled me aside.

On the flight back to Europe, the man next to me kept brushing my arm with his. I kept moving away. I felt him staring. I worked hard to keep my face turned away, so that he would not strike up a conversation. I arced my shoulders toward the window and made a hard shell of myself for all twelve hours. Still he brushed me whenever he could. I had no means of escape.

Finn's claims about Lucomo—that it was safe, fair, equal—kept tumbling like a stone down the hills of my mind. I didn't think such places existed. I'd never seen a society like that. I'd never met a man with so much confidence, either. It did not occur to me to see his argument during dinner on behalf of an absolute monarchy as the symptom of a great and troubling disease; instead I saw his sense of humor, his modesty about the whole thing, as a sign of humility, grace, even.

When the plane landed at Frankfurt and I stepped into the aisle, the man seated next to me found a way to touch my waist and brush himself against my rear as he reached for his bag in the overhead. I elbowed the man—*hard*—but it was irrelevant. He'd gotten what he wanted.

Furious, I slung my bag behind me, a feeble barrier, and inched forward. The man gave me a wink as we stepped off the plane. I briefly regretted not taking Finn up on his offer of a ride home. But I told myself that I'd done the right thing.

It took Finn ten days to show up in Lisbon. When he did, I was ready.

10

THE INVITATION came from the French embassy: a classical concert by a Lugesque trio. I wondered only briefly how Finn had discovered my address before recalling that it was registered with the consulate as part of my visa.

I spent the morning shopping for a suitable dress. My habit of years past was to seek out unfashionable dark clothing that minimized my power. But now my power was different, and I could wrap myself in all the fabrics I had always avoided, the kind that would rip with one real step.

At the central department store I selected a silk dress, cut on the bias, with delicate shoulder straps, and a matching jacket with a stiff collar. The store's seamstress hemmed the dress to my knees and added the excess fabric to the jacket, so the hemlines matched.

I put on Rally's red lipstick, then fiddled with my hair in the mirror, braiding and pinning it atop the side of my head in a knot. The salesgirl tossed me a cluster of silk flowers. As the ribbon-wrapped stems slid into place, there I was: a Frida, looking for my very own Diego.

◆ ◆ ◆

I made it through embassy security without any stray cupping of my bottom. *I must have dressed correctly,* I thought to myself, *I must look like another man's property,* before realizing, with a little chirp of relief, that it was because I was in an embassy and such an assault would be an embarrassment.

The ballroom was like that of any nice hotel, a modern room slapped here and there with faux-royal gilt, the chairs all a teeny bit knocked about, the draperies all slightly frayed at the hems. A hundred or so seats faced a trio of black-gowned goddesses cradling string instruments. The atmosphere was fevered; Finn had not yet arrived. Half the audience chatted away while the other half drank cocktails and stuffed canapés into their mouths.

The French ambassador to Portugal was a matronly bundle of suiting, topped with a puffy shock of lacquered brown hair. A small man, her aide, stood three feet behind her and tapped away on a BlackBerry. The aide gave me *that* look—the one everyone gave me back then, unable to stop themselves—and so I stepped forward and told him my name. I was introduced a few moments later. Madame Ambassador shook my hand, saying, I think, what a pleasure it had been to watch me run. As that was the extent of my French, I thanked her politely in English. "You have your own runner in the family, yes?" I touched my hand to her elbow. Nobody could resist me, especially not this stout bureaucrat.

"Stephanie, *yes,* how kind of you to remember!" the ambassador exclaimed, shifting languages seamlessly. "We are hoping for Athens."

As my face fell at the mention of Athens, I was saved from embarrassment when all at once, everyone around us stood taller. No trumpet sounded, no flock of birds was released, no announcement was made, but the whole audience felt it. The room changed as it had at the bar when he had appeared with the singer. Changed like the crowd used to, when I walked onto the track.

The only adornment on Finn's suit was a small lapel pin, with enamel stripes of lavender and green, to signify his rank. As people shook his hand, they disappeared entirely inside his frame, their heads coming up to the middle of his necktie. Hand to hand, nod to nod, he moved gently through the crowd, in my direction.

The ambassador caught my expression as I watched him approach. "He's a hard man," she offered quietly. "You would be better off with someone more . . . normal."

"I'm not very normal, though, either," I replied.

"I suppose every girl, even one like you, wants to be a princess," the ambassador mused, "deep down." She blew out a condescending sigh, as if it was the stupidest wish she could imagine.

My nostrils flared. I hadn't spent my life playing with Barbies, wearing tutus. I wasn't some nobody who fantasized about being special. I'd run twelve thousand miles in the dirt. I *was already special*. "We all have different destinies," I said flatly.

She gave the faintest nod, a politic simulation of an apology. "Of course," she murmured as Finn swiveled from the nearest circle and took up all our space.

"Caroline," he said. "Madame Ambassador."

She curtsied and after a moment, I followed. The delicate cross of the legs, sinking without tilting my pelvis. It was painful.

Through the windows, the sun emerged, shining onto my shoulders. Destabilized, he lost his manners and glanced at my body. "I missed you," Finn said to me unexpectedly.

"I missed you, too," I replied quietly. Locked in, we forgot ourselves, until one of the musicians sneezed. I blinked to find everyone else in the room watching.

"After you." Finn motioned, indicating the rows of chairs.

I was to learn later that this was quite the gesture, to let me sit first. Nobody was to sit until he sat. They were not to eat until he ate, nor speak until he spoke. But I didn't know this—or perhaps I took pride in ignoring my sense of it—and I'd been standing too long. I clattered down like a pile of little porcelain bricks. Finn sat to my left, so near that the wool of his trousers brushed the hem of my dress.

When the lights went down, it was my turn to bloom like a lily. I heard Finn's every breath, the air ballooning in his chest. I wanted to *be* the air, wanted to pass through his lungs, to dissolve into particles, to enter his bloodstream, to flush beneath his skin. But I did not turn into air and fly into his mouth. Instead I sat perfectly still.

The music was lovely, full—it must have given me pleasure; I am sure that a smile played around my mouth, perhaps my hand flew to my heart at a crescendo—but all I could think about was that I wanted to follow him into a dark room. Yet I was terrified that if I did, we'd never see each other again.

When the trio finished, we clapped in our seats. Thirty seconds passed before I realized that everyone was waiting for him. "Want to be a tourist?" I asked.

"I'd like that."

I followed him outside. A bulky armored vehicle idled, Otto at the wheel, Dix minding the rear passenger door. I kept my distance. When Finn motioned toward the car, I shook my head. "I'd rather walk," I insisted. "It's not very far away."

Young Otto and Young Dix glanced at each other, then at Finn. He waved them off. We fell into step, Otto ten feet ahead, Dix ten feet behind, walking east, *up up up* the city's endless staircases. Seared by sunbeams, sweat soaking through my dress and the placket of his shirt, we rose high enough to overlook the whole of Lisbon and its sea of terra-cotta tiles. Eventually Finn snagged my index finger with his, stopping me in my tracks. "Where are we going?" he asked.

"Saint George's Castle. I thought you might be at home there," I teased.

"Sow Yor-hey," he corrected me.

I rolled my eyes. "You speak Portuguese."

"It's not *that* hard."

The roads to the castle were small ramparts, graded low, made for trucking goods back and forth. We walked very close. I wondered aloud what circumstances would have brought us here in the past—a man and a woman, unmarried, approaching a castle together—say, in the seventeenth century. Finn thought about it briefly and responded that we might be a nun and a priest, who, having witnessed a miracle out in the countryside, had made our way here to share the news with the king. "I'd rather we were spies," I declared, "here to infiltrate the regime."

"We'd still be *dressed* as a nun and a priest." At that we slowed our gait, hands together, heads bowed piously. Enraptured by make-believe, we walked the parapets and ramparts, the keeps and staircases, inventing past lives.

"I'm a woman of revenge, here to kill the king," I offered, "to cut his throat with my own hand, to watch his blood pour down his nightshirt."

"I'm a prince of another land, here to take the throne."

"Would you?"

"Heavens no. It's lonely enough being the prince of one land."

At the castle's well, he dug in his pockets for centimes. Together we made wishes and flicked them to the dry bottom, where they clinked against a treasure trove. My wish was to see Finn again. I flipped another to be sure. "You must be a very big classical music fan," I said when it landed, "to come all this way for a concert."

"Absolutely," he said. "Now let's get down to it. Are you going to marry this person you're living with?"

I suppressed a smile. "I don't know," I said slowly. "What do you think I should do?"

"I think you should *not*."

"Why not?"

"If you were married, you'd have a hard time dating me."

"You date a lot," I said factually. "How can two people keep things even when one of you is being rated in the paper? I'd date you if it could be private. But that doesn't seem possible."

"No," he agreed, after a moment. "It's probably not."

An unpleasant truth. Still, relieved that he hadn't pretended otherwise, I suggested that we get dinner. We made our way down the hill to a little café. The restaurant was the Mozambican one that Hanna liked—but oh, who cares about the restaurant. When we sat down, I took my jacket off, revealing the silk gown with its narrow straps cutting into the sculpt of my shoulders. Finn nearly fell off his chair. We barely touched our food. I remember he looked into my eyes before we ordered and asked if I was hungry and I said always and then I just let it *hang* there.

When the coffee came, Otto brought over a square package wrapped in brown paper. "I have something for you," Finn said, sliding it across the table. It was a biography of Frida Kahlo. The first page was inscribed with his phone number. "So you can return it," he said. "I won't wait another year to see you."

I clutched the book and smiled down to my toes. "Thank you."

"Did you see the exhibition that came here?"

"I did."

"But you haven't read the biography?" He seemed crestfallen at the very possibility.

"No," I told him, running my fingers over his dozens of dog-eared pages, pleased that soon I'd discover what they marked. "Diego, for the record, made me think of you. His commitment to 'the people.' It's very like you."

"Diego Rivera was a communist."

"Wouldn't you have been one in his shoes?"

"I believe in equality of opportunity." He shrugged. "I don't think governments should limit the choices people can make with their lives. I think they should protect and support their citizens with the basics and let everything else be a choice."

I thought about that for a moment. To my surprise, I agreed. His perspective dovetailed nicely with my own feelings about athletics, that love of the starting line. As I paid the bill—I insisted on paying—he asked me back to his hotel. I declined.

"There's something between us," he said, confused. "Am I wrong?"

"I'm not available," I told him.

"You can leave your boyfriend."

"I can't picture anything but my heart being broken," I said unambiguously.

"I'm not asking you to marry me." And he said this like it was a gift, like he was being casual, but it was the very thing that I wanted and so it was the thing I hated most to hear him say. Because it was the single card I had to play, I stood up and kissed him on the cheek, losing my breath as my lips touched the edge of his, and then I walked out of the restaurant and hailed a cab.

But I left my jacket on the chair.

❖   ❖   ❖

At home in the apartment, I dashed into my room, avoiding Rally and Hanna. I paged through the biography to the first corner Finn had folded back twice. It opened with a letter: "It's not love, or tenderness, nor affection, it is the whole of life, mine that I found when I saw it in your hands," Frida wrote to Diego. "In my mouth I have the taste of almonds from your lips. Our words have never gone outside. Only a mountain knows the insides of another mountain." It was life itself that I drew from Finn—the thrumming rush of blood—and in him I saw the core of a mountain that mirrored my own.

The next day, a messenger showed up with a box wrapped in brown paper. My jacket was folded inside, with a note: *I will think of you tomorrow, tomorrow, and tomorrow—and the day after that—please call me.*

11

THEN MY MOTHER died. I was staring at the phone, thinking of calling Finn, when it rang.

"Caroline. It's. Mum," my father said, his voice halting and empty. ". . . She's. Gone."

"Gone where?" I was confused, at first. I didn't understand.

"She fell sick in the night. I took her to hospital. She went into surgery. She died about an hour ago. I've been sitting here waiting for my hands to work the phone. They say it was an aneurysm. I am so—she loved you so much." He lost his voice entirely then, choked by sobs.

It took a moment to sink in.

"Caroline, can you hear me?" my father rasped. He didn't want to, but he would say it again, if he had to.

"I heard you. I'm—I can't believe it. I mean, I believe you. I'm sorry. Oh god," I mumbled, rising to my feet, automatically seeking out my passport, searching for a bag. "I'll be there as soon as I can."

I stuffed clothes into a duffel, emptied the medicine cabinet, and left the apartment within minutes, hailing the first taxi I saw. I sat stunned the whole ride to the airport, rendered weightless by distress. The ticket agents were kind. They gave me the bereavement discount and ushered me through security in time to catch the last flight up to Amsterdam, where I changed planes for the eleven-hour flight to Johannesburg. Even with the discount, it was nearly two thousand euro. I found myself wishing it had cost more. I loathed myself for being so far away. It seemed like if I could hate myself enough, if I could be punished, then maybe she would come back.

I found punishment soon enough: I hadn't stretched properly and began swelling with pain the moment we took off. Soon each muscle contracted to its shortest stance. Even for me, even in that state of self-flagellation, it was unbearable, and it did not bring my mother back.

I took the drugs left over from Scoria Vale. Dilaudid, a powerful opiate. Flexeril, a muscle relaxant. The pain was soon replaced by a warm fuzz. Knotted tissues slackened, fell limp. I slept until the pills wore off six hours later, and everything in me contracted again with a vengeance. Then I remembered why I never took these kinds of drugs—because taking them never ended. I was in such intractable spasms that I could not even retrieve another dose from the overhead. When we landed, the stewardesses had to roll me off the plane in a wheelchair. I let them take me through security like that, and then I curled into a ball in the back of a taxi with my bag and ate another handful of pills.

The taxi bumped along the highways. The taste of red dirt rising in my throat, I opened the window and let in the diesel, the smell of home, a world run on generators. At our exit, onto the local roads, people surrounded us like the car was simply another person, talking loudly and laughing and exchanging in all eleven of our languages. We merely paused at the handful of stoplights, the driver lowering his window, waving others by, taking his turn with a heavy foot. Cars did not stop at stoplights in Johannesburg, then, day or night. My hometown is a place of constant negotiation and bone-deep resistance to oversight. It was safer to figure out the timing needed to move through it for yourself.

My father wasn't alone when I arrived, though he was *indeed* alone and would *be* alone *forever*. Our neighbors Dora and Cassy bustled about the house, cooking and labeling casseroles that my father would never eat. He sat crumpled on the old tweed sofa, staring at paperwork from the funeral home, coughing intermittently into the sleeve of his sweater. He'd had a miner's cough my whole life, though now it sounded worse than ever. When he saw me, he began to cry, tears catching in the crags of his face.

"I'm so sorry, Caroline, I'm so sorry you didn't see her," he sobbed. I'd never seen him cry before and it made everything worse. I sat with him on the sofa like that, telling him not to apologize, that I was wrong to be gone, for hours and hours.

I don't think we slept. My father opened a bottle of gin. Without thinking of the consequences, or the medication already coursing through my system, I joined him. We drank one set of doubles, and then another, none of it mattering or making a single difference except that finally we must have passed out. Luckily, I woke up several hours later— in an armchair, with a splitting headache. I thought for a moment that I must be at their anniversary party.

But then I remembered my mother had died and it hit my stomach like a cannonball, and then I was clutching a toilet and throwing up. My father came in and held back my hair. "Dignified mourners, that's us," he said. I cackled midretch. It came out as a kind of dinosaur noise, and then we were both laughing, my head in the toilet and my father slumped next to me, coughing intermittently, on the floor of the bathroom.

We drove to the funeral home with her best dress, the one she'd bought for the Olympics, and some pictures for the makeup. Purchased a dove-gray casket with white silk lining, pretty standard, I suppose, the middle tier. Drove to the church. Met with the priest. Chose hymns for the service. We wrote the obituary for the newspaper and mailed it in with a photograph.

My mother was descended from British settlers who had taken land in Zimbabwe, then called Rhodesia, three generations earlier under the employ of the British South Africa Company. Colonel Swan, my mother's grandfather, forcibly possessed six thousand hectares and planted citrus about three hours from Salisbury, now Harare. The soil, cultivated for so long by the Ndebele people, was good; the oranges and grapefruits took right away. I have one picture of my mother from the Swan farm, and that is the one we sent to the newspaper. In hand-me-down men's trousers, the too-big waist cinched with a bit of rope, she sits impatiently on her bicycle, its basket full of oranges. The fine dust of the road stripes down the middle of the tires and clings to her boots like powdered sugar.

My mother told me that whenever it rained on the farm, that fine dust turned to silver, the plants doubled in size, all the flowers opened while the crickets sang in chorus, and ripe oranges fell from the trees. That was why they had colonized the land, because it was so fertile. That's what men do in this world to fertile things: put fences around them and make them procreate at any cost.

The farm is where my mother grew up until Robert Mugabe's party, the Zimbabwe African National Union, began to repatriate the land. When the Swans left Rhodesia with their passports and two duffel bags, my mother was sixteen. Her two older brothers were killed. I don't know how, exactly. I was never told. She couldn't explain other than to say, *It was a long time coming. We should have left sooner. We didn't belong there.* Her life changed overnight. In a moment everything she knew was taken from her. We had that in common. We had so very much in common.

My mother's reading room was made from hoarder's piles of newspapers. Any mention that I'd ever had. Nothing was too small, not even local newsletters and church bulletins. My medals lined the wall, the Olympic gold hanging next to my second-place rosette from St. Margaret's, like they were equivalent. The free spaces were tacked with postcards I sent every week. In the view from her chair, mine was a life well lived, well worth sacrificing her own happiness for.

The grief of losing a parent takes many forms. I don't know what it must be like to lose a parent when you are very young, to grow up without a mother. I am sure it is a shapeless void that follows wherever you go, and you must be always attempting to fill it in—to discern fact from fiction—to find yourself reflected in the myths of the person you can barely remember. I am sure that it is very, very hard.

But I knew my mother. I knew her and loved her desperately. No haze obscures my memories of her. They are clear as a church bell on a cold day. Losing her was a hard shock. She put me first. She gave so much to me that there was not enough left for her own self. I don't think I quite understood the ramifications of that until years later.

In fairy tales, the ones I would someday read to my own daughter, the princess at the heart of the story rarely has living parents to worry about. Sleeping Beauty's parents die long before she wakes from her hundred-year nap; Cinderella's mother, and then father, die and leave her to the indenture of a wicked stepmother; Rapunzel is stolen from her parents by a sorceress; Snow White's mother dies in childbirth, and her stepmother sends her away with the huntsman. When biological parents do appear, they are fathers in jeopardy. The original Beauty, she of *La Belle et La Bête*, trades herself to the Beast to grant her father his freedom. Like so many, she goes from her father's clutches to her husband's. With a mother around, daughters are safe, but without one, they are prey for princes, witches, and beasts alike. They are killed for their insolence, sacrificed for their male counterparts, imprisoned for their desires. Mothers cannot appear in fairy tales because there is no room in the stories for both women.

❖   ❖   ❖

"Harriet Jane Swan Muller was born in 1949, in a stall filled with tack on a hay-strewn floor, in the barn of a citrus farm, three hours from Harare, when it was called Salisbury. Under repatriation she made her

way here in 1974 to attend secretarial school, by taking—and I believe
this is in order—a horse, a bush plane, a train, and a bus. She was a
secretary for two years until she met my father at a protest. After they
were married, she gave her time to the UWO and to me. As many of
you know, I had a running career. My mother took me all over the
world. As my chaperone, she only saw the hotel, the route, the airport.
We counted. Twenty-three countries she had been to where she saw not
one museum or cultural site. Only continental breakfast rooms, buses,
sidewalks, and pharmacies. She never complained, not once; she was
not wistful or sentimental. She concentrated on my success." At this I
lost my composure, gripped the podium, tried to focus. I choked out
the rest. "She loved us so deeply, she put us first, she loved my father
and me more than life itself and she cared for her community and adopted country. And she will be so missed that to say now the words *I
miss her, I miss you*—that's the faintest expression of what I feel. Thank
you for coming."

The ceremony was graveside. I plunged my hand into a wet pile of
dirt and threw a grip's worth across the gloss of my mother's coffin. The
dirt landed in a ball, then blasted apart, like my family. No walk has
ever felt as grand a betrayal as the first steps away from my mother's
grave. Later I clipped one of my dirtied fingernails and pressed it between the pages of one of her scrapbooks. I did not want to lose the last
specks of earth between us.

The reception was in our house, spilling out into the dry garden
under a borrowed tent. My father clutched my hand through the whole
evening. I felt woozy, alternating between lethargy and panic, like I was
constantly being woken from a bittersweet dream only to be told the
building was burning down.

Zola called from London while I was refilling the sandwich trays.
Now an associate at a white-shoe law firm, she'd negotiated the finer
details of my sponsorship contract after the Olympics, and we'd stayed
in touch that way, though we were no longer as close as we'd once been.

She invited me to stay with her at Christmas, if I was returning to Europe. I promised to think about it.

As the mourners began to leave, the funeral home dropped off the flowers. They filled the rooms, lining all the walls, replacing the legions of empty glasses and plates on the tabletops. In the very last armful, there was a bouquet of white dahlias and fragile ferns. The card bore my name. Inside was a note in Finn's bold hand:

Dear Caroline: I was so surprised when you didn't call (vain I know) that I asked Otto to stop by and make sure you were all right. I am so very sorry for the death of your mother. My father died when I was twenty-five and nothing anyone could do or say was helpful—it was the greatest hurt—but I'll try, anyway. C. S. Lewis wrote, after his wife died, that no one had told him that grief feels so much like fear. No one told me that, either, but it's true, and so all I can do is tell you in turn: Grief feels so much like fear—but it is not fear. It is loneliness. I would beg of you to let these flowers soak in the rain at your mother's graveside until they're nothing but mulch. Let them wait by her side in peace this first night when you yourself cannot.

> *With deepest love and solace—*
> *Ferdinand II*

It *was* a great hurt, a wound, a hole in my heart, and the fluttering in my chest did indeed feel *exactly* like terror. But unlike the terror of my fall in Lisbon—that time in the rain, when my rear had smacked on the ground and I worried that my new hip was broken—there was no adrenaline, nothing that could rise up and free me. The fog of grief pressed me down. I thought of my mother alone there in the dirt and I wanted to take her from her coffin and hold her in my arms. I told myself to get up, get up, get up, whispered this aloud until I was standing with the keys to my father's Volkswagen. It was late, and I was full of

pills, but I got behind the wheel and made my way back to the ceme-
tery, darting inexpertly through every red light. I laid Finn's flowers
against the muddy heap of her grave, told her how much I loved her,
and said goodbye to her once more.

This time when I walked away it did not tear at my heart so dear. My
grief was lessened by the weight of a petal, but it was enough, and I slept
through the night.

12

WITHIN A WEEK the rest of the flowers brought by the funeral home began to turn. Yet even in their rot they did very little to cover the lingering presence of my mother. With every inhale it was as though she were around the corner, in the kitchen, making a coffee.

During that time, I suffered from the constant *forgetting* that my mother was dead. *I simply forgot.* Every afternoon at four, I picked up the phone to text her. Did she want to go for a cycle because I'd been feeling terribly down? Has she noticed that Daddy's cough seems worse? Did she think we ought to plant all these flowers? Should we have the leftovers of the *pap en vleis* Cassy had made, or should we go out tonight? But there was no one to answer her phone but me. It sat powered off in a leather tray in her office and I couldn't bear to move it. My father kept asking me to take it to the tech shop, along with her computer, so someone could print out every message she'd ever sent him, and then he would make a strangled noise and say, *Never mind, I'm not ready.*

He was trapped, my dad. He was absolutely lost without her. Each morning when I brought him a coffee, he crumpled. I knew it was because of how much I looked like my mother, even with all the changes.

My father's pain filled every room so completely that there was no space for my own. I read Finn's note again and again, and his other notes, and all the pages he'd dog-eared in the Kahlo biography about Frida and Diego and their love for each other. I thought about what it must be like to have that much love, and in my father's vacant eyes I saw what it was like to lose it.

Between his staring like a vegetable, my forgetting, and waves of my own terrible grief, I grew edgy. I could not stay in South Africa. While it felt the biggest cruelty to leave, I told myself that my father would grieve like this whether I was there or not.

In the end it was the doctors who pushed me to depart. Drs. Swane-poel and Singh had their offices at the public hospital where my mother died. I'd had my emergency surgery there, the first one, before they sent me to America, but in the haze of trauma I didn't notice its flaws. Now, returning for a follow-up appointment, all I could see was the peeling paint on its cinder-block walls, the decades-old ambulances, the wait-ing room that was always full. With Scoria Vale to compare it to, our hospital now looked unbearably worn-out to me. Underfunded. *The place where they could not save my mother.*

Both doctors were eager to replace my right knee. Sooner is better, they insisted. They wanted to do an MRI, too, said I'd have to go to the private hospital in Sandton, pay out of pocket, seek reimbursement from the sponsor's foreign insurance company. They warned me that it might cost far more than I was comfortable with, but they were certain it was necessary to move forward. As I envisioned emptying my bank account in order to go under anesthesia and into the twilight where my mother now lived, I felt such a tremulous wave of fear that I nearly ran from the office into the parking lot. I felt absolutely certain that staying for the surgery was the wrong thing to do. I wanted to see a few more things, to live more, before I lost another year (or worse) to recovery. I did not want to get back into a hospital bed and wait for the future to begin. Dr. Singh made me promise to come back before my sponsor-funded healthcare ran out. I agreed but didn't mean it for a second.

It was easy to arrange my departure. A widowed friend from the UWO, Winni Diedrichsen, agreed to move temporarily into the guest room. She needed to repair large sections of her roof, anyway, she said, and it would be a convenience for her not to have to sleep in the dust. I was grateful for that lie; I could tell she felt so sorry for my father, and that she missed my mother, too. My father seemed pleased with this arrangement and told me not to worry. "Your mother would want you to live your life," he said in his space cadet voice. "Winni can watch out for me."

I organized my mother's papers and checked their finances. There were, to my surprise, no savings to speak of. It appeared that my mother gave me all they had when I left home. Their accounts had the equivalent of five thousand euro in checking. There was a letter from the union to my father with the date he needed to return to work, in order to receive his full pension in five years. The wet tenor of his cough—it seemed unlikely that he would meet the deadline. I did what I could to make it easier. Their statements revealed that the house was nearly paid for. Without hesitating, I paid it off, and the funeral bills, too.

That left me with about three thousand euro, enough to get back to Lisbon, pay my expenses for a while, and then . . . I didn't know what. I was as lost as I'd been a year earlier.

I booked my ticket back to Lisbon with a heavy heart. Neither Hanna nor Rally had called. They'd sent emails, the easiest way to tell me they were sorry. I realized how much depth our friendship lacked. I stood behind them, accomplished enough to make them feel special and naive enough to find them special in return. In the daylight, as I looked for the kind of jobs they would never deign to apply for, or mourned my mother decades before they would understand this kind of grief, I hardly rated.

I thought about how alive Finn made me feel. The seed, the anchor he'd planted without meaning to, still rooted in my gut. I opened my mouth to speak, to tell my father about this man I'd met, this man who cared about me, but—my father was already gone, staring out the window like someone had shot him with a tranquilizer dart.

I walked to the internet café, traded wrinkled bills for tokens, and spent the afternoon reading about Lucomo, the web pages loading with agonizing slowness. I pictured myself renting a room in Cap-Griffe and meeting him in one of their tiny streets. I inquired with an employment agency over email. Someone wrote back immediately; there were no jobs at the moment, she wrote, for foreigners. *Not a one?* No. Every listing at the moment solely permitted Lugesque. I checked flights to the nearest airport and found that I couldn't afford to fly there, or even to stay a single night in the five-star hotels of Lucomo. I couldn't afford a rented room, either; real estate rates there were astronomically high.

But it didn't matter. I didn't need some elaborate plan to run into him. I had his phone number, and the next morning, I ginned up the courage to call.

❖ ❖ ❖

I dialed with bated breath—only to be told that the number I was typing in did not exist.

I tried again and received the same message.

I read the inscription again and counted: country code, area, number, and then—odd—it seemed that it contained four extra digits, separated by a near-imperceptible dash on the end. I dialed the first twelve and waited. The line beeped a few times, a noise that was not really a ring. Then—silence.

"Hello?" I called out.

Nothing.

"Hello?"

The line went dead.

I called back and this time, when the silence answered, I typed the four extra digits.

It rang. A phone number *within* a phone number. And rang—all the way through to his voicemail. "You've reached the mobile of Ferdinand Fieschi. Please leave a message and your call will be returned promptly," said a man's voice, not Finn's. A long beep.

"Hello. This is Caroline Muller. I wanted to ring and thank you for the flowers." I thought about giving our phone number, but—what if my father answered? I didn't want to explain. "I can try you at this same time tomorrow, perhaps, and maybe we can connect," I said. "So"—I checked my watch—"eleven in the morning tomorrow. I'm, um, I'm two hours past GMT. If you could translate it to your time zone, then we will work it out. Thanks ever so. Goodbye."

◆   ◆   ◆

He answered right away the next day.

"Hi—"

"It's Caroline—"

"I know—"

"Right." I gripped the receiver like it was tethering me to Earth.

"Are you okay?"

"No," I admitted. "Not at all."

"How can I see you?"

"I don't know," I said. "I've got an open return to Lisbon on KLM, but . . . I suppose I don't have to. Where are you?"

"Milano," he said, sounding out the *a* and the *o*. "A conference for textile manufacturers."

"Starting a clothing line?"

He snorted. "Not yet. Everyone here does business in Lucomo."

"I've never been to Milan."

"Come and meet me."

His request hatched a flock of butterflies from beneath my navel, rising in my chest, darting from rib to rib. I twirled the phone's cord around my finger and looked out the window. I could see the patch of dirt outside our house, the tall fence topped with barbed wire, shreds of errant plastic bags waving from its spikes. "Is Milan nice?"

"The food's great, but it's fucking freezing this time of year," he said. "Do you mind?"

"No," I replied softly. "I suppose not."

After we hung up, I called the airline. The cheapest flight to Milan was five hundred euro, leaving the next day, routed through Doha. Not bad. I put the phone down and looked out in the living room. My dad was holding the television remote, staring at the box, which was off. He blinked gently, coughed into the sleeve of his shirt, and closed his eyes.

I picked the receiver back up. After giving my ticket number, I was placed on hold. Five minutes later—minutes I ticked off in frustration, knowing the charge was at least ten rand a minute—someone got back on to say that it had all been taken care of. I was booked on the evening's red-eye to Amsterdam, and then a connecting flight to Linate, Milan's smaller airport. The ticket was already paid for, and the return portion of my fare would be refunded.

My first feeling was relief. I needed the money. Then—nervous fear. Did this mean something? Did I owe him? I called Finn, but it went straight to voicemail.

"Hello. Caroline again. I appreciate your buying me a new flight, which, I suppose, means you know my arrival time so . . . thank you. But now I have to buy dinner. Don't choose anywhere too expensive, though. Okay. See you . . . in Italy. Bye." I smiled as I hung up.

My smile stayed in place for hours, refusing to budge, snapping back and forth across my face as I packed, hugged my father goodbye, and called a taxi for the airport.

◆　◆　◆

I arrived in Milan on December 10, 2003, wearing a camel wool coat and sweater, faded jeans, orthopedic clogs, and carrying a small black duffel bag. I'd kept limber on the plane, stretching in the freezing exits every ninety minutes and rolling my ankles, wrists, knees, and hips, pretending I didn't see the people watching me. I arrived undamaged. With the slightest bit of makeup on, my long hair brushed down past my waist and an unkempt fringe heavy across my eyes, I could have been any normal young woman.

I spotted him from leagues away. Finn stood beneath the arrival hall's dramatic armature looking like any normal thirtysomething man—waxed jacket, white shirt, dark trousers, and battered brown boots. I skipped up behind him and placed my hand on his elbow, expecting him to lean in and kiss my cheek. Instead he wrapped me in a hug. When we should have both released, we didn't. It was one of those hugs where you're stunned with bliss at the feel of the other person, because they're truly holding you, making you whole.

He mumbled *hello* into my hair. I was buried somewhere in his neck. When I breathed in, he breathed out. Our chests aligned with a satisfying roundness. Before we could kiss—we very nearly did—I let go. *Patience,* I told my beating heart, taking his hand and leading him to the street. I aimed for the bus bench, digging in my pockets for change. The shadow of a bus—no, another of his trucklike SUVs— pulled up, eclipsing every other car in the queue. Finn moved to open the door. I held him back. "Do you mind?" I asked, jutting my chin. "After the flight I'd rather prefer to stand on the bus." I wanted to be with *him*, not with the men who seemed to follow him everywhere.

Otto shook his head. Finn's lips formed a tight apology. "It's not always up to me."

I let myself be helped into the cavernous backseat. When the door closed it was like the world had been put on mute. A thick shell of bulletproof glass and reinforced steel insulated us against every sound. Otto drove us across town, through the gridded maze of traffic, in complete silence, until we arrived at a glossy black building with neither address, nor sign, nor doorbell.

A valet appeared and held open the door. Otto remained in the car. Soon we were inside a private club so secretive that I hesitate now even to describe it. But I think of it as the first place where I began to separate from the outside world.

It was quiet. Not cold quiet, but warm quiet: Carpets so thick they swallowed the sound of our steps. Walls upholstered with fabric so dense I couldn't hear myself breathe. We were taken through several large rooms and into a smaller one, with a roaring fireplace and a table laid for two. There were no menus; we did not even order. The food simply appeared, one delicious dish after another, pickled vegetables, cheeses, meats, truffle-bedecked risotto, and herb-crusted sablefish.

Finn asked about the funeral first. I confessed everything I'd felt, about the way the house smelled and my father's tears, and how desperately I'd wanted to get away but that I didn't know where to go anymore. "You didn't want to go back to Lisbon," he said evenly, but there was hope.

"No." I was relieved at the sound of my *no*. Saying it made it real.

"I was afraid we were in a fight."

"I was about to call you." I reached out and held his hand, and there in the dark of his private club, with the fire's heat on our faces, I felt happy—truly happy—for the first time since the funeral. All those doors between us and the street. I marveled that this secret world had been here all along, nestled inside the one I walked through. "I wanted to call you."

"I've thought about you every day since we met," he said, brushing the palm of my hand. "You said you couldn't date me. Is that still true?"

"I actually—" I hesitated, then told the truth. "The problem is still the same. It's you. I am not . . . I cannot . . . I cannot be . . ."

He gazed at me across the table, breathless, senseless, waiting.

"I cannot be broken," I finally said, and couldn't look at him. "I've already been broken."

"What if we could be casual, and private? Like this?" Finn asked.

"This is *not* casual."

"I don't know what you want," he said, frustrated. "You won't be casual; you won't be serious. What do you want?"

"I want—tomorrow, and tomorrow, and tomorrow," I said, my voice so frail that it came in a whisper. "I want . . . there to be no end." Saying this felt like an ending unto itself—to admit to such want was to ensure that it could never be satisfied. For a moment there was a crack in the world, and it seemed that everything between us was over, but then—before I could stop myself, I was climbing atop him—and I wanted to be the air in his lungs—and we were gripping each other like I was oxygen, and we were dying, and there was nothing but the two of us.

Finally, he broke away and placed his forehead to mine. "Are you asking me to marry you?" he whispered into my ear.

"I am," I said. "I am. I'm all or nothing."

That was how we got engaged.

13

WE LEFT THE CLUB in a daze. A new car waited for us; this one was smaller, low to the ground. Its seats and walls were quilted with a suede so peanut-buttery that I was afraid to touch it. I sat gingerly, aware of the dirt on my shoe soles, fidgeting with the window buttons. One turned out to be a partition. I slid it closed. Finn touched the third finger of my left hand then, the soft spots between my knuckles. "Use a twist tie," I told him. I didn't care. All I wanted was for him to belong to me.

"What's that?"

"I mean, I don't mind about a ring."

"No, I'm asking what a twist tie is." Finn was puzzled.

"The paper and wire thing that holds a loaf of bread shut," I explained.

"Of course. I see." But he didn't see.

"You've never opened your own bread," I said in teasing disbelief. I wondered if he'd ever even bought any.

"In Lucomo bread comes in paper bags." He kissed me into silence.

Streets later I looked up. "Where is *he* taking us?" I gestured to the partition.

"Nowhere in particular. It's safer to move around than it is to stay still." Everything he said to me in those days, even when it was banal, mirrored my own desires and beliefs. "Let's get a ring," he insisted. "Please. *Cara* Caro," he teased, "precious and dear. Don't you want to live up to your name?"

"Aren't you supposed to go off on your own? Isn't it terribly—what's that French word—*gauche,* for me to choose?"

"*Gauche, oui. Goffo en Italiano*—but not quite either. Maybe . . . *tacky*?" He didn't change accents but somehow managed to fit the languages to his own voice, his own manner of speech, as though he owned them.

"*Takkie*?" I asked, confused.

"Tacky."

"*Takkie,*" I said, pointing to my shoes. "Jozi for 'shoe.'"

"No, *that's goffo,*" he laughed, grabbing my clog. "I don't know if it's a shoe or gauche or tacky for you to choose because I don't have any experience. As you'll be the one wearing it, I think you ought to choose." I was lit aflame to hear him say he had no experience—that he'd never been truly engaged, that what he'd told me about Lidia was really true, no matter what the papers said.

❖   ❖   ❖

We went to a gilded arcade, one of those glass-topped intersections of expensive stores near the city center, and beelined for a tiny shop. The door was locked; inside, the jeweler, an elderly man with papery skin and white whiskers, stood motionless, stooped over a velvet tray. At our knock he looked up slowly, then shuffled to the door.

The cases held the standard treasures you might see in any store—necklaces and rings and bracelets—and I lingered over them, enraptured by their sparkling facets. I paused over a diamond the size of a fingernail and realized Finn could buy it, if he wanted to. I glanced over, searching for his reaction. But Finn stood yards away, in the back of the store. "This way." He tilted his head.

The papery man pressed a button underneath the counter. The walls slid away to reveal a small door, an elevator that was otherwise invisible. As at the club, we were being taken to a private room. Finn would probably not, I realized, make such a purchase through a glass window. We stepped through. The jeweler did not follow. We dropped down several floors. "What is this place?" I asked.

Finn bit the edge of my ear. "A private collection."

The lift opened into a small salon, where the restrained violins of a classical symphony curled from an antique stereo. Paneled in dark woods and velvets, the space generated an intimacy all on its own. I felt my shoulders drop.

At the back, a dignified woman somewhere in her forties sat behind a large desk. Behind her was, I presumed, an imitation Rembrandt. A loupe hung from her neck on a thick gold chain. Her hands smoothed the surface of a padded suede blotter. With a wave she indicated that we should seat ourselves across from her. She did not rise, as everyone else did for Finn.

"Signore Fieschi. How may we be of service?"

"This is my fiancée, Caroline Muller," Finn said. "She would like to see some engagement rings."

The woman took my left hand in her cold fingers and examined it carefully. "One moment." She rose, unfolding an array of cranelike limbs, then compressed herself through a narrow doorway. A moment later she returned with a tray full of rings so distinct we could have been in a museum. A pink diamond, big as a pendant. *This one belonged to Marie of Austria*, she said, *whom you may know as Marie Antoinette*. A blue stone flanked by a shower of diamonds. *It was said this belonged to Catherine the Great. This here was Romanov; this one from an empress in the Chin Dynasty. This,* she said, holding out a hammered band of yellow gold with small ruby, *belonged to Cleopatra.*

I found myself drawn to a sunshine diamond. Ten carats, emerald cut, set atop a thin band between two matching baguettes. It was the size of a piece of candy and heavy as a paperweight. The woman parted her lips when I asked where it had come from. After a moment I realized she was attempting a smile. She was pleased with my choice, apparently.

"The center diamond was originally cut from the raw for a Medici daughter, who wore it as a single earring. We were lucky to acquire it from a private collector a few years ago. Its color is a unique variation on what is often called a canary diamond. The baguettes were matched from a necklace belonging to Elisabeth of Bavaria. You'll see"—she held out the loupe and pointed the lamp over my hand—"that the color is nearer to orange, or even pink, than to a true yellow."

It was like a cloudy wisp of sunrise had settled on my finger and frozen so that we could gaze upon it forever. Even down in that velvet basement, it caught the light and cast a halo of lemon-hued rainbows so vivid I could taste them. Its gold band, brighter than my medal, would have taken my father a week to dig out of the ground. Anchored beneath it I felt as though I had found my place in the world.

We made no more conversation. Finn took my hand and said a polite goodbye to the woman, and we rode the lift back up. In the main shop we merely nodded to the old man and left. There was no till, no price given, no charge settled. Three steps into the arcade, I stopped. "We didn't pay," I cried, reaching back toward the door. "We're thieves!"

Finn drew me to the street, bemusement altering the roughhewn turn of his cheek. Such details were for other people to handle. *Oh*. I shoved my hands in the pockets of my coat and blushed. He reached for my lapel. "Is this warm enough?"

"It's fine, honestly."

"We've got time."

"Until what?"

"Until we have to leave for Lucomo." He put a hand on my waist and spun me closer.

"You don't want to stay in Milan?" I circled my arms around his neck.

"No, Caroline. I have a quite nice house." He smiled.

Wet snow landed on the tips of our noses. The air, blustering with the storm, turned cold. "This feels awfully fast," I said aloud, without quite meaning to.

He put his forehead against mine. "You want out?"

I shook our heads. "No."

"Then we shop. You need a better coat. It's not a negotiation."

"Isn't Lucomo famously sunny?"

"Three hundred days a year. But for the other sixty-five, it's cold *and* windy. We've had real snow this year. *Twice.*"

"Did it stick?"

"No. But it's still cold."

"One shop."

"Of my choice. This is how things are from now on. I take care of you."

I liked this game. I liked everything about it. We tumbled into the car, entangled. We kissed for blocks and blocks, the world passing by around us in silence, the ring blazing. I had a flash of understanding, why so many people obsessed about jewelry: Because it was validating to be so adorned. Finn had distilled my worth into an object—a ring so beautiful I couldn't have dreamed it up—and placed it upon my hand for all the world to see. But when we arrived at our destination, he slid the ring from my finger and pocketed it. "I'd hate for the announcement to come from a salesgirl," he said plainly.

I felt its absence as profoundly as if he'd taken my finger along with it, but I nodded agreeably, determined not to appear needy. I followed him into the store—Fendi—and up a golden staircase, past floor after floor of bright leather handbags and shoes and dresses. The tanned Italian couples browsing the shelves glanced at us but were given no time to stare, as for the third time that day we were ushered into a small private room.

Legions of furs were brought for me to examine. I chose modestly, at first, a mustard wool coat, double-breasted, with dyed-to-match fox cuffs. I'd never worn fur before—never even considered it—and the purring softness of it astonished me. At Finn's encouragement, I settled on a second—a short tea-toned mink jacket with a velvet collar. At some point my camel coat was whisked away. I mewled a complaint, asking for it back, but Finn insisted on a third coat, "for the cold." Though I didn't believe it could be that cold in Lucomo, I allowed it, because the garment he selected was so extraordinary. It was a dark green cape made from beaver fur, with a large hood. It reached almost to the floor and looked very nearly medieval.

I wore the tea-colored jacket out of the store. We exited through the back, into a secluded courtyard, where the small car waited. The green cape and mustard coat were zipped inside leather garment bags—a giveaway from the store that was probably more expensive than anything I'd ever owned—and placed gently into the trunk. I tumbled into the backseat, comfy now, slinging around on those buttery seats like they were mine. I was so exhilarated by the kissing, the engagement, the special treatment, the jewels and furs, that I felt very nearly drunk.

We nosed out of the courtyard, turned a sharp corner, and then—the fur brushed my throat, and the drunkenness gave way. A foul taste crept across the back of my tongue. I was wrapped in the corpses of animals, animals like I had been once, slaughtered for my comfort.

But Finn gazed at me so gently, topaz eyes soft in his beastly face. He slid the ring back on my finger. As it weighed me down, my tongue was washed clean. The foul taste faded. And instead of pitying the beings that clothed me, I told myself that in wearing their skin, I was animal again, protected by and living for them.

By the time we arrived at the special gate at the airport, where the road splits off to the private hangars, the taste was gone entirely. I relaxed in a way that I didn't know was possible. Butter melted throughout my joints, spreading its grease over the links between my faculties. Every muscle—every ligament—turned to dough. I felt the ceramic and plastic of my hip grow warm and alive in its socket. I was *safe*. In Finn's version of the world, no one could harm me or touch me; no one could even see me. The last few years became, in that instant, a memory. I shook free of that intermediate era, that precarious, vulnerable youth, in the moments when Otto opened the car door, and Finn drew me across the tarmac to the tiny golden jet that seemed too small to contain us.

◆ ◆ ◆

The Gulfstream, lined in kidskin and rubber, encapsulated us like we were pearls in an oyster. Every edge had been rounded, padded for comfort; you could shake us up like dice and we'd come out clean. There were four armchairs in the first section, where Otto and Dix took their places. We passed into a middle area, where recliners faced each other. Finn paused, and crouched beneath the low ceiling to kiss me. I kissed back, but shyly, and glanced nervously toward Otto and Dix.

"They don't exist," Finn said. "You'll get used to it. Look." They clicked headphones over their ears, the two men turning themselves off like the androids they were.

"It's creepy," I insisted. Finn blew back my bangs and led me farther down the aisle, to the third and final section. Behind an upholstered panel hid a long sofa, a bar, and a television.

Finn pulled out the woven seat belts, neatly tucked away into the sofa cushions, and we buckled ourselves in. Then he reached up to the ceiling, pushed a button, and the upholstered panel extended to close us off from the rest of the plane—a giant version of the partition in the car. And with that, we were alone, at long last.

He kissed me. I scrambled for him, undoing his seat belt as the plane sped across the runway, lifting its nose—

And then he pulled away. "I was thinking about something."

"Let's not," I said, reaching for him. "Let's not think."

Finn exhaled. Set his shoulders. Straightened up. "What if we wait?" he asked.

"Wait for what?"

He tilted his chin just so, eyes flickering—and then I understood what he was asking. "What if we wait until we're married?"

"We can get married right now," I said, my fingers working the buttons on his shirt. "Get the captain. Isn't it the same as a boat captain?"

"No," he said. "There are laws that govern my body," he quipped, taking my hands from his shirt, holding them tight in his own.

"Welcome to the club."

"Not a joke. Legally, I need Amelie's consent to marry."

"I don't want to wait."

"You want to marry me?" Finn asked. I nodded, staring at the curve of his neck, the slab of his shoulders. "What I want is to wait."

I thought he was kidding. I pulled at him harder.

"I'm serious. You might change your mind."

"I won't," I insisted.

"You're not listening to me," he said, frustrated now. "Please try to hear what I'm saying to you."

I ran my hands over the heft of his forearms. "What if we're not sexually compatible?"

"Let's make a deal," he offered. "Give me ten days. Ten days in the Talon should be enough for you to see how it all is."

"Where will I sleep?"

"In the barracks," he suggested. "You can have Otto's bunk."

"Ha. Ten days. But then we get married."

"If you stay." When he kissed me again, I bit him hard enough to draw blood. He kissed back harder, dripping blood into my mouth.

I loved it.

❖ ❖ ❖

Finn knew more about power, the reversal, the ownership, the transmitting of it, than anyone I have ever known. On that flight, he took what I believed had been my only leverage—our desire for each other— and repossessed it for himself. He managed, in those strange moments as we hurtled through the atmosphere, to make me the one who was controlled. Even the biography he'd given me was a form of restraint: the letters highlighted, so that they outshone the story of a woman who loved a man who abandoned her over and over.

But I didn't see it that way. I saw our relationship as a glorious deliverance from the earth into the kingdom of heaven. In every moment I'd spent with Finn, we had been guarded, cosseted, cared for, escorted, protected. No one brushed me in the street, no security at the airport groped our bodies, no shoulder but Finn's touched mine, no elbow fought for armrest real estate, no seat-backs plowed into my aching knees. In our few moments in public spaces, the service created a bubble around us that no one could breach. It was an extraordinary relief to no longer feel vulnerable. To *believe* that *I* was no longer vulnerable. I fell into the deepest sleep of my life on that plane. It isn't until you feel safe that you realize how difficult it was before, when you were constantly afraid, as though you have been hearing a noise in the background for so long that you cannot pick it out until someone turns it off. And when you hear the sound of silence, it's sweeter than you knew anything could be.

I woke when the landing gear began to whine. Finn tapped away at his computer. Out the window, beneath the white of the Alps, moonlit forests unrolled in hills of emerald.

"Is there coffee?" I set my hand on his shoulder.

"On the boat," he replied without looking up.

"The boat?"

"We land in Italy, drive to the boat, and then we'll sail around the coast."

"Why?"

"Security," he said flatly. "They vary the pattern."

"What about a helicopter?" I teased.

"We outlawed them. Medical emergencies only. I try to set an example."

"I was kidding."

He blushed. "You're going to have to start tapping your nose when you're teasing."

I shook my head. "That takes all the fun out of it." Out the window, netted by a bright scatter of stars, the half-moon shone its flashlight over the terrain. As the plane banked to the runway, I spotted a faraway stone villa, sequestered beneath a carpet of vines. "Ooh," I mumbled, pressing my nose to the glass. A rusty gate guarded an abandoned garden. "I bet it doesn't even have electricity. I want a house like that, someday."

"Churn your own butter?"

"I don't churn," I said, squeezing his biceps. After we found gravity, I tried to put on my shoes, but my feet were so swollen from the journey that I couldn't even get them up to the arch of my foot. "I'm rather swelly when I travel," I admitted, embarrassed.

Finn barked an order in Italian. Two minutes later, Otto handed me a pair of men's loafers. They hung big on my feet, slightly roomy at the back, but I curled my toes and clamped them on.

We exited into the quietest hour, about three or so in the morning. Another bulletproof bus waited. In the backseat, Finn kissed my palm, then closed his eyes and slept. Out the window I watched this new world flow past. The roads wove in and out of modernity; for every new building, there were ten that were hundreds of years old. An hour later we arrived at a small port, where a white yacht the size of a small cruise ship bobbed against the pier.

We made our way through the empty harbor and onto a metal gangplank. An officer in a sharp white uniform, like one of heaven's admirals, welcomed us aboard. "*Signore*"; she bowed. "*Signorina*"; a nod.

Finn responded with a flicker of eye contact, the smallest of acknowledgments, before glancing away. Meanwhile my hand was already halfway out to shake hers. The officer pretended not to notice. By the time I'd retracted it, she'd led us to a large living room. She retreated through a doorway, returned with a tray of coffee and sweets, and disappeared again.

"We don't shake hands?" I asked Finn.

"It's not social. This is her workplace," he explained. "You'll adjust."

I picked at the breakfast, my appetite disappearing as the boat heaved into the sea. Finn's phone pinged constantly. He answered one call and had a brief conversation in rapid Italian. I didn't understand a word. "Who calls at three in the morning?" I asked as he snapped the phone shut.

"Roland. It's half past four."

"Who's Roland?"

"Roland is my chief of staff. He handles everything."

"Everything?"

"Everything." Finn winked. "He said that when we arrive you should rest, and I should do the work I was supposed to do yesterday, which, I can't really fight him on that." The boat slowed its pace, the engines growling. "This is our stop," he said, taking my hand. He helped me to my feet, held up my new coat.

Together, we rose through the narrow passages of the ship, and faced, at last, Lucomo.

14

THE FIRST TIME I saw that marble prison, I stood on the teak deck of a yacht in the Mediterranean Sea, in men's loafers lent to me an hour before. As I have explained, I thought myself mature, but I knew so very little. For example I had no idea that everything I owned from then on would feel as borrowed as those shoes.

The very first part of Lucomo that I could identify was the cliff of the outer Talon, curving like a hook into the sea. A hundred meters of bare slate soared dry above a white band of crusted salt. The rocks closest to the water were damp from spray and coated with algae.

Atop the curving cliff, three iterations of castle huddled together, interlocked by courtyards and arches into a single grand palace. I found the sections easy to identify: The trio of stone towers, ancient as the cliff below, guarded the westernmost edge. The second expansion had a smooth limestone exterior, flat and gripless, punctuated with arrow slits. That part was pure Gothic, from a time when conflict meant pouring boiling oil atop the peasant soldiers of your enemy. The third expansion, built as a personal residence for the royal family in 1750, was made of spotless white marble. On the rock face below its foundations, wild dahlias dared to sprout, bobbing from lonely cracks laced with neon lichens.

As the yacht nosed its way toward Cap-Griffe, a medieval storybook rose, page by page, from the rocky bay up along a switchback to the castle. Slender town houses painted in pleasing pastels nestled against each other like an advent calendar.

Eastward, Le Chappe's glittering glass skyscrapers sparkled in the moonlight. Along the coast, beachside bars and umbrella stands were wrapped for the season in waxed canvas, like oversized presents.

But we did not sail for the old town, for the city, or for the beaches. Instead we banked sharply to the west and rounded the edge of the outer claw. There—jutting like a razor blade from the sea-darkened slate—was a thin slice of dock. The yacht shouldered up against it, bobbing heavy in the waves, while Finn's white-uniformed sailors tied us down to massive, rusted iron rings.

We exited down a metal ramp and were met by a pair of armed Gardiens in their green military suits, the same type who'd been bulging around Finn in that Lisbon bar. Their wool overcoats were damp and ringed with frost; they'd been waiting outside for us. *They must be terribly cold,* I thought, casting them a compassionate glance. But their hard eyes were glued to the horizon; it was as though we were not there, for they did not acknowledge us in any way.

We passed through an iron door set in the rock, into a small cave filled with monitors and communications equipment. An elevator waited. We skyrocketed upward for several stories, until we reached a tunnel: a long, dank passageway, chiseled by hand through the interior of the cliff. The bright fluorescent bars along the ceiling, lighting up one after another, *brr-buzz-ding* as their gases caught the light, did little to alleviate the impression that it was a modified dungeon. Finn took my hand.

The hard walls sweated—and so did I. My breath fell short, inhales shuddering through the tightness in my chest. Without choosing to, I walked faster, stepping in front of Finn. In a single month I had crossed half the planet, buried my mother, become engaged to a prince, and was now trapped inside a medieval correctional facility with no visible way out.

"Are you claustrophobic?" Finn asked.

I shook my head and aimed for the dark at the end of the tunnel, choosing to believe that it was a light.

◆　◆　◆

The tunnels are original to the castle. When the Talon's first stone was laid in 870, the first hole was dug beside it—to fortify the castle down, as well as up. For hundreds of years, with the aid of these underground passages to hide its populace or punish its enemies, as needed, the Talon endured many conflicts—and survived them all.

Until 1100, when the civil war between the Guelph and Ghibelline families overwhelmed the region. From then on the Talon was burned monthly, the residents of Cap-Griffe slaughtered weekly.

In 1310, after two centuries of continual assault, the castle's population had dwindled to a mere fifty starving Ghibelline soldiers. Flanked to the north by Guelphs, to the south by a raging sea, their boats long since incinerated, the soldiers had no food besides what they could catch—some fish, and the occasional rat.

That's when Giancarlo Fieschi, a recently retired mercenary fleeing the violence of Genoa, nosed his boat into the city's empty port. The soldiers watched Fieschi scramble over the scorched remains of the harbor and climb the streets of the deserted village. When he was ten yards from the Talon, the dying soldiers raised their skeletal arms and pointed their last arrows at him. Fieschi pointed, in turn, to his boat— stocked with salted meats and barrels of beer.

The soldiers lowered their weapons.

With a single feast, Fieschi took possession of the castle. He dispatched the two strongest Ghibelline men into France with white flags pinned to their uniforms and a message for the Avignon Pope, allied with the enemy Guelphs. *This castle is no longer a battlefield,* he wrote; *it is become a slaughterhouse. I have taken control of the Talon and from this day forward, it will be neutral, a home for peace, neither Guelph nor Ghibelline.* Fieschi promised to provide a home for all surrounding residents in times of war, to put peace before all else. He sent a similar letter to the Holy Roman Emperor, ally to the Ghibellines, with the addition of an olive branch: Fieschi's first act of neutrality would be to christen the region in honor of Etruria's long-dead King Lucomo, a man famous for his respect and courtesy.

Both sides, tired of sacrificing their respective armies to certain annihilation on the Talon's cliffs, agreed. Fieschi's Lucomo soon attracted hundreds of families eager for its promise of peace. *Pax*, the first word on Finn's stamp. Within fifty years the second expansion began, and the castle itself doubled in size. The population of Cap-Griffe increased to two thousand, then ten. The Talon became a rock, impenetrable, guarded by a devoted legion who knew how to close it up like a clam. The magic city bustled once again with life and outgrew its boundaries. The populace of Lucomo began to settle farther and farther to the east, eventually claiming forty miles of overgrown hills that sloped to the sea. Piétons, the pedestrians, lived here in the west; Marins, the sailors, lived to the east. And all the while, the Fieschi family remained, here, in the castle.

❖   ❖   ❖

I followed Finn through a maze of staircases locked off from each other, a metal keycard swiping us through each portal. The last had a steel door thick as a bank vault's—and then, on the other side, in one blinding moment, the Talon assembled itself around us.

The stones built up the walls. Forests of trees shook free of their branches, rolled off their bark, chopped themselves into joists, erected great halls and armories, while courtyards laid their tile. A natatorium dug itself an emerald spring. Greenhouses filled themselves with flow-ers. Armored cars drove into a garage massive as an airplane hangar. Peach and crimson rugs grew like grass beneath our feet, while water-falls of velvet drapes spurted over the windows, pooling over the floor in swaths of palest rose.

Vines rocketed from the ground, snaked across the walls, and stitched themselves to the ceiling, becoming living chandeliers that de-scended every few feet. On their ropy tendrils, porcelain flowers burst forth in eternal bloom, lightbulbs twisting into place behind their pet-als. Ceramics and jewels launched themselves from vitrines, entwining themselves in the sky above our heads to form a crowded aviary packed with jeweled birds. Ascending on feathers dipped in liquid gold, blink-ing beady sapphire eyes, the birds turned to glass.

Great fireplaces, crackling against the winter air, burned like forges. Their smoke plumed out along the corridors, wrapping us in a lilac-shaded fog that smelled of burnt cedar and fresh-cut vanilla pods.

The force of such beauty is meant to destabilize a person. I was no exception.

15

I BREATHED IN WITH EVERY two steps of my right leg, breathed out with every two steps of my left, as Finn led me down a broad hallway, the floors tiled in islands of black and white stones, like a nightmare. The walls were hung with hundreds of staggered portraits, interconnected by enamel leaves and branches: a sculpted, three-dimensional family tree. Every twenty feet or so, the enamel boughs diverged from above to encircle a set of double doors. We stopped at a pair lacquered in red, where a brass plaque, the inscription reading *Gloria II,* was set in the marble.

The red doors opened to an apartment bigger than anywhere I'd ever lived. The lounge had enough antique sofas for twenty. To the left, a writing room held a petite archipelago of desks; to the right, a breakfast nook; then the bedroom, its pair of queen beds showered in orange silk. It took thirty full seconds of gawping with my mouth open to realize that Finn stood waiting for me to speak. "What a dump," I finally managed. "How can you bear it?"

"This isn't my apartment."

"Who lives here?"

His eyes flicked to the walls. There materialized dozens of elegant specters, bound in gilded frames. The first was a Renaissance figure in a dress of virgin blue, her profile a pointed nose and rosy cheek. Her neighbor was dressed for a hunt in an embroidered riding habit; the next shimmered like a satin cake. "The Gloria Apartment is traditionally given to the consort. That's you," Finn murmured, touching the nearest frame. "Maria the Simple, fifteenth century. Madeleine de Valois, sixteenth century. Beatrix Mantes, I think called Beatrix the Rich, seventeenth century. Antoinette the Pious, eighteenth century. That one," he said, pointing to a sour-mouthed woman stuffed into a velvet hide, "is Gloria of Trieste, who founded the casino."

"She looks like a Dickensian matron."

"And you claim to be uneducated."

"*Masterpiece* plays in all the world's hotels."

"It was painted," Finn explained, "*before* she learned how to gamble. Gloria the Savior." His phone wiggled in his shirt pocket; he pressed a hand to it and frowned. "I'm sorry. I've got to go."

As if someone had pulled a cord in my back, I yawned. Finn kissed the palm of my left hand—the diamond on my finger glowing from within, like everything else in this room—and then he left.

I crept through the rooms, examining the portraits lining the walls. There were twenty-seven in total. Starting with the double-peaked hat of Alessia of Siena in 1398, each woman reflected the styles and trends of her time. There was no portrait of Queen Amelie, Finn's mother—or any of the other thirty-six natural-born daughters of the monarchy. This was an apartment for imported princesses only, a landing pad for those who married into this family. All twenty—now twenty-one. Soon I would be up there: Caroline of Johannesburg.

A shadow rose in the corner of my eye.

Startled—*had a portrait moved?*—I backed into a chair.

The shadow turned white. A porter—another bleached uniform— was silently carrying my bags into the closet. When he unzipped the duffel and began to unpack it—his stranger's hands touching my clothes—I flapped to his side. "Please don't do that," I begged. "I only need to know which drawer I should use."

"*Signorina?*" The porter blinked. "I've been instructed to put everything away."

"No, thank you."

"As you prefer," he sniffed.

It was then I realized that I'd insulted him. "I'm sure you would do a very fine job," I backpedaled. "But I would like to put my own clothes away."

"As you prefer," the porter replied again, and departed.

Alone with the roaring fires, I pulled the drapes shut, cutting off the electric blue of the predawn light, and sat on one of the beds. It was a downy cloud, layered in comfort. All I had to do was lie down; no tucking my pelvis, arranging my legs, padding myself with pillows until I found a restful position like every other bed I'd slept in since the accident. I pulled the eiderdown up to my neck and surrendered to the kind of sleep that I had when I ran, back in the days when I could be sated, and emptied.

◆　◆　◆

A knock. Then another. I opened my eyes. "*Signorina,*" a woman's voice said, loudly. "You are required." I sat up, looking for the source of the voice, but the room was empty.

I stumbled from the bed. "Hello?" I called out. No one came. I peered into the closet. Nothing. I walked through the sitting room, the breakfast room, the writing room. Empty.

I opened the red doors with a sweaty palm. "Hello?" I called out warily, craning my neck. But there wasn't anyone in the hallway, either.

"*Signorina?*" The voice was definitely coming from the sitting room. Yet the only faces belonged to the portraits. I turned slowly in a circle, dozens of dead eyes burning into me. When the voice sounded again, close this time—"*Signorina?*"—I nearly hit the ceiling.

"WHERE ARE YOU," I shouted, and that's when I saw the crack next to the portrait of Gloria.

"May I open—"

"Yes, yes," I breathed. With a click, the wall holding Gloria's portrait swung forward. A young woman in white stood at attention inside a secret hallway. "What's your name?" I asked.

"Ensign," she said, pointing to the single star on her collar.

"Ensign what?"

"We are rank within the Talon, miss."

"You're nameless? That's ridiculous. How demeaning," I thought, and said it, too—it was out of my mouth before I could stop myself.

The officer's cheeks turned red. "Yes, *signorina*."

I had demeaned her. Not the title. "I'm so sorry—" I began to apologize.

"*Signore* is ready for you," she finished. The ensign waited impatiently while I slapped water over my face and bound my hair into a hasty braid. Then she took me down the black-and-white hallway to a pair of dark blue doors. A trail of enameled dahlias, sharp as knives, circled round the door frame. The inscription read *Ferdinand II*. At the ensign's gloved touch, the doors sprang open. We ascended a wide staircase directly into an office, where Finn sat at a mammoth desk, typing away on a computer. His ceiling contained no birds; in fact it contained no ornament at all. Everything in his office was gray, from the stone floors and ceiling to the drapes and furniture.

"I'm nearly done," he said without looking up from the screen. "Have a poke around."

Finn was the only thing in color, I thought—but no, the portraits, too, were bright. In this room there were no men or women. There were only figureheads.

Like the paintings in my apartment, they were mostly from other centuries, except for one: A satin-skinned, Barbie-doll-looking 1960s

blonde over a background sponged with pastel splotches. Hair in a bee-
hive, supporting a massive crown. Her mouth a cruel smile.

Finn glanced up and caught me staring. "That's Amelie," he said.
"From her coronation."

I tried to think of something nice to say. "It's a beautiful painting,"
I managed. It *was* beautiful, in a sickly-sweet way.

"It's tremendously weird," he said. "Don't be polite." Just then, a
thin man in a dark suit somehow emerged from the edge of the room
and began gliding silently toward Finn. Sharp nose, bony chin, narrow
hands, each holding a BlackBerry, the man hovered above the paved
stone floor like he was weightless. "Caroline, meet Roland, my number
two," Finn said casually.

Roland bowed in my general direction, creasing precisely ten degrees at the hip—acknowledging me in the barest possible way. Before
I could open my mouth to greet him, he was upright again—and aiming a surprisingly violent eruption of rapid Italian at Finn.

He was going a mile a minute. I watched his Adam's apple bobbing
in the narrow rope of his throat, the words twisting and flying around
Finn and me like a curse. Goose bumps rose on my arms. Finn, however, seemed unmoved and waited patiently, still typing away at his
computer, allowing the tirade to flow past him like a breeze. Yet beneath Finn's stillness I sensed him crackling with displeasure. When
Roland finally paused for breath, Finn stood abruptly and barked out a
forceful "Sì, ho capito, sta' zitto," which even I could tell meant something along the lines of "buzz off." Then—"I'm sorry," to me, in English.
"Roland has forgot his manners." At the reminder of my presence, Roland swiveled fluidly—and shot me a deathly glare. Finn stepped out
from the desk, placed a hand on my hip, and nudged me toward the
nearest door. "Would you mind excusing us?" he asked me. "There's tea
in my study, you'll find it if you keep walking, yes, just through there."

As he pulled the door shut, I caught one more glimpse of Roland,
vibrating with fury; once it clicked, the man was back at it, a fire hose
pouring rolling vowels. Finn raised his voice in return.

I lingered in the hall, listening to what little of their argument I could understand. From Roland I grasped *giornalista* and something that sounded like the word *unfortunate* over and over, and Finn's forceful *No, no, no*s, the same in any language.

Then Roland said something that made Finn laugh—a sincere, big chortle—and their conversation changed. The words were still coming quickly, passionately, but without a trace of the previous menace. Whatever they were battling over was, for now, resolved.

It occurred to me that one of them might open the door and find me still listening. I felt myself backing away, retreating out of instinct.

I believe now that my inaction stemmed from two things: one, the sense that Roland was a predator, that he was not to be crossed; and two, the more insidious thing, a bone-bred inclination to give men their space, to allow them room to fight—let, as they say, boys be boys. To assume it was none of my business.

I shook off my discomfort as the result of not enough sleep and unanticipated conflict in a new place, and explored the residence. It continued with the same impersonal gray banality as Finn's office. There were no photos, no knickknacks, no shoes slipped off in doorways or trousers folded on chairs. The stainless-steel kitchen's refrigerator held trays of prepared foods; the cabinets were filled with pre-apportioned snacks. His life was serviced, it seemed, all round.

It was only once I discovered his private sitting room that I found any evidence that he was not living in a hotel, that he himself was not a piece of furniture. It was cozy, sort of; a fire roared in another hearth so big you could stand inside it. A tray laden with tea, sandwiches, and sweets rested on the sideboard, though that felt catered, too, in its own way. But the walls were fully lined with overflowing bookshelves, entirely nonfiction, on seemingly every topic: biographies of world leaders, polemics on the tech boom, academic philosophy, chemistry books on minerals.

There were little framed pictures tucked between sections, selected mostly, it seemed, for their comedy. A photograph of a boardroom table stocked with men, watching a woman pop out of a cake, had the twenty-five-year-old Finn's face cut out and glued over hers. Below was a cheeky note from the French president that had something, I thought, to do with goats, a word I only knew because of chèvre cheese. Another, from a famous film director, showed the two of them lying across the deck of a yacht in matching Speedos, heads on crooked elbows and grins beneath their sunglasses, Finn holding a sign that read *We the Mermen!* In the corner a bulletproof vest hung on the coatrack. Some-one had written in permanent marker across the back, *For dropping bombs!* A framed note adjacent, written on Arabic letterhead, said in English: *My friend: Stay safe in the brave new world of toilet warfare!* Accompanying it was a news article about an accidental explosion at the Lucomo embassy in Paris that had destroyed a WC.

I opened a book lying on the table—*The Soviet Union Under Brezhnev and Kosygin*—to keep me company, poured myself a cup of tea, and curled up on the sagging, overworked sofa. As with the Kahlo biography, I discovered that Finn had dog-eared and double dog-eared—folding a triangle, then the corner back again—the pages he found interesting. He seemed to be drawn to betrayals and corruption between long lists of Russian names. To me only Brezhnev was vaguely familiar. I began at the introduction. By the time I understood that he'd been the leader of the Soviet Union for eighteen years, through my early childhood, Finn arrived.

He was smiling brightly, as though his argument with Roland had never taken place. I closed the book, looking at him quizzically. "Are you all right?"

"Pfft," Finn snorted. "Roland's a pussycat."

"I'd be crying. Does he speak to you that way very often?"

"He's been here since before I was born. We're a family. Sometimes families don't put on their best behavior. I'm sorry." He lifted the book's cover. "You *do* like history."

"Don't be too impressed. I've discovered that Leonid Brezhnev and Yuri Andropov were different people, and that neither of them was Mikhail Gorbachev."

He settled in across the sofa, pulling my feet into his lap. "What do you think?"

"Of Brezhnev? Nice eyebrows. Why are you reading this?"

"Soviet politics are like their literature—ruthless, dramatic, fascinating. For example, there's a phrase in here," he said, tapping the book against his knee, "'the useful idiot.'"

I shook my head. I didn't know the reference.

"It means a person who perpetuates propaganda without knowing it. Ronald Reagan, famously."

I smiled uncertainly.

"Doesn't matter," Finn said indifferently, sliding the book underneath the sofa to save me from further embarrassment. "Anyway. What do you think of my apartment?"

"It's a hotel."

"If you'd lived in this jewel box your whole life, you'd long for gray chairs, too."

"Tell me all your secrets," I demanded.

He laughed and grabbed my foot. "Where do you want to start?"

"Middle name."

"I've got several. Amelie Arturo Henri-Louis Eduard."

"Your mother's name is your first middle name?"

"And her father's name. There's a system to it."

"How do you take your tea?"

"Two sugars and lemon. You?"

"Neither sugar nor lemon. I'm a purist. Would've pegged you for cream."

"Never. I'm lactose intolerant."

"What a terrible thing to be in this part of the world."

"It's like being color-blind. I don't really know what I'm missing."

Our back-and-forth popped the balloon of my exhaustion. "How does this work?" I asked bluntly, sitting up. "What happens next?"

"You'll meet Amelie. Then we ought to start planning the wedding."

"What's to plan? I'm sure we can dig up a priest in a week."

"You say that now," he said evenly, taking my feet in his hands, pressing against the knotted tendons. "You haven't seen the country. You haven't even seen the whole *house*." He smiled. I kicked him lightly; this was no house. He bit one of my toes in reply, then began kneading my feet. I closed my eyes, and he launched into an explanation of Lugesque politics that mostly confused me, but nonetheless got across the point that the elites of Cap-Griffe expected to be consulted on everything that Finn did with his life, like where he'd gone to college or in this case which woman he would marry. Native-born Lugesque were 17 percent of the population, but to the crown, they were a significant demographic. Their six ministers were the only people, aside from Amelie, who were capable of amending the country's laws.

"I hope you enjoy explaining things," I told him, glancing around the room at all the books, almost counting them. His gaze followed mine, and I could see what he was thinking—if I wasn't joking about not knowing the difference between Brezhnev, Andropov, and Gorbachev, then I had a lot to learn. "We didn't have news of other places except the USSR until I was ten, and obviously even that didn't stick. It was like—the whole world was all sort of a fantasy, one that came rushing in all at once," I tried to clarify. "I think that's why I like going to museums, and castles, and old places. Because otherwise I can't differentiate any of it in my brain. Otherwise I can't understand."

"I'm not judging you," he offered genuinely. "I like who you are."

After that I recall we fell into each other, kissing again. At some point we realized it was dinnertime, and he heated something from the refrigerator—I think it was a lasagna—and we ate it with our plates on our laps. Around midnight he walked me back to my apartment. At the red doors, we kissed goodbye. When I arched, pressing for more, he left.

It was rather like training a dog. He needed me to get used to everything, first to like it, then to love it—and all the while to want him desperately.

It worked.

16

ON MY SECOND DAY in Lucomo, I awoke to the sounds of a fire catching. By the time I sat up, whoever had set it was already gone from the apartment. A silver pot of coffee gleamed from the breakfast room, steam rising from the spout, beside a bowl of sun-ripened fruit and a stack of books about the history of Lucomo.

I floated from the bed on airy limbs. Plowed through two pears, a banana, and the whole pot of coffee while paging aimlessly through the various tomes that had been brought, presumably, for me to absorb. *Lucomo and the Renaissance* had lots of beautiful illustrations; *Fieschi: A History in Twenty-One Crowns, 1320–1910* was extremely dry, but it had a whole chapter on Savior Gloria, the gambler, she of the puckered portrait. *Wartime Riviera* was more recent, examining Lucomo's involvement in the two world wars, but since I couldn't have told you which one involved Franz Ferdinand and which had the Beer Hall Putsch, I felt self-consciously stupid and closed it. The last book, that year's red leather *Michelin Guide to Lucomo,* wasn't exactly thrilling, but at least it was easy to read.

I resolved to try again later. I took the hottest bath of my whole life and wrapped myself in a towel heavy as a blanket. In the closet, my cotton clothes—those jeans and long sweaters—felt cheap and ragged, compared to the exquisite sheets of the bed, the weft of the bathroom towels. *They don't belong,* I thought.

The leather garment bags winked at me. I pulled out the green fur cape, spread it over my naked shoulders. In the mirror it was obvious that *it fit,* I realized, in a way that *I* didn't. It fit this room—this circumstance—seamlessly.

Someone knocked at the secret door. I peeked around the jamb to find a therapist in white scrubs already setting up a massage table. She—a woman whose name I've long since forgotten—led me through a gentle series of unfamiliar stretches, strange angles that, to my surprise, helped a great deal. Then she pounded my already-slackening tension away.

Finn appeared around noon, dressed casually, the cuffs of his shirt rolled up, to take me to lunch. I grabbed the cape and followed him through the maze of underground passages. We didn't take the elevator this time, but exited instead into a tiny kitchen where two Gardiens ate lunch at the table, daylight streaming through the windows. I had to blink a few times before I realized we were inside a house.

Its staircase had sagging treads from centuries of use; the door-jambs were matte, their lacquer long worn off. A mixture of communications equipment and sailing memorabilia lined its rooms. Regatta flags were tacked along the ceiling—the oldest one I could see was dated 1821—and a corkboard held decades of sentimental family notes and photos. Grade-school Finn, sitting at a three-quarter angle and smiling like any other boy, was pinned next to a note that read, *Finn 0, Fish 100,* in faded ink.

"We're in Cap-Griffe," Finn announced, grabbing a scarf and oil-cloth jacket from a peg.

"Is that your coat to take?" I asked.

"Every coat is my coat." He slid his arms through the sleeves. "Actually, this was my dad's coat."

"Was this his house?"

"It's been a guardhouse for five hundred years. But he was close with them," he said, looking at the young Gardiens cleaning up in the kitchen. "The older ones, anyway." At the thought, he gave a wan smile, then swallowed his feelings. "Come on, it's a bit of a walk."

The street outside was so narrow that I first mistook it for an alleyway. The air tasted of salt, smelled resinous, like the sun-soaked bark of an evergreen tree. I stretched my arms out, touching my fingertips to the houses on either side. Finn did the same, though his palms lay flat. "Godzilla," I teased him, ducking under his arm. "How can a city be so small?"

"People were smaller eleven hundred years ago. When I was about twelve," he reminisced, "I was already this big. I hated coming down here."

"That's cute."

"You're supposed to pity me when I say things like that."

We walked on together—and relatively alone. The young Gardiens tailed us, but at a distance; their digital colleagues, miniature camera lenses, glinted from the eaves of every building. I marveled at the flawless perfection of the village. The town houses, with their colorful façades and jewel-box windows, shone with pride. No detail was too small—not the brass doorknobs or the carved wooden shutters, carefully waxed against the humidity. Even the Christmas wreaths, tied with plush red ribbons, were pristine. Cap-Griffe's cleanliness was so complete that I myself felt immaculate by association.

Piétons bustled to and from their houses with bundles of cut flowers and paper bags of groceries. Some stood chatting in their gardens, coffee in hand; others marched purposefully toward one of the three roads that led to the busier cities. Their "pedestrian" bodies were wrapped in sensuous fabrics—suedes and flannels, oily wool, cashmere—necks and fingers sparkling with diamonds over skin so plump and juicy that at first sight they looked twenty-five. But their postures gave them away, stiff movements like mine that usually come with age. The Piétons were not young; they were in their fifties, sixties, and even seventies. The sea air and safety that cocooned them had paused time, suspended their youth under glass.

When we arrived at the harbor, we descended into a fog so thick I could barely see the waves lapping against the pier. Through the arch, a gravel road began, marked *Basse. The low road.* "Are we at the edge already?" I asked, surprised. We'd been walking for fewer than ten minutes.

"Cap-Griffe's population is eight hundred nine," Finn told me. "Le Chappe is fifty thousand." He pulled a baseball cap from his pocket and placed dark glasses over his eyes. "My elaborate disguise." He raised his scarf over his distinctive jaw.

"Does that really work?"

"If I'm not in a suit, or clean-shaven, I could be a German on holiday."

We turned the corner. Apartments and hotels shot skyward from the mist, their narrow foyers guarded by uniformed bellmen. At the next road—the *Moyen*, the "middle"—a snaking line of shark-nosed sports cars hummed, moving mere inches at a time.

Finn led me up a staircase pinned between two skyscrapers—then another—and another and another—lined with shops, a retail assault. Specialty boutiques that sold twenty-euro cans of tinned fish or a hundred colors of cashmere socks. Most people we passed had the air of the tourist; rich ones, but tourists all the same. As Finn predicted, few gave him a second glance. They were too busy living out their own fantasies of being princes and princesses, flicking their wrists as money shot out like a web, to notice the real-life one standing among them. Those who did, doormen mostly, gave the smallest of nods, which he politely returned.

More stairs. I panted, I huffed, I flung the cape over one shoulder and felt the color rise in my cheeks. L'Original, the casino, big as a museum, came into view. On its spacious patio, mink-wrapped couples gathered around a bonfire. I paused, hand on my chest, pretending to watch them while I took an extra breath.

"I thought you liked walking," Finn teased.

I pinched him and kept moving. After two *more* flights—so narrow there were cutouts where we waited for foot traffic to pass from the other direction—we arrived at last on a mezzanine, zigzagged with strings of bistro lights over restaurants of every flavor. We walked the length but entered none. At the very end, Finn reached for a modest door that read simply *Il Piatto*. The Plate.

Il Piatto was charming, plaster walls and dented wooden joists. Its handful of tables had paper tablecloths and muslin napkins. The waitress gave Finn the same gentle nod as the doormen had, then took our order matter-of-factly and returned with a mountain of sweet and savory breads, each in its own paper bag. I tore into an almond loaf ravenously, finding a hidden trove of raisins soaked in sweet liqueur.

"See? Bags," Finn said, pointing to the bread. "No twist ties."

"This is the best thing I've ever eaten," I marveled through a mouthful.

"Our secret." Finn grinned. "Piéton pathways maximize profit. Easy to resist a shop from the interior of your luxury car with a chilled bottle of champagne. Harder to ignore when you've climbed six stories."

"Where are we in relation to where I woke up?"

Finn took the saltshaker and the bread, the dishes of sugar cubes and butter, our cutlery, and our napkins and set them out across our table in a long line. "Here's the Talon," he said of the saltshaker, "and here's Cap-Griffe"—the butter. "Around the corner is Le Chappe; that's us"—the bread. The knives and forks went end to end, becoming the seashore, and the sugar cubes became towns: "Next is Fils-sur-Mer and Crete Marin. They're mostly French in heritage. They end here, at the seaport. That's where the 'Italian' bit begins," he said, with air quotes, "and the land curves up again."

"Italian?" I inflected back.

"Lucomo is far older than Italy," he said, folding his napkin into a strip. "They're the ones who are Lugesque." He set the napkin down to indicate the seaport that separated the bustling Gallic Piétons from the sleepy Roman Marins (and farther north, Italy from France), then added the seaside villages that made up the serrated blade of the Lucomo dagger. On the other side of the seaport were the soon-to-be-expanded Mare-Dio, San-Berno, and Lo Scopo, the hill towns of Lucomo's pointed tip. Their beaches were rockier, he explained, but Finn was certain that over time they would be as dense as those in the west. Real estate development was at the heart of his long-term economic plan.

As I crossed my arms and looked at the miniature world he'd built, Finn pulled a tourist guide from a display near the front door and opened it to a photo of a metal skeleton arcing backward. "Here's what Lo Scopo will look like. Terrazzo will be the finest building in Europe," he said proudly. "Saltwater swimming pools, commercial-grade kitchens. A landmark." The commodity of Lucomo real estate was stable—more than New York, he claimed, more than Hong Kong, more than London. I didn't know anything about the manipulation of real estate. What it meant to build shiny empty boxes and pump them full of money. I perceived value as a solid index based in reality. Not as a fluid one, based in the shifting sands of opportunity.

The brochure's pictures of the village surrounding Lo Scopo, home to generations of Marins, showed clusters of modest buildings. "That will all be landscaped," he said casually, closing the pamphlet and sending the present into the past. "The Marins will be given better housing."

"*Given* housing?"

"We provide state housing for the Marins. Otherwise they could not afford to live here. We need restaurants," he said, smoothing the tablecloth. "We need nurses, teachers, cleaners. The real work of this job," he explained, "is meeting everyone's needs. You'll help me keep the balance." The warmth of his smile, that sunshine beam. "They'll adore you."

We held hands across the table. The cook roasted an entire fish and laid it out over a bed of rice. Finn cut the neck; pulled the spine from it, clean and white; and it seemed to be mine, for I was boneless in his presence.

◆　◆　◆

The rest of the week was spent the same way. I would awaken each morning in the Gloria Apartment to find that ghosts had silently placed fruit and coffee at my bedside and lit the fires. Then I sat and tried to absorb the information in my stack of books, until Finn broke through around lunchtime.

The general history I found confusing at best, but the specifics stuck, especially the stories of Lucomo's royal women. I loved Gloria's, that in seeking pleasure she saved Lucomo, and read the chapter devoted to her several times over.

When teenage Gloria was first imported to Lucomo in 1840 to marry septuagenarian Louis the Elder, she came with the reasonable expectation that she'd have one baby, maybe two, before her husband would keel over and die. Then one of said babies would take over, and she'd drink champagne in the sunshine, a fat, happy dowager in the richest country in Europe. Unfortunately for Gloria, Louis would live into his nineties—and the monarchy was *dead broke*. The past several Fieschis had repeatedly spent the Lucomo coffers down to the bare wood in ceaseless attempts to keep up with the Joneses of Milan and Versailles; the marble palace, recently built, had barely any furniture.

Aside from giving birth and playing whist in a dank tower with a passel of moldering, witless aristocrats, there was very little to keep Gloria occupied. Four children later, she began to complain of a severe depression that began every November and lasted until the end of February. "I fear I am too Nervous for this Southern Sea—I hear it in my

Sleep and it Calls to me," she wrote to her sister Giulia in 1848. "Do you know of a Cure?"

Her sister recommended the famous thermal springs of Bad Homburg in Bavaria, to warm the body and soothe the mind. Gloria traveled there at once. The springs were warm, that was true, but after a week she was still *ailing*—still *exhausted*. Gloria wondered if she was dying.

A brave maid whispered that *madam might want to see the casino. People said it had baccarat. Laudanum. Ostrich feathers, champagne, caviar, and music.* Gloria gripped the bedpost and ordered the maid to start lacing her corset.

Within an hour Gloria was tossing handfuls of ivory dice at the Spielbank Bad Homburg, and the evening evaporated, along with her depression. As she clutched a newly won stack of enameled chips, she realized that it was not Lucomo's rocky winds that ailed her. No. It was not the damp. It was not the chill. No. *It was boredom.* She'd been dying of boredom.

Two days later, high as the Pope's hat, Gloria finally exited the casino, blinking in the afternoon light. She owed six thousand ducats, today's equivalent of fifty-four thousand euro, a decent loss by any standard but particularly for a twenty-six-year-old mother of four whose only means of repayment would come from pleasing her octogenarian husband. Yet Gloria didn't care about the money, she realized—no, in fact she was looking *forward* to returning—wait, no, more than that—she was *desperate* to return.

She dashed off a letter to Louis. *Torno presto. La fortuna si siederà accanto a me,* she wrote. *Fortuna*: the second word on Finn's stamp. *Coming home soon. Fortune will sit beside me.* The corset was laced back up. Gloria returned to the casino, took a hostage, and departed town.

The fortune bouncing beside her on the velvet seats of her carriage was a person: François Blanc, the casino's architect. At Gloria's direction, and with the last of Lucomo's funds, Blanc built L'Original, Lucomo's own seaside château of vice. Recalling her own desperate urgency, Gloria forbade the Lugesque from ever playing a hand. White-gloved foreign hands dropped their money on the felt, and when the ball stopped bouncing, the ungloved hands of the Lugesque were there to collect, their fortunes growing with every loss.

It was Gloria who filled Lucomo's vaults with gold and its beaches with striped umbrellas. Thanks to her, this peaceful windswept out-cropping was transformed into the golden oyster of the Mediterranean, an endless palace of pleasures, where champagne drips like sweat be-tween heaving breasts and cigar smoke lingers in the haze that drifts off the sea. Peace brought prosperity. Since then—except for the brief pe-riod following the Second World War—everything in Lucomo has cen-tered around this world of indulgence.

◆　◆　◆

I began dreaming about a future that had no boundaries or borders, no limitations or problems, swaddled in safety and buoyed by endless, be-nevolent wealth. Each morning I read more, learned more. Each after-noon I met with a therapist who eased my suffering with a skill and grace that I had not known possible, and felt my pain recede. Each night I stayed up until midnight, talking with and kissing this divine man, weaving him into my skin and bones. Finn whispered promises of all the things he would give me once we were married—the things he would do *to* me, *for* me, *with* me. *Caroline the Strong,* he called me. He painted a dizzying narrative of two lives spent intertwined between power and sheets, from up there in the Talon, making people's lives better from a life of luxury.

I'd been so afraid that if I stopped moving, I would break down, but the quality of this pause, as I got to know Finn, the rhythms of the Talon, and life in Lucomo, surprised me. It did not feel like stillness. It felt, instead, like a world unfurling itself to me, perhaps because I be-lieved that it was within my control—and that it was, as he told me, within Finn's control.

Aware that such infinity could still slip from my grasp, I wanted to be married as soon as possible. Finn kept saying he would not be able to discuss the wedding until I met his mother. I asked a dozen questions about her and received limited answers. "She's a sweet person at heart." "You'll love her." But Finn's vague portrait did not line up with the cruel smile of the woman who sneered down upon me every time I entered his apartment.

On the seventh day, a true cold front appeared. The temperature dropped ten degrees in an hour, plummeting below freezing. It happened so fast that the fog froze to every surface in what Finn told me was called *la brina,* a rime. The rime clung like crystallized spray paint, dyeing the trees white to the very tips of their branches. Frost formed in lacy curls on every stone, every road, every wall. Even the moss froze.

Now the green fur cape came with me everywhere I went—my blanket, my protector—and I was delighted to have it. How modest my camel coat seemed now. How naive.

◆   ◆   ◆

On the evening of the eighth day, a note appeared:

The queen requires your presence at 8 A.M.

Nothing else was written. There was no way for me to reply, to decline or ask questions. *Was I to meet her alone? Would Finn be there?* I rushed down the hall to see him, but an ensign waved me off. There was a meeting of the ministers and Finn could not be disrupted.

I ignored the ensign. Tried the handle. It was locked. I pressed my ear to the door and, sure enough, heard a passel of men's voices shouting at each other in Italian. The ensign looked away uncomfortably as I strained to understand, but I couldn't decipher more than a single word here or there. Eventually I gave up and walked back, dejected, to the Gloria Apartment.

A dinner for one had been plated, for me to eat alone. I left it untouched and spiraled into a panic. *What was I supposed to expect? How should I act?* I would have called my own mother, but she was dead, and the second I remembered the fact of it the anguish was so enormous that I pushed her from my mind. I would have called my father, but I hadn't told him a thing about Finn—and I hated to confuse him or burden him in any way. In resisting my own grief, I made my father's sacred. I wanted to call him *after* Finn and I were married, so I could say with certitude: *You don't need to worry about me. Everything is fine.*

Hanna, Rally, and Duarte, my fair-weather friends, were not worth calling. That left—*Zola.*

We hadn't spoken since my mother's funeral. During our brief chat, I'd said nothing about Finn; not to Zola, I realized, or to anyone. I tried to use my cell phone, but it only had a South African SIM card and wouldn't connect. I picked up the heavy desk phone and heard no dial tone. I tapped the hook switch, but nothing changed.

After a moment, a voice spoke. "*Signorina?*"

"Pardon me," I apologized, thinking I'd interrupted someone else's call.

"This is the operator," the voice said. *Oh.* "Who would you like to reach?"

It was six P.M. in the UK; I assumed she'd still be working. "Uh. Clarence Cast, London?"

"*Momento.*" Moments later, the line began to beep.

"Zola Mbatha's office," said a man's clipped voice. Clever Nick, Zola's secretary.

"Hi, Nick, it's Caroline Muller. May I please speak with Zola?"

"Hello, darling. She's in a meeting, then dinner with clients, but I'll make sure she calls you back. Your cell phone?"

"Oh. No. I don't have the right SIM. Um . . . I don't know the number. Did it show up?"

"The ID is blank. That's odd," he said, drifting off. ". . . This ought to be working . . ." I could hear him fidgeting with the phone's buttons.

"It's my end, I'm sure. I'll call again. When will she be free?"

"She's in the weeds for . . . at least another week . . . we'll find time."

"I'll call back with a number," I assured him.

"Is there anything I can do in the meantime?"

Clever Nick had six or seven brothers, I recalled, and Zola did call him Clever, so I guessed he'd know as much as anyone could. "I'm meeting my man's mother. Any advice?"

"Is she nice? The mother."

I thought about her portrait. "I don't think so."

"I'd expect the standard gauntlet of possessive resentment. Hold tight. If she insults you, don't let her see. If you can help it, don't say a *word* to him. It'll only end in a fight. I realize that sounds terribly sexist. But my brothers Dave's and Peter's partners would tell you the same thing."

"That's as good as it gets, Nick. Thank you."

After we hung up, I poked my head into the corridor. But there was no ensign to be found. "Hello?" I called out. "Hello?"

I tried the orange doors, where we'd come in from the courtyard, but they were locked. I tried—well, I tried every door. *All locked.* The ensign was gone from her post at Finn's, but the passel of men was still shouting. I tried the handle again; it was immovable.

I was both locked out of Finn's apartment and locked *into* the Talon.

I leaned against the wall and sighed. At the very least, Clever Nick had given me some guidance. *Didn't I love a competition? Didn't I love a challenge?* And then there was Finn's insistence that I'd love her. I told myself to take him at face value. That I should believe him.

Back in the Gloria Apartment, a steaming pot of chamomile tea waited. Fresh logs had been placed on the fire, sap snapping. "*Hello?*" I yelled out. But there was no one there.

I curled up in the padded nest of my bed and tried not to worry myself further.

17

DAWN BROUGHT a cold apartment and curiously empty breakfast table. No fire. No delicious coffee, brought by invisible hands. I supposed Amelie and I were to eat together.

With an hour to spare, all I could busy myself with was my appearance. I considered my artless cotton clothes and felt like an idiot. *If I ironed my jeans and T-shirt, and picked all the nubs from my sweater . . . ?* It would have to do. Resigned, I wrenched open a closet door—and found myself suddenly in possession of nearly a hundred dresses.

The first dripped with golden pleats and ran through my palms like mercury; the next was a gauzy slip so delicate that the fabric snagged against the pads of my fingers. A lavender column flowed like heavy cream; a flowered tea dress had been starched stiff as a butterfly wing. An endless parade of filmy things, each more fragile than the last, floating above piles of pointed-spike shoes.

When did these appear here—in the night? I tried to remember the last time I'd opened the closet. Yesterday? Maybe the day before? I couldn't be sure. I'd so completely relaxed into the rhythms of the Talon that I no longer even thought about putting my own clothes away; I simply shed them on the floor.

I tried on one inappropriate, ill-fitting dress after another. A pale blue shimmer, fit for a prom queen, was several sizes too small. The butterfly-wing tea dress was closer to my size. Yet when I zipped it shut, the waist and elbows pulled tight as a string, trussing me up for a roast. I nearly split the sleeve with the flex of a biceps. Off it went. Next was a yellow sleeveless dress, lovely but too cheerful, insubstantial—and it was *short*.

A multicolored pile of discards grew as I went clockwise round the room. I'd nearly given up when the last cabinet sprang open to reveal a soft suit. Done exactly in my measurements, it was made of a matte gray silk. A crisp white blouse hung beside it.

In the stacks of pointed-spike shoes—these were in a variety of sizes—I found nothing appropriate, or comfortable. I'd read somewhere that one was never supposed to wear heels on certain kinds of wood. *Was that these floors?* I wondered, looking down at the herringbone pattern beneath my feet. *Or was that about boats?*

I realized then it was all trickery. A test. *How many women had touched these dresses?* I picked at them, seeing the wear, now, the tear—some had bent at the zip, others were frothy at the hems. A white cotton day dress hid brown makeup stains inside its collar. I wondered who'd squeezed inside these one-size-fits-none costumes for Finn's doll collection. My hip let out an ache.

I snorted. *Fine.* I pulled a handful of acetaminophen from my bag and chewed them up. I showered, blew my hair dry carefully, and wore no makeup. Tucked the white blouse smartly into the gray trousers, hung the jacket neatly over my shoulders. I put the borrowed loafers, the ones Otto had given me on the plane, back on. Now that the swelling was down, they were comically roomy, but it was this or the orthopedic clogs. I doubled up on socks and strode toward the door as soon as the clock read 7:50.

I ran smack into a stern-looking older woman in a green Gardien military suit. Tall as an oak, sharp as an axe, no makeup on her grim face—only a pair of tortoiseshell eyeglasses, the lenses thick as the bottom of a drinking glass. Each wrist bore a watch, set to different time zones.

"Gosh. Pardon," I said, too loudly. The words echoed down the hall. "I'm Caroline."

"Schätze," she called herself. "I am *the* private secretary of *the* queen." Curious. Because of my father, Rainer, whose Namibian German dialect was frozen in the nineteenth century, I knew that *Schätze* was German for *sweetie*; calling this tough bit of leather *sweetie* was rather like calling a tall man *tiny*, a sort of inverse joke. But her accent wasn't German, not exactly. Intermittent high notes, placed on *the;* the squared-off sturdiness of her vowels; and her extreme height all seemed to indicate that she'd originated from Scandinavia, though I couldn't tell where.

"Very nice to meet you." I used both hands to pump her iron arm up and down. Schätze retracted herself a moment before it would have been polite—*definitely* Scandinavian—then turned away and began striding briskly down the hall. Ten feet later she glanced back, slowing with the most temporary of pauses.

I was supposed to catch up. I stood firm. "May I ask a question?"

She stopped, her face dispassionate, and waited begrudgingly for me to continue.

"How am I to address Amelie? What is—what is the customary way to behave?"

"You may," she said slowly, "address her as Your Serene Highness. It *is* customary *to* curtsy. Do *not* speak until *she* asks you to."

"Until she asks me to," I repeated. "Thank you. Is there anything else I should know?"

Schätze didn't blink. "Miss?"

"I mean—well—is there anything that I ought to take particular care of? In order to make a good impression."

Her mouth turned down at the corners. "It's not for me to say." Then she began marching again, all through the hallway to the final pair of doors, painted a rich purple.

As Schätze flung them open, a soundtrack of insistent, cacophonous birdsong filled our ears. There, among a strange cluster of oversized metal birdcages, filled with taxidermized parrots, fifty-nine-year-old Amelie waited impatiently.

◆　◆　◆

I possessed a basic set of facts concerning Her Serene Highness Amelie Arturo Alexander Gloria Fieschi, Queen of Lucomo, Duchesse of Burgundy, Marchesa of Lombardy, Contessa of Savoy, and Baronne of Meaux. Born in the Talon itself, in 1944, as World War II began to end. At fifteen, upon the death of her father, Arturo, she was crowned queen. She was married one year later to Armand Robert Brevard, of the French-colonial textile fortune Brevards. Finn was born in 1969. Armand died in 1995. There were no other children.

Amelie sat in an overstuffed armchair four times her size, feet crossed at the ankle and knees bent modestly to the side. Two cups of coffee, one presumably mine, steamed on a filigreed silver tray table to her left. She wore a sweater set and trousers, her wispy blond hair held back with a velvet headband, like any other pensioner. I could tell that, like many women of her generation, she'd spent a lifetime dieting without exercising; at fifty-nine she'd already shrunk from svelte to frail, a scaffold of glass encased in parachute silk.

As I strode across the room, the reverberations of my cloddish steps rattled the coffee cups in their saucers. Amelie shuddered with such profound distaste that I stopped in my tracks, feeling as if I'd broken the cups, though of course I'd only caused them to tremble. I remembered to curtsy, and did so very badly, rising awkwardly. It was clear from Amelie's marble gaze that I was to remain still. She regarded me like I was a horse, impassively rating the quality of my flesh. I kept quiet by counting my breaths and got all the way up to fifty before she spoke.

"You may sit." She offered the command like it was the most

gracious of gifts. Her voice surprised me; it was musical and deep, a river rushing through the cavern of her body.

I took the nearest chair, a spindly antique that felt like it might break beneath my bulk. Amelie's tiny hands began to flit about her shoulder, as though she was digging something out—yes—it was—it was a neon-green . . . bird? Yes. *A living bird.* A small tropical-finch-like creature emerged from her cardigan and gripped one of her translucent fingers. I realized the soundtrack of birdsong was not digital but real; the birds in the cages behind her—there were a dozen, no, two dozen— glowed with lifelike fervor because they were alive.

Amelie sighed, exasperated, and glanced at the clock on the wall. She seemed to dislike that it was eight in the morning. She took a coffee from the tray beside her and let the second remain where it was. I nearly spoke, ready to apologize for waking her, though I had of course been summoned—but I remembered Schätze's instructions. *Do not speak until she asks you to.* I kept my mouth shut.

Amelie stared expectantly. I said nothing. She raised a penciled eyebrow. I did not react. She drank her coffee. Cooed at her bird. Adjusted her necklace, a thick rope of pearls, arranged over a silk scarf with interlocking Fs.

I lowered my eyes to the ground.

At that, she cracked a perverse little smirk and boomed out a question: "Who are you?"

Ah. So this is how we're going to start. I answered clearly: "My name is Caroline Harriet Muller, and I'm an athlete, Your Serene Highness."

"Caroline," she said firmly. "Not a Carrie, I hope."

"My mother called me Caro, Your Serene Highness," I reported.

"You did not attend secondary school or university."

"That's correct, Your Serene Highness."

"You were baptized Catholic?"

"I believe so, Your Serene Highness." I had no idea if this was true.

She sipped her coffee and did not look up. "You are not employed."

"I'm under contract, Your Serene Highness, with an athletic company."

"This contract will soon expire."

"That's correct, Your Serene Highness."

"You have no means of employment."

"I am recently retired, Your Serene Highness."

"No," she corrected me, "you have *no* means of employment. You are *seeking* a means of employment, which is to say, you seek a position here." She touched the Fs on her scarf.

"I see, Your Serene Highness." My voice was faltering, half-full and scratchy; I was caught off guard by this hateful game. I cleared my throat. "Yes, I suppose I do."

"Why are you qualified for this position?"

My mind went blank except for the obvious. *Because your son . . . is in love with me?* But that didn't seem to be what we were discussing. I tried to parry. "I'm not sure what you're asking, Your Serene Highness."

"That's absurd," she countered, running a beige fingernail gently along the wing of her bird. It cocked its head, turning its beady eyes to hers. I couldn't tell if it was pleased or terrified. "Come now," she encouraged me. "Make an effort."

"I hold the record for the women's marathon," I tried. "I'm an ambassador for the Special Olympics. I'm accustomed to speaking in public—"

She interrupted me. "That does not concern us. What are your *qualifications*?"

"I'm sorry, Your Serene Highness, but I don't understand the question," I told her.

She rolled her eyes, dragging her claws through the bird's feathers. It tightened its grip on her finger; it was definitely scared. "Have you"— she squinted—"ever been pregnant?"

"*Oo-oh,*" I hiccupped. "No, Your Serene Highness."

"Can you *get* pregnant?"

"I . . . I . . . ," I stammered. "I believe so, Your Serene Highness."

"Belief is not sufficient. We must have proof."

My cheeks burned. As I desperately searched for a response, I unwittingly waited her out.

"You must understand," she sighed finally, opening her hands. The neon bird flew away instantly. "No one may govern Lucomo except natural-born Fieschi children. In the *direct* line."

"I didn't know that, Your Serene Highness."

"You've been given plenty of books," she snorted. "Are you illiterate?"

"I read carefully, Your Serene Highness, and slowly."

"We made a treaty with France and Italy in 1870, after Italy was unified and France began the Third Republic. This treaty recognizes our sovereignty extending solely from the House of Fieschi. If there is no Fieschi heir, there is no government. If there is no government, there is no nation. Do you understand?"

"I do," I said, forgetting the honorific. She arched an eyebrow. "Your Serene Highness," I followed up quickly.

"You're very pretty," she stated abruptly. "And you don't dress like a slut. That's refreshing." I almost choked. "Your mother is dead," she said next. Plainly, like she was describing the color of my hair.

Tears welled up. I tilted my head back a fraction to keep them from falling. *I never want to let this woman see me cry*, I thought—*never, ever*. "My mother died last month. My father lives in Johannesburg. He's a miner." My voice wavered but did not break.

"Condolences," she said automatically, hollow as the cages that hung behind her. "Your parents were political activists who sought to overthrow the government. Do you deny it?"

They sent letters and went to meetings, I almost snapped. *If you think that's what brought down apartheid, then you know even less about the world than I do*. I managed to hold my tongue and gave the best response I could come up with in the moment: "Apartheid does not find many defenders, Your Serene Highness."

"Are you political?"

"I believe in fairness," I replied sincerely. "I believe in equality of opportunity, Your Serene Highness. Finn and I share many of the same beliefs."

"Hmm." The cold-blooded smile from her portrait appeared. "You are handicapped. You require a great deal of medical care."

"I . . . yes. Yes. I am, Your Serene Highness."

"How can you bear children when you are so indisposed?"

"I'm already recovering, Your Serene Highness. That's why I stopped running."

"Is it hereditary?"

"No, Your Serene Highness."

"That's good. It is *very* sympathetic," she murmured. "That's *very* helpful. Now there's only one thing to do." The vicious slash of her lips widened, exposing a row of miniature teeth.

She wanted me to ask. "What's that?" Amelie tilted her head expectantly. "Your Serene Highness."

"An exam," she said enthusiastically. "We'll have an exam. Off you go!" She struck her hands together in a delighted, insane little clap, then rang a small silver bell at her side. Then—she opened her book and stared at the pages. Perhaps she read. I couldn't tell. Either way she did not look up.

I remained on the chair, unsure of what to do. After fifteen long seconds, the door opened and through it Schätze, the Green Giant, beckoned for me to rise.

"Goodbye, Your Serene Highness," I said.

Amelie did not reply. Schätze offered me a pitying glance as we exited. After another string of corridors, we arrived at an office. It was white, all white, a small red cross painted on the door. An upholstered table was covered in paper. I was told to remove my clothing and wait. I did as instructed, wrapping myself in a cloth gown, nervously anticipating what I assumed would be an examination of my joints.

A middle-aged woman appeared with a clipboard. "Hello, love," she said in a friendly South London twang, flipping the pages. "I'm Dr. Finney." At the sound of her accent—she was the first person in this entire country with whom I shared a native language—I relaxed. *Finally*, I thought, *someone who understood, a doctor who was on my side*. "We'll do the exam and take some blood, get some samples, quick as we can," she explained.

"What am I being examined for?"

She suppressed a laugh. "A pelvic exam. I'm an obstetrician. Didn't no one tell you?"

"No."

"Well, not to brag, but I've done a million of these and I'm fast as lightning. Easy peasy pudding pie. Go on, lie back for me, that's a good girl," she pattered, pulling out the metal stirrups. I cannot believe that I complied—but, too stunned to do anything but obey, I did. Like a good girl I put my heels in the supports and lay back. "Scoot forward. Open up—bit more—again—well done." The doctor parted my labia with gloved fingers, aimed her flashlight, then marked something down. "Not in this day and age," she muttered to herself.

"Not what?" I asked.

"Hymen. They insist that we check. Silly. I've not seen one since medical school," she said, shaking her head as she coated the plastic speculum with lubricant. She raised a gloved hand. "This discharge, very nice," she said approvingly, separating the egg white of it between her fingers to observe the stretch. "When did your last period end?"

"Two weeks ago," I heard myself answer. *Is this really happening?*

"How long's your cycle?"

"A month, I guess."

"Fine, fine." She swabbed the interior of my vaginal canal, then bagged her findings. "All right. Scoot again? Well done. This will be a bit cold, love—there we go. Good girl. I'm going to sound your uterus. It'll be a bit uncomfortable."

◆ ◆ ◆

Schätze deposited me in my room afterward.

Once the shock wore off, I stood up, removed the diamond ring from my finger, and set it on the bedside table. I did so without thinking or feeling. Driven by instinct, I simply *acted*.

I did not write a note. Finn did not deserve an explanation. I would leave as I had arrived: as my own person. After a moment's thought, I left my duffel behind; I didn't want to be stopped. I pulled on the mustard coat with matching fox cuffs, because he'd given my camel coat away and I guessed it was the least expensive of the three. I pocketed my toothbrush, passport, wallet, cell phone and charger, and exited through the Gloria door, where an ensign stood sentry in the hall.

"*Signorina?*" she asked politely.

"Which way are the public rooms? I've been told to have a look."

"This way." She gestured. "I'll take you."

I followed her down through the orange doors, the ones that had been locked the night before, into an ostentatious foyer, gilded and upholstered within an inch of its life. A tour group, roped off in the next room, glanced hopefully in our direction, but their faces fell when they realized I wasn't anyone important. *No, I was no one,* I told myself, *though I was given a free pelvic exam at the behest of the Lilliputian monarch they were so desperate to see, so perhaps I was special by association.*

I unhooked the velvet rope, squeezed past the tour group, and strolled right out the Talon's front doors.

18

IN THE MAIN COURTYARD, I joined a group of ruddy-cheeked tourists led by a loud man brandishing a German flag. It took no more than a few seconds, though in my silk suit and fur-trimmed coat, I didn't exactly blend in with their anoraks and jeans. I kept my face turned down as we filed onto one of a half dozen red buses marked *LUCOMOTOUR*. Yet I needn't have worried. Nobody asked my name, only counted my head. As soon as it was full, the bus wheezed, the door closed, and we were hauled out to France.

The bus was coated in dirt, flakes of skin smeared on every surface. The toilet reeked all the way through to the front. I curled up in a ball and tried not to touch anything. Lucomo disappeared out the greasy windows as I replayed my conversation with Amelie. *Are you illiterate? What are your qualifications? Your mother is dead.* Yes. My mother was dead. My mother was dead, I was casting about for a life raft, and I'd chosen the wrong one.

The exam. I was used to being examined, of course—I had done nothing but go to doctors and physios for the past two years. I was used to doing whatever was asked of me. But to be poked and prodded so intimately and expediently, as though it didn't matter what I thought or how I reacted—as though pretense was unnecessary, as though politeness itself was irrelevant—it was humiliating. I thought of myself as an animal. A *free* animal. Amelie treated me like I'd been born in a cage, like one of her birds.

Did I want *to have children?* My mother told me that it gripped her like a fever—that she woke up one morning and it was all she could think about, a feeling that did not pass until I was born. A grasping for life, she called it. I missed my mother so badly in that moment that I raised my head and glanced around the bus to see if she was on it. I searched for her face through the window, praying that she would appear on a corner or in the driver's seat of a passing car.

Amelie. Someone's mother, too. Finn didn't call her Mother. He called her by her first name for a reason: Amelie was brutal. She was not a "sweet person" that I would "love." *He ought to have protected me from her. From the way she spoke to me. From the speculum, pushing me open; the thin metal ruler in my uterus, measuring my worth.* I wanted to tear his skin apart for hurting me.

I sat there fuming, practically *broiling* in my mustard coat, but couldn't move an inch to take it off. Between my anger, the slimy bus, and the coughs and malodorous gases of the tourists around me, I was paralyzed. I closed my eyes and tried to pretend I was outside, on an empty road, alone. *Two, twelve, eight,* I repeated quietly, my lucky numbers, over and again: *two hours, twelve minutes, eight seconds.* When the seat next to me became vacant I noticed the bus had stopped. The driver was speaking to someone—me—in German. *"Ihr Hotel liegt um die Ecke,"* he was saying forcefully, directing me to the street. *"Ecke."*

I had no idea what he meant beyond the word *hotel.* Nevertheless I exited the bus and walked in the direction of his pointed finger. We'd left France and stopped somewhere on the Italian Riviera. Most everything was closed; this close to Christmas the town was deserted, its streets covered in muck and overflowing piles of trash. The sea crashed loudly to my right, and the wind blowing off it was near to freezing. I pulled my collar up to my ears and pressed on.

There was an open business, a restaurant. A waitress with one of those life-threatening Italian tans stood outside in a puffy jacket, lighting an extra-long Marlboro Light. As I passed by, snow began to fall. The waitress broke into a tremendous, golden smile, gesturing to the slow-moving crystals with her cigarette. The smoke made me ill. *First the foul bus, and now this repellent town. The world around Lucomo was awful,* I thought, frowning reflexively. The waitress ignored me, caught a flake on her tongue.

I stepped carefully along the damp sidewalks, toward where the man had pointed. Some of the bus's passengers stood outside a two-star hotel. I went right in. The owner, wrapped up in aubergine polyester, gave me a rehearsed bob of the head.

"May I speak English?" I asked.

"Naturally. Name of the reservation?" she replied.

"I need a taxi." I dug a euro coin out of my pocket. "Would you mind?"

"*Prego,*" she agreed, picking up the phone. "Where are you going?"

"To the airport," I said.

"*Aeroporto,*" she said to the phone, and hung up. "*Momento.*" She flipped her palm toward the door.

I turned—then thought better of it. "Do you know where I might buy a SIM card?"

"International or Italian?"

"International."

"Thirty minutes, twenty euro." She took a plastic card from the register, scanned it, popped the SIM from its casing, took the money from my hand, and deposited the small plastic chip in return. I thanked her and sat on the bench, putting my phone back to rights. But it wouldn't turn on. The battery was dead.

Before I could find an electrical outlet, a dented minivan ground to a halt at the curb. My taxi. I sat dumbly in the middle, the other row empty of any luggage or travelers. The van reeked of body odor and cologne. I coughed repeatedly and tried to open a window, but the child locks were on. The driver, listening to Italian talk radio, seemed oblivious to my discomfort.

The van's shocks were worthless, the roads pitted with holes, of which we hit every single one. Every house out of the window was grungy, covered in bad political graffiti. *Disgusting.* Trash clung to the soiled streets. *Revolting.* It took about forty-five minutes to get to the airport, and I became severely nauseous.

The airport wasn't much better; it was older, then, unrenovated, and looked more like a bus station than the architectural aerie it became a few years later. I walked to the departures counter, purchased a ticket for the next flight out—I would need to go to Amsterdam and endure a short layover before the next flight to Jozi—then made my way to the gift shops, where I bought travel-sized toiletries and a novel to read on the plane.

It felt incredibly peculiar to perform these simple exchanges. The motions were familiar (remove wallet; insert chip card, type PIN; say thank you) but no longer comfortable. After eight days of being waited on hand and foot, I found this sudden return of responsibility to be enormously stressful. At each interaction, I wondered if I was doing my part correctly. Every glance from a stranger felt heated and intrusive. Stepping down the unfamiliar hallways, being jostled by strange bodies like a dinghy tossing in a storm, I became smaller and smaller.

The queue for security took half an hour. Every time someone near me moved, I worried that I hadn't properly anticipated their movement and that we would accidentally touch. One of my legs jiggled uncontrollably, and my breathing was uneven. The security officers eyed me warily. So did the businessmen behind me. *Why is everyone looking at me?*

I tried to remind myself that this was normal life. Normal people looked at you however they pleased; they didn't cast their eyes to the floor to defer to your emotional space. Normal people accidentally smacked you with their backpacks. Normal people tried to cut you off in line. Normal people were sweaty and overperfumed. Normal people stared hungrily at young women in mustard fur coats with long hair and beautiful skin. Normal people lived this way.

I myself had lived this way every day of my life but the previous eight. A nice vacation, but that was all it could ever be: A stopover. A pause. A mistake. Finn had not even asked me if I wanted to have children—had not even raised the question. If he held me at such a remove, we could never share a life. That life. *His* life. Not ours. I'd met a man I loved and none of it was real; I felt as though I'd won a lottery, only to find out it was a hoax. I tried not to cry, but the tears leaked out anyway, dripping off my chin and spotting the fur of my collar.

At the gate, yet another queue. Stale air baked in the hot breath of a thousand travelers. I couldn't stop staring at a cluster of spots on the neck of the man in front of me. When he glanced down at his ticket, inadvertently brushing the spots against the worn-out coat, one burst. Oil on dirt, white pus on flannel. I forced myself to look away, and landed on the gate agent, with her pancake makeup and ill-fitting uniform. *I bet she would do anything to be a princess,* I thought. Her painted smile surrounded a trash heap of coffee-stained teeth. *I bet she would do anything. Not me,* I thought, my ego so big it wore me like that purloined suit. *I won't do anything. I won't be disrespected. I am Caroline Muller and I am important.* Thoughts that were nothing but capricious arrogance.

South Africa waited for me on the other side of the tunnel, with its stultifying inequality, its cemeteries full of the murdered. I dreaded it. I didn't want to beg Wits for the coaching job I'd already rejected. I didn't want to spend the rest of my life looking for someone I could imbue with all my hopes and dreams. Someone I could follow down the track and watch climb to the top of that wooden box again. But it was my only option.

People shuffled forward. I clutched my ticket and passport readily.

It was nearly my turn. Yet, as I was about to step up, bony fingers gripped my elbow and plucked the paper ticket and passport from my hand. I jerked away, feeling a seam tear in my coat, but the fingers didn't loosen their grip. They belonged to Roland, standing firm as a steel girder outside the ribboned queue. Otto and Dix hovered a few feet behind, avoiding my eyes.

"*Signorina* Caroline." Roland's voice was low, discreet.

"What are you *doing*?" I sputtered, vainly attempting to squirm free from the vise of his grip. It did not ease; he held me still. His eyes were darting around the airport, and only half his face was even visible. I wonder now if he ever did look me in the eyes, if I ever saw that face in full. I must have—I lived with Roland for over ten years—but that is how I will always remember him, as a hissing, shape-shifting snake of a man, bruising the elbow of a twenty-four-year-old girl in an airport.

"*Signore* is troubled. You must not go," Roland insisted. "Please. It will hurt him."

"That's none of your business." I prickled as I felt pressure building up in the line behind me. I was holding it up and people were starting to stare. Roland, meanwhile, was unfastening the ribbon with his free hand. When I pinched him, hard, he let go of my elbow. But he kept my ticket and passport. "Give me those," I hissed. The businessmen behind me in line at last looked concerned.

Roland gave them an embarrassed grimace, as if to say, *Women! What can you do?* And then he gestured for them to go ahead. "*Prego,*" he said to the men.

"*Grazie,*" they said politely. The businessmen stepped around me easily, this crazy woman who was no longer a member of the line, merely an inconvenience. The ribbon was clicked back in place and now I was outside of it. Passenger after passenger gave their ticket to the pancaked agent. Between bright smiles, she glanced at me once, then again, worry creasing her brow. I nearly called out to her. As the words

This man is trying to take my passport rose in my throat, Roland pressed a mobile phone into my palm, the display reading *FII*.

"Please," he urged. "If you speak with him, you may go."

I held it to my ear. "What do you want?" I snapped.

"Caroline, I'm so sorry," Finn said right away. "I had no idea. I had no idea she would act out like that." *Act out.* Like she was the child and he the parent. "Please," he begged. "I'm so angry." He was wildly upset. Far more upset, I realized, than I'd assumed he would be.

Finn's distress worked upon me like a tonic. I bowed my head away from Roland, trying for privacy. "I don't know what to say."

"Say you hate me."

"I don't." I softened. I wanted to hear him out. "But I wonder if you might secretly hate me. How could you let that happen?"

"Caroline, I'm so in love with you. Please don't leave like this. Please come back. At least allow me to apologize. I can explain. Let's not leave it this way. Please. I'm—I break." His syntax faltered—the sound of his otherwise faultless composure snapping—and with it went my resolve. I sighed, hung up the phone, and handed it back to Roland.

With one last glance at the flight I didn't really want to take, I turned around and went back through security, past the black nylon corrals. Finn's henchmen trailing, I returned my ticket—you could do that, back then—and Otto escorted me out of the airport. Roland and Dix stayed inside. "What are they doing?" I asked.

Otto pursed his thin lips. "They will take a different car." No more of an explanation was given. I know now that they stayed behind and paid off the worried gate agent, bought the security footage, and had all evidence of my aborted departure erased from the airport.

As I buckled myself in, a parking officer approached Otto's SUV, ticket pad in hand. The officer glanced briefly at the plates—then walked away. We were not to be ticketed; we were not even to be seen.

When we crossed back into Lucomo, I felt the deepest relief to once again be on its clean, smooth streets, among its dewy rich. It wasn't, I realized then, that the parts of Italy surrounding Lucomo were dirty. It was that Lucomo was so clean that everywhere else looked filthy by comparison.

◆ ◆ ◆

In an inner courtyard, Finn waited, pacing up and down. The second we pulled to a stop, he wrenched my door open, dropping to his knees on the running board. He rested his forehead on the cool silk of my trousers, murmuring apologies. Otto scattered to his rat hole, giving us space.

"I'm so sorry." Finn's topaz eyes were bloodshot, his neck and cheeks red from misery. "I should have expected this. I should never have let you meet her alone."

Without thinking I ran my hands through his hair. *Don't make it easy,* I chastised myself. *Don't break.* I repossessed my hands and sat on them. "I agree," I said flatly.

"Amelie—she's *afraid,*" he said. "She behaves this way out of fear. Succession is extremely important. She went about it the wrong way, I know."

"What's she so afraid of?" I asked. "You've been here for seven hundred years."

"It's not as easy as that," he muttered, his head still pressed against my thigh. "Lucomo is complicated."

"Well, you can either explain it to me," I said calmly, "or you can drive me back to the airport."

Finn stayed on his knees but looked up, hope brightening his eyes. "You really want to know?"

"I really do."

He exhaled heavily and sat up a bit straighter. "First promise me you will never repeat this. Not to anyone."

I arched an eyebrow.

"Promise," he said again. "No matter what you decide to do."

The wind howled through the courtyard. "I promise," I agreed, the words dying in the cold. He clicked his jaw back and forth nervously. "Spit it out."

"How much do you understand about debt?" he asked carefully.

"My parents had a mortgage from a credit union."

"*National* debt," he specified. "The leveraging of an economy for growth."

I shook my head. "Not much."

"Nations borrow against income, our gross domestic product," he said slowly, "to generate growth." I gave a quick nod; I did know that, even if I couldn't define the term on my own. "A nation's ability to borrow at favorable rates depends on their stability. In a monarchy the line of succession is part of that stability. It's very important to maintain, because broadly, stability equates to economic power."

I looked at the palace around us. "It seems to me like Lucomo is doing fine."

"It's not a new debt. When Amelie ascended in 1959, the economy was distressed. Do you remember when I said we had to pay reparations? She found herself in charge of a bankrupt country. She tried to acquire a sovereign bond, but without an heir she was unable to."

"You weren't born yet."

"Not until ten years later. So—she took on private investment. It is . . . highly leveraged."

"What does that mean?"

"It means a fifteen-year-old girl authorized a personal loan to the family, even as the money went to the country. It revived the economy, but the interest was very high, which kept her from repaying the principal. The debt is now very valuable."

"How valuable?"

"It's now slightly over one point two trillion pounds." Finn waited, gauging my response; it took me a moment to comprehend.

"You owe someone one point two trillion pounds?"

"I'm resolving it. We're in an economic boom that will push us through this," he reassured me. "Europe is thriving."

"Is this . . . common?"

"No. That's why you *must* keep it to yourself. You can't tell *anyone*," he insisted again.

"I don't see why this resulted in someone looking for my hymen this morning."

"If I'd died in that car accident, without an heir, there would have been immediate instability. Instability creates a credit crisis. Our assets—which means much of the nation—would be taken as collateral by the lender. We could, theoretically, dissolve the economy in a single afternoon."

I thought about how so much of my own meager money had disappeared when the rand last fell. "I wish you would have told me from the start."

His eyelids flickered up and down. He was shamed—but optimistic; there was still a door open between us. "I've spent my life gathering the resources to repay this. It's being handled, and you'll never have to worry about it." He bent his head to my knee once more. "I'm in love with you, Caroline. I didn't tell you because—I wanted to avoid conflict." He turned his cheek. "I've ruined everything."

"Maybe." One of my disobedient hands floated to his face.

"This isn't how I wanted this conversation to go."

"Me either."

"So you're not against having children."

I thought about how desperately I wanted to fill the mother-shaped hole in my heart. "No," I said softly, "I'm not against it."

"I'm in love with you," he repeated. "I'll do anything you ask. Anything."

"I'll think about it."

"*Anything*," he repeated. "I'm so sorry. Can you forgive us?"

My index finger traced his jawline. He was forgiven—of course he was forgiven.

That was Finn's specialty. Being forgiven.

Because in a way none of it was his fault.

❖ ❖ ❖

The next morning, I powered up my phone, but it didn't connect; the SIM card I'd purchased in Italy wasn't able to communicate with the towers in Lucomo, either. I sighed, dropped it in the pocket of the yellow coat, then picked up the landline and asked the operator for Clarence Cast. When Clever Nick answered, "Zola Mbatha's office," I pushed him to get Zola out of her meeting. "It's a legal matter," I insisted.

Nick sighed. I could tell he didn't believe me. "Okay . . ."

"Caroline," Zola said when she answered, "you don't have to pretend. Are you okay?"

"I'm not pretending. I need to hire you."

"The sponsor wants to renew?" Zola assumed. "I knew we'd get traction off that *Trib* sports piece on your speech in Shanghai. Well done, by the way, nicely written. Listen, whatever the offer is, don't fight it. I'll look it over but it's a gift they want you. I'll find the time this week, I promise."

"It's nothing to do with that."

"Then what is it?"

"I—well, I'm getting married," I said, moderating it a bit.

"Oh! To that gay guy from Portugal? Congratulations. Allow me to be the first to welcome you to the European Union. But you don't need a lawyer."

"Not him. I—I don't know how to say this."

"Out with it."

"I'm getting married to . . ." Like a child, I whispered: "Ferdinand Fieschi. I'm—I'm in Lucomo."

There was silence on the line.

"Zola?"

"I'm here," she said quietly. "Where are you calling from?"

"The palace. The Talon. They call it the Talon."

She sighed. "All right. I'll—*Christ*. Don't sign a thing. All right? Not a single solitary thing. Someone puts a pen in your hand, you *open your hand*. That pen falls to the ground. You are functionally incapable of writing as of this moment. Do you hear me?"

"Yes."

"Has anyone taken pictures of you?"

"They have cameras everywhere, so I suppose their security has."

"But no tourists or anything like that?"

"I don't think so."

"Good. Keep it that way. I'll . . ." She clicked away on a keyboard. "I'll call back later today."

"I don't know the number."

"Ask someone to get it to me."

"Sorry about the long distance."

Zola laughed. "I'll bill you."

"Starting when?" I had so little money. All I could think was that the ticket return would still take days to clear in my account.

"It's three hundred fifty pounds to talk, darling, we have minimums here."

"Zola, I don't have that kind of money."

"Don't fret. It'll get worked out."

"Okay." I sounded more squeak than woman.

"You did the right thing to ring me and it'll be fine," she said reassuringly. "Talk to you shortly."

After she hung up, I opened the Gloria door and motioned to the ensign, who rose to attention immediately.

I scribbled *Zola Mbatha, Clarence Cast,* and her phone number on a piece of paper. "Can you make sure this person has my direct line?"

"Of course," the ensign said flatly.

"Thanks so much," I said, following it with a dismissive nod—my first ever.

I'll admit it. It felt good.

❖ ❖ ❖

Our last race together was the Comrades, the fifty-five-mile ultramarathon, ending in Durban, in 1998. After we finished—eight hours, patinated with salt, shaking like dried leaves at the finish line—Zola put her hands on her thighs and began to giggle uncontrollably. The giggle became guffawing, horking, snorting. Soon she was laughing so hard she was crying. I stood bewildered, wrapped in an aluminum blanket to keep the heat in, asking what was so funny. Finally Zola stopped yowling long enough to choke out an answer. "That's it for me," she wheezed. "I found the endpoint. I found enough."

"Enough?" I didn't know the meaning of the word.

"Yes." She turned to the crowd walking up the hill, the sonic wall of their cheers. "I'm full."

"You don't want to qualify?" Zola was the strongest marathoner in the country and a shoo-in for Sydney.

"No," she said, knowing it was true, feeling her own disbelief. "I got what I wanted."

"Don't," I pleaded. "I can't go without you. This is the beginning."

"Caroline, you ambitious little cheetah," she said. "For *you*. It's a beginning *for you*. This is an end for me. I'm—I don't want to pass through cities. I want to change them," she said, stretching her hand out to the urban sprawl of city and townships, then back to the Indian Ocean. "I'm running a different kind of race."

"There's no other kind," I argued, confused.

"There's so much more," she contended, watching the horizon. "There's a whole world."

"You made me a runner, Zola. You can't stop."

"I can do anything I like," she replied. "I'm not the reason you run, Caroline. You don't need me running ahead of you. You only want to pass me, anyway."

◆　◆　◆

The phone rang an hour later. "What do you want out of this marriage?" Zola asked clinically.

"Hello to you, too."

"Caroline, this is serious."

"I want him to marry me next week *like he promised.*"

"Sure. But let's get some other options on the table."

"And put up with six more months of being pushed around? A year? I don't think so."

"If you wait, you'll have more leverage."

"His mother had someone give me a gynecological exam."

I thought Zola would be as upset as I'd been, but she made a positive noise. "Mmm."

"Not *mmm*. It was awful. And what if it goes wrong? I didn't get a period until a year ago."

"That's your hard line? Getting married immediately?"

"Yes. I'm not asking for something new. *He already promised me this.*"

"What else do you want?"

"I don't know what to ask for. I'm useless, Zola. I don't know how to do anything."

"That's not true. What have you loved doing over the past few years?"

"Uh. Traveling, I suppose, living in a new place."

"For god's sake. What's the biggest problem in the world you can think of?"

"Well . . ." I crossed my arms. "Since I fell—and listen, it's not like I'm complaining, I know how lucky I am—"

"Shove it on the humility," Zola snapped, "get to the point."

"—I want to do more for the Special Olympics. I want there to be more people who can compete."

She jotted it down, ballpoint scratching. "What else?"

"My dad's not doing very well. Anything I could send him would be a help—I think he'll have to take an adjusted pension—"

Zola coughed. The miner's union had long excluded nonwhite workers; only white miners were eligible for pensions. She didn't need to say it, we both knew it. "Why am I surprised that you're only thinking about this now?"

"It didn't affect me until now."

Zola let out one of her big honking laughs, incredulous. *Predictable Caroline,* I knew she was thinking, *Caroline in her bubble.* "Here's what I'm going to fight for," she said sternly. "Money for your father. Staff of your own. A charitable budget to do with what you please and official support in all your endeavors. A bonus for each child. Shares in family investments. A trust of your own, at least one property in your name—"

"Zola, why would they give me any of that?" *They're one point two trillion pounds in debt,* I did not say.

"Because of what you bring to the table."

"I thought . . . I brought a lot. I'm a good public speaker. I'm an Olympic medalist. But all they care about are children."

"My point exactly. You're young, Caroline. You're twenty-four. Even with everything you've been through, I bet you could still get pregnant from a sneeze. I'm asking you," she said, sounding sad. "Is this really what you want?"

I thought about Finn, about the way our bodies fit together. The way whole rooms adjusted to his presence, and the power he held, power that I assumed I would share. Out the window, I could see the sea rolling along the beaches to the east. Lucomo, pristine and untroubled. I couldn't bear to tell her that I wanted more than Finn. I wanted the comfort, the safety, the cocoon. I wanted to escape the ordinary life I'd fallen into. I didn't want to admit that I needed to be important, to once again live a life that was special. So all I said was: "Yes. I want to be married as soon as possible."

Zola paused. We sat in the silence. I waited for her to tell me to walk away even as I prayed she would let it go. "Be very careful, Caroline," she finally replied, an edge in her voice. "Open your eyes."

"He loves me. I love him. I do."

"That's not what I mean," she croaked, a sound high and strange—but I didn't understand. Let me say, honestly, that at the time I don't think it was possible for me to have seen past what I wanted. That's the thing about competing, about aiming for the moon and landing on it. It's easy to become certain you can have anything you set your sights on, that wanting is itself enough of a reason to do anything at all.

I waited for her to explain, to push, but she didn't. We'd run thousands of miles together. She knew where I was, mentally. She knew that I was not a complicated person. "Thank you, Zola," I finally said.

"Call you back." She hung up.

I was left alone in the Gloria Apartment, my only friends the ghostly women on the walls. But they were dead and gone. I wish I'd listened to the one living person whose voice broke through those rooms.

19

THE WEDDING WAS NOT, in the end, delayed any further. A ceremony was followed by a formal reception where I met all of Cap-Griffe. It took place on December 24, 2003, exactly thirteen days after my arrival. It was modest, I believe, as royal weddings go, and simple: I awoke, wrote a letter to my father, and dressed.

The gown was duchesse satin, worn over an ivory silk turtleneck and stockings. It had very little embellishment—there was no time for lace bodices or pearl beading—so once it was buttoned in place, I sat on a tall wooden stool while fresh lilac blooms, plucked from the Talon greenhouses, were hand-stitched into its hems. With each step their delicate scent would release, and linger on the air.

A technician braided a stranger's hair into mine, forming a rounded nest, the purpose of which was the underpinning of a tiara. The Dahlia Diadem, as it is called, was made from white gold bent into branches. Diamonds, cut in the round like drops of dew, studded the edges. Though it weighed about as much as a pair of winter boots, the nest docked it firmly against my skull and rendered it immovable.

Items that were new (the dress), old and borrowed (the tiara), but nothing blue. This struck me as the type of detail my mother would have paid attention to. I shut my eyes to banish the thought. *She's not here. I can't bring her back. I don't need my parents at my side on my wedding day,* I told myself. *That's an absurd tradition, a remnant of a world that gave women away as property. I am my* own *property. I'm making a choice. I'm winning a prize.*

When the clock struck eleven, the green fur cape was set about my shoulders. I followed a pair of ensigns to the Marian Cathedral, the sixteenth-century marvel that sits on the easternmost aspect of the Talon. The sun, pale yellow in the winter sky, gave little warmth through the winds that whipped atop the cliff and blew the fog clear across the sea. The cathedral's blue-and-gold windows—*Four Visions of Mary*—were visible that day all the way from the pebbled beaches.

The outer doors opened to the sounds of a string quartet playing Vivaldi's "Winter." Someone took my cape and handed me a bouquet of lavender dahlias, wrapped tightly in forest-green ribbon; someone else straightened my skirts. The inner doors swung open, and there stood my future: Finn waited for me in the round of the apse, showered in rays stained blue and green. Under a silk veil coating me like a dropped web, I walked, alone, to meet him. Candles flickered all around, dancing in the dry air of the unheated cathedral, the temperature low enough for steam to evaporate from our lips. We faced each other and listened as a shrunken priest spoke in Latin.

Amelie, Roland, and Schätze sat up front. The other pews held an ocean of strangers, bundled in furs. Soon the priest tied our fists with green ribbon. Finn and I exchanged yellow bands of gold, mine narrow, his wide—and then we were married.

It took fifteen minutes.

There was no license. We signed our names below his parents' on the page of a Bible so old that I worried the paper would come away on the nib of the pen. I wrote my name as Caroline Harriet Muller Fieschi. As I dotted four small "i"s instead of two, I became Her Serene Highness Caroline, Princesse Consort of Lucomo.

Outside the church, the Talon stood transformed. The wind had vanished; crates of doves were released, flocking all around us. As we were led back to the palace, the birds kept pace, landing along the stone walls and parapets, weaving through the porticos.

Our next destination was the coronation room. Its walls were painted with real gold between enormous panels of water-lily murals by Monet. A triumvirate of wooden chairs—thrones, I realized, sitting in one—was the site of our official portrait. I wore the diadem and a striped sash of lavender and green; Finn wore a gold-and-silver crown, the inside padded with velvet. Between clicks of the shutter, he reached for me. When his thumb found the uncovered space above my wrist, the rest of the world fell away. We were but two sovereign bodies, once separate, soon to be whole, spilling over with longing. I was repeatedly told not to smile, but it took ten minutes to get myself to stop beaming, even though the scar tissue in my cheeks had already begun to ache.

◆　◆　◆

The reception was held in the Talon's largest chamber, the Grand Quartz, a multistory rose-pink ballroom with faceted quartz walls and high ceilings painted a brilliant blue. Three tiers of balconies surrounded a dance floor opening seamlessly into the courtyard. Every surface overflowed with fresh dahlias, towers of chilled champagne, and frosted cakes.

We did not circulate, but rather stood to receive our guests. Desire made us luminous, exquisite. In the photos from our wedding day, both of us trembling, fizzing with want, he's so handsome and clear-eyed that it's impossible to imagine he could ever fall out of love; it appears that I myself had been grown like a crystal in a fountain of youth. Starry eyes, full lips, hair so thick it seemed to sprout before one's eyes. As rapacious stares surged from the approaching Lugesque, I focused on the feeling of Finn's arm against mine, the gentle sweetness of his breath.

Even Amelie's cruel sneer was replaced with something resembling admiration. She kissed me on the cheek—and as she did so, patted the silk across my stomach. I flinched at her touch, though she seemed not to care. "How is your pregnancy coming along?" she asked quietly.

I checked for Finn's reaction. He had none; he was busy embracing Roland, whose serpentine face seemed to reflect Finn's happiness. "Forthcoming, I hope," I whispered nervously. Amelie gave me a pinched, insincere simper, and moved on.

Two hundred handshakes later, my legs ached from standing, the purple lightning bolts of acute pain storming my nerve endings. I gritted my teeth and kept going. My body outlasted my mind: during the five hundredth handshake, I stared blankly for ten seconds, put on pause, my palm clamped around a slim hand extending from a wrist covered in bangles. White-painted claws carefully pried my fingers away. "Gosh, I'm sorry," I blurted, taking control of myself.

My victim laughed and came into focus. A woman, wearing a severe black gown, the same color as the hair that hung straight to her waist. Her moon face, swelled by fillers, could have been thirty or sixty; she was in fact so pale and otherworldly she could have been the moon herself. "I am Atena Ricci," she introduced herself, her English heavily accented. "My husband, Domenico."

An elderly man, his sparse white mustache like a flattened doll's broom, bowed slightly. "Pleasure." A gold cross pinned to his ascot signified that he was a member of Finn's cabinet; enamel pins spelled out his rank.

"The pleasure is mine," I repeated, as I'd done so many times already.

"Best wishes," they replied, and then it was on to guest number five hundred and two.

◆ ◆ ◆

The wedding was a compromise for everyone except Finn and me. Nearly everything Zola tried to negotiate—the budget, the bonuses, the property, the shares, the assets—the Talon agreed to grant *only* if I acceded to a large, formal wedding, in one year's time, with the maximum PR and tourism efforts, all of it pending the outcome of a more complex fertility examination. I'd passed the first one with flying colors, its simple inquiry proving that I had an acceptably sized uterus and two ovaries that released eggs, but the Talon wanted more. They wanted to inject me with dye, photograph my interior, count my ova. I refused further testing and the further delay it would cause, while Zola seethed on the other end of the phone at my stupidity. I simply insisted on being married as soon as possible. *He promised to marry me. He promised me I could have anything I wanted.* That was it. That was the only thing I wanted. I was, as ever, single-minded.

I was, however, forced to sit before the wedding for an interview. Schätze had procured a list of every race I had run. What did I recall? Who did I remember? What struck me about the city—the track—the fans—anything? Who did I run with? Who did I have sex with? Did I do anything bad? Schätze's tone was not judgmental. This was for national security, she insisted. It did not matter what the answers were, as long as I told the truth. Under the guidance of her uncompromising and relentless inquiry, I dredged up details while Schätze typed. Entire races were reduced to the following:

> IAAF Marathon, Seville, Spain. Seville was more agricultural than I expected. It was a Sunday in August and I chafed badly, didn't drink enough water. Sonia Gonzalez and Ari Noguchi did a ten-miler and pasta dinner with me the night before. All my other training runs (early morning and evening) were solo. Rena Jong was there. We used to run together often, but we didn't then, I think that's when her knee problems started. We were in residence there for nearly a week. [Caroline stayed in the hotel for three nights, four days] Pete Driscoll [from Ohio USA, see LOSING VIRGINITY, ATHENS] and I spent one very nice evening in the old town of Seville.

Soon the document was almost twenty-five thousand words long, but it was nonetheless an insufficient record of my life on the track. The memories were diminished to the words on the page, as though Schätze had snatched them from me, consumed them in full, and returned only their hard rinds, turning my first sexual experience into a loss, for example, instead of a gain. I went to bed that night hating words—hating how they could take something so big and make it so small—and feeling terribly lonely.

I feel the opposite now. These words are freeing me as I collect them, as I put this in order, how it all came to be. Even if I'm deluding myself, making myself look good where I ought not to.

When I woke the next morning, safe and comfortable, fire burning, coffeepot gleaming, it seemed right to leave my old life behind. To write it down and file it away. At the end of the second day of questions, after I had told Schätze everything about what came after—about my accident, about Lisbon, about my mother's death—it was the past. I was about to begin a new kind of life, one that had no more hard edges.

Zola was able to secure a stipend for my father, and a charity budget, under Schätze's supervision. I thought the budget was generous. Fifteen million euro a year, mine to spend on whatever I pleased, as long as it was charitable, provided that I produce two children, an heir and a spare, by whatever means necessary. In those days before our wedding, all I wanted was to attempt pregnancy. I agreed readily.

At this Zola became irate. "You're a pushover," she said angrily.

"I'm a pushover," I repeated. I didn't care who thought that. Let them see what I was willing to do, who I was willing to become. Let them see how much Finn and I loved each other.

Zola did not attend the wedding. She was too busy to make the trip on such short notice, she said. *Swamped with work.* We both knew she thought me foolish. I thought her unfair. When we hung up I knew that we probably wouldn't speak for some time.

As for my father, he replied to the letter I sent on the morning of the wedding with a brief note of his own:

Best wishes. I am happy for you, and must admit that I am much relieved, in my heart, that someone is taking care of you now that Mummy is gone. It's very kind of you to send money home and I wish I was too proud to take it, but it will be a big help. Winni has got me hooked on bridge. Please come and visit soon, and bring your—what a word!—your husband. I hope he is a good man. Love, Papa.

It was, in its own way, the perfect wedding gift, for he absolved me of any responsibility. I wish that grief hadn't pushed us apart, but my mother had been the polarity holding us together.

◆   ◆   ◆

When we reached seven hundred, Finn and I glanced around furtively. "Our" guests, five glasses of champagne deep, were no longer paying us any attention. We inched backward in tiny steps until a line of revelers blocked us from the rest of the party. A draught from a nearby exit beckoned with cold fingers. Finn stepped sideways into the narrow passage, clasped my hand, and—we ran for it.

I expected we would go to his apartment, or perhaps mine. I had no idea of the tradition. He led me in the opposite direction, until we popped out of the north side of the Talon—where Roland waited behind the wheel of a dark sedan. My shoulders sank. "Roland," I whispered, disappointed. I wanted to be alone with my husband.

"Don't think about him." Finn kissed my neck. "Think about us."

We were driven away from the Talon to Italy, up a hill that seemed nearly to be a mountain. It reminded me of where we'd first landed in Finn's plane. The same velvet sky stretched above us, the same bright stars and dark forests. The car turned down a narrow lane pocked with holes. Three such country roads later, the last running parallel to a high stone wall, we reached an opening guarded by a rusty gate. Roland pulled the hand brake and eased open the metal wings. When he returned to the car, he brought the cold with him, the pine-needle fragrance of a wooded night so fresh I had the sense we could drink it.

Beyond the gate lay a large garden. Dead grasses shivered across patches of lawn; knotty rosebushes hooked over rickety trellises. A bloated pond, skimmed with lichen, flowed over its own iced edges. At the end of a path, carpeted in evergreen needles, sat a wide stone cottage. No light glowed from within the rounded windows, and no smoke puffed from its ancient chimneys—yet it managed to exude a warmth that stretched across centuries. A small inscription was laid over the door. "Villetta Dell'Asilo," I read aloud. "Anno 1634."

"It's the house you saw from the air. The one you wanted."

"That's . . ." I was momentarily speechless. "You listened."

"I listen to everything you say whether I want to or not. It's rustic— no electricity yet," he said apologetically. "I've had a bed put in, though, and food in the cellars." No electricity meant the service could not operate from here. They'd have to stay down by the gate. We would be truly alone with each other, for the first time, in every way.

The knob turned with a gentle click. Finn carried me over the threshold—he had to duck beneath the door's squat frame—and into the cottage.

"It used to be a nunnery. This"—Finn indicated the parlor on our left—"was the common room. Long tables would have gone the whole width." He waved his hand, made stripes between fireplaces. "There's a porch there, in the back. The kitchen is across the corridor," he said, kissing me across the foyer. "Downstairs are the cellars, where you may churn your butter. Upstairs are the bedrooms."

The main staircase twined around a banister smoothed by the touch of a thousand bygone hands, up and around to the second level. We kissed on every step. The bedroom held exactly one enormous wooden bed and what appeared to be a full season's stockpile of firewood, and then we fell into each other. An explosion in the pit of my stomach. The feeling of his skull beneath my palms. The push—the pull—holding on—letting go.

◆   ◆   ◆

The very beginning of our marriage was one long kiss. Marriage is elastic that way: As it happens, each day is an adventure unto itself, taut and exciting. Later it is as though entire years have slipped your grasp. Memories dry out; turn brittle and shatter like glass. So you move carefully among them, for fear of being cut.

We spent over two weeks, from Christmas past New Year, sequestered in what Finn laughingly assured me was indeed called a *"matrimonio"*-sized bed. He became the source of all my happiness. His breath was my breath, his skin my skin. Our bodies and the roaring fireplace were all the warmth we needed. It took but one match to get going and then we never let it go out, not once. Smoke billowed out the windows day and night. Our linens took on that wooded scent. Time disappeared. It could have been a thousand years ago or a thousand years from now. And I was embodied, in full, at last.

It snowed for three days but didn't stick. Then it rained for five, a hard storm that fell in buckets. The water leaked everywhere, dripping down the walls and pooling in the low spots of the brick floors, into the fireplace, evaporating in pops from the burning wood at all hours. I can still hear the sound.

Finn hauled dried meats up from the cellars. I sat on the counter, wrapped in a sheet, eating berries by the handful while he cooked on the hearth. We delighted in making plans. The kitchen would be renovated, but not too much—enough to make it usable—and the cellars would be restored and restocked. The parlor walls would be covered in tapestries to keep in the warmth. Our bedroom would gain nightstands, mirrors, a chest of drawers. The other rooms would stay empty until we could make them into nurseries.

The Villetta anchored us to each other. Inside its walls, it was always raining, and we were always in love.

20

SIXTEEN DAYS after our wedding, we packed our things and returned to Lucomo. Damp leaves left streaks across my trousers as we crossed the enchanted garden. Beyond the gate, Roland waited behind the wheel of yet another shiny car. We let ourselves be folded inside its shell, the engine turned over—and suddenly it was not 1634. We were not isolated. We were only a few hundred feet from modernity, after all.

The Talon released my official biography, our coronation room portrait, and selected images from the reception to the press. An official celebration—what they called our *anniversaire*—was scheduled for the following Saturday. It was decreed that the borders would be closed to outsiders: We belonged to the Lugesque first.

❖   ❖   ❖

When the bells of the Marian Cathedral rang noon, Finn and I clasped hands on the highest tier of the three towers. From it we could see every faction of the Talon and all the streets of Cap-Griffe. He wore formal morning dress, dark as the wet slate of the cliffs. I wore an ivory wool gown with long sleeves, insulated by paper-thin layers of cashmere and silk. A collar of diamonds and pearls was locked around my throat.

We strolled the length of the balustrade for an hour. Hands cupped like clamshells, rotating from side to side. The energy built, a swarming buzz, as throngs pressed the streets and yachts filled the harbor. I watched as our faces were pasted on a billboard in Le Chappe, one strip at a time. Once the nation's pitch reached a fervor, Finn and I descended through the castle and embarked on an official procession through Cap-Griffe, on an emerald carpet nearly four miles long.

Over the next six hours I was grasped by every person in Lucomo. It began with the military, their smiling faces differentiating them at last—a crooked tooth here, a cluster of freckles there. Then the Piétons, many of whom had attended the wedding. I noticed they had the same round cheeks of the Talon portraits, pink and doughy, while the last group, the working-class Marins, had the sandy hair and sharpened features of those who waited on us hand and foot. Roland, I realized, was Marin, as were Otto and Dix. The service were nowhere to be seen. *We don't need them*, Finn had told me. *We don't need protection from the Lugesque. They would never harm us.*

With each baby that squeezed my index finger, each hot cheek that brushed my own, surges of approval steeled my spine, lifted me up so that I sailed across the ground. That night I didn't even feel the sheets of the bed; instead I lingered above it as the walls around me shivered with life. It was an earthquake whose aftershocks did not stop for days and days.

This happened when I set the record. It's exhilarating to create joy, to heave it into the world and catch it back at double strength. It is a feeling worth doing almost anything for.

❖ ❖ ❖

The morning after a race, my mother and I always hunted for newspapers. She collected them all; whether it was my last name and time, a fuzzy dot-print of my head in a crowd, or the finish-line photo from Sydney, they all rated storage. As such, I thought that news coverage was generally a net good and asked the ensigns to bring every paper they could find. While Finn was in the shower I spread them all out on the bed. *If my mother could have seen these,* I thought, *it would have made her so happy.*

I turned the pages and read them to her silently. FERDINAND FIES-CHI, CROWN PRINCE OF LUCOMO, WED CAROLINE MULLER, OLYMPIC MARATHONER, IN PRIVATE CEREMONY, the *Tribune* wrote. Every paper had quotes describing a quiet but devoted friendship and subsequent decision to marry: "Caroline has a gentle nature," moon-faced Atena told the *Times*. "She is a perfect match for Finn in every way. The whole country is delighted on their behalf." *Considerate,* I told my mother, *if deceptively familiar.*

"Many of Lucomo's wealthiest residents choose to depart during the film festival, the yacht classic, the San-Berno Stakes, and other large public events. The couple's decision to have a private wedding and Lugesque-only reception was seen by many as a savvy and thoughtful diplomatic concession by the princesse to honor the dignity and privacy of the residents of Lucomo. In choosing the Lugesque, Caroline has gained the goodwill of a lifetime," wrote a *Times* reporter. "By comparison, the celebrated 1999 nuptials of Prince Edward and Sophie, Countess of Wessex, which packed the once-elegant streets of Windsor with plastic trinkets and drunken revelers, seem a greedy spectacle, one that Lucomo's residents were pleased to avoid in their own country." I'd intended no such thing, but the Talon found the perfect way to spin our decision, remade us so effectively that it was very much like reading about a complete stranger. There she sat, in an Italian-language newspaper, on her gilded throne; there she stood, kissing the cheek of a stunning Lugesque woman at the reception like they were old pals. I tried to remember the woman from the photograph—tall as Finn, hair like a lion's mane—but she truly had not made an impression.

I couldn't recall meeting most of the other guests, either, but then, I never remembered the faces of the people I saw on the sidelines. I absorbed no more about them than I would a single tree or shrub. I'd accepted the current and let Lucomo wash over me, dissolving inside Princesse Caroline the very moment she came into being.

Almost everything I read was positive, save for the coverage of my appearance. Many papers ran photographs of the moment I broke the world record alongside an image of this new face and softened body, a candid photograph that Schätze had staged. In the gray suit, I stood in front of a pink Cap-Griffe town house, lit by a cotton-candy sunset. The cruelest speculated viciously about the change in my facial features. HOW TO CATCH A PRINCE, wrote the *Mail*. ALL YOU NEED IS ONE HUN-DRED THOUSAND POUNDS AND FIVE MONTHS OF SURGERY. Kinder newspapers noted that "in the right light, thin scars are visible across the line of her jaw from the reconstructive surgeries following her fall in 2002."

I'd expected to see something negative, but I hadn't known how badly it would hurt. When Finn returned from the bath, he found me staring at a zoomed-in picture of my face with lines drawn across it and quote bubbles from cosmetic surgeons suggesting that I'd had my nose, cheeks, chin, lips, and teeth all remade, alongside a to-the-ounce esti-mate of the weight I'd gained since I stopped running. At the sight of the number—the one I used to obsess over, the one I tried so hard not to think about now—I began to cry.

Finn snatched it from me and threw it into the trash, then began gathering up the other papers. "Caro, honey, no, no. Who gave these to you?"

"I asked for them," I said, defending the staff. "It wasn't anybody's fault."

"We don't allow unfiltered newspapers in the house. I promise, it's a boundary you'll come to appreciate. The press—they've ruined my every relationship. They even told me that my father died before Amelie had a chance to call, filmed my reaction. Look at this one, claiming you had surgery to find a husband. Profiting from your pain. It's better if you never look."

I sniffed. "I wanted to see what my mother would have."

"Think of it this way: The Caroline you see in the newspaper," he explained, "is not you. She's a representation of you, who goes all over the place, into people's homes, and offices, and train cars, but she's not *you*. Whatever anybody says about her isn't about *you*. The more separation you have from her, the better."

I'd been a gawky teen in the newspaper since puberty, but only when I *won* something. It was factual and affirmative. Finn was right: The treatment of Princesse Caroline was different. As I folded the *Courier,* my eyes snagged on an article about a journalist killed two days earlier in France, near the road to Lucomo. GIORNALISTA UCCISO IN INFORTUNA TRAGICO. The odd feeling, the same one I'd had when we left Milan, crept up my throat. The argument I'd heard between Roland and Finn flashed through my brain—the two words I understood, *giornalista* and what I thought meant "unfortunate," *infortuna*. For a brief moment, the greasy newsprint pasting the words across my fingertips, I felt a shifting disembodiment. I wondered if these papers were real. I counted the days. *No. Coincidence.* That conversation had been weeks ago. According to the paper, this happened two days ago.

"Caroline?" Finn asked, watching my face. "What?"

"I—" I paused. He bent over my shoulder, reading the article.

"Oh, that," he said. "Sad. We have speed limits for a reason."

"No—I heard you say these words, before. When I first met Roland. Your fight."

His topaz eyes lost their clarity, turned opaque.

The page fluttered in my hand.

"This is what I mean," he said gently, taking it from me, folding it up. "The media makes us paranoid. Mark, a friend from university, a journalist, was killed in a motorcycle accident in Turkey, in early

December." His jaw clicked. "I asked Roland to make a donation to the school, a scholarship, in his name. Roland didn't want to. He's against journalism in general. He doesn't think I should support any institution that harms us. That's what you overheard. That's why he was so mad. He was fighting with me on what he sees as my behalf." Finn reddened. "Do whatever you want, Caro. Read whatever you want. But it's not good for you. Trust me. I know."

The odd feeling disappeared. Compassion arose in its place. I reached for him and we became wrapped up in each other—the solution, I thought, to any conflict between us.

21

MY FIRST MONDAY in residence as Princesse Caroline was not what I expected of what I'd once laughingly referred to as "chair," the game of sitting. I assumed that I'd sleep in, then start in on our seven hundred thank-you notes. Instead I was utterly readjusted, from nose to tail.

It began at dawn. An ensign appeared in the doorway, averting her eyes with practiced courtesy: I was to meet Schätze in the so-called baby ballroom, the Petit Ange, immediately. I managed to grab a banana as I trailed after the ensign's spit-shined boots.

The ballroom held a maze of rolling racks bearing the full inventories of Fendi, Gucci, Giambattista Valli, Prada, Armani, and Valentino. I squeezed through a tunnel of sweaters, pivoted at a wall of trousers, and ducked through the gaps between blouses until I burst into a small clearing. Schätze perched woodenly on one upholstered armchair, clicking away on her laptop.

Still wearing clothes my mother had picked out for me, I was unsure of what to do. I had the awkward thought that Schätze and I might have to make small talk. But with the flick of an impatient finger, she summoned a flurry of ensigns, who pleated a barrier of large mirrors between us and the merchandise. Moments later, a parade of models began streaming in twin rivers round the edges.

They looked at me so hopefully: baby blue cashmere, gathered tangerine cotton, black silk yarn, maroon chiffon with spaghetti straps. The models aimed straight for me, standing briefly at my side, their colors reflecting against my skin while Schätze squinted, deciding yes or no. Her choices were plucked from the mannequins' lithe bodies and set aside. I noted that she seemed to favor luxury versions of athletic clothes: tanks like longline sports bras, compressive and wide-strapped, mohair mock-neck sweaters, cashmere golf polos, leather track pants, and legions of long-sleeve dresses. "It's important," Schätze clarified, "to emphasize the accomplishment in every way."

I nodded enthusiastically—I thought I was being seen.

The evening wear was more international in scope and had been previously arranged. Schätze only needed to examine each against her calendar before they were sealed back inside thick plastic garment bags. The gowns were so elaborately sewn, with mountains of pleats or yards of beadwork basted at strange angles, that I couldn't imagine how they'd fit on my person. Schätze nevertheless grunted with satisfaction, accepting them tidily, until a rainbow bracketed us.

The last gown to be plasticked was orange, bright as the sun, its empire waist belted by a fat inch of gumball-sized sapphires that I wanted to roll around my tongue. "What's this one for?" I asked, reaching for it.

She glanced at it. "A wedding."

"Isn't this awfully bright?"

Schätze's stony eyes blinked. "This is my job." She snapped her fingers. "Yours is to read." An ensign appeared with a dozen white plastic binders. "They are in order," Schätze instructed. "The first event is tonight. Prepare yourself."

I opened the binder marked "January." The first page was titled with that day's date and the seal of the French government. There was a sketch of a gauzy tulle confection from Christian Dior. Then a seating chart: Amelie, Finn, the French president, his wife, and I were seated at the center of a long dais. Women's names at my right, men's names, the six ministers, at Amelie's left.

"Atena Ricci," I read aloud. "I know her."

Schätze reached over and impatiently flipped the page. A yearbook-like spread, with small photographs and dozens of names, had been prepared. "You know *all* of these people," she said peevishly. "You met them weeks ago," she clucked. "At your wedding." I felt my cheeks grow hot. I'd met seven hundred people at the reception. Surely I was not supposed to recall all of them? "You must pay attention, Caroline," Schätze instructed. "You have one hour to study."

◆　◆　◆

I spent the next fifty-eight minutes trying my best to memorize the names and faces of the evening's seating chart. But with only a banana in my stomach and no coffee, my head swam and I couldn't keep them straight. As a cheat I wrote out the names of the men and women who were to sit on the dais with us, in order, on a little scrap of paper.

When the hour was up, an ensign appeared. "Time for exercise," she announced.

We descended into the basements—past the kitchens, the garage, the tunnel entrance—until we reached a cavern filled with dark shapes over rubber flooring. Machines came into focus, then people; between the Pilates Reformer and the resistance swimming pool stood a collection of highly athletic women in white scrubs, their names embroidered above the words *Team Caroline*. After a startled moment, I realized that it was a state-of-the-art training facility—all for me. My hand flew to my heart, holding back a rush of gratitude as I broke into a smile.

Popping forward one at a time, energetic as squirrels, trainer Farah, masseuse Delia, and acupuncturist Jessica introduced themselves. The last, a small woman in her fifties with a black bob, her scrubs labeled *Dr. Shan-Tai Sun*, circled me slowly, taking notes. "I'm Dr. Sun," she said, putting a pair of calipers to my waist. It didn't faze me; I raised my arms automatically, letting her pinch and measure my fat. "I'll be your attending physician." Not only was I was used to this kind of assessment, I'll admit that I felt relieved by it.

A small table held one single place setting: hard-boiled eggs, raw spinach, and grilled chicken breast. Dr. Sun indicated I should sit. "Starting tomorrow we meet promptly at seven A.M. We will try different breakfasts for a month or two, to see what's most effective. I've ordered an MRI machine. It'll be here in a month or so; in the meantime, we'll use an ultrasound to chart you out. It's helpful that you don't drink alcohol but tell me if that changes."

An MRI machine? In this building? For my use? I could hardly believe it. "Thank you, Dr. Sun." Overcome, I shook her hand too tightly. "Delia, Farah, Jessica. I'm so grateful for you." They returned my beaming smile with warm ones of their own. "*Signora*," they said in a sweet unison, heads bobbing.

"Call me Caro," I insisted. "We're colleagues."

I tore into my sad athlete's lunch, the plate empty before I felt even the slightest bit full.

❖　❖　❖

I was, to put it politely, out of shape. Two minutes of barre squats spilled lactic acid into my thighs and rear like a chemical burn; I panted, broke a sweat. On the Reformer, I froze, abs failing, my left trapezius screaming painfully as it compensated. In the resistance pool, my shoulders quickly gave way. Dr. Sun, jotting observations on her pad, couldn't help but scowl; she was not impressed. I tightened up, gritted my teeth, and worked harder.

Afterward, limp with fatigue, I was led back to the Gloria Apartment, to be cleansed and prepared for the evening. It was so pleasurable: the luxury of someone else lathering the hair with their knuckles against my skull, coating the strands in slick conditioner; sweeping soft brushes across the tip of my nose; dripping perfume down my neck,

dabbing it at my wrists. The gentle pressure of unfamiliar hands apply-
ing felted tape to the bony protrusions of my feet. I stepped carefully
into the open circle of tulle Schätze called a dress, and then I was
rushed down the hallways to a hidden sanctuary abutting the Grand
Quartz.

Finn was already there, waiting, a cloud hovering over his brows—
yet when our eyes met, his wide smile appeared, and whatever scratched
at him was swept free.

Hands fell upon us once more. Someone adjusted Finn's tie; a
lavender-and-green sash was pulled across the bodice of my dress. As
one last pin was placed in my hair, twisting the strands tight, I tucked
my cheat sheet into one of the kid-leather gloves sheathing my wrists.

A beetle-green ball gown, like a taffeta umbrella, topped by a blond
head dripping in diamonds, shimmied into place—Amelie. She seemed
unusually large, costumed like this, less frail. The orchestra struck up a
bout of "Lucomo, My Lucomo," the official Fieschi anthem, and the
doors opened. Amelie stepped forward, then Finn, then me, precisely
two steps later.

❖   ❖   ❖

Through a parted sea of ladies bobbing, gentlemen bowing, I glided inside the vacuum of Finn's wake to a raised platform, a dais, with three
thrones. We took our places. The ministers, the six elderly men pinned
with gold crosses, strode behind six glamorous women dressed in white.
They formed a hallway of shining hair and gleaming teeth through
which the president and First Lady of France were brought to us.

The first woman in white was a girl barely out of her teens. I expected
her to tremble—she was delicate, mothlike—but she didn't. Instead a key
turned in her back and she performed with the precision of a mechanical
toy, presenting a concise dip to the president as the angle of her shoulders
provided the exact indication of where he ought to step, to Atena, glowing like a midnight ghost. As Atena pulled him forward, the delicate girl

pressed herself upon the First Lady, and so on. Watching all six pass them and move toward us was like watching a corps de ballet toss dancers from one side of the stage to the other. Except I was not a dancer and did not know how to catch. By the time the president landed at my feet, I stood gawping, a stunned member of the audience pulled unexpectedly upon the stage.

"Madame." He spoke first, reaching for the hand I was too foolish to hold out.

"Mo-onsieur President," I stuttered. Amelie's beady eyes hit me with a cold glare, though it only served to slow me down. I heard someone cough. "I . . . am . . . so . . . pleased to meet you," I finally managed.

He kept my hand in his grip. "I hope so, madame."

"You must forgive me," I begged, wanting desperately not to offend. "I did too many burpees this afternoon."

He was puzzled but intrigued. "Madame?"

I made a squat-and-jump motion, with everyone watching. "Burpees?" I turned to Finn. "*Qu'est que c'est le mot pour* . . . burpees *en Français?*" I asked, "What is the word for ___ in French" being the only French I knew. Amelie raised a plucked eyebrow so hard it hit the ceiling.

"*C'est . . . burpee, je pense.*" Finn said the word in a French accent, then shrugged in a very French way, all mouth and eyebrows. "*Comme les grenouilles,*" he offered. *Like the frogs.*

The president's eyes flew open wide. "*Ah oui, à la gymnase!*" he exclaimed, making a little squat with his legs. "*Avec les bras!*" He raised his hands, adorably, to the roof.

"Exactly. And I am . . ." I leaned into his ear. "Famished."

"Burpees are an exercise of Satan," he said kindly, patting my hand. "You are very funny, madame." He shook Finn's hand warmly, then bowed deeply to Amelie. "Your new daughter is a gift." Amelie smiled with satisfaction. I did not think it genuine for a second.

As our chairs were pulled out, Schätze found her way to my side. "Best not to butcher a language that you do not speak," she whispered

in my ear. I lowered my eyes, mortified. She patted my shoulder en-
couragingly. "Something to work on."

◆ ◆ ◆

During dinner, I mostly spoke with the First Lady. We discussed her
own fitness routine, the demands of maintaining one's athleticism
while traveling. I invited her to join me in the gym the following day.
She shook her head. "You may do the burping," she said. "I would rather
do *le jogging*."

The first thing I used to do after dropping my bag in any new city
was go for a run. "Along the sea. Of course, you must," I encouraged
her, trying to hide my disappointment. Luckily, a distraction: oysters,
piled high atop a bed of snow, materialized between us. "These are
local, I believe," I told her, a fact from the binder bubbling up of its own
accord. "Harvested from Mare-Dio."

"This golden oyster," the First Lady mused. She loosed one from its
barnacled shell with an authoritative flick and swallowed it whole. "Interesting species, bivalves," she said. "Turning the ocean's filth into
pearls. The ideal symbol for this place." Unable to discern whether or
not it was an insult, I bared my teeth in an uncertain smile. She lifted
another shell, squeezed a lemon over its trembling flesh, and offered it
to me. "Go on."

I felt its heart beating on my tongue and tried not to gag.

◆ ◆ ◆

After dinner, we danced a waltz alongside the president and First Lady.
My amateurish steps were unbelievably clumsy, though Finn took care
to sweep me up when I faltered. When the second song began, the
women in white dresses took the hands of the ministers and joined us,
crowding the floor. "Can we sneak away?" I whispered in Finn's ear—
accidentally marking the edge of his shirt with a smear of makeup.

"We can't leave until Amelie leaves." His smile wooden, he tightened his grip on my waist, taking on more of my weight. "I'll keep you upright. Try breathing through your mouth. It's sufficiently similar to smiling." I rubbed at the stain, without success, and grimaced. Finn pulled me in and chuckled in my ear. "You're a mess."

"Don't I know it. Distract me. Tell me about Schätze. Why does your mother have a Swedish giant for a pet? With a German name? And why do I feel like . . . I want to impress her so badly?"

"*Hah*," he let out, breaking his control. The couple next to us glanced over, startled. Finn winked at them; they flushed with pleasure at his attention. "She's German, but from Flensburg, the part that's basically Denmark, so she understands our . . . combination identity. Amelie met her—gosh, twenty years ago? No, thirty, I was a boy."

"You said *gosh*."

"Your very sweet influence." He pulled me closer, not caring that it meant my makeup was smearing into his shirt again. "Schätze was the housekeeping manager at the George V in Paris. Amelie was smoking out a back window and saw Schätze sternly addressing the staff about Lugesque protocol. Amelie hired her on the spot. They're peas in a pod."

"Do I get a pea? For my pod?"

"You'll have to borrow her for now. Everyone is very fussy about who gets to work up *here*." I felt him begin to wince, his facial muscles twitching against my temple. "If my face is burning, you must be dying. Yes? Right. Let's find the EU people. They're very dour. We can let loose and frown."

I smiled for real, then. Though I walked two steps behind him, I thought, we were a team.

◆ ◆ ◆

The moment Amelie retired, Finn whispered that I could leave, if I wanted. I almost knocked over a table in my dash for the exit. Safely in

the hallway, behind closed doors, I kicked off my high heels and padded home barefoot, the cool tiles a balm against my swollen toes.

In the gray apartment, a waiting ensign unzipped my dress, folded
my sash; she even held out her arms for my slip. Once I was naked she
retreated, turning out the lights as she went, closing curtains and doors.
I was getting used to it, the staff being around us all the time, making
every single action just a little bit easier. I drew a silk mask over my eyes
and fell into a glorious sleep.

In the morning Finn was at my side, reeking of cigar smoke. He
took the pins from my hair, amused by how many he found. We dressed
for our pursuits—his clothes a fine suit, mine spandex—and took our
breakfast together. I got scrambled egg white and fruit. He got toast
and sausage. I frowned, stealing a link from his plate.

"Do *not* make Dr. Sun mad at me," he warned. "I'm on strict instructions not to interfere with her experiment."

"I have a fast metabolism," I countered, depositing it in my mouth.
Finn drew an X over his lips before zipping them shut and throwing
away an invisible key.

"You get three secrets," he said. "That was your first."

"I don't have secrets," I replied, kissing him goodbye. "I don't need
them."

We parted in the great hall. Prince to his office. Princesse to her gym.

22

TAKING CARE OF MY BODY became once again my full-time occupation. It was a relief to return to the only job I'd ever really known. I relished the order, the illusion of control. From then on, weekday mornings were made from resistance-pool cardio, Pilates, and strength training, followed by ninety minutes on the massage table and twenty minutes of acupuncture. After a few days I no longer needed anti-inflammatories to sleep. Within weeks, I no longer needed them at all. Dr. Sun expressed confidence that if kept on track, my right hip and knee would not need to be replaced for decades.

Over the lightest of lunches, I read the day's binder. Afternoons were built for evenings, with the pleasure of my exterior adornment. Pleasurable at first—and time-consuming. I soon spent the same amount of time grooming myself as I once had running. The only way to run twenty-six miles is to run twenty-six miles, and as with running, there were no shortcuts: Good fake hair is tied on strand by strand. It can take a whole day to get right once you add in a cut and color. Same with fake eyelashes. For that you've got to lie on your back while someone tapes your eyelids closed and painstakingly attaches one single lash at a time. All forms of extended hair need to be refreshed every few weeks.

As for unwanted hair, laser treatments take full afternoons and must be repeated every week for at least a year. That's at least three full days per month, if not four, which in the end is anywhere from thirty-six to forty-eight days per year spent solely on hair care. Even the most passable of manicures requires not only steady hands and a file but potions and paraffin wax. If you don't want it to chip, you ought to let the polish cure for an hour, so you're looking at two hours, once a week, twice if you're active, like I was. Good facials really ought to be preceded by a steam bath; good steam baths ought to be followed by saunas; and honestly, if you're already doing that, you might as well do a light chemical exfoliation and a moisture wrap.

In this manner, all the rough edges of existence were sanded away. My brief life of independence seemed, in retrospect, unbearably coarse. I could barely believe that I'd managed to live in this body—this body that had ached so constantly—without help in an outside world that looked so rough to me now, so fundamentally insecure. I couldn't believe I'd met with so many random physical therapists—*were they even qualified?*—in the living room of Rally's apartment. I couldn't believe I'd lived without the care of a physician who knew my every ache, or that I'd ever washed my own hair.

Stress flared briefly during the unfortunate week that Schätze spent her lunch hours attempting to get me started with French and Italian. In Finn's mouth the languages played like symphonies, but when I repeated the phrases Schätze indicated with the sharpened tip of a pencil, they tripped from my self-conscious tongue like caricatures. Schätze said my Italian accent sounded like I was in a mob movie, my French like "a Quebecois trout fisherman." I had some vocabulary but found the Romance grammar impossible, with its illogically gendered nouns (did you honestly have to *memorize* the gender of every object? Why was *vagina* male?) and infuriating habits of moving the subjects around willy-nilly. "Are you staying long?" transliterated was "Stay you long?" "Did you sleep well?" was "Have you well slept?" The verbs applied differently; you weren't "twenty-four years old," you "had twenty-four years." I hated that I couldn't keep up. Since I didn't have much experience with formal study, Schätze had to instruct me to do the most basic things, like write the words down on paper. She gave me a set of children's workbooks but I didn't retain much. My mind was a sieve, resisting things it didn't understand by allowing them to pass through unattached.

After a week I stole away to Finn's office and sat on his desk, begging him to let me speak in English, at least for a few months, until things adjusted.

"Can't you conjugate while they do your nails?" He tucked my hair behind my ear. "*Io amo, tu ami, lui ama,* I love, you love, he loves."

"During nails I go back to the binder."

"It's really too much for you to add a few verbs?"

"It's making me so frustrated. I can't feel like an idiot every day."

Finn puffed his cheeks, blew out a dissatisfied sigh. But I got what I wanted. The language books were hidden away.

I remained a body. I worked out, read the binder, let myself be groomed like a pony, and then we entertained, or were entertained ourselves. The days were all the same. The nights were filled with handshakes, gowns stitched tight around my thighs.

There were enough parties to fill a Bible. Remembrance Day begat the Italian Prime Minister's Visit begat the Opera House Fundraiser begat the Yacht Club Schooner Day begat Amelie's Birthday begat the German State Dinner and so on. Our primary job was to appear: Lucomo's luxury hotels hosted a great many companies, for conferences and meetings and exchanges, and the corporate bodies were titillated, into excess and agreement, by our mere nearness. Million- and billion-euro ideas might be dreamed up anywhere, Finn told me, but they are far more likely to be realized among million- and billion-euro people.

Our married life happened in the spaces between. During the rare evenings we had to ourselves, we tried to get pregnant. In the morning, he would be gone again, and I would be alone with only the dissolution of my most perfect self into that day's plastic-bagged dress as a goal.

◆   ◆   ◆

It wasn't until a Friday in early May that I had my first day without commitment, the afternoon free and stretching out before me like a question. At lunchtime, I let myself into Finn's office. The cabinet ministers, the men with gold crosses, were streaming out of a large conference room.

Christ, they were old. In dusty suits, shoulders dotted with flakes from their thinning scalps, they shuffled by, liver-spotted hides clutching leather folios. I nodded politely to each, noticing their yellowed teeth, wondering if their bones were that yellow all the way through. I thought briefly of their yelling at each other that first week in the Talon and envisioned the spittle flying. Finn was last, his bulk emphasized by the meagerness of their carcasses.

"How do you tell them apart?" I asked, as they were swallowed into the hall.

"Domenico Diplomat has that wee mustache."

"That's it?"

"I grant you that Francis Finance and Simon Seaport were perhaps separated at birth. But I think Hugo Hotel and Rocky Road look quite different. Hugo's tie is always tucked into his shirt. And he's a viscount."

"What's the different between a count and a viscount?"

"Number of teeth," Finn deadpanned, folding up a paper airplane and aiming it at me. It sailed past my head and into the fire. "To what do I owe the pleasure of this visit?"

"I've used up all the world's hair." I tugged at the waterfall of honey flowing past my hips. "We've achieved Peak Princesse. There's nothing left to do."

"Stand somewhere photogenic. Look moody. Everyone loves a moody girl."

"I'm free for hours. Can we have lunch?"

"Not a chance. I'm on calls through nine P.M.," he announced, wagging his eyebrows. "We're securing financing for projects that don't even exist yet." He pulled out a freshly drawn plan of Lucomo with forty-five green squares on it. "New buildings, all mixtures of commercial and residential." As I ran my fingers over the plans, he swiveled his computer monitor. A three-dimensional rendering of condominiums connected by staircases, platforms, and escalators appeared on the screen. The layout was identical to that of the stone pathways of Le Chappe, but instead of cobblestones and wrought iron, the computer world was made of futuristic silvers and ebonies—polished cement, curved steel.

"This will be Lo Scopo in ten years." He grinned, clicking through the simulation. "We have so many investors that our banks are struggling to process the collateral fast enough."

"Collateral. Is that the same as money?" I asked playfully.

"Anything of value. Investments are leveraged against other growth opportunities and developments in a daisy chain," he said, like it was obvious. "We have a very strong position. You're my good-luck charm." He pulled me in.

"Me?"

"They're spending millions to watch you walk down the street." The phone began to ring, its shrill urgency biting away our intimacy, but he ignored it.

"Is that so?"

"It is," he said, squeezing my thighs. "You should go out to lunch."

"By myself?"

"I would," he said. I scowled. "Phone a friend."

"I don't have any friends," I admitted.

"Domenico's wife, Atena, likes you. Call her." We were interrupted by Amelie, for whom all doors opened without a key. Bird struggling under her sweater, she spoke in French as though I weren't even there.

"*C'est l'heure pour . . .* ," she began, and in my ears it faded to a long stream of prattle. Roland surfaced from his crack in the wall, along with three secretaries in drab suits, and another ringing cell phone, and then Finn was back in his leather throne and I was invisible to everyone.

I shrank away. Doors closed firmly behind me as I retreated to the Gloria Apartment, now my "office"—the place where I had my hair done and hammered out correspondence. They'd given me a desktop computer to keep notes on people I met. I searched for Atena. We had most recently chatted at a party for an investment brokerage, about a new restaurant she wanted to try called Mayot. I kept reading. Her wedding gift was the sterling-silver typewriter that I typed thank-you notes on. It had a special key that had FINN & CAROLINE in a banner below the stamp with the three towers, and two more that had elaborate engravings of our initials. It was the perfect gift from a diplomat's wife. I picked up the phone and spoke to the operator. "Atena Ricci, please."

"One moment." Then a beep.

"*Allora,* Caro!" Atena answered, traffic honking in the background. "A treat." She sounded surprised. I had a sudden vision of her long black hair swaying in the breeze.

"We never seem to have more than two minutes to speak. I've been meaning to tell you that your lovely wedding gift is so useful to me," I said. "I thought it'd be a nice excuse to invite you to lunch. If you're free."

"*Dolce.* I would love," she said. "Lunch is my favorite meal."

"Mayot," I offered, hoping it was correct. "One o'clock?"

"Of course, I have been dying to go," she agreed. "See you there, darling. *Ciao.*"

◆　◆　◆

Otto escorted me to the bottom of the Le Chappe steps. Tanned thighs propelling me upward, under a dress barely long enough to *be* a dress, hair rippling in caramel waves, I was immediately recognizable. People called to me as I climbed, reaching for their cameras. I waved gently, never losing my composure, the unflappable star of a play set on a StairMaster.

There was a commotion as I reached the top. I found Otto engaged in a heated argument with a wild-eyed woman, her cheeks striped candy-apple red, who kept repeating my name, each time more agitated than the next, *CAROLINA, CAROLINA,* while Otto shook his head and said, *No, no, no.* He caught my eye and jerked his head toward the restaurant. *Go.* The woman let out a bloodcurdling screech. Dix put his hand on the small of my back and pushed me around the corner.

Atena waited near the restaurant's front door, in a high-necked jumpsuit with long sleeves, her face shaded by a straw hat with a brim wider than her shoulders. "*Ciao,* Caro!" she called out gaily, as though I weren't running from anything. We kissed each other's cheeks like old friends. I glanced back toward the steps. The woman was gone, removed by the service, though the tension remained. The pedestrian traffic had slowed, tourists collecting like rain in a gutter, enjoying us for the spectacle we were. Dix seemed angry. Otto looked uncharacteristically uncomfortable.

"Something strange just happened," I told Atena. "Give me a minute." I beckoned Otto. "Who was that?"

Otto collected himself with each step, became a statue, betraying nothing, by the time he arrived at my feet. "A drunk." Three more Gardiens appeared, muttering into their earpieces as they moved smoothly past. I watched them step into position, blocking off the stairs, my heart beating overtime. *What's happening?*

Atena rested her gloved hand on my forearm. "Let's get inside. *I'm* barely upright," she insisted, taking ownership of the urgency. I was so distracted that she practically had to shove me through the restaurant's foyer. "The shipping people wanted to play baccarat last night. I bet an antique vase and lost it." Otto stepped into position, becoming the door itself, turning the lock. "It was very precious," Atena kept on, trying to draw my attention. "But it was also very ugly."

A maître d' in his cropped jacket escorted us to a terrace, where kelly-green booths shaded by triangles of sailing canvas were hidden from the surrounding streets and windows. Ours had an entirely unobstructed view of the sea. I slid onto one side, Atena the other. There were very few customers. It occurred to me that the restaurant had been emptied out deliberately.

"You are so kind to ask me," Atena said right away. "It's a rare honor."

Her way of saying I didn't have a lot of friends. "I'm adjusting . . ." I paused and fiddled with the place setting. "I'm sorry. I'm a bit shaken."

She raised her hands defensively. "Breathe, Caroline. The security is very good."

"I'm sure it is—"

"We are getting off to the wrong shoe, I think." Worry generated a single crease between her eyebrows. "Breathe." I took a deep breath. She inhaled along with me. "In and out," she encouraged me. "Everything is fine."

A bottle of champagne arrived. "Monsieur Mayot has taken the liberty of preparing your lunch himself," the waiter explained. "Is this okay? He wants to make such a nice meal for you."

Atena looked triumphant. I very nearly declined the wine—then decided against it. It struck me as unwise to expose the particulars of my health to someone I barely knew. So I nodded, and when the waiter poured us each a glass I took the offered flute, tapped it against hers, and drank.

The champagne fizzed in my throat and filled me with warmth, its effects instantaneous: My panic receded and the world was briefly lovely, sitting there in buzzy Le Chappe. The sun baking the May air around us, the glass towers reflecting the blue and white of a sea already crowded with summer yachts. I listened for further yelling, any sign of conflict, but there was nothing—only the roar of Lamborghinis, the giggles of tourists.

"Everything is safe," Atena cooed. "Be calm. The adjustment must go on."

I took another sip. Then I downed the rest of the glass.

"You have been set a great challenge," she said sincerely. She removed her gloves, tugging at each finger, then folded them gently and glanced up at me. "I can see you are having a hard time. Yes?"

Almost nobody acknowledged what was happening to me—really, it was only Finn, and he was mostly impatient—and I was so surprised that I almost cried. "It's hard to keep up," I admitted. "I don't think I'm doing a very good job. Finn is so used to this life and he doesn't . . . he doesn't understand."

Atena blinked sympathetically. "May I ask a question?"

"Atena," I replied, "that itself is a question. Be normal."

She pursed the pillows of her lips. She did not want to be normal.

"Yes. Ask me anything." I placated her.

Atena turned melodramatically to the sea. Apparently this was a question so large that we should not even make eye contact. When she spoke, she did so with great care. "Have you not asked your mother-in-law for guidance?"

"I don't want to bother her," I answered honestly. "She is very busy." I didn't say that Amelie had spoken to me directly on three occasions since we returned from our honeymoon, and that it was only to ask the same question she asked on our wedding day: *How is your pregnancy coming along?* After a beat, I said, under my breath, "Also, she is very scary." Then I winked.

Atena laughed and clapped her hands together. "You have said it."

"Have you ever been close to her?"

"I don't think I am . . . how do you say? Acceptable company."

"What?" I goaded her, refilling my champagne. "How could she think that?"

"She does."

"I don't believe you. Give me an example."

"I hope it does not offend."

"Atena," I hissed, "*offend* me. I'm demanding it."

A shy smile crept over her, those rounded eyes darting secretively around the emptied restaurant—then she leaned in and whispered. "Once we held a dinner for the Dalai Lama. It was at our country home as he is very fond of animals. Amelie sent cleaners while I was picking up my dress. By the time I was home she had put in all new furniture."

"Did you get to keep it?"

"No." Atena shook her head, wicked disbelief on her face. "I got a bill for it. And I didn't get the old stuff back, either."

At that moment our appetizer arrived. Two bowls of chilled cucumber soup drizzled with honey and olive oil. It tasted like an open bud gently toasted by the sun, the essence of that late-spring day, and I found myself unable to focus on anything but the movement of spoon to bowl to mouth. My portions in the Talon were always fresh, the catered event meals adequate, but oh, I'd been missing out.

"Mayot has three Michelin stars," Atena said, scraping her own bowl clean. "But you must be used to such things."

"I live on egg whites and sous-vide filets."

"What!" she exclaimed. "We have the most Michelin stars of any city in the world."

"I'd love to go out more. I want to meet more people, make a bit of my own life here."

"That can be arranged very easily. The wives of the other ministers—Aurora, Chiara, Benedetta, Marcella, and Vida—perhaps you ought to ask them to lunch."

"You think they'd be interested?" I thought of their machined moves, their brittle smiles, their ancient husbands. I wondered if they had any imagination.

"Of course. We are the official ladies-in-waiting of Lucomo."

"I didn't know that."

She became the tiniest bit sad. "Amelie has never needed much from us." Aside from the formalities they executed at the beginning of every event, the six women were rarely included, I realized. They were always seated near us, but never close enough to speak. "I suppose you could say," Atena tendered softly, "that we've been waiting quite some time for you."

◆ ◆ ◆

We left the restaurant tipsy—I drank three glasses of champagne—and made our way back through Le Chappe, stopping in any boutique that caught Atena's eye. I encouraged her to express her taste and offer her opinions. What was lost between our languages she made up for with funny faces and well-timed gestures. I didn't have any means of payment, but nobody seemed to mind. With a wave of the hand they wrapped up my purchases. In the end we each had at least ten shopping bags.

Atena seemed so pleased merely to attend me—to lavish me with attention—and it occurred to me that she had probably spent years fielding questions from the other members of the Piéton aristocracy about her official role at the Talon without ever having much to report. In Cap-Griffe, we strolled up the alleys until we reached her town house, a white stucco manse covered with lush ropes of flowering vines. "Magnificent," I observed.

Her spherical face crinkled, ever so slightly, with joy. She kissed me goodbye, squeezed my arm. "It is very nice to know you better," she said. "I am so glad."

"Me too." I squeezed back. "See you soon? You'll call the others?"

"Yes. Tomorrow, Caro. See you then!"

I nearly skipped the whole way back to the Cap-Griffe guardhouse. I'd made a friend.

◆ ◆ ◆

Schätze was displeased. "*Signora,* you cannot simply purchase things," she said, waving a pile of bills as she barged into the writing room, where I sat at the computer, typing up notes on my conversation with Atena.

"I thought it would be impossible without a credit card, but they said it was no trouble."

"That's not what I mean. You've spent far too much. You've shown preference. It is—it is not done." She towered over me, trying to bully me with her size. I decided that it was time to see what would happen if I deliberately did not react—so I kept typing and didn't say a thing. Schätze's face reddened as she waited for me to answer. When she was near to purple I gave in.

"I *do* have preferences," I said slowly. "And I don't know why you're bringing up the cost because this dress," I said, plucking at the fabric clinging to my waist, "that *you* chose, was the price of a car."

"The Talon did not pay full price. There's a process."

"Whatever your process is, I *do* need money of my own. I need a card."

"*Signora,* I will see what I can do. But *do not* do this again."

"We can afford it," I assured her.

"*Signora,* promises were made."

"Not by me." I felt myself starting to harden.

"*Signora,* it's *rude,*" she exploded. "You made a mess."

"You'd better clean up after me, then, since it's such a crisis," I said mockingly. Without making eye contact, I rose from the desk and walked out the door.

That was, I think, limited as it may have been, the first instance of my asserting any form of independence with the staff. Within an hour, an official Bank of Lucomo credit card with my name on it was delivered, along with a new cell phone, tied to a Lugesque number with four digits on the end, the same security as Finn's. A stack of papers printed in unreadable Italian legalese accompanied it, marked "return" and stuck all over with plastic tabs for my signature. I plowed through the lines, dashing off my name again and again, so eager to complete the chore that I did not even bother to try to make sense of the papers in front of me.

I worried things would be tense between Schätze and me after that, but the next time we saw each other, she didn't act the slightest bit bruised. Everything was fine. I was delighted to discover how easy it was, to know my place in the hierarchy. Below Amelie and Finn, sure. But above *everyone* else.

23

EVERY CLIQUE has roles determined by comparative truth: a cook, a gambler, a glutton, a neatnik; the acerbic one, the forgiving one, the funny one. We can be any of these roles within the elastic net of friendship, even if in other circles we're considered terrible cooks, or intolerant of risk, or unfunny. There's always room, in a group. As I looked through the sparse notes of my spreadsheet, trying to match them up with their decrepit husbands, I imagined that Atena, Aurora, Chiara, Benedetta, Marcella, and Vida probably all had their roles already. *Who could I be to them?* I wondered—before realizing that I had a role already: I was the one in the castle.

Atena organized lunch for all seven of us at Sea Club Aquilegia, a private beachfront tucked into the curving scythe of a jetty on the edge of Mare-Dio. Otto took me there in a wooden speedboat, skimming the coastline, to avoid the heavy weekend traffic. We were officially in the eastern half of Lucomo, where the skyscrapers gave way to rocky shores and large private estates. He aimed for a small pier where a neon-orange banana boat, *Marcella* written on the back, bobbed in the waves. Otto tied us up, cut the engine. As I climbed onto the dock, he didn't follow; he intended to sit there and wait.

I scanned the road. Two ostentatiously bulletproof SUVs—Otto's men, dispatched to examine the club in advance of my arrival. Behind them, in a line, there were a fire-orange Lamborghini, one dented Vespa, one teensy-weensy vintage convertible, one aggressively cantilevered racing bicycle, and one . . . white horse. Yes—I squinted—a living horse . . . tied to a post. *Huh. Maybe these women were more interesting than I'd thought.*

"Otto," I asked gently, "could you maybe not sit here like I'm a child on a playdate? I'm sure I can get a ride home."

"No," he replied immediately.

"Why not? The service are over there."

"Do you remember the crazy woman who was screaming in Le Chappe yesterday? Did you hear what she said?"

"I'm not scared of being yelled at."

Otto frowned, then turned away, pressing on his earpiece, whispering a stream of Italian. *Sì, no, blabi blabi, signora, sì sì.* He let go of the earpiece and turned back to me. "The lady was screaming that she wanted to cut off your breasts. Obviously we did not let her do that. But, in the mail, you received six death threats this week already," he said. "And we found a plot to kidnap you on the internet."

"What?" I actually didn't believe him. Not at first.

"You are safe," he told me firmly. "If I leave, maybe not."

I glanced around nervously, the idea sinking in. *Did someone want to shoot me?* Christ, they could. Here I was on a dock like a big golden target. "Tell me more," I demanded.

"No. This is not good for you. You should not think about it."

"Then why did you tell me?"

"Because you asked. And because I sense you do not take us so seriously."

I tried calling Finn twice in a row, but he replied with a text—*Don't stress about the security. We'll talk about it later. Go have fun.*

"*Signora* is secure," Otto said sternly. "Please have trust."

I swiveled on my heels and examined the club. Aquilegia comprised a few dozen beach chairs and cabanas, an outdoor bar, and a restaurant built precariously across the massive jetty. It was mostly empty. A single bartender stood at his post, pouring a line of martinis, while a waitress walked a bowl of water out to the horse. The only customers sat facing the beach, their low-slung chairs arranged in a semicircle of six. It seemed safe enough. I gathered my wits and approached.

The six women were so busy laughing and poking fun at each other, lighting cigarettes and rubbing sunscreen over their shoulders, that I made it all the way to their umbrella before anyone caught sight of me.

"Caroline!" exclaimed a topless brunette, dripping with gold chains and tanning oil. Five pairs of sunglasses swiveled my way. "You are right on time!"

"Should I be late?"

Atena, in a white linen jumpsuit and shaded by another huge hat, stood to kiss me on the cheek. "*Nobody* is *ever* on time in Lucomo. Traffic."

"I boated. Is that the right word?"

"Why not. Isn't it so much easier?" Marcella, namesake of the banana boat, stood, a leopard-print swimsuit wrapped around her like a shoelace. Her hurricane of reddened hair cascaded over both of us as she planted a lip-gloss-gummed smack on my cheek.

The others stood and round we went. Without evening heels to prop her up, Chiara, the topless brunette, was barely five feet tall, and muscular like a gymnast beneath her oiled hide. I remembered her most clearly from an event to do with luxury handbags at which she'd cleaned out the stock; the orange Lamborghini was almost certainly hers.

Aurora, the youngest, the one who looked fragile enough to disappear on the wind, shook my hand shyly, with no grip, and called me *Your Serene Highness* in her butterfly voice. In a modest one-piece, accessorized with a single gigantic diamond ring and baseball cap, I pegged her for the dented Vespa. "Please call me Caro," I said. Aurora smiled so nervously that I almost pinched her.

Benedetta, in a mod Pucci caftan, swept in with a gentle hug. "How are you, *dolce* Caro?" Benny kept her hair cut short, dyed platinum blond, and curled like Marilyn Monroe. She looked to be in her forties, which in Piéton time meant she was possibly seventy.

Gigantic limbs lifted me from Benny. "Vida," I mumbled, pressed to her bronzed shoulders. Vida was the lion-maned woman I'd been photographed laughing with on my wedding day. "How are you?"

"I'm starting to feel like my own person again," she said, patting a strawberry C-section scar. Benny and Marcella nodded knowingly. Aurora appeared too terrified to react, while Atena and Chiara looked on with the tolerance of those used to being excluded from conversations about childbirth.

"I cannot wait until there are robot wombs," Vida proclaimed. "Then we'll have true equality."

"Not for the robots," Benny muttered, collapsing into her lounge chair.

"It's a vicious cycle," Vida agreed.

I laughed—loudly, not politely. I hadn't expected her—or any of them—to be funny.

The bartender appeared with a glittering tray of martinis. Still shaken by Otto's admission, I found myself eager for a drink. Vida pulled a seventh chair into the semicircle, and I took my place, merging seamlessly as the water dampened the sand beneath our feet.

◆   ◆   ◆

We baked in the sun for a few hours, wading intermittently into the azure basin of the sea. The surgical scar on my left hip shone a bright white; I covered it with my hand, but no one stared, they were too polite. Vida and I swam all the way out to the nearest buoy, kelp catching against our feet. I smiled when she swam harder than I did. Vida had no interest in letting me win. That was something I understood.

The parking lot began to fill up with cars, the surrounding beach chairs with people. By the time we sat down to a very late lunch, the restaurant was almost full. The seven of us, ranging from my twenty-five to whatever Benny was, were one of several such groups of women. As I unfolded my napkin, I felt a breath of clarity—was it *normalcy*?—singing through me like a choir. I was a grown-up, all of a sudden, a married woman out to lunch with friends.

We chatted over our salads about cities we liked, books we'd read. No one asked me any direct questions—they already knew where I was from, they knew about my running career, they knew everything about me—yet somehow that was neither awkward nor bothersome. They were well practiced in the art of one-way communication.

Over coffee, I raised the issue of my budget. "I have some funds," I offered. "For charity. I was wondering if you might wish to help."

They looked at each other carefully. "How much?" Atena asked.

"Fifteen million a year."

Atena nodded gently. Not enthusiastically. Perhaps it wasn't as much money as I'd once thought. Aurora cleared her throat. The others fell silent.

"I sense a *but*," I said.

"Is it," Aurora asked gently, ". . . yet available?"

"What do you mean?"

She twisted the gigantic ring on her finger. "Is it not," she asked quietly, "for *after* you have borne your children?"

I turned pink. Aurora's husband was the finance minister; she would know the specifics.

"You must," Atena said, patting my arm, "drink nettle tea every morning."

"Forgive Atena, she is reincarnated from the fourteenth century," Vida interjected. "Clomid is much more effective. It makes the eggs go *boom*."

"My daughter had luck with Lupron," Benny added.

"I don't think any of it works," Aurora whispered softly. Vida reached over and scratched the top of her hand.

Atena changed the subject to an upcoming wedding that apparently we would all be attending, sparing me any further embarrassment. After lunch we threw ourselves back in the sea; three hours later, the party broke up. In a misplaced attempt at bravery, I ignored Otto down at the pier and asked Marcella to drive me home on her banana boat. She kept the pedal to the floor, like it was a go-kart and the sea was a track. This had the surprising effect of holding us above the waves—skimming, rather than falling—and I shrieked with delight, urging her on: *Faster, faster!* We were back at the Cap-Griffe harbor in under fifteen minutes. Otto had trouble keeping up but never lost us. Marcella nosed her boat into its slip, and we walked up the hill together, laughing happily, *what a riot*. At the guardhouse, I shifted my beach bag from one very sunburned shoulder to the other and bid her goodbye.

"Ouch," Marcella said of my red shoulders. The corner of her mouth twitched; I had the sudden idea from the gesture that she *pitied* me. She covered it by moving fast, stepping backward, waving goodbye. "Take care," she said. "Really."

"You too," I called after her. As the guardhouse elevator whisked me upward, I replayed it in my mind. It was pity, absolutely. I told myself that it was only because of the sunburn.

24

THOUGH I WAS DEPOSITED into an immediate ice bath by a frustrated Dr. Sun, who lectured me on the dangers of alcohol and made me promise to have Otto procure virgin cocktails for me from then on, I went to bed with a fever and woke the next day with peeling skin and a pounding hangover. I skipped my workout, took a contraband handful of acetaminophen, and snoozed the morning away. Finn appeared in our bedroom around eleven and began to undress. I slid my eye mask up on one side and frowned. "What are you doing?"

He pulled a sweater over his head. "I don't like to travel in a suit," he said.

"What?" I rubbed my eyes. "Where are you going?"

"It's where are *we* going." He tapped the burn-free white triangle on my rear end. "Up we go, party girl."

"You told me to make friends," I groaned.

"I didn't say you had to go from zero to sixty." He pulled a blousy shirtdress from the closet. "Can you tolerate this? They already packed you."

"What. Is. Happening?" I demanded.

"The Villetta," he said with a broad smile, dangling a set of keys. "The renovations are done."

"Hold on," I said, putting my hands over the keys and closing them in my fist. "I want to discuss what Otto said yesterday. About death threats."

Finn swore, shaking his head. "He shouldn't have told you that. Look: Don't worry. People will focus on you, with, as you have seen, some irrational fervor, but you're always safe. They have a lock on . . . everything."

"That doesn't make me feel better."

He pushed his forehead against the doorjamb, as though nothing in the world were more boring than this particular topic. "Can you please trust me?"

"Tell me why I shouldn't feel scared all the time," I demanded. "Explain it to me."

He closed his eyes and swore again. "I'll take you to the service on our way out, and you can see for yourself. Okay?"

Ten minutes later we were deep in the bowels of the cliff below the Talon, in a room full of beeping computers and flashing video monitors. Green-suited Gardiens were stationed throughout, drinking coffee as they stared down the images. "There are cameras on almost every corner in Lucomo." Finn pointed to the feeds rolling over from scene to scene: the casino, the public areas of the Talon, the staircases of Le Chappe. "Within our borders we own the phone lines, the cell phone towers, and the broadband. By law we can read any text message, any email, any notification that concerns our safety." He nodded to a Gardien, who changed his computer screen over to a running stream of data.

"Her lunch yesterday," Finn said. The Gardien typed *Sea Club Aquilegia* and selected yesterday's date. One of his monitors played a cubed collection of videos—the seven of us sitting in the sand, the cars in the parking lot, the highway leading to the club, the interior of the restaurant. Another displayed a stream of text messages in Italian; with one click, they were translated into English. The Gardien rolled back so I could see them clearly: *Caroline is here!! Ask her to come to Calliope's party on Friday. Oh I couldn't, besides anyway I hear she's horrible to talk to.* I watched my own body wade into the ocean, hand on my scar. *She looks so unhappy,* texted one of the diners; *maybe its because she can't move her face,* was the reply, then: *lol what would happen if you dumped a drink on her?* Someone else: *I watched her eating, she cut the food into such small pieces, so sad. Their dessert looked amazing but none of them touched it.*

Stung by the words—and utterly humiliated by the act of being watched as I read them—I turned away. "I've seen enough," I said quietly, backing out of the room. Finn waved *thanks* to the Gardiens and followed me out. Once the door was firmly closed behind us, I said: "That was mean," and started walking away.

But Finn dashed in front, using his bulk to block my exit, unwilling to let me remain upset. "*No kidding,*" he contended. "Why do you think I didn't want to show you any of this? Look, now you know. If it's any consolation I've seen much worse things about me. This jaw?" he asked, holding my hand to his face. "These thighs? You don't want to see what the French president texted about my thighs."

I couldn't help but laugh. "I'm sorry."

"It's fine. I don't care. Really, I don't. You shouldn't care, either. All you have to do is trust that the service see all of this, and they handle it, and they *never* make mistakes. *Fiducia.* Trust."

The third word on the stamp. "It doesn't feel right," I said uneasily. "It's wrong to . . . *spy* on people."

"You think we have the manpower to spy?"

"I bet they read their girlfriends' texts."

"It costs three million euro a year, that room. The budget doesn't extend to curiosity." He snagged the edge of my shirtdress, tossed his head toward a staircase. "Come on. Forget about it. This way."

❖ ❖ ❖

Otto drove us to the renovated Villetta. I wasn't really able to ignore him, like Finn could, but I felt more like he had a defined, meaningful role in our lives. Nevertheless I wanted this world to be ours, and I asked him to leave us at the gate. Otto looked to Finn for confirmation, who nodded. I tried not to feel irritated at how they ignored me.

The gate's padlock opened with my key. The no-longer-rusty wings swung aside easily on smooth new hinges. The long drive had been leveled, potholes filled, gravel distributed precisely. The garden had been tamed; the stones of the house were brighter. The front door, with its friendly latch, still opened at my touch. We entered to find the world we had imagined on our honeymoon made real.

With its cozy furniture and warm fires, it was a home for a family. It had downy sofas, running hot and cold water from a boiler we lit by hand, and fireplaces, and that was all we needed. The rain still snuck in through a few of the windows, but aside from that, we were alone for the first time since our honeymoon.

It was that weekend that we conceived our first baby.

❖ ❖ ❖

Without knowing I was pregnant, we returned to the Talon and resumed our routines, with the addition, for me, of thrice-weekly outings with my new friends. We made a lovely flock, the seven of us: Vida and I were the tallest and strongest, all carved biceps and flaxen tresses; Atena, the eccentric goddess on her white horse; Aurora, the delicate sweetheart; Chiara and Marcella, the firecrackers; Benedetta, the fashionable doyenne, with her platinum hair and vintage clothes. The Talon dubbed us the "Ammaliatrici," meaning a group of charmers or bewitchers, and the name stuck like glue.

We were routinely delivered to a variety of locations throughout Lucomo, followed by a professional team of photographers employed by the Talon. The pictures were distributed to the media, along with "select lifestyle reporting" (tightly controlled puff pieces) on Atena's impeccable town house, Benedetta's vintage yacht, Aurora's modern country house, and so on. We dined at the Yacht Club, the Polo Club, and all the Michelin-starred restaurants, where Otto worked behind the scenes to make sure my drinks were nonalcoholic. We lounged on beaches, we went sailing, and of course, we shopped. Armed with my new credit card, I could purchase anything I desired—though it seems I was drawn, and encouraged to be drawn *to,* those things that would already complement my wardrobe. My "taste," seeded by Schätze and reinforced by the approval of others, was being shaped without my noticing.

We graced the pages of dozens, then hundreds, of magazines— monthlies and Sunday supplements—the clothes we wore selling out everywhere. It was hard to avoid the coverage, since the Ammaliatrici ate it up; it wasn't too bad, though I was routinely criticized for not smiling enough. But whether I smiled or not, there were immediate responses on Finn's real estate charts. Cash offers dotted our trail. Wherever we went, Finn made money. And whatever money he made, Amelie spent.

I will admit she spent it magnificently. On Lucomo Day, the anniversary of Giancarlo Fieschi's arrival, Amelie hosted a grand masquerade ball at L'Original for two thousand people, including all of Cap-Griffe and a pointed selection of Lucomo's most valuable legal residents. She wore a spectacular bird costume, bright as her neon-green parrot. Finn dressed as Giancarlo, the first Fieschi, in a rugged medieval seaman's outfit. I was a shepherdess, in a flouncing skirt and ribboned stockings; the ladies-in-waiting were my flock of sheep.

We threw dice on felted tables and took cards from the dealers, but it didn't take long for human beings to become the game. It was decided that my sheep would hide throughout the building and I would have to catch them one by one like a real shepherdess. Bets were placed on which sheep would prove the most elusive; the Ammaliatrici were given a five-minute head start.

Benedetta, encumbered by the bulky woolen grapes of the sheep costume and fundamentally lazy, was the easiest to find as she simply sat down in a chair and pronounced herself dead. Chiara, distracted by the lure of a poker game, was next. I looped my shepherd's crook around her arm and scattered her cards to the floor. She bleated with rage, downed a martini, and ordered the dealer to reset. Marcella managed to wedge herself inside the dealer's pit of a blackjack table, but her fiery hair, poking out the top, gave her away. Vida simply *ran,* darting to and fro across the room at a speed I could not match. I wagged my finger at her and changed tack, searching for Aurora, who was discovered hiding in the cashier's box between towering stacks of euro.

That left Vida and Atena. I requested a net from the Gardiens. They whispered among themselves, and with a wink, Dix handed me a bazooka-like personal cannon and instructed me to fire from at least three meters' distance. I snuck along the upper balcony, stalking Vida until someone trapped her in conversation. I aimed, fired, and captured my prey, along with two extremely startled Trappist monks.

"ONE LEFT!!!! Twenty minutes!" screamed an excited woman whose Marie Antoinette hairpiece, decorated with wooden ships, teetered dangerously over a candelabra.

The flames began to lick a miniature sail. As a panicked ensign doused the woman with a bucket of ice, I took advantage of the commotion and snuck into the nearest ladies' room. A drunken reveler had left a black silk mask on the vanity. I locked the door, stripped down to my slip, removed my shepherdess wig, freed my hair from its skullcap, donned the mask, and reemerged into the party incognito.

As I crossed the room, people looked at me, this masked, half-naked woman, but all the reserve and respect that had barricaded me for the past few months was suddenly absent. I felt the heat of their stares like someone pressing between my shoulders. I sidled up to the bar next to a group of men wearing foxhunting costumes, middle-aged and paunchy beneath their short red jackets. As I waited to order, they talked among themselves as if I weren't even there. "*Bellissima*," I heard one of the men say, approvingly, of me.

"There's talk of legalization," another said.

A third one laughed. "He'd better not. The end of duty-free."

"Can you imagine," the first said, "submitting an itemized receipt?"

"You break it, you buy it?" they cackled. "No thank you."

"Coursalis," a familiar voice bellowed, "I thought I saw your boat." I tilted my head far enough to spy my husband at the edge of their circle, slapping the man on the back. Before Finn could spot me—he wasn't expecting me in this outfit, but I was his wife, he knew my silhouette as well as his own—I slipped behind the couple to my left.

I watched Finn contort himself, blending in; laughing too loud, smiling too wide, baring all his teeth. The men's chests puffed so broadly that I thought they might explode. I wiped my eyes, disbelieving that he could so quickly become unrecognizable. *How is it so easy for him, to change, like this?*

Someone backed into me, knocking me to the floor without apologizing. No one helped me up. As I brushed the dirt from my bare knees, the thrill dissolving with a few specks of dust, I noticed creamy wool frizzing the edge of a nearby doorway. *Atena.*

I crept along the wall, rubbing my hands together. Atena had her head down, whispering intimately with someone I couldn't see. "The air hostess says the *two-year-old* is his. A boy." The voice was Marcella's, speaking in English. I paused and listened.

"What about the other one? The bartender?" Atena asked in a low voice.

"The girl's at boarding school. They came to an agreement."

"You think she has no idea?" Atena shifted her weight, then glanced around; she was still being hunted, after all, and so before she could run I grabbed her around the waist. Her muscles contracted in genuine shock, and she remained startled even as she saw my face. "Caro, you have killed me!" Atena cried, laughing, trying to wave away her panic. "Oh, that was really scary."

"Gossip was your downfall. I feel awfully sorry for whoever you're talking about."

"*Hey*," Marcella shushed us. "*Aurora is right over there.*" Little Aurora perched at a half-moon blackjack table, losing badly to a hooting Chiara. Meanwhile Francis Finance, her husband, across the room with the men in the red jackets, was actually putting his hand on a woman's thigh, like a pervert in a nursing home.

"Aurora's been trying for a baby, hasn't she?" I asked.

Atena paused for a moment, glancing at Marcella, as if she was looking for permission—then gave me a heavy blink. *Yes.*

"Don't feel *that* sorry for her," Marcella said. "She doesn't have a prenup."

❖   ❖   ❖

The next day a slightly hungover Finn and I curled up in bed. Over pizza we recalled snippets of the party, the wildness of it. As he combed my hair with his fingers, I recalled Atena and Marcella's gossip. "Did you know Aurora's husband has secret children?" I asked. "With a bartender and an air hostess?"

Finn's fingers stopped moving. "Who told you that?"

I didn't answer; I wasn't going to sell them out. "Isn't that awful for her? She's trying for a baby."

"Yes, but who said it?"

"I'm no rat."

"I don't believe it. If Francis Finance tried to reproduce he'd puff out a cloud of dust."

I smacked him on the thigh. "Don't be disgusting."

"Don't give me disgusting visions, then."

"Speaking of. I saw you last night, with a group of men. In red jackets?"

"Oh, that's embarrassing," Finn said, pulling my hair over his face, cringing. "They didn't say anything to you, did they? They're so crass."

I took my hair back. "They were fairly busy making jokes about prostitutes."

"Pure chat. *Macho*," he said sarcastically, then sighed. "Ugh. Well, with luck I'll never have to introduce you. They're friends of my Brevard cousins," he explained. "Russian, mostly. People call them *Lucien*. A kind of derogatory joke—that they're not Lugesque. They live here, they invest here, they build here. They're too rich to ignore."

"It was like *you* were in a disguise. You weren't yourself."

"I never get to be myself except for when I'm with you," he said plainly.

We spent the rest of the day watching old movies. The next morning, it was simply another party we would barely remember.

25

A WEEK LATER I returned to the casino. A movie was being filmed there; Marcella wanted to flirt with the lead actor. Upon entry we were enveloped in billows of manufactured smoke. Gripped by an inescapable nausea, I promptly vomited into my handbag.

"Caro." Atena's eyes twinkled. "Are you *sick*?" She emphasized the word with hopeful expectation. The film crew bustled around us, someone yelling "Duck" as a ladder swung over our heads. I grabbed the nearest trash can and vomited a second time, as discreetly as I could. "Come now," Atena said soothingly. "Let's get you to the doctor."

❖ ❖ ❖

In the same medical bay where I'd been examined less than a year earlier, Dr. Finney drew blood from my arm and disappeared. I waited impatiently. She returned with a smug, winning smile.

"Positive," she said to me, simultaneously picking up the phone. "Positive," she spoke into the receiver, and then she was talking to whoever it was, letting them know I was four weeks pregnant, and all I could think was that I wanted to be the one to tell my husband.

I raced down the black-and-white hallway, catching Finn as he burst from his office.

"Caro," he murmured. "We did it."

"They told you."

"It doesn't matter," he told me. "Nobody matters except us."

◆   ◆   ◆

At seven the next morning, like I had every day for months, I made my way to the gym. I hoped Dr. Sun wouldn't have the television on; the Athens Olympics had begun and I was trying to avoid the marathon. Every time my mind even *skirted* the idea of it, I shook with hurt, my life's grief rolled into one hard ball in my chest.

Usually the facility was alive with sound: pool jets turning on, mats being dragged into place, or at the very least, the water-cooler chatter of Farah, Jessica, and Delia. Yet today it was curiously silent, the lights turned off. I poked my head through the doorway, confused. "Hello?" I called into the emptiness. The top of Dr. Sun's pint-sized head was just barely visible through the office window. "Where is everybody?" I asked, barreling into her space.

Dr. Sun pointed to the doorway—the boundary of our worlds—and obediently I backed into it. "On a much-needed vacation," she reported, stapling a stack of papers. "Congratulations, by the way."

"What do you mean, vacation?" I reached over the top of the doorway and absentmindedly did a pull-up.

"No more work for us. *No jostling*," she explained, in a tone that suggested she didn't agree, pointing at my belly. "Exercise other than walking is no longer allowed." She paused mid-staple, considering another comment, before deciding not to elaborate further.

"That's absurd," I said for both of us, doing another pull-up, this time with my knees bent.

"It's what Dr. Finney says." She reached over and folded my legs firmly onto the ground. "I'm serious. No more gym time."

"Does Finney have a control group of retired pregnant Olympic athletes somewhere?"

"Obstetrics is not my area." Dr. Sun scowled, switching off the overhead light.

"You're leaving me," I complained.

"No, Caroline," she said with some sympathy. "We're *taking time off*. Dr. Finney is working on a new plan." She led me to the door and locked up. "It's good to rest."

"You always say I have to keep moving. Motion is lotion."

"Pregnancy is . . . different," she said pointedly, herding me away. "Take a walk. Clear your head. Have a nap. There's no stress." She gave me a firm smile. *Time to go.* Dr. Sun wanted to get out of this conversation. "Okay?"

I made room for her to pass. "Enjoy your vacation."

With obvious relief, Dr. Sun patted me on the shoulder and ducked into the hallway, already clutching her car keys. I made my way to Dr. Finney's private office, next to the exam room, and knocked.

"Yes?" Wedged behind her desk, the doctor was squinting at her computer, too distracted to look up.

"Dr. Finney," I began, ready to make my case for why I should be the exception to whatever rules she might have. She held up a hand.

"Sit, sit," she said. "I'm preparing your regime." She typed and pointed and clicked.

I took a seat and studied the room. I'd never been in here before. Books upon books upon leather-bound books; a wall-sized mosaic of five different diplomas in gilded frames. *Five of them? Was that possible?* I thought about my own sad certificate, ordered from the government. It came on cheap translucent paper from a dot-matrix printer, the sides torn off, printed in all caps and the date written in red ballpoint pen. Dr. Finney's were on linen, written in Latin calligraphy, signed with flourishes and stamped with golden seals. They were regal, like my Olympic medal, and they struck me with just as much authority.

"First, obviously, no more parties, no more sneaking champagne at lunch with the girls, hmm? Given your condition and the nutritional requirements of pregnancy, there are some studies that show that activity ought to be limited . . . ," she began, volleying figures my way. I tried to disagree at one point, saying, I think, that it didn't make sense to connect my quads or my calves to my uterus. *I needed to move. I needed to move every day or I would lose my mind.* She cocked her head—as though I were a child who needed to be taught the difference between fact and feeling. "That's your opinion, but it's not scientific, now, is it? When *you* were in charge, overexercising and undereating so you could be the fastest . . . well, just look what that did to you . . . no period for years, months and months to get pregnant, not right at your age, not at all . . ."

I receded as she listed my failures. By the time she finished her lecture I was primed to believe absolutely that Dr. Finney knew best and that I knew nothing. She told me I was to take it easy and spend most of my day resting, and above all else, stay in the Talon, to keep my pregnancy private until it was considered fully, absolutely viable.

◆ ◆ ◆

The Talon became my whole world. Forbidden to go to the gym, and bored senseless inside our dull gray apartment, I took to wandering the castle, loitering in the greenhouse or lolling in the mosaic-tiled pool, counting the gilded stars on its ceiling. After a few weeks of this I resorted to sitting on benches, watching the staff perform their daily chores. This proved far more interesting than expected. There was so much to be done: paving stones to be swept, tapestries to be beaten, vases to be dusted, horses to be groomed, guard dogs to be trained.

At first I was greeted with confusion—*Signora?*—but after a few days of persistent curiosity, I was accepted. If an ensign was polishing silver, I was pointed to a chair next to an open window, the filigreed patterns described in halting English. If the ballroom was being set for an evening meal, I was served a ginger ale in the kitchen while the cooks spun their copper pans, doling out spoonfuls of sauce with a wink. I witnessed the birth of a litter of mastiff puppies belonging to the Gardiens, their mother licking their mewling mouths and closed eyes. I grew to love the buildings, their great sprawling masses of hard stones and fine silks, and I came to realize that we more than merely provided for the people who kept them upright. We—Finn and I, and now this baby, the economy of our living bodies—were responsible for these other lives in their entirety. The palace needed masons to repair the marble of its veneer, conservation scientists to restore its paintings, farriers to shoe its horses. The staff could not exist without us. They needed us. *They needed this baby*, I thought, as the chauffeurs rubbed down the bulletproof cars with their melon-colored chamois cloths, *as much as I did.*

I loved being pregnant. Every single person smiled at me—even Otto and Dix, they couldn't help it. I was radiant, so full of hope that it spilled out of me with every breath. I smiled whenever Amelie asked, *How is your pregnancy coming along?* because at last I had an answer. *Very well, thank you.*

Finn made time to bring me sandwiches in the afternoon, and he was permitted to come home early from the events I was no longer allowed to attend. A projector was set up for us in the gray apartment's formal living room. The ensigns loaded films on the reel, like in a cinema, and it helped pass the time, for a while.

I miscarried at thirteen weeks. It happened on a weekend in the country house and could not be stopped. I woke in the middle of the night with cramps and a soggy pair of underpants. I hobbled to the bathroom, blood running down my legs; climbed into the enamel basin of the tub; and prayed. But prayer, even in my nunnery, did nothing at all.

◆ ◆ ◆

"It's those country roads," Dr. Finney clucked. "You can't bounce around like that. It's *immoral* to be so careless."

"They're not that bad," I tried. "I've been staying on the grounds, and I wanted—"

"That's the trouble, right there." Dr. Finney stopped me cold. "Hear yourself?"

"I don't think the roads were—"

"Not that. *I wanted*," she mimicked me, shaking her head. "It's not about what *you* want. It's about the *baby*. The baby who is now *no longer with us*. You must promise to be much more careful," she insisted.

Poured over with shame, I agreed.

From then on, my movements were constantly monitored, though my mental health remained unexamined. I put on a "brave face" and tried not to complain. I reminded myself every morning, as Otto stood outside my bedroom door and waited to escort me to the gym, that I was lucky that someone in the world would take care of me the way the Talon took care of me. When Dix put his hand on my shoulder, stopping me from rounding a corner as he spoke into his earpiece, I told myself to be grateful that I was a princess in a castle. I'd bet my whole life on running—and I'd lost. I was the one who'd chosen not to find any other form of employment. I'd refused to educate myself or take the only job offered to me, the one back at Wits, in South Africa. What would've happened to me if I were still in Lisbon or Johannesburg? I'd have been in traction somewhere, cheap hip and discount knee already rotting on my right side. I'd barely be able to walk, much less have a baby.

I got pregnant again two months later, and had another miscarriage, that one at six weeks. It was indistinguishable from a heavy period, globs of clotted brown jelly between thin bursts of new blood. If I weren't constantly being tested, I don't think I would even have clocked it as a miscarriage. Dr. Finney interviewed everyone that time—Otto and Dix and Roland and Schätze and Finn—trying to find out exactly what I'd done wrong.

I know now that many, many women have five- and six-week miscarriages—it is so normal, there is nothing to be done about it, it is not anyone's responsibility or fault—but Dr. Finney never told me any such thing. She only made me feel as though I myself had caused them. And I, to my eternal regret, believed her.

◆　◆　◆

This is where time becomes liquid and difficult to measure. When Dr. Finney could not pinpoint what she called a "precipitating incident" for the six-week miscarriage, it was decided that assistance was needed. I was put on a program of fertility drugs and forbidden to go to the gym.

My breasts grew huge. I held masses of water, ballooning with bloat. I was alternately constipated or diarrheal, with matching moods: so uptight I ground my teeth, or so loose and louche that I barely recognized myself. They did work, though, the drugs. They flushed out every egg in my system. I tested pregnant two more times but was not able to carry either past five weeks.

Around us Lucomo boomed, the new construction loud enough to hear from within the Talon itself. The green squares of Finn's plans began to fill in with metal exoskeletons. The population swelled by 5, then 7 percent. Finn was always on the phone, negotiating, currying favor or carrying it from one party to another, stoking and stroking strangers' egos until they erupted, spewing assets into our chasm of wealth. His zeal became mania, every conversation ending with the word *billion*. Whenever I questioned the amount of money he threw around—especially as the sovereign bond of massive debt had not yet been resolved—Finn would dazzle me with explanations that I didn't understand. I *was* told *very* clearly, however, that because we were married, and his personal assets were part of the leveraging process, a great deal of paperwork required my signature. Unable to read the Italian legalese, I signed them blindly as they appeared, usually a stack on my desk with a sticky note from Roland reading *Si prega di firmare prontamente e li invierò.* "Please sign promptly and I will send them."

And Amelie kept asking how my pregnancy was coming along.

After these incidences of "the question," I would wake in the night, wander out to Finn's office, and talk to her portrait. *All you've done is inherit your position and get married and bear a child who runs everything for you. Inheriting money and getting married and having children are experiences, but they are not accomplishments. You're not someone I look up to,* I told the portrait. *You're not better than me. You're not more of a person than I am. You don't know more about being alive.*

But of course, I never said these things to Amelie. I merely stood alone and said these things aloud to the only person who could hear them: myself. *You are worthless, you are nothing, you are nobody, your opinions don't matter, your accomplishments are meaningless,* I said aloud, again and again. *You don't matter.* The embittered sparks of my own frustration never left our apartment.

Without my fitness routine to mark the time, I began to wake later and later, sitting listlessly in the gardens for hours, trying to read but unable to focus. Finn's early efforts to pay me extra care each day wore out—I think he began to feel superstitious about it—and soon we rarely saw each other. He rose early and came home late.

After I miscarried for the fourth time, Finn tried to cheer me up. We took the boat to beaches across the sea, on the northern coasts of Morocco and Tunisia. I loved that vacation. I wish I could recall more than what is indicated by the photos we took with what was then a very expensive digital camera, but they come in those flashes exactly: the two of us lying on tasseled towels over sand too hot to touch; rich stews served in earthenware containers; olive oil fresher than any olive. Wine in our room on the boat, sipped in privacy, in secret.

The service lurked behind us, but as the trip was impromptu, there were no events, there were no requirements, there was no performance.

We were as alone as we ever got. I came to consider those sandy climates, with their exquisite food and muezzin calls and cultural fixation with marriage and family, as the places where I received the undivided attention of my husband.

I was being reshaped, my self-determination stripped away each time someone washed my hair, my self-esteem draining out with each unwanted period. The Talon controlled what I ate, where I went, what I wore, who I spoke to. The only undetermined variable was Finn's attention, and that became all I could imagine wanting out of life.

◆ ◆ ◆

All the while, I missed South Africa. I longed for its forthrightness, for its landscape and buzzing, living difference. Somehow we could never find the time to visit; I was told the security requirements were too complicated. On the calendar we always had things to attend between pregnancies and miscarriages. And if I am being truthful, I did not really want to go. I missed it abstractly. I missed the *idea* of it. I missed the way it felt when people like me thought everything would be different. Everything I loved about it was from those precious years of change, before the dream sputtered and plateaued, when I looked every day toward a finish line and my mother was there to cheer me on.

There was no *rush*, Finn assured me. My father reported that his cough was subsiding. *There was no rush.* When there was a baby, my father would certainly come and visit. There was no rush at all.

I wrote long letters to Johannesburg every month, describing the Talon and its heartbeats: each flower, each antique chair. My father wrote back, telling me about the weather in South Africa or news from his friends. Winni had become his companion, which I liked, because they seemed to find some happiness with each other, and the money that Finn sent every month kept them afloat.

It all went by so quickly that the day he died in the yard of a heart attack we hadn't seen each other in over two years. Winni wrote with the news and said that my father wished to be cremated, that he did not want a memorial service. I am still surprised that she did not call, though perhaps she did; it's not as if I answered my own phone, even the mobile. She promised to send his ashes.

When they arrived two weeks later, in a thick plastic bag, I walked the *Basse* road all the way to the beaches, in a large hat and sunglasses. The service gave me little space. At the crowded summer shore, Otto grumpily stripping down to trunks behind me, I waded through throngs of tomato-skinned tourists. On the far side of the breaking waves I opened my fist and dropped a handful of bony fragments of my father into the sea, so that he would be of Lucomo, too. I cried myself to sleep that night, hours before Finn finally settled beside me, stroking my hair.

I was an orphan at twenty-six who had now miscarried four times. I felt utterly alone in the world, except for my husband, but he was always busy—always working. After that, what had been a strong desire became a matter of obsession. We began IVF.

26

JANE WAS BORN in the early hours of September 21, 2006, in the Talon's medical bay. After the scheduled cesarean's opening salvo, one long incision across my abdomen, Finn stepped outside and paced the halls, unable to stomach the reality of it. Amelie, double-masked and wrapped up in scrubs, remained behind.

Subdued by opiates in the spinal block, I calmly accepted his departure and blinked hazily through the separation of my abdominal muscles. When they began to cut into the uterus, I didn't feel a moment's pain; it was only strange, to watch the pink and brown amniotic fluids be sucked up through their tube. But when Dr. Finney pressed down to force Jane's head through the opening, my blood spattered across her goggles, and I became *absolutely terrified*.

I tried to reach across the sheet, but immobilized below the shoulder, only my arms stretched forward, grasping at nothing, flapping helplessly in the air. The nurses pushed back on each shoulder and held down my hands. Dr. Finney gave the nod to release more fentanyl into the spinal block, and then I was in a warm bath, drowning in heat, while they birthed my baby.

I watched helplessly as Dr. Finney put a suction cup to Jane's tiny mouth, pulled the mucus from her lungs, and handed her to Amelie, who kissed her head and rocked her back and forth. I tried to yell *GIVE ME MY BABY* but the words died in my throat, eradicated by some combination of sedation and fear. After the longest minute of my life, Amelie, her scrubs stained with our blood, finally handed Jane to me. I clutched her to my chest, slimy and precious, this being I'd pictured countless times over the nine heinously worrisome months of my pregnancy.

I am pleased to report that she was exactly as I'd imagined, but better. I knew—does this sound crazy?—I knew her face before I saw it. I knew her tiny fingers, her tiny toes. I even knew her eyes would be silver, bordering on violet, that they'd never gain more pigment. She was smaller than a bottle of champagne. I was reoriented, a compass pointing to her, the new center of my universe. I named her Jane, after my mother, who had been Harriet Jane.

The Talon didn't like the name Jane. Amelie insisted it was too plain. She was baptized as Jeanne Marianne Ferdinand Amelie Arturo. Finn called it a compromise, but I never called her Jeanne—never ever; it wasn't her name.

Twelve hours after her birth, I was hoisted upright and given a thick pad to wear. The loose bag of my uterus, already shifting within its truss of surgical stitches, was massaged into place, my trunk wrapped tight in white gauze. A lovely blue dress went over my head. Finn took my hand and we were marched outside onto the Talon's central lawn with baby Jane in my arms, so everyone could see. I remember the dizziness as the flashes went off, and the surreal feeling that my uterus was about to spill onto the ground. But Jane belonged to them—*she belonged to Lucomo*—and they had a right to see her, so I kept still. If you look carefully in the photographs you can see a small stain on my belly where the incision began to bleed through the gauze. I'm smiling like it's the best day of my life.

◆ ◆ ◆

When Jane was three weeks old, Amelie appeared in our apartment as I was coming out of the toilet, Jane on my breast, trousers half-down. When I turned the corner and spotted Amelie curled in a chair, quietly drinking a cup of tea, I nearly screamed. "Hello," she warbled, bending her head in a regal invitation. "You may sit."

Four new words: *Hello you may sit.* You could have knocked me over with a feather. I finished buttoning my pants with one hand, Jane's drool pooling on the edges of my top. I sat in the nearest chair, wincing as the incision in my belly folded. I clutched at the nearest fabric—a cashmere sweater—and draped it over the twin bulbs of breast and skull. But Jane yowled; the fabric was too thick. It scared her. Pulling back the sweater, I searched the room for a replacement. Amelie let out a heavy sigh, untied the silk scarf from her neck, the one with the interlocking Fs, and waved it in the air. I reached for it, painfully; once it was in place, Jane settled down.

"I understand she's doing very well," Amelie stated.

"Yes," I agreed, forgetting her honorific. "She's doing very well."

"She looks very much like you."

"She looks exactly like my mother," I said, stroking her round cheeks.

"I'd like to spend more time with her." Amelie set her cup down firmly; it was a statement, not a request.

"She's a bit disgusting at the moment. Her gas clears the room." At that, Jane bit my nipple, and I winced. "Christ," I muttered, sticking my finger in her mouth to break the hold. Jane mewed, then readjusted and kept drinking. Amelie's neon-green bird snuck out of her sweater and perched on her finger, snapping its head to and fro, focusing its bright eyes on Jane.

"Excuse me, Your Serene Highness," I apologized, glaring at the bird.

She seemed amused. "I had a baby once, you know. I am very familiar with how sticky it can be. Perhaps one of the nannies should start bringing her for tea."

"If you please, Your Serene Highness . . . ," I scrambled for an excuse. "She has a strict nap schedule—"

Amelie straightened her index finger, dispatching the bird. It took flight, sailing around the room and screeching. I wrapped my arms protectively around Jane, tucking her head under my chin. "Schätze will coordinate," Amelie said, rising from her chair. I struggled to do the same, clutching the slippery scarf while trying not to suffocate my baby. Amelie let me rise. By the time I was upright she waved me back down again. "No, you may sit," she sighed benevolently, as though she was being kind. "Goodbye." She turned on her heel and left.

I fell back down on the sofa, gobsmacked. At last, Amelie had spoken to me—but as ever, the topic was the same. *Children.*

◆　◆　◆

One month later, Atena threw a baby shower. I wore a pink-and-white-striped dress and asked the technicians to braid my hair—in those days, a lustrous tangle of burnt honey—and lace it with fresh flowers. My skin had begun to tan in the sun, to show little freckles. I'd kept some of my pregnancy weight. I looked happy.

On my way out, Finn called me into his office. A shoebox, my name written in calligraphy on the lid, waited on the edge of his desk. Inside, wrapped in swaths of violet tissue paper, was a pair of mules, embroidered with beveled amethysts and a diamond fleur-de-lis. They had the proportions of another century, though modern inserts were delicately stitched into the footbed, and the sole was a fresh piece of leather.

"What brought this on?" I asked curiously, sliding my foot into one. It fit perfectly.

"They were Savior Gloria's. I thought you might like to have them."

I put the other shoe on. The jewels shimmered. "These aren't real?"

"They are."

"What if they come off? They're sewn on. All it takes is a snag."

"The stones are not *particularly* valuable."

"They're valuable to me."

"I'm glad." He beckoned to the door. An ensign knelt at my feet, opening her hands to indicate that I should step out. She seasoned the bottom of each sole with a cheese grater, then helped me to slide them back on. Another ensign came up behind her, carrying six mono-grammed Goyard totes, three in each hand; in each bag nestled an-other labeled shoebox. "For the Ammaliatrici," Finn explained. "These belonged to Gloria's own ladies-in-waiting."

I arrived at Atena's country estate towing a red wagon piled with one baby, snug in her carrier, and six gifts. I felt wonderful. No Clomid coursed through my veins, inflating or deflating my mood; no bruises pocked my thighs or abdomen from shots of Lupron; there was no vomit in my hair, no surgical staples catching against my underwear. The path to Atena's front door, across a garden filled with sweet grasses, was peppered by a herd of white horses grazing up to her very doorstep. A fluffy white cat, wearing a ruby-encrusted collar, sat flicking her tail in the foyer. Beyond, the sprawling manse was filled to the rafters with nearly three hundred Piéton women.

Chiara, Marcella, Benny, Aurora, Vida, and Atena accepted their gifts with delight, pulling the shoes from their bags and trying them on while everyone watched. I could see how right it was, to have brought these gifts, to have elevated these women above their peers. *Finn always knew precisely how to behave,* I thought, *when it didn't even occur to me.*

Amelie didn't grace us with her presence until an hour later, and so for a while, I was the most important adult there. Jane was passed into a thousand arms and given a million kisses. She had but to mew to be bounced, rocked, attended until she smiled. I was placed in a large chair to receive the Piéton women, one by one. They brought a Lu-gesque custom: handwritten cards bearing their secrets for being a mother. Their advice generally fell into two camps: either the rules of folk wisdom, such as "never let your children swim after drinking milk," or remedies of the natural world, like arnica for bruises and bur-dock root for sour stomachs. Marcella's card, however, was uniquely thoughtful: *It does not matter what you do, as long as you do it with confidence. The best mother is simply one who can be counted on.*

Drenched in such kindness, everyone moving around me in prearranged orbits, I felt myself shift neatly into position. I had at last achieved the one thing that everyone wanted. It was so much *more* than when I was merely beautiful; it was deeper, inclusive, a glue. I drank in the attention, greedily, from a golden cup.

◆ ◆ ◆

I was given another gift: We were finally permitted to create our own apartment in the Talon. The third floor of the residence, mostly dormant guest suites, would now be wholly ours. A team of architects had designed a four-bedroom apartment with several living rooms, a playroom, a nursery, a chef's kitchen, spa bathrooms, and a walk-in closet. The renovation happened in the space of two short months; hundreds of hands make light work. Jane's nursery was completed first, decorated in the most royal of colors. Lavender and orchid and mulberry painted the walls; thistle and mauve upholstered her furniture in quilted velvets. From the moment she opened her eyes each day from then on, she was inundated with it, her righteous color, her birthright.

I took on two older Marin women to cook and nanny for us: Marie and Lola, both squat and bosomy, always quick with a kind word or a helping hand. Every morning they hung their personalities on a peg by the door and merged flawlessly into our lives.

Jane was an excellent baby. She fattened up quickly and slept for long periods of time unaided. Finn was so tender then. He did move into our second bedroom to get a full night's sleep, but he would come in every morning and lie in bed with us and skip meetings while we drank coffee and stroked her tiny eyebrows. He helped me put on her socks and change her diapers. He took us to the country house for languorous weekends, where we kissed by the fireplace as baby Jane napped in the downy embrace of the sofas. And Finn would cook, and cook, and cook, doing all the meals on the gas stove and serving them by candlelight. This joyous, intimate idyll lasted for months. I floated around in a dream, my fat baby clutching at my breast.

But how quickly our lives shifted back: I was no longer playing the part of glamorous young wife. I now had to be the world's most perfect mother. Four-month-old Jane and I were dressed and tidied for photo ops at upscale playgrounds, cafés, charity luncheons, and afternoon teas so that anyone important, or anyone who worked for someone important, could catch a glimpse of us as they passed through Lucomo. Vida, who had a two-year-old son, was often with me; Benny sometimes, too, with her granddaughter. But Marcella, whose children had recently gone off to university, and childless Chiara, Aurora, and Atena, were naturally excluded. I barely even noticed their absence. I only tried to make it through each day.

◆　◆　◆

When Jane was six months, Dr. Finney informed me that it was time for two things: first, to stop breastfeeding, and second, to resume my next cycle of IVF. I broke down at that and stayed up all night crying in Jane's room. Finn found me around three and gently led me back to our bed. He canceled his appointments for the next day, spending the hours reminding me that this was my role, that it was necessary. Once we were finished, I could have my own life. I would have my charity budget. He promised me that I would be free. All I had to do was have one more baby. All I had to do was get it right one more time.

I was doing well, physically. After Jane's birth Dr. Sun had revived me with a strict high-protein diet, daily strength workouts, massage, acupuncture, and a new schedule of calibrated treatments. Weekly injections—hyaluronic acid to lubricate the joints, alternated with batches of stem cells taken from my bounty of postpartum body fat, to stimulate muscle growth—kept my arthritis pain at a two, sometimes a three. My bones had regained much of their density and my joints stood still, their degeneration miraculously paused. I was twenty-seven years old and felt better than I had at seventeen. This was, according to Dr. Finney, the ideal condition for conception. I was put once again into the inert fog of IVF.

27

MOST DAYS, Jane was cleaned up after her early-afternoon feeding and brought in her carrier to Amelie. Her grandmother would tickle and coo at her until Jane fell asleep, and then my baby would be returned to me. She was adorable, and unfortunately, Amelie adored her. She even let Jane spit up on her. I was terrified of the ease Amelie had with her, like she was Amelie's baby, not mine; I hated that she was never returned on time, not on my schedule, only on Amelie's. At least twice a week Jane would be kept long enough to take her afternoon nap in that damned menagerie of caged birds, even as I waited nervously in my apartment down the hall, feeling the inescapable pain of a mother whose infant was needlessly out of sight.

One afternoon I couldn't take it and shoved my way past the ensigns to find Amelie smiling fondly as her clawed companions clung to the cradle's edge, hopping curiously and dangerously close to Jane's peach-thin skin. Instinctively I darted forward, bending over the cradle to cover Jane with my torso. Almost all of the birds scattered in terror, save for the neon-green one who lived in Amelie's sweater. It landed on my back, dug in with its claws, and left a deep gash on my shoulder as I tried to shake it free. In terror I lifted Jane to my breast, fled the room, then locked myself in our apartment. I refused to put her down and cried for an hour, shaking, as Marie disinfected and bandaged the wound on my back.

The next day, Amelie herself came to pick up Jane—two Gardiens close behind her, their strapping bodies a living threat. She didn't attempt an apology, but instead behaved as though I was the one at fault. "The birds are very protective," she told me sternly. "You shouldn't startle them like that."

"They're going to peck her eyes out," I muttered.

"Pfft." Amelie dismissed me and lifted Jane from her bouncing chair as I stood frozen, the Gardiens casting their shadows on the floor between us. And though Jane was returned without a scratch hours later, I nonetheless, from that day on, could not bear my baby's absence without a deep pit of fear opening up in my stomach.

One morning I was sitting on the lid of the toilet, pinching my thigh for an intramuscular shot of progesterone while Finn shaved. He drew the razor down his skin, lips pulled to the side, before pausing—razor in hand, as though it was an afterthought—and saying, "Oh. I completely forgot to say, earlier. It's a bit last-minute, but Amelie's going to bring Jeanne to the party tonight for the Red Cross."

"Babies don't like parties," I snapped, depressing the plunger.

"Amelie only wants her there for an hour. She'll be brought right back to you."

"Will she, though?" I put the used syringe in its red plastic box.

"What does that mean?"

"I'm afraid sometimes that she won't give her back." I faced away from him as I turned on the shower.

Finn put down his razor, still half-masked with cream, and stared at me. "Caro, you're shooting yourself up with liquid insanity. No one is going to take her away."

I stepped into the tiled cavern, a drop of blood dripping down my leg from the injection site. "You don't know that," I said, wiping it off.

"I *do* know that," he sighed. "You used to be rational."

I let the water cascade over my head, drowning him out. *Why did I even bother to bring it up?*

Thereafter, instead of challenging my husband, I became preoccupied with keeping my daughter away from her grandmother. This did not go very well. It began with canceling on a visit, then staying in bed with Jane and claiming we both had a cold. And one fateful night, when Jane was eleven months old, it finally resulted in my lifting her from her crib and taking her down to the boat.

◆　◆　◆

As we were falling asleep the night before, Finn offered another of his last-minute strategies when he "remembered" to mention that Amelie would be taking Jane to the Vatican to be blessed by the Pope in the morning. *Without us.* I hadn't assented to this—I hadn't even been asked—and I declined. "No, that won't be happening." I sat up straight. "That's not possible."

"She wants to take her." He yawned, rolling onto his stomach. "What can I do? I've got work. You can't travel. Dr. Finney's orders."

"Tell her *no*. That bird is going to peck her eyes out. I can see it in its face. It's dying to."

"Please don't be upset." He opened one eye, looking at me so wearily, like he was tired of my being upset. He *was* tired of my being upset. We'd had mere months of a relationship before I began to rotate between pregnancy and miscarriage. I knew—he never said it, but I knew—he thought it would all end after Jane was born, that I would return to "normal." I couldn't believe he would let his mother take my eleven-month-old baby from me—but there was no use arguing. I was so tired. I didn't complain any further, that night, about the Vatican. I closed my eyes and let myself sleep. Two hours later, my eyes flew open. Finn was snoring.

I crept out of bed, packed an oversized Gucci handbag with a bottle of formula, toothbrushes, swimsuits for each of us, clean underwear, and a small plastic bag of my father's remaining ashes. I put extra baby food and formula into a shopping bag. Pulling my green cape over my nightgown, I lifted my daughter from her bed, swiped Finn's keycard from his pocket. Then I took the passageways down to the vault door that would lead us to the boathouse elevator.

The vault door was locked. I swiped Finn's key, Jane in my arms, bags hanging off my shoulders. The passage was unusually crowded with large wooden crates, their splintered edges snagging the lace of my nightgown.

Where are we going, Maman? Jane didn't use real words yet, but I could see her thoughts. She'd never been in the tunnel before. Her eyes grew wide at the thousand-plus-year-old chisel marks. "We're going on a trip, darling," I whispered. "You mustn't be afraid." I pressed up against the wall to pass a tall stack covered in a strange alphabet. The letters were squared off, similar but different; Cyrillic, I guessed. *Cyrillic?* Even in my exhausted, impulsive state, it struck me as odd.

I set our bags down and ran my free hand over the sides, looking for loose panels, but they wouldn't budge; they were nailed shut. I put my nose to the seam and sniffed, coming away with the distinct scent of ammonia. There was another note, something familiar, but I couldn't quite place it.

Jane let out a loud cry, pulling me back into focus. I picked our bags back up and clutched her tighter. *This tunnel is very scary,* she telegraphed, fear in her eyes. "Yes, darling, it is a bit. But we are *very* brave." I controlled my breathing and kept moving. We took the elevator down, past the damp Gardiens standing sentry, and boarded the boat.

An ensign appeared, looking worried. "*Signora?*" she asked. "What is going on?"

"A little trip. We'd like to have some fun. Wouldn't we, darling."

Yes please, Jane gurgled.

"A warm beach, please," I said to the ensign. "Tunisia, perhaps." I'd liked it there best, on my miscarriage holiday. I handed her the bag of baby food and formula. "Pop this in the galley."

The ensign nodded and disappeared.

Jane's sweet face, so trusting. "We're going on a trip, baby," I told her as we curled up in our stateroom, warm under the green blanket of my cape. "A holiday for mummies and babies." The engine fired up; the boat began to rock in the waves. I fed Jane the bottle from my handbag, and she fell asleep on my chest. Relaxing into the rolling motion of the boat, I closed my eyes, too.

◆　◆　◆

In the light of dawn, the view from the yacht was the same one I saw every day: the northwest coast of the Mediterranean, the Alps in the distance. After laying a sleeping Jane flat on her back, I tiptoed to the door and cracked it open—but there was no one on the other side.

There was nobody in the hallway, nobody on the deck, nobody anywhere. We were still tethered to the cliffside dock. I searched furiously for the captain, at first, and when I found the bridge empty I decided I would settle for any staff member. "Staff!!" I shouted, marching around the boat in sheepskin boots and a nightgown. "*STAFF!*"

There was no answer. Each open door revealed a vacant room. The hallways were empty, the staff quarters, too, even the bathrooms. The only people on the boat were the two of us.

I returned to our stateroom to find Jane stretching herself awake. She let out a hungry yowl. I checked the bottle of formula, but she'd emptied it the night before. I hoisted her on my hip and took her to the galley. It was still empty of people—and the bag of formula that I'd packed was nowhere to be seen. I opened the cabinets to find that someone had removed every scrap of food from their shelves.

Maman, I'm hungry, Jane whined. I checked the empty cabinets again. She began to cry. "Don't be dramatic," I scolded, bouncing her up and down as she wailed into my eardrums. *Maman, please,* Jane said, wrinkling with sadness. I pulled out one milkless, hormone-swollen breast to comfort her. As usual she bit my nipple. It was so painful that I shrieked.

And at that perfect moment, Amelie appeared in the doorway. "Hello, baby," she cooed. "Who wants a hot breakfast?"

Jane unlatched immediately. *I do, I do!* she cried.

"Maman is confused," Amelie said carefully. A team of Gardiens appeared behind her, blocking out all the light. "She forgot to tell us about your special sleepover. Did you have a nice time?"

Jane's screams grew louder. "Oh, Jeanne, little baby," Amelie said, frowning. "So unhappy!" The Gardiens took their places at my side, ready to tear my daughter from my limbs. Unnecessary. I would never let anything bad happen in front of Jane. When Amelie held out her slender arms, as I knew she would, I handed over my daughter. "Come with Mamou. That's it." Amelie settled Jane on one hip, like I just had—and then she turned and marched right off the boat. The Gardiens followed.

I walked last. All five of us rode up the elevator in silence. The long corridor was swept clean, bereft of the wooden crates; they'd been whisked away in the night by the Talon's ever-moving hands. Amelie trotted ahead with Jane, ignoring me as she whispered sweet some-things against Jane's velvety skull. I shuffled behind, dejected, the Gardiens between us.

◆ ◆ ◆

Finn was furious with me. "Are you fucking crazy? Have you finally lost your mind?"

"Don't swear at me." I was crumpled on the floor of our bedroom, still in my nightgown, fiddling with the edge of the rug.

"You took our baby onto an empty boat in the middle of the night without telling anyone."

"That's the least of what I'm entitled to do."

"What if something happened to her?"

"It wasn't empty when I got on. There was an ensign there. I gave her a command. And they pulled away. But *then they turned around.*

And they took all the food, Finn. Your mother had the whole thing ruined."

"Caroline, there was nobody on that boat," he said slowly, looking worried.

"Ferdinand, *yes there was*," I said, just as slowly. "We *pulled away from the dock*."

"Caro, that didn't happen." He sat on the floor next to me.

"There were crates in the tunnels," I remembered. "Hundreds of them. Russian writing on the side. They disappeared."

"That doesn't make any sense."

"They were there," I told him. "It all happened."

Finn paused, trying to determine whether or not I was out of my mind. After a brief staring contest—I won—he gave up, opened his phone, and called Roland. They spoke briefly in Italian before he folded it shut. "There was a shipment of food," Finn asserted. "Could that have been what you found?"

"I don't think so. The crates smelled like window cleaner, and like . . ." I trailed off, nose twitching as I attempted to conjure it back up. Then a flash of my father's rarely washed safety vest—and the scent that clung to it from years of blasting—surfaced in the back of my throat. "Hot metal," I blurted out. "It was like a penny on your tongue."

"A penny on your tongue?" Finn repeated. I nodded. "Caro," he said tenderly, "that doesn't make a lot of sense." He took one of my hands and faced it palm-up, tracing the heart line back and forth with his index finger.

"Why would crates for food have a different alphabet?" I asked.

"People reuse wooden crates for all kinds of things. It's not a plastic bag, Caro, you don't just throw them out."

"I don't know," I replied, shaking my head. "I just don't know."

"Dr. Finney says the fertility drugs can make you paranoid. Do you feel like that? Paranoid?"

"Paranoid? *You don't believe me.*" My voice had risen to a shriek; I was losing control. "It's not irrational, Finn. I'm not irrational."

"I understand that you feel strongly about this," he said, calm and steady, as if I were a child on the verge of a tantrum. "But I really don't think you need to be *quite* so upset."

At that condescension, the alarm bells ringing in my head took control. "You can't take my baby away," I told him desperately. "She can't just *take* my baby."

"Nobody is taking her from you, Caro." Careful, but firm, wrapping his arms round my shoulders. "This doesn't have to be a big deal. It's a short trip. It's the Pope. They'll be back tomorrow morning. Can't you try to see her side?"

"It *is* a big deal," I cried. "Jane is *mine*."

"She's *ours*," he corrected me, "and she's *fine* and she's *safe* and she's *happy*. I think—I think it's been a lot, Caro. I think you need a break." He swallowed and reddened and clicked his jaw and I could tell—*he was my husband, I knew him*—he knew exactly why I was upset.

"You don't really think that it's okay for her to take our baby."

His eyes flashed, turned dark. He got red all over. He was about to lie.

"Don't lie to me," I said.

Click, click, jaw to the left and right. He was not going to tell me the truth. He was deciding to side with his mother. "You're having a tough time, Caro. I think you need a little space from Jeanne. You're forgetting that there's an adult in there."

I peeled his hands off me and stood up. "I don't believe you," I told him. "You *know* she had that boat turned around. She did it to hurt me. To make me look like a fool. You *know* it."

"Caroline, please," he said, exasperated. "Nobody had anything done to you."

I locked myself in the bathroom and cried. He'd lied to me, for what I perceived to be the first time in our marriage.

28

AS MY BABY WAS LOADED onto the golden jet and flown away, I fumed hard enough to break a sweat, poison spilling from my pores. How easily Amelie had made me look foolish. She'd ordered the boat back, she'd had them remove every scrap of food, she'd made it look like *I* was a *crazy* woman doing *crazy things* in the middle of the night—and then she'd gone ahead and taken my baby. It made me want to rip something in half. I ached to run like I hadn't ached in years. All I wanted to do that day was run out the doors, after my daughter, feet pounding the pavement along the coastline down to Rome. I wanted my bones to shudder; to feel every ounce of pain.

The phone rang, interrupting my rage. I cracked the door, took a peek; the apartment was quiet. Finn was gone. I answered. *Atena.* She asked me to lunch, suggesting a small restaurant in San-Berno, a locals' place, she said, and offered to pick me up.

I tried not to look crazy. I wore a floor-sweeping linen dress in powder blue, one that accommodated my IVF bloat, and simple gold jewelry. No nail polish or makeup. I parted my hair down the middle and began to brush it from the ends up, the way the technicians did. But in my clumsy fervor I snagged a batch of extensions and accidentally ripped them out, a patch of my natural hair coming with it. The sight of the bloodied tangle in my palm, the plucked roots like miniature tubers, prompted an electric urge to keep brushing, brushing hard. I got two more patches out from the back before an ensign knocked. Quickly I balled up the clumps of hair and secreted them away in my pocket.

Atena waited in a vintage black two-seater Ferrari, a white silk scarf knotting her hair into a turban. Dix pulled up behind, blocking her exit. Otto motioned for her to get out; they wanted to drive us. Atena refused. "I think not," she said to him firmly. A minor argument ensued. She won. Dix moved the SUV. I slid onto Atena's teeny-weeny passenger seat and clipped myself in. "*Dolce* Caro," she said, putting her hand to my cheek. "How are you?"

"Wilted."

She winked. "We'll have a drink. Some sun. You'll revive." With that, she slammed the car into reverse and roared out of the palace.

❖   ❖   ❖

We took the *Haute* road, the one that winds above the coast. It was August of 2007, tourists everywhere, the traffic so dense it looked like a dealership. That summer the whole world was rich, and Lucomo most of all, a sausage stuffed to the ends with creamy, fatty opulence. The men who built the banks, the men who filled the vaults, their underlings, and hordes of companions.

Atena had a lead foot, racing fearlessly between shark-nosed fenders. Her '62 Ferrari, a tin can lashed to a rocket, smelled powerfully of gasoline. Every shift of the gear was nauseating, but the adrenaline of it was stronger. I tilted my face to the sun. It was a strange and welcome relief, not to worry about Jane for a moment—not to feel her in my arms—to be an adult again. *To feel risk*. I told Atena to drive even faster.

When she was busy changing lanes, I snuck the nest of torn hair from my pocket. *Maybe Finn's right,* I thought, releasing it on the wind. *Maybe I need a break after all.*

By the time we reached San-Berno, the town of Piéton palazzos that could never be rented or sold, the tourists had thinned out and mostly disappeared. The restaurant, a modest place built over a rocky breakwater, served locals. It had plastic roll-up walls, a poster of Magnum ice creams. One man sat in back, a fluffy cocker spaniel sleeping beside him. The bartender leaned against the window, reading the newspaper, coffee in hand. After we entered, both men nodded to Atena, lifted their drinks, and exited to the deck. The dog continued to sleep. Aside from her fluffy snores, we were alone; Otto and Dix remained in the parking lot.

Atena went behind the bar and poured two glasses of pastis, adding the cold water and ice that turned them opaque. "The menu is limited," she explained, plucking two packets of crisps from the wall. She waved at the empty tables. "Take a seat." I set myself down, took the glass from her as offered. "So," she said squarely. "How are you?"

"Very well," I said uncertainly. I didn't know what she'd been told.

"Mmm. And yet, your husband calls me to cheer you up." She shrugged, popping a crisp in her mouth. "So—what is going on, Caro? You must tell me. I am here for you, but I am not psychic."

I turned my eyes to the gulls dipping and diving over the sea, the silence an answer unto itself. We watched the birds until our glasses were empty. Atena rose and refilled them from behind the bar. "The service can't hear you, not here," she pointed out. On the peaceful beach, the Marins stood in the water with their fishing poles stuck in the rocks. "They're friends, the owners. You can speak freely."

It came out in a whisper. "Amelie took my baby this morning. She made me look crazy."

"How did she do that?"

"I was on the boat."

"In the day?"

"In the night."

"It was planned?"

I did not want to say it—*oh, but I did, I wanted to be validated.* "Amelie wanted to take her to the Vatican. But she's *my* daughter. So I decided we would go somewhere else."

Her response was an expression of pure horror. "Caro," she tried to say gently, cocking her head. "You must not do such things."

"But I wanted to—"

She cut me off. "You may want to do many things, but you must not. I think you are overtired," she said sincerely.

"She can't take *my baby* whenever she feels like it."

"Amelie is a difficult person," Atena observed, "and used to getting what she wants. This is very important, to give her what she wants." At this she became serious. "It is the *law.*"

"My husband took her side," I tried to explain. "It made me feel so small."

Atena put her hand over mine. "You cannot believe she would hurt your baby."

Amelie loved Jane, I knew that. "That's not the point. She's *mine.*"

"You must calm down," she said. "You must not think the worst of others."

"I wasn't, Atena. I'm not."

"Caro, you are not born here. You don't know what things were like, before. After the war things were very difficult. We returned to a sub-sistence life, almost. It is through Amelie we have thrived. If Amelie arranges something, it is because it has some meaning. If she wants to take Jane somewhere, to show her off, it has purpose. It is on your be-half," she said sternly. "It is on *Jane's* behalf."

"I don't see how it is beneficial for Jane to be without her mother."

"Jane is safe, is she not? She has the best care in the world. She is surrounded by guards. She lives in a castle and you are waited on hand and foot." Atena—who'd always been so deferential to me—was suddenly animated. Regardless of our status she was twice, possibly three times my age and possessed of an influence I couldn't imitate or ignore. "Amelie's will is the law," she repeated. "Caro, you are so important. You have many friends who support you and want you to be a success. You must not make believe that you are above the law," she insisted, voice cracking. "All of us—myself included and your husband—have spent our whole lives following the law. If you disregard the law, you are disregarding our very personhood." She shimmered with hurt.

Here was this woman who had to drop everything when she was told to, who dressed up like an animal so I could hunt her at a party, who faded away when she wasn't wanted, who reappeared on demand, and I'd wounded her.

I wish I'd been able to understand at the time that Atena was invested, above all else, in supremacy itself. Aristocrats need crowns to distract from their own empires. Queens and princesses are targets for the slings and arrows of the working class, while people like Atena sit in their country homes and file their nails. But I didn't. What I understood was that everyone around me believed the Earth was shaped like a cone with Amelie at the top and the rest of us below. And so I believed it, and felt duly ashamed, for wanting to put my own needs above the rules that everyone else had to follow. "I'm so sorry," I told her sincerely.

Atena composed herself, flicking the apology away. "There is nothing to forgive. It is my role in this life, to support you."

"Even when you don't want to?"

"I always want to," she said, still holding my hand. "I am your friend. You are used to this, are you not? You have always been the most important woman in the room." I thought of my mother, then, standing on the side of the track for so many thousands of hours. Zola's mother, whispering in her ear, encouraging her to invite me to join the Elephants. Atena didn't let go. "You will be a success, Caro," she assured me. "Everything will be well."

◆ ◆ ◆

We left the shack wearing a pair of wan smiles. We didn't speak on the drive back to the Talon; there was nothing else to say. Atena hugged me goodbye with a compassionate smile.

In our apartment, technicians in white coats waited. Of course. These endless appearances. Face painted, body swaddled in yards of silk, spritzed with perfume, dotted with jewels. The technicians said nothing to me about the little bald patches, and I pretended not to see their uneasy expressions as they carefully tied on new skeins of hair.

When Finn returned from his office and happened upon his impeccable wife draped across a chaise like a present, he looked satisfied—happier, in fact, than he had in months. I was surprised that I could please him with something so simple: by performing wellness in the language of the rich. "You look very nice today," he said, kissing me on the neck. "How was your day to yourself? Did Atena call?" As though our argument had never happened.

"We went to San-Berno, a little place where nobody bothered us."

"Was it nice to have some time away?"

"It was," I conceded. "Does that make me a bad mother?"

Finn loved when I asked questions like that—to imply that I'd made a mistake, so that he could assure me I was forgiven. He always forgave me, no matter what, as he himself was forgiven. His whole world was about the trespass, living in the dark of the shame and the joy of its absolution. "You're a wonderful mother," he said lovingly, truthfully. "The boat was a misunderstanding. It's been very stressful. Maybe we should take a break from IVF." Finn was really glowing. He was so pleased.

"I'd like that." I took a sip of my water and twisted my ring around my finger. These tiny allowances meant so much to me then; my body had been repossessed and along with it my mind. Someone knocked. Finn changed into a tuxedo, and then we were sweeping through the hallway like so many nights before. Except for one thing. During the cheese course, I threw up under the table.

29

MY SON WAS BORN on February 12, 2008. The second month, the twelfth day, the eighth year, or as I thought of it, two hours, twelve minutes, eight seconds, my record in the marathon. I thought someone might break it that day, but it held, and Henry was born with all the luck and fortune in the world. He simply *was* a Henry, I told Finn. Naturally Amelie decided his name wasn't sufficient, either. Henry was christened Henri-Louis, after Finn's middle name and his father's uncle.

Henry began life as a very difficult baby. At six weeks old he started a period of colic that still makes me shudder. It was a nightmare. He would scream for forty-five minutes, I would feed him, he would sleep for two hours maximum, and then he would wake and begin screaming again. Blubbering, sobbing, weeping, howling. Crying is a social act; meant to be heard, and responded to. It changes meaning if it goes unanswered. It becomes a weapon. Yet babies have no other way to express themselves. I felt so sorry for Henry, even as I lay beside him, stretched to my wit's end.

Once again, Finn moved to another bedroom so he could get a full night's sleep—but to avoid Henry's screams he went to the one all the way in his gray apartment. This time he did not come back every morning to see us; his presence only made Henry scream harder. Exasperated, my husband stayed in his office at all hours, leaving me alone with Henry's maddening wails.

Henry's screams boiled my insides until they turned to gas, expanded beneath my skin. I would choke on it, that white steam, lose my breath until my vision went blank, my brain firing so many neurons that I no longer had the capacity for eyesight, and I had to clutch the nearest wall so that I didn't fall over. It was unbearable. I wore out around the edges. I was never awake—never asleep—never here—never anywhere else.

Yet no one else could soothe him. I wore earplugs and sound-dampening earmuffs and kept his bassinet within arm's reach of the bed. Sometimes, when it seemed like he would never be well, I raised a hand to my little bald patches and used the acrylic pincers of my fingernails to pluck the regrowth.

I continued to sign paperwork. In my stained nightie and construction worker's ear protection, running on an average of three hours' sleep, I signed 463 documents in 3 months. Usually Roland appeared in the early afternoon with a stack of clipboards. That's when I was at my most dreamlike—one hand on the bassinet or pressing my temple, I signed each sheet, initialed each sticky tab, from bed. I didn't read them. I was too tired.

❖   ❖   ❖

I tried a variety of movement-based remedies: I had an ensign drive us around in all the rumbly vintage cars. I took Henry to the stables and let the horses tickle him with their velvet noses, bathe him in their warm, grassy breath. I tried eight different prams, rolling them along the black-and-white hallways, but Henry screamed all the while. Eventually it became clear that he could remain calm in my arms—*if I was moving*. After that I dragged myself in laps around the castle, beams of moonlight showing the way.

We took our paces, night after night. I often found myself haunting

Finn's gray apartment, arguing with myself over whether or not to wake him and ask for help. Sometimes I made it into the office and paced around his desk with Henry in my arms, hoping that the sounds would ricochet across the apartment, that his cries would break through the velvet curtains lining Finn's walls, that my husband would understand that even if he couldn't help our baby, he could help me.

It was one of those nights that, paused in Finn's desk chair to nurse, I noticed a pair of birthday cards on his desk with a sticky note reading *Si prega di firmare prontamente e li invierò*, a sentence I knew by heart as it dotted my own desk constantly: "Please sign promptly and I will send them." One envelope was addressed to Honor, the other to Edouard. Honor's had a Degas dancer on it. Edouard's was childish, a goggle-eyed monster. Neither had yet been signed.

Assuming they were for the children of staff, I signed them on our behalf. *Happy birthday, love from Finn and Caro,* I wrote, sealing the envelopes and crossing out Roland's text on the sticky note, the usual indication that the task was complete. As I capped the pen, disturbing Henry, he started up again. I rose to my feet and bounced him up and down, murmuring comfort in his ear, walking the Talon until at last we managed to catch some sleep on a sofa in the stable. Henry had wanted to nurse, and so I pulled a wool pony blanket over us and we drifted off. In the morning, awoken by the movements of an apologetic groom, we made our way back to the apartment through the Talon's morning bustle of vacuums and feather dusters. I handed Henry to Marie so I could take a shower. By the time I was cleaned up, his wriggling body was placed back in my arms. I stuck my earplugs back in and the cycle continued.

❖ ❖ ❖

Somewhere in the midst of this black hole, I received news of my long-awaited budget. I would be given, at last, fifteen million euro to disburse each year from then on.

I picked up the phone to call Zola for advice—and put it down. Aside from polite exchanges of handwritten cards on Christmas and birthdays, we no longer had any semblance of a friendship. I was mortified even thinking about it. *Zola, help me give money away, I don't know how!* Her Christmas card last year was a photo of her standing next to the firm's new sign, *Clarence Cast Mbatha*; she'd become a named partner. All elegance, now, in a matte burgundy suit, with a stunner string of pearls, her hair cut very short.

I pictured Zola being driven by a chauffeur she paid from the house she owned to the polished office that she'd helped build, commanding respect already earned by a lifetime of hard work and dignity. She was always a better runner than me; she paced better, knew herself better. I wondered what she thought of me, or if she ever thought of me for longer than the moment she signed my holiday card. I wondered what it was like to own your life, to be in control of it.

I dialed Atena instead, who knew exactly what to do.

◆ ◆ ◆

I left Henry with Marie, arriving at the Gloria Apartment at the appointed time to discover a conference table had been installed. It was laid with stacks of binders and proposals from every major charity in the world. The ladies, armed with silver pots of coffee and fountain pens, sat waiting.

They argued passionately on behalf of one dispossessed group or another: refugees, the homeless, victims of human trafficking, the illiterate, the sick, the poor. Then they argued again about what each meant for Lucomo. What issue would pull at the heartstrings but still be relatively blameless? None of Lucomo's populace should be made to feel targeted or responsible in any way; political neutrality, really, was the most important thing. Disabilities were a natural fit, meaning the Special Olympics were still in, as was the EU's handicap accessibility working group, which, while not technically a charity, would have my participation funded from this budget. Cancer, and other noncommunicable diseases, were acceptable. Homelessness and refugees were high need, but as so many of Lucomo's residents prided themselves on having built their wealth, it seemed, the ladies agreed, like an impossible cause.

It was decided that deeper vetting of our choices and early outreach would be conducted by Schätze's staff over the next month or two—work for accountants and lawyers, I was told. Once approved, I would be included in the final round of confirmations. I'd get to meet in person with the charities and have my say about the best way to give my time and money over to their causes.

A calendar was sketched out. The money had already been partitioned: ten million for donations, four million for expenses. We would meet with the final charities by June 1 and aim to hold our first event by July 15. As we were about to wrap up, I noticed something was missing. "There should be one more," I said, searching the pages in front of me. "Million, I mean."

Schätze set her hand on my folder. "That's reserved for expenses specifically related to your attendance—security, hair, makeup, clothing, and transportation, that sort of thing," she said through a tight smile. "I believe that's everything." The ladies sighed with relief. Unconvinced, I motioned for Schätze to follow me into the hallway.

"Is that correct?" I asked. "It's not fair to make *this* budget responsible for my hair care and security when the Talon is already responsible for those costs."

"Caroline, it's always been partitioned," Schätze said patiently. "The Talon, and the family, while intertwined, do have quite a bit of separation with regard to accounts. Diplomatic functions are supported by one budget; business development, like attending a cocktail party, another. *Some* of your social engagements are paid for by the Talon. *Others* are maintained by your personal assets. It depends entirely on the day."

There was always another reason, another secret for me to trip over. "I didn't realize."

"It's not your job," she replied. "Don't be embarrassed. We've made a lot of progress, you and I."

"I'm not," I tried. "I'm *disappointed*. It feels like a hidden fee."

"If you'd rather mail checks, I suppose that can be arranged. However—the strategy, as it stands, of using your appearance to encourage matching donations is . . . extremely effective. I think you'll find at the end of the next fiscal year that the extra million is what helps you draw another fifteen, even twenty million, from other sources."

From the sitting room came the rattling sounds of cups landing in their saucers. The scrape of chairs being pushed back, everyone readying themselves to leave. "I'd like to discuss this further," I pushed.

Schätze extended one heavy hand to my shoulder. I think it was meant to be comforting, but it felt like I was being held still by the playground bully. "I don't want to . . . wear your shoes," she said hesitantly, testing out the idiom. "I don't want to eat steamed chicken or wear the makeup, you know. So I hope you can believe that I am always doing my best to make this work, but *my role* does have its own difficulties. Please don't complicate it. We'll meet again in six weeks."

As the exultant ladies-in-waiting streamed into the hall, heels clacking against the stone, heads held high, so proud of what we'd accomplished, I felt . . . nothing. I'd looked forward to this for so long—yet now it seemed another hallway through which I was meant to sweep, another set of gilded rooms in which my only use was to stand like a statue. Nobody needed me to think. Only to glow. Crestfallen, I picked Henry up from the nursery, Jane from the playroom, and spent the evening pacing him around the apartment, begging him to stop crying.

30

ONE DAY IT FINALLY STOPPED, and in my screaming baby's place lay a perfect angel. He had his father's and grandmother's topaz eyes, and round cheeks beneath a heavy Gallic brow. He smelled of sunshine, and his laugh was so irresistible that I forgot he'd ever cried.

I retreated for the weekend with my children to the country house, bringing only Marie to help cook and clean. Jane was frequently frustrating in the way that small children are, but her little storms calmed as quickly as they arrived. We took long walks in the forest and spent hours in the garden, and I felt myself healing with Henry's every gurgle. Spring was arriving; I would bloom anew along with it.

When Monday came I wasn't ready to return. I called Schätze and informed her that I was taking the next month off. "He's been crying for so long," I told her before she could argue. "I need peace or I'm going to fall apart."

Schätze, to my surprise, agreed. "I suppose that's fine. We don't *really* need you."

After we hung up, stung by her plain acceptance of my uselessness, I resolved to return better educated. The lineup of charities was full of interesting problems: food poverty, medical care, the Special Olympics, and of course, handicap accessibility; I was as capable as anyone of learning more on those subjects. I enlisted Marie's help in ordering dozens of books, memoirs by former employees and nonfiction books about the various subject areas, and they were delivered a few days later.

Finn joined us for one perfect evening. He called from the road, telling me to send Marie home. An hour later he marched up the driveway. I waited in the doorway, Henry on my hip, stains on my clothing, and twenty-month-old Jane peeking through my legs. "Papa!" she squealed, charging toward him at full speed. She tripped, but he caught her before she hit the ground, rescuing her from a skinned knee. Jane wrapped her tiny arms around his neck and started to talk. "Papa, *fort*," she said.

"*Sei molto forte.* You're very strong."

"No." She frowned, shaking her head. "Fort!!"

Fort, I articulated, tracing the symbol for a house in the air.

"Yes," Jane said grandly. "*Big* fort." *Adjectives?* Finn mouthed. I nodded proudly. "*Big* Papa," she noticed, saddened instantly. "Too big?"

"Papa can share my room," I told her.

We tumbled inside. Jane dragged Finn into the parlor. Its grand sofas had been pushed into a square, facing each other, pillows lining the floor. Sheet corners were tied to various lamps and chairs. The dining table was covered in crayons, and a frosted cake with child-hand-sized holes gouged out of the side. Through the windows, laundry billowed on the line, drying in the sun.

"You're an architect," he exclaimed, rubbing his nose against Jane's.

"*Sì*," Jane agreed. "Henry only poos."

"That's Henry's job," Finn told her seriously. "It's your job, too."

Finn rolled up his sleeves and washed the eight thousand dishes that had accumulated throughout the afternoon. We bathed the children, put them in clean pajamas, read a bedtime story. In front of the fire, in our sofa fort, the world was reduced to the four of us at last. "Caro," Finn whispered over our children's sleeping heads. *Yes?* "Thank you for everything." With that simple act of appreciation, I felt the last of Henry's cries vanish from my body.

"I needed that," I acknowledged. "I needed you to say that."

Finn had to leave in the morning but returned the next several weekends, lazing in bed with me and the children, mornings of black coffee and milk. Things were so good that I remember feeling frightened they might end, remember thinking that I'd do anything to love so deeply, to feel so loved and safe. I spent the weekdays snatching time during the children's naps to read the books we'd ordered, working hard to understand each organization that my initiative might fund. At the end of the fourth weekend, Finn convinced us to follow him back to the Talon.

❖ ❖ ❖

Home in our apartment, suitcases had been stacked on the upholstered bench in my dressing room. The bags were heavy, already packed. An outfit hung from the mirror: a blue-and-white-striped swimsuit, white jeans, a white sweater, white-soled shoes, and a straw Panama hat. *Boat clothes.*

"Finn?" I called out. "What's all this?"

"We're going out with some investors," he said apologetically. "We were having such a nice time, I forgot to bring it up."

I let his avoidance slide. "All right. We'll *keep* having a nice time," I said, lifting my dress over my head and squeezing into the jeans, slowly. Everything was still a *little* too tight.

"You're a vision," he said, curbing my self-consciousness.

"Are the kids packed?"

"It's not a child-friendly boat."

"Oh." I paused, frozen. Henry was only five months old. I'd never been away from him before. "You didn't forget," I admonished Finn. "You *avoided* it."

"Caro, it's got to happen sometime," he entreated. "It'll be fun. We'll go snorkeling and get sunburned."

"Who's going to—"

"Amelie, but also Marie and Lola," he said, wrapping his arms around me. "Come on. I thought we'd moved past this." I laid my face against the heat of his shoulder and felt the panic rise up—my children being taken from me—and then further panic still—of what another fight would do to the togetherness we'd had over the last month. It would shatter it.

"Whose boat is it?" I asked, searching for sunscreen. "*Lola—*"

"A friend of my cousin Roger."

"Roger who? Lola, is there sunscreen in here?"

Lola called back, "*Sì, signora.*"

"Roger is one of my Brevard cousins," he said cautiously. "No? Okay. You've met him. He's a bit of a glutton, he has a mole on his nose—"

"Shit," I said, disappointed, then slapped my hand over my mouth.

Finn laughed. "Oh my stars, *profanity.*" He grinned.

"The man who brought a prostitute to Henry's christening? Isn't he married?"

"The very same." He let out an apologetic groan. "Marta. She always looks ever so slightly ashamed. Probably don't mention the christening. They weren't *actually* invited."

"Noted. Anyone else?"

"The boat belongs to a relatively important shipping magnate, Alexei Coursalis. His wife's called Dasha. Francis and Aurora will be there, too, I think, and some other friends of Roger's."

"The things I do for you."

Our peace maintained, Finn held my hand all the way down to the harbor.

◆ ◆ ◆

Coursalis's 325-foot superyacht made our scant 75-footer look like the maritime equivalent of a battered Honda Civic. Eight floors, fifteen staterooms, crew cabins for twenty, two ballrooms, an aft swimming pool, and a helipad on the promenade deck. It was both excessively white—every surface, the ceilings, the floors—and excessively outfitted with animal products. Dead sharks were immortalized against the walls; white jaguar skins were the rugs in our stateroom. Ivory everything, even the light switches.

Roger Brevard—part man, part mole—greeted us by kissing me wetly on the cheek, almost at my mouth, his hand on my waist. I recoiled and stood behind Finn like he was Otto. Roger then led us to the aft deck, where a crowd was gathered around a large bar. His wife, Marta, a slight woman with huge brown eyes, drooped wretchedly as I pried the meat of Roger's groping hand off my waist for the second time. "Nice to see you again, Marta," I told her.

"I'm sorry about Roger," she replied. "Honestly." Then she excused herself.

The crowd of thirty—fifteen couples in all, strangers to me except for Aurora and her husband, Francis—parted, opening a seam through which the boat's startlingly porcine owner, Alexei Coursalis, emerged. I disliked him immediately. Coursalis's hairline looked drawn on, thanks to the thick stems of a recent transplant, and although he was deeply tanned and clad in high-end sport clothes, nothing could hide the paunch that flowed over his belt like a bag of wet pudding. He hugged Finn as though they were old friends. Before I knew what was happening, Coursalis's damp hand was raising my fingers to his dried-out lips.

"The most beautiful woman in the world," he panted, supposedly a compliment, but there was a sly violence in it. I repossessed my hand and ran the back of it carefully down my trousers. "*Your Highness*," Coursalis appended, bowing. It was slightly incorrect, and slightly mocking. I could tell from his leer that he didn't enjoy speaking to women who forced him to consider whether or not we were more than objects. I glanced at Finn again but he was waving to someone and deliberately avoiding me.

"*Signora* is fine," I corrected Coursalis, while Finn turned back and said, "Caro." I smiled and tried not to let my irritation show. "Caroline," I compromised.

"Caro! Darling Caro. Caro, this is *my* wife, Dasha, and my daughter, Sonia," he said, the emphasis on *my* pointing out again that first and foremost I belonged to Finn.

Two fox-faced blondes of indeterminate age, swells of injectable filler caulking the welds between a constellation of recently installed body parts, made little smacking sounds in the general direction of my cheek. Alexei herded Finn over to a knot of chest-puffing men, all similarly attired in high-performance sportswear. I was left to the attentions of Dasha and Sonia, who paced around me in catlike little circles, flicking their tails, excited by my presence. We discussed the prices of real estate in London—they couldn't believe how expensive it was becoming to live in a boring neighborhood like Belgravia, but they're not making any more land, of course—and how thrilled they were that they would soon be living in their new apartment in Finn's development in Lo Scopo, an upgrade from the building in Le Chappe they legally called home. Dasha spoke excellent English, with a strong Balkan flavor. Sonia, on the other hand, had an overpronounced upper-class British accent, the vowels tucked back and abused. *Hice* instead of *house, yiiis* to every question. Dasha made a series of stereotypically gender-specific inquiries about my life: Where was I planning on sending my children to school, was I going to this year's Alta Moda, who made my dress? Over their shoulders I watched Alexei Coursalis lead my husband around the room like a prizewinning horse. I didn't understand why we were there; the man was coarse, like the hard globes of his wife's breast implants, and completely insincere, like his daughter's put-on boarding-school accent. The other guests were of the same vulgar caliber. Only dainty Aurora, with her unaltered face and body, looked even remotely human. She waved gaily from the other side of the room. I waved back, relieved to see her.

By the time we were shown to our stateroom, our bags were already unpacked, the contents in the closet. Next to Finn's navy blazers and cashmere sweaters hung a collection of filmy dresses I'd never seen before. I puzzled over an open-back midi so sheer it was practically lingerie. "Schätze would *never* approve."

"She's not heeeere," Finn said playfully, coming up behind me, kissing my neck. "Try it on, Caro. Try. I promise, I'll take it right off."

◆ ◆ ◆

We emerged for dinner flushed and rosy. After a spirited negotiation— *It's too much! No, it's exactly right*—I wore a cocktail slip of mushroom silk. Finn knotted a rope of diamonds round my neck—sparkling stars, heavy as ice cubes—that he said was a gift he'd been waiting to give me since Henry was born.

At the table, Finn and I sat pressed together—thighs knees fingertips—while the guests prattled on, occasionally squawking in an attempt to draw our notice. I could tell they were disappointed that we didn't mingle, but I didn't care. I spent all my days floating on the river of other people's attention. It was easy to take it for granted. That night, I was in love with my husband, the summer air was warm across our skin, and the whole world seemed as if it would belong to us forever.

After dinner a band struck up. The floor of the swimming pool was raised, the water draining away at the sides. Lackeys polished it dry with linen dishcloths, turning it into a dance floor. We held each other close, barely dancing. Three songs later Finn was pulled away into a conversation. I took a seat at the bar, floating in the afterglow and gazing out happily into the velvet night. But I was soon disturbed.

"Caro," Alexei Coursalis said, creeping up behind me, a man-shaped smirk, "you are sitting on the largest penis in the world."

After a stunned moment I collected myself. "I don't believe metaphor qualifies."

"The seats, Caro. They are upholstered in whale foreskin."

I bit the inside of my cheek; nevertheless a sneer fluttered uncontrollably over my face. "I pity the rabbi," I said dryly.

Alexei chuckled. "You are very quick, Caro."

"I'm the fastest woman on earth." My well-worn, forever comeback.

"I don't believe so, madame." He pulled out his BlackBerry and opened a news report from a week earlier. "Mary Chepkemi of Kenya has lately set a new record."

I glanced at the screen. Chepkemi had an IAAF trial in 2:12:03, beating my record by five seconds.

At the sight of that number a great elevator in my chest plummeted to the ground. I blinked. Alexei sniggered, greedy eyes wet with glee. *He was delighted to have been the one to tell me*, I realized. *He was over-joyed to knock me down a peg.*

"How nice," I managed, rising from the penis stool. I waved to the bartender. "Bring the best champagne you have, please, gobs of it," I ordered. The bartender's eyes went to Alexei, who nodded. I ground my teeth in frustration but managed a wide smile. "Everyone," I called out, tapping a glass with a knife. "Everyone!"

The crowd turned to listen. Finn was between two of the men, that same look on his face from the masquerade ball so long ago—the ugly look—the one that made him like them.

"Mr. Coursalis has informed me that Mary Chepkemi of Kenya has broken my record, over a whole week ago, which means I've let a whole week go by without congratulating her. Please help me raise a toast to her accomplishment. Does someone have a video camera?"

One of the staff produced a small digital camcorder. I took two glasses over to Finn, dragged him to the bow of the ship, and rotated so that the twinkling lights of the Lucomo shore were behind us. The cameraman gave a thumbs-up.

"Hello, Mary," I said to the camera, Finn at my side. "I've recently had another baby, who has kept me so busy that I didn't know until this very second you'd broken the record. I am so incredibly happy for you, my sister from Kenya," I said, brushing away the tears that fell down my cheeks, "and now this achievement is yours to hold. You've advanced the sport for everyone. You are welcome in Lucomo. I'll keep you in my heart, forever," I said to her, meaning it. "Congratulations to you, Mary Chepkemi. God bless you and keep you safe." Finn and I raised our glasses, the moon winking in the background. The ship's guests, invisible to the camera's lens, yelled *Cheers* along with us. Coursalis's voice was the loudest.

◆ ◆ ◆

I didn't speak to my husband then, even though he whispered *I'm sorry* into my hair. I didn't speak to him when he put his hand on my thigh how I like it. I didn't speak to him as we walked back to our stateroom, and I certainly didn't speak to him as I brushed my teeth and he knelt on the floor and apologized. When we crawled into bed, I looked at the rugged trunk of his neck and imagined snapping it.

It was the only thing I had, that record; the only thing in the world that belonged to me and me alone. The only thing that couldn't be moved or changed or altered; the last part of me that hadn't been re-made by my husband. And now, it was gone. There was nothing to separate me from the other women on this boat. I, too, was simply property. I lay there drowning, a tide of grief coming in and out over the undertow of my ever-increasing ego. All the vicious thoughts I'd had earlier about Dasha and Sonia were turned back upon myself. "I want to talk," I said at last, sometime near dawn.

Finn opened his eyes. "Okay."

"You didn't tell me." I spoke quietly. "You let that . . . *man* . . . tell me."

"I didn't know how. I was hoping you'd . . . hear about it."

"You could have left a newspaper on the table or something."

"You're right," he agreed. "I could have. I'm . . . I don't know what to say, Caro. I've been busy. I'm overworked. It was upsetting and so I avoided it."

"You always, *always* do this," I said. "You never want to confront anything. Tomorrow and tomorrow and tomorrow with you. This *domani* lifestyle. Everything is your responsibility, so *nothing* is."

"You knew this would happen. You *knew* it would," he pleaded. "I'm sorry that I didn't—that I *don't* know how to handle it. There is no handbook in a marriage for how to tell your spouse that the most important part of their identity no longer belongs to them."

"All you had to do was tell me in private, where I could react to it by myself."

"I know that. I'm sorry. I screwed up. I'm really and truly sorry."

"I want to get off this boat. If you're sorry you'll get a helicopter here right now."

"We can't. Okay? We can't. These people have a lot of money in Lucomo and we agreed to be here." Finn shook me off and got out of bed. "I'm going to go work out."

He left me alone in that room full of dead animal parts to cry by myself.

◆　◆　◆

The next two days were spent smiling publicly and fighting privately. I believed our mutual trust was consistently and almost irrevocably damaged by Finn's unbreakable habit of conflict avoidance. He believed I was finally processing the end of my athletic career and shifting the blame to him. I insisted that he didn't have to allow a stranger to deliver the most heartbreaking news of my life in an objectifying power play. He said it was an accident and I would have to find a way to forgive him. *I DO EVERYTHING FOR YOU,* I said over and over. *I LIVE MY WHOLE LIFE FOR YOU.* He responded, *I do everything for you and everyone else. I take care of this whole country. My life is bigger than our family. You know that. You've known that from the beginning.* Round and round we went, never finding a resolution, neither party ever satisfied.

◆　◆　◆

On the final evening, I sat alone after dinner as the band played. Aurora fluttered to my side, then folded herself up into a ball. "I think these weekends will be fun, until they happen," she whispered. "Then I spend the whole time thinking about swimming for shore."

"I don't know why we had to come."

"I suppose if none of the wives came it would just be another meeting."

"I miss Henry and Jane," I said without thinking. Aurora tried to compose a reassuring smile, but it came out half-baked and gloomy. "I'm sorry." I tapped the bench. "I know you've been trying."

"We *did* try," she said, anchored by the past tense. "It turned out that he's sterile."

"What?" Her husband was the one with those extracurricular children. "Are you sure?"

Taken aback by my directness, Aurora stiffened. "He had mumps as a boy."

"He's been sterile his entire adult life?" I knew it was rude to press, but I couldn't help myself.

"Yes," she said firmly, batting away my curiosity.

"That's . . . that's very surprising."

Aurora's dainty fingers dug into the padded edge of the banquette, eyes turning hard in their innocent sockets. "It was to me, but why is it surprising to *you*?" Her tone—sharp as a razor—startled me into self-awareness.

I backed off. "Forgive me. I'm so rude." I ran my hands through my hair, catching a flaxen knot and untangling it. "I've not been sleeping well. Everyone stays up so late."

Aurora relaxed her grip and put her arms round her knees. "Me either. If I have to hear Sonia Coursalis say *dear old London* in that phony voice one more time I'm going to toss her overboard."

"Do you mind if we sit here and don't talk?" I asked.

"Love to."

We sat in pleasant silence for an hour, letting the wind play with our hair, the party wending and weaving without us. I replayed the night at the casino in my head. *If Marcella and Atena weren't talking about Aurora, then . . .*

I watched Finn work the room, mostly speaking to men but occasionally holding polite conversations with women. He didn't glance at their bodies or behave inappropriately; he never had. He'd always been the politest man alive. Whomever Marcella and Atena had been gossiping about, it wasn't Finn. They hadn't wanted to tell me who it was, so they'd lied. That was all right, wasn't it? They didn't owe me other people's secrets. They didn't owe me everything.

I told myself to let it go.

31

WE RETURNED HOME. I curled up in bed with Henry and Jane. Finn stayed out until dawn, somewhere, with Coursalis and Brevard. When I asked in the morning where he'd been, Finn said that he was taking care of our family, and that he didn't want to fight about it. "I don't want to fight, either," I insisted.

"Let's leave it, Caroline. Leave it until you forgive me."

"I don't know how long that will take."

"Then it's a good thing we're married, isn't it?" With a wan smile, he retreated to his office. It was an offer of time—and a reminder of the boundary. There was no world outside of our marriage.

We weren't broken, not exactly, but after that, we took our space. He slept in the gray apartment most nights. It was the start of a pattern, or perhaps the start of my realizing the pattern in which I couldn't make a dent. If I challenged my husband, if I openly pointed out something he'd done wrong, a heartfelt apology would be followed by distance— punishment, for asking him to change.

❖　❖　❖

The kickoff meeting for my initiative happened shortly thereafter with a nonprofit that sent physicians to war zones. I stayed up late the night before, sorting my notes and writing the relevant pieces of information on a stack of cards. I wanted to show that I had some familiarity with the world of emergency medicine, enough for the organization's dashing doctors to hold a conversation of substance with me.

Yet the Gloria Apartment's conference room contained no rugged physicians on break from the Gaza Strip—only some very professional-looking lawyer types. Zolas, but softer. They introduced themselves as the director and associate director of development. *The fundraising staff.* "Let me know when the physicians arrive," I said, turning for the door.

There was an uncomfortable pause. "That's . . . it's us for now," the director said. "We don't typically relocate our medical staff for meetings at this stage."

"No?"

"We don't have the funding for something like that. We're stretched pretty thin."

I was mortified. Of course. *Of course they wouldn't fly a trauma surgeon working in a war zone to meet with a bored princess.*

"That's a different meeting," Atena said, covering generously. "We've overscheduled her." The other ladies chuckled congenially as I took my seat. *Ha ha.*

The director launched into her pitch. "For the July fifteenth event, as everyone has confirmed—yes, yes?" Eight heads bobbled in agreement. "We're planning a deconstructed opera. It'll be exquisite," she declared, fingertips held together like she was holding a precious jewel. "A few short pieces, a speech from a member of the medical staff, followed by an auction, anything you're able to resource. Tours, spa weekends, we've discussed that, and maybe dinner at *someone's* house . . ." Her voice sloped up. Atena tilted her chin gracefully, a martyr for the cause. "Wonderful, Ms. Ricci, thank you. Maybe, and I'm thinking on my feet here, if we hit a certain number during the auction, then we 'open up' a tier with you, Your Serene Highness, something social? Tea, perhaps, or a tour of Cap-Griffe. Do you see where I'm going with this? Does this make sense?"

Yes. It made sense. I smiled dully. The director trumpeted on, her voice a melody, while I became the smallest I'd ever been. I watched it play out, knowing I was nodding when I ought to, smiling when I ought to, while the rest of me shrank away. Beneath my skin, a membrane grew, thickening until it touched my organs. I squeezed myself behind it. Soon I lived inside a hard shell that could not be breached.

After everyone left, I dumped my notes in a drawer. What was the point?

I spent the next month planning parties.

◆   ◆   ◆

The parties of July and August 2008 were extraordinary. A thousand swimmers sprang from beach chairs and crowded the bay, diving under and resurfacing for a synchronized routine that could be seen for miles. Acrobats climbed the buildings in Le Chappe, turning the skyscrapers into their personal circus. I gambled at the casino for spina bifida, cheered on Vida at a polo match for endangered waterfowl, shook thousands of hands and posed for ten times as many photos. I took tea fifty times with as many strangers, sitting stiffly in the court-yard, Jane and Henry garbed in starchy frills.

All throughout, I woke up at dawn and did sit-ups, push-ups, glute med lifts. I pumped my arms in tiny circles, sandbags weighing down my wrists, dipped my rear to an inch above the floor in one-legged pliés at the barre. Longing for explosive motion, I lured one of the Gardiens into a pull-up contest. I won. After that they didn't let me do pull-ups anymore. The point was not to make me strong. The point was to burn away all the fat and shape my muscles, so they looked good under clothes.

Once again, my body became a vessel for my willpower: the will to stand and smile. Once again, my body put other people to shame, except this time it was other women. Every woman who took tea with me glanced from my calves to her own, at my carved, but not enlarged, biceps, with envy. I pretended it wasn't happening. I hid behind the shell of myself while Princesse Caroline smiled. I started to die inside.

I wasn't the only one having trouble, though I didn't notice Jane's unhappiness until it reached a fever pitch. At the opening of a hotel tearoom, the photographers assembled—and then Jane removed her clothes. At the sound of the clicking shutters, she yelled, the same noises over and again. We went home immediately. When again, the following day, Jane undressed and began shouting, a top child psychologist was brought in to examine her. Echolalia, he called it. "It's perfectly normal," he told me. "It's possible she feels that cameras take your attention away from her. Perhaps you ought to take a break."

"Of course she feels that way. It's true. You must tell my husband," I insisted. "Tell him."

But this advice was swept under the rug. Finn derided the yelling as "the yips" (*all Lugesque children are expressive, she's merely nervous*) and Amelie insisted that the best course of action was to bribe her. The policy became that Jane would be given a new toy or some sweets each time a camera appeared. To my absolute disgust, it worked. After two weeks of this, Jane relished the attention of cameras. She knew her angles better than I did. She screamed when she didn't get her way, but instead of teaching her to self-soothe, the palace rewarded her. Her first word had been *maman,* her first sentence *When is Papa home?,* and now she mostly said *I want,* the words laced with a condescending Veruca Salt cadence—*I want it now.* I began to wince at the sound of my own daughter's voice.

We clashed wickedly over this. Finn's position was that public life was indeed intrusive. He himself had been spoiled into accepting it, and he'd turned out fine. I argued that he would make Jane into an egomaniac. He replied that leadership required what I called egomania and he called confidence. And so on and so forth—but his word was always the final word. He was my home, the father to my children, the son of this country; I didn't stand a chance. I was an adjunct to power. I was not its source. I was merely its reproductive resource.

The past five years had utterly distilled us. Finn was the same person that he'd been when we met and when we married. But I'd grown six people, one after the other; I divided and subdivided into pieces, as his understanding of me, his empathy for my experiences, subdivided, too. I felt often that it came down to one problem: Finn remained an individual while I became a group. He no longer understood me, and in turn, I resented his independence.

32

THE EVENING OF Sunday, September 14, 2008, the Grand Quartz
was appropriated for the closing event of a weekend summit entitled
the Human Scale Conference. Modeled on the World Economic Forum
held annually in Davos, Switzerland, the HSC agenda was a mix of
speeches and presentations from political and corporate leadership
about the state of manufacturing across the globe. The costs for the
closing party were underwritten by PRAIF, the People's Rights Accountability Initiative Foundation, a nongovernmental organization
that lobbied for the rights of orphaned children from developing countries. PRAIF was *also* the pet project of Dasha Coursalis, its funding
secured primarily from her husband's shipping empire.

The ballroom was dazzling: Candles burned atop invisible glass
shelves, the melting wax pooling flat above our heads. Five-hundred-
foot banquet tables were set with a thousand plates of filigreed silver.
An orchestra played at one end of the room, where cocktail stands were
already piled high with discarded coupe glasses. Massive arrangements
of wisteria and lilac filled the spaces between troops of stakeholders
and stockholders celebrating fresh allegiances.

It was the same as so many nights before. Hands waited to cross mine, cheeks burned with the anticipation of a kiss. An American banker whispered conspiratorially to a Lugesque banker. A minor British royal chortled indecently at Roger Brevard's mole, which by then was practically molesting its own waitresses. Attachés, liaisons, and other bureaucratically named spies leaned into each other in a minuet that curled and bobbed wherever my eyes happened to fall. I watched these people of power secreting their ideas upon one another, in a ballroom in which I was the designated jewel, and it seemed like life would never change.

Behind the dais, Alexei had been seated at Finn's left. How Coursalis had risen in our estimation—from acquaintance to cohost. Dasha, seated to my left with daughter Sonia, banged on about a winery.

"I brought several cases for you to sample," she was saying. "I'm sure you'll recognize the label. It's really very famous in South Africa."

"South Africa? The label?" It was easy to ignore most of what anyone said if you repeated their words back to them. I was the world's most flattering mirror.

"It has little stars all over it, yes?"

"Little stars," I agreed, though I had no idea what she was talking about.

"We've changed everything except the label. You will love it. There are waterfalls in each room. It is extraordinary there, you know. South Africa is also so very, *very*"—she giggled convivially—"cheap!"

"The rand is very favorable to the euro," I agreed carefully.

"Did you know, the workers value the wine so much they take it as their pay?" She tsked, astonished. "We would never work for so little in my country. But the Africans are so *happy*."

I cringed. "It's not that they value wine, it's that they're rarely given another choice."

"It's the custom."

"It's a shameful custom and it's illegal. If you own a winery, you must pay a wage."

Dasha didn't even blush. "It's *so* complicated, of course," she demurred. "You must come and see it. We will have such a nice time." Moments like this were where I felt the utmost powerlessness. People think that if you manage to get in the room with the people in charge— if you commandeer a seat at the table—they have to listen to you. That you won't be ignored. That may be true, if you earn your place. But not if you marry into it. "I'll ask Roland to plan something," Dasha said confidently. She did not believe I had any power at all, not even to decline an invitation.

"PRAIF is an interesting charity," I said, changing the subject. "How did you choose it?"

"I myself am adopted. My adoptive parents were older, with different . . . ways than perhaps you and I have of raising children. I could have been happier, somewhere else," she said. A flash of emotion appeared—not enough to shift the dedicated arrangement of her facial muscles, though a tear glossed the corner of one Prussian-blue eye. "That is why I made PRAIF. To lobby on behalf of the voiceless."

I felt a twinge of pity. "That's very bold of you." Her head was lolling a bit on the twig of her neck; she was past buzzed, closing in on drunk. I pressed further. "What's the operating cost? I'm very curious—my initiative has only made donations so far, but I'd love to start something of my own."

"Ohh," Dasha said, hemming, bobbing into her wineglass. "It's difficult, you know, to compare, because every business is so different. Our service is legislative"—she tapped one finger against the surface of our table—"which is *very* expensive." She widened her mouth and twitched her eyes playfully, like it was a joke, then turned to her daughter and pinched her. "Sonia, you must listen. Sonia is *very* interested in charity."

Sonia wiped away her boredom with an instantaneous fake smile. "Oh yes," she said through her mouthful of marbles. "Horses. There are so very many wild horses who never receive medical care." Sonia's ongoing imitation of the world's dumbest people was not merely vocal; it was ideological, right down to the bone.

Unable to respond politely, I stared out at the crowd. Hundreds of men, feeding at the glittering trough of the banquet tables, jaws crunching, silver knives scratching golden plates, cabernet sloshing from their mouths while their wives dabbed away the spills like mommies. Here and there sprouted a firm stalk of neck and pointed shoulders: a woman on her own, a woman there to work, stiff as a board as she tried not to drink her single glass of chardonnay too eagerly. Dasha, meanwhile, was snout-deep in her fourth.

"What will your foundation . . . do? Have they told you?" She asked this casually, looking unconsciously to Roland, folded into the nearby shadows. *Why did she keep looking to Roland like that?*

"Told me?" *Why persist in assuming I would be told what to do?*

"So much to avoid. Medical services and research"—she pointed to a small section of disheveled NGO workers—"that kind of *work*"—the word said like a euphemism—"has so much *disclosure*." She stuck out her tongue, *yech*. "Documentation." She raised a finger and her glass was filled a fifth time. The staff then removed her plate of food—completely untouched—and she was relieved by its departure. "Time for dessert. The chocolate, oh, I love this country's chocolate."

"Mother," Sonia chided, tapping the wine, "we're on a stage."

Dasha flushed. "Easy to forget one is on display."

Reflexively, I scanned the room, but very few people were looking at us; they seemed to be *clutching* each other. And several of them, extraordinarily, were on their BlackBerries. *Odd,* I thought. Odd because it was rude—but odder still because it was forbidden. I'd never seen anyone except my husband use a phone at one of these dinners.

At that moment, Finn squeezed my shoulder, beckoning me into the hallway. Automatically concerned for our children, I followed in mincing steps, hobbled by the gown's compressive embrace. "Triple the liquor," he was instructing the ensign in the hallway. "Cigars. Champagne."

"AreJaneandHenryokay?" I asked breathlessly.

"They're fine," Finn reassured me, one hand in a stop sign, though the color was gone from his face. "Follow me." He nearly *ran* to our apartment. I kicked off my shoes and wiggled behind him. By the time I caught up he was already jacketless, hunting for his BlackBerry charger. I noticed the slump of his shoulders; there was an emptiness about him lately, more silver in his hair. He'd lost weight.

"What's *wrong*?" I demanded.

"Some of our assets are . . . becoming unstable." Finn made a beeline for the closet and changed into a sweatshirt, a sign that he intended to sit in his office until dawn. "We have to reduce our exposure." I'd absorbed enough of his vocabulary by then to know he meant *sell off whatever he'd invested*.

"You mean you're going back to work." Even as we were personally at odds, when we were together in public, I felt like I had some small use; that I was working to support him as he in turn supported Lucomo. But without his body near to mine, I felt vulnerable and pointless, my use abstract. "You're going to leave me alone with those people."

"Some of *those people* are going to lose a great deal of money. We could lose ours." He didn't elaborate further. I found that lack of candor surprising; he normally loved to talk about money but tonight he was bloodless, the vigor let out.

"What makes you so special?" I sat on the bed—and my dress ripped up the thigh. Finn, startled by the noise, actually looked at me.

"What are you saying?" He glinted with wolfish curiosity.

"I mean . . . if you sell something that everyone knows isn't valuable, who would buy it?"

"Nobody knows, Caro," he said. "Not yet. That's the point. *You're* what makes me special. I need you to keep the party going. We have ninety minutes until the exchange in the States closes."

"What do you mean nobody knows? They were all on their phones."

"Their knowledge is limited. They know that one bank is tanking. The real problem is the American insurance company backing the assets. None of those people will figure that out until tomorrow, maybe even the next day. We've got half the world's corporate leadership sitting out there, Caro. Five trillion euro in collective market power. If you can distract them, we just might come out ahead."

"How on earth am I supposed to do that?" I wasn't being snide. I was genuinely looking for guidance.

"Keep them drinking. Offer a . . ." Finn swiveled, scanning for ideas. "Try a . . . charity match. *Yes . . .*" He drummed his fingers against the bedpost. "That'll work. They'll get mobbed by those NGO wretches. Match whatever. Get them drunk. I don't want any of those people to be smart tomorrow. I want them to be *useless.*" He rifled through my wardrobe until he found what he wanted. "Here."

He'd chosen a blood-red gown of cady silk, meant for the opera. I stepped into it, watching the fabric pool dramatically across the floor. Finn went to the racks of shoes and selected the Gloria mules. I slid them on. He pulled the pins from my hair and let it fall down my back. "Good," he said approvingly. "Go."

I returned to the ballroom, the dress waving behind me like a flag. As the double doors opened wide, trumpets sounded. The bankers, wives, and workers froze in place. The trumpets sounded a second time, and as I stepped forward, everyone was forced to look at the crimson princess in their midst. With a snap of my fingers, the ladies-in-waiting flanked me, three to a side, in their white gowns. We descended upon the party in a strategic line, touching backs and wrists, giving out free samples of our precious atmospheres as the waiters shoved triple-strength cocktails into open hands. *Won't you sit down. Won't you please enjoy the party. The* princesse *wishes to make an announcement. Please, put down your phone. Please take your seat.*

I made my way to the dais, where the abandoned Russians blinked nervously. To the shifting crowd, I spoke in a clear voice.

"We would like to extend the hand of Lucomo in gratitude for your generosity to PRAIF and all the other NGOs that have received promises from you during the HSC. I'm pleased to announce that we've decided to match any donations made tonight, *and only tonight,* from your companies to the assembled charities," I declared. The NGO workers became instantly sober; the businessmen looked pained. "Funds, space, resources, and time are acceptable. We will match in kind. You have until"—I looked at my bare arm sardonically—"let's say . . . four A.M."

The NGOs took flight, landing on the businessmen before they could move a single inch. As the room rearranged, I took my seat, smiling as though nothing were wrong. Coursalis leaned across Finn's throne. "I see Finn has left."

"His Serene Highness Ferdinand the Second is currently with our son," I said icily. "Someone wishes to speak with you." I made eye contact with the nearest wrinkled suit and beckoned her. "What's your name?"

"Gillian Peters," the woman answered. "UNICEF." She made an awkward bow.

"Gillian Peters of UNICEF, I'd like you to meet Alexei Coursalis. He's in shipping and he likes to give away money." Coursalis, annoyed, made the mistake of shaking her hand. As Gillian Peters launched into her pitch, I turned away.

"Dasha, that's your cue." I elbowed the crumpling woman at my side. "Get donations for PRAIF. I'll match it."

"Oh, that's not necessary," she mumbled. "I have the only donor I need."

"It's free money," I reiterated slowly.

"I don't have plans to spend it." She spoke thickly, through a rubber mouth. "And it's *not* worth what it takes to hide it." Dasha reached for her wineglass, missed it, and managed to knock over a bottle of mineral water. Her eyelids attempted to sag, though since they had two modes—open and shut—it had the effect of making her look like she was being electrocuted.

"She's not feeling well," Sonia interjected. "Mother," she seethed, grabbing Dasha by the wrist. Dasha teetered back and forth, like an inflatable puppet outside a petrol station.

I was not a complete idiot. I knew that wealthy people used all sorts of instruments to maintain their fortunes, and that charity was one of those many instruments. However, I assumed philanthropy was genuine, if selfish; a way of choosing one's own commitment to social service in lieu of allowing the government to choose for you. Not in this case. PRAIF was, I realized, a smoke screen built on a sympathetic truth, intended only to put Coursalis in proximity to power, to use other people's legitimacy—in this case, ours—to build his own.

But I didn't have time to babysit the Russians. The first round of cocktails had emptied quickly. Businessmen were trying to get out of conversations, checking their watches, their phones lighting up inside their pockets. I sprung up and worked the room with the ladies-in-waiting, connecting broken clusters of people to each other. Cakes and cookies appeared, chocolates and berries; more drinks; more sweets. Soon, the guests lost their inhibitions, lighting cigarettes and dousing them in the mush of their sugared plates.

I whispered to the orchestra and directed a troop of ensigns in their blinding livery to clear the dance floor. The cellos struck guitar chords; the trumpets sounded bass lines. I swirled a red streak across the ballroom, reaching out at the edges, drawing people in. The flautist took a microphone and set free her own voice, a guttural scream.

In sweaty gowns and pitted dress shirts, our little corner of oligarchy danced while the global economy's first precarious domino tipped, and then fell. And, exactly as Finn intended, our guests were so distracted that they couldn't do a single thing about it.

33

THE NEXT AFTERNOON I was in a store full of fuzzy bunnies and wooden blocks, buying trinkets for Jane. A crowd had formed outside, pushing against the glass, their shadows darkening the shop. I looked for Otto, but he'd joined them. The crowd wasn't peering through the store at me. They were watching television through the window of a café across the street.

"MARKETS COLLAPSE IN THE BIGGEST DROP SINCE THE GREAT DEPRESSION." Behind a worried-looking reporter was the logo of one of the world's largest investment banks. I cracked the door, careful not to ring the bell, and watched. Global markets were plummeting in panic while crude oil shot to 150 euro a barrel. The financial firms, whose executives filled our hotel rooms and paid the insane bills, who partied here and conferenced here and funded Finn's projects, were declaring bankruptcy by the dozen.

The assembled crowd were hotel maids and doormen and busboys and drivers, crossing the road as they changed shifts. I let out a small sigh—and inadvertently drew their focus. "*È la principessa!*" a little girl told her mother, tugging at her sleeve. The mother looked, the crowd followed—and then I was the center of attention, the television ignored. "What do you think about America, *signora*?" the girl's mother asked, fear in her voice.

"I am sure it will not affect us," I said, backing away. "There are many strong economies."

I was always a terrible liar.

They saw the discomfort on my face. It unnerved them, loosed them from their moorings. They flickered with confusion, a dawning, unfamiliar feeling of distrust.

I dipped my head and tried not to run into the waiting car.

◆ ◆ ◆

Traffic was impossible. The conference's hungover CEOs had already jetted away on company planes to face their boards, but in a response I could not have predicted, the midlevel executives decided that instead of fleeing for the airport, they would give in. Every bar was on fire. Women in stilettos exploded from doorways and fell out of Lamborghinis. Champagne corks popped like revolutionary gunfire. Credit cards were inserted again and again into the pockets of their guillotines. An army of Zegna-clad subordinates collectively opened their wallets and dumped the contents into our sewers, as if such a sacrifice would heal them, make them whole.

When we passed the inert body of an unconscious banker, the uneaten half of a sandwich staining his starched cuffs as it oozed from his open palm, I pulled the Maserati's window curtains shut and sealed myself off from the unsettling atmosphere of Le Chappe. Clutching Jane's new toys, remembering the shop owner's kind face, I wondered, once this fierce panic wore off, how many other people would buy three-hundred-euro bunny rabbits.

❖ ❖ ❖

Within a day the insurance company Finn relied upon was down-graded by the credit agencies. He remained in his office, Roland at his side, the ministers waiting. I fought my way past them, asking what was happening. Finn tried to wave me away—"Caro, not a good time"—before remembering to thank me for giving him a head start. "You spent your whole budget for next year," he commended me. "That was very generous."

"*Excuse me?*"

"It's ideal. It's many of the same charities you'd planned for, but the timing was perfect. You helped." He was pleased that I'd done my part.

If I'd known—that money was mine—I mean, I had plans for it—I had ideas—it was going to help me carve out my own space—I would never have given it away—certainly not to trick anyone. I stood there with my guppy mouth opening and closing, saying nothing at all, until the ministers descended like flies and I was pushed out.

❖ ❖ ❖

The beginning of the crisis felt like a gunshot, shocking but presumably recoverable, before it turned into a cancer. Economies are curious things. It is as if they function purely by agreement, as if the under-standing that money is available creates more money, and the fear that money is limited will dry it up. Lucomo was a great mechanical clock of money, wound every day by the influx of investors, our hands tick-ing forward to the future with each and every *yes*. Then, at last, an alarm bell rang, and we were pulled out of sync.

September is the last month in the third quarter of the fiscal year, and so the anxiety to balance the year's end against the loss was far more pressing than it would have been in, say, March. Luxury tourism, our primary economy, disappeared practically overnight: Within a week 75 percent of the year's remaining bookings were postponed, meetings suspended, vacations delayed, all of it ostensibly "to be rescheduled." The remainder of my initiative events for 2008 were quickly canceled.

It was, frankly, a relief. I felt so useless at those parties, forever sneaking one hand behind my head to yank out another strand of my thinning hair. When a stack of personal entreaties from the affected organizations appeared, requests for the promised donations, I sent checks. I suspected it would be the only proactive thing I would do until my budget was reissued in 2010.

I was right. My desk soon held stacks of declinations for political events, too. The chancellor of Germany politely explained that Lucomo was unfortunately, at this time, the very opposite of austerity, but that she looked forward to returning when things were better. The princess of Japan wrote to thank us for the chrysanthemums we'd sent on her birthday, along with her regrets. The queen of Sweden was unable to leave her country at this time of crisis; the First Lady of France hoped I was well and that we might see each other on a less fraught occasion. The sole acceptance was from the mouth breathers of Liechtenstein, for whom the chasm of this deepening recession was but a mere ripple.

In late October Vida and I went shopping in Le Chappe, Talon photographers in tow, but in the vacancy, all the tourists gone, it felt like we were performing at a closed-down theme park. I'd never noticed how few people actually lived there, day in and day out. It was a shell of a place.

Finn worked constantly, growing ever thinner and drawn. He missed Henry's first steps. I didn't say anything. I let him believe that the night he saw Henry rush headfirst toward the nearest doorway was the first time.

Christmas Eve was our fifth wedding anniversary. We spent the morning in church, under the blue Marys where we'd said our vows. I mentioned this to Finn once the service was over, some comment about how much time had passed, but he was on his BlackBerry already, speaking to someone who either equally disregarded their own family or did not celebrate the holiday. Finn didn't come to dinner—he didn't even sleep in the building that night. I don't know where he went, but it wasn't home with us, and in the morning, I didn't bother to ask.

34

THOUGH LUCOMO was crumbling around us, the beginning of 2009 is notable for being one of the very few periods in which I personally had nothing to do every day but go to the gym and play with our two small children. As such I remember it with great fondness, aside from the increasingly obvious fact that my husband no longer found me even remotely interesting.

Finn and I were briefly thrown together one afternoon for a photo shoot at the frozen seaside, an attempt by the Talon to reiterate Lucomo's image as a haven untouched by the troubles of the world. On a bright, sunny day at the end of February, the beach chairs were unwrapped, models were oiled up and planted into the icy waters, and Finn and I were told to walk through the surf holding hands.

I was costumed in an alarmingly sexy one-piece slit to the navel, the legs cut well above my hips. Finn was allowed to stay covered up, in a linen shirt and trousers, but he pulled me close, his fingers grazing the exposed rise of my hipbone before moving down my thigh. I melted, closed my eyes and lost myself in the current—

Then the photographer called out, "Got it." Finn stepped away so abruptly that I tripped and fell over. Dazed, I sat back on my heels. Finn was already walking away.

"Hey!" I cried, brushing the sand from my forearms. "Where are you going?"

Finn paused, looking back at me with a pained expression. "I don't have time to fool around, Caro. I'm already late." He walked to the *Basse* road, got into the backseat of a Talon SUV, and was driven off. I stayed in the sand, cheeks hot from the rejection, tears welling in my eyes, waiting for the world to come back into focus.

❖   ❖   ❖

In March, Marcella invited us all for a girls' dinner at her residence in Cap-Griffe. The five-story marvel was set back from the road by a walled garden and a copse of overgrown trees, with boughs of lilac whose dried winter skeletons had to be parted like a curtain. As the branches shivered and snapped back into place, I ran smack into a private security guard wearing a dark suit. A cord ran from his ear into a box at his waist. He looked at me unblinkingly and refused to move.

I stared at him curiously. Plenty of visitors to Lucomo had private security, but I'd never known any in Cap-Griffe; we had enough national security of our own. After a moment, Otto came up behind me and motioned for the guard to resume his watch along the covered path, and I was allowed through.

The house was enormous, a burnt-orange stucco mini-château with lacy metalwork and painted shutters, surrounded on all sides by high trees obscuring an even higher wall. The windows were dark on every floor but the first, where antique panes of glass shone with friendly candlelight. Marcella waited at the door, her red hair unkempt and matted like a shroud. "Theatrical," I said, kissing her cheek. "When did you get private security?"

"It's becoming necessary," she snipped. "These immigrants, you know." Before I could inquire as to which immigrants, exactly, she was referring to, she'd stepped inside. Chiara, Benny, Aurora, Vida, and Atena were already milling around the dining table, cocktails in hand. Broiled fish and salads were heaped in huge dishes on the table; we were to serve ourselves. "My entire domestic staff was hired away by some Chinese woman," Marcella snarled, pulling at the yarn skein of her hair. "She offered to pay them *double*." For the first time in our friendship, the seven of us were alone.

"It's becoming unlivable," Benny agreed. "They're so pushy, and *so* rude."

"They?" I finally got in.

"These new residents," Atena said pointedly. "The '*Lucien*,'" she said, making exaggerated air quotes, their nickname for those who were not Lugesque. Hobbled by austerity, Europeans had spent the last six months of the crisis unloading their Lugesque real estate at fire-sale prices. The buyers hailed from the robust economies of China, Russia, Nigeria, Indonesia, and Brazil—all the world's 1 percent finding a tax-friendly bargain here in Lucomo.

The rest of the meal was a litany of complaints. It was bad enough that Amelie was allowing the cruise lines to come and dump cut-rate slobs on our doorstep every week, but at least those people *left*. This new batch of Chinese, on the other hand, had no taste and no respect for the delineated social superiority of the Piéton wives of Cap-Griffe. They were hiring all the Marin laborers and paying them *far* too much. They were practically *looting* the stores. None of them spoke French or Italian and they *barely* spoke English. They had absolutely no sense of history, but the Africans, everyone agreed, were the worst; they had the rudest security, after the Russians—well, maybe tied with the Emiratis. Which, if you thought about it, made sense given that most of their countries had been established in the last twenty years. They weren't even civilized, not really.

I watched it all unfold, moldy disgust spawning across the back of my throat until eventually I contributed that I myself was an African immigrant from a young democracy.

"That's totally different," Atena said, batting the notion away.

"I don't believe so," I countered. "I was born there, and now I live here."

"You're not some dictator's daughter laundering gold Krugerrand at the casino," Chiara said. "I saw one last week. The nerve."

"Which dictator?"

"How should I know? They all look the same."

"Did the casino cash it?" I asked.

"Naturally. It's currency." Chiara raised her shoulders—*What can you do?*

"That's the same thing then," I replied. "It takes two . . ." I trailed off when Chiara shot me a dirty look. I wasn't supposed to make her feel bad about herself. I was supposed to be outraged, too.

Atena smoothed things over, as usual. "We've been considering hiring *our* own security," she said. "A man followed me home the other night. It made me *so* nervous. He watched me go through the gate like a Peeping Tom." She sounded exactly like the hysterical Afrikaners of my hometown.

"It's getting so overrun. It's not good for the economy," Vida insisted. "It's never good to inflate wages." She stabbed at her salad. "You need to speak to your husband, Caro. He needs to vote with the ministers to outlaw wage inflation. We give the Marins so much already . . ."

As Vida talks, the building changes. The walls fly away from us; the candles blow out. Suddenly we're in a white-walled compound in Johannesburg. I'm four years old, clutching my mother's legs, one of her secondhand pumps between my fake-patent-leather shoes and frilled anklets. My mother's left foot taps up and down. She's talking to someone; she's tense, but she's trying not to seem that way.

The woman she's talking to, the woman who owns this house, is telling my mother that *it's very important that the UWO does not interfere on the issue of wages or they will lose the support of the Women's Union because she is paying absolutely everything she can to her domestic and if the UWO wants to take money out of her pocket, against her family, it will not have her support.* My mother is polite but insistent, saying she is certain *there is a way to satisfy every mother in this circumstance,* but her foot is tapping, tapping, the frustration building until we leave and get in our beat-up Opel. My mother buckles me in, muttering that she can't argue with this woman because all this woman's ideas come from her husband. She does her own buckle, then slams her hands against the wheel. *These women have no idea what they can afford,* she says, and then she ruffles my hair and says, *Caroline, I love you and I know you'll grow up to be a good person.* She sighs and releases the parking brake, and off we go to the next house.

I blinked. I was in Cap-Griffe. They were still talking. *These women have no idea what they can afford.* I'd thought I'd come so far. But I hadn't gone anywhere at all.

I was not my mother; I didn't know how to adjust the moral disequilibrium between us. All I could think was that Vida was wrong, but I knew that saying so would make her feel small, and what was the point in that? So I said nothing. I focused on my meal; I stayed in my lane. I reached to the back of my head and pulled out strands of hair.

When Marcella located the digestifs, I excused myself. I didn't have the stomach for any more talk and stepped outside, the cold air preferable to conflict. As I crossed the garden, the wind picked up, stripping the lilac bushes of their few remaining leaves.

"Caro, *wait,*" Marcella called, her voice barely cutting through the wind. I turned back. Through the window, I saw her grab a cashmere wrap before following me outside. "I need your help with something."

"I'm rather tired. Tomorrow?"

Marcella craned her neck. Her guard was still standing firmly along the path. She motioned for me to follow her around the edge of the house, where the trees of her garden, even winter bare as they were, shaded us from the Cap-Griffe security cameras. She then produced a thick black plastic phone from within the folds of her wrap. "It's only a phone call."

I laughed at the object, heavy as a book. "Is this a car phone?"

"It's a satellite phone," she whispered. "It can't be monitored."

Curious—who on earth did she want to call?—I remained still. Marcella took my stillness as agreement and began to dial. "*Allora* . . . *Sì*, she is here." She handed me the phone.

"Yes?"

"This . . . is Honor." The voice of a young woman, a teenager maybe, polite but unsteady.

"Hello, Honor," I said uncertainly.

"I would like to come and visit and I thought you might help." The girl's words came out in a rush.

Marcella was biting her nails. "Honor, forgive me," I said evenly, "but . . . how do we know each other?" Marcella's face clouded over with frustration. I put my hand over the receiver. "What is this about?" Before Marcella could answer, the girl broke into tears. I could barely understand her. "My mother lost her job . . . I thought you might want to help . . . don't then, I get it . . . but it's so strange not to meet him and now that I have a sister and a brother, I thought—"

"Honor, calm down," I tried. Marcella, meanwhile, was furious. Knuckles white, clutching her wrap. Baffled, I raised my hand in defense.

The girl gulped. "I'm so sorry, this was a mistake," she said, and then the line went dead.

"Marcella, what the—"

But Marcella's fury did not abate. She snatched the phone back from me like I'd broken something precious. "That was horrible, Caro," she hissed. "I can't believe you did that."

I remained mystified. "Marcella, I honestly *do not know* what I was supposed to say."

Ruffling like an irritated horse, Marcella lowered her head. "So, we go back to pretending," she muttered. "I thought you were a nice person."

"This is crazy," I whispered, angling my head under hers, trying to get her to look at me. "I'm not pretending anything."

"You sent the girl a *birthday card*. Why? If you're going to act like this?"

"Sent who a birthday card?"

"Honor. Your husband's daughter." Marcella stared at me like I'd stabbed a puppy. "With the bartender."

My husband's daughter. With the bartender.

As her words landed, the ground fell away from beneath me. The house loomed, tilting dangerously against the sky. For a moment I thought it might fall right on top of me. A memory lifted, bubbling faintly to the surface: *The birthday card I'd signed and sealed in Finn's office when Henry was screaming, the one I'd assumed was for the staff. Addressed to someone named Honor, with a Degas dancer on it, a card for a teenage girl.* I fumbled for support, hands slicing the air until I found a post and steadied myself against it. Marcella watched my floundering with suspicion, trying to determine the degree of truth in my confusion. Meanwhile the blood drained from my skull and leaked out into the night. "I sign a lot of cards," I offered weakly.

Marcella understood, then—I genuinely didn't know. "I, I th-thought—" she stuttered, reaching for me, trying to pull me in, to smother me in an apology. "Honor's at school with a friend of my daughter. She got in touch about a year ago. I thought I was helping." I backed away in horror. The leaves rustled beneath my feet, alerting the guard, who came into sight as Marcella hid the phone beneath her wrap.

"I'm awfully tired," I squeaked, and then I was running, down the path, through the gate, back to the guardhouse, the stones of Cap-Griffe moving beneath my feet like a river, I was jogging in place in the elevator, the staircases running like escalators, the hallways streaming past, the apartment door locking behind me.

35

ONE THOUSAND SIX HUNDRED TWENTY-FOUR STEPS in a flat-out uphill sprint from Marcella's door to my bedroom. I didn't even realize that I'd been running until I stopped. Calves trembling with adrenaline, obliques and glutes quivering with that inimitable, honeyed aftershock, the buzzing high. My hips were warm, whole. I heard an eerie laugh, my own, as I peeled off my shirt, then my trousers, the waistband soaked through with sweat.

Disoriented, I sat half-naked on the floor of our bedroom and tried to sort out what I knew. *The mother a bartender*, wasn't that what Marcella said, and before, at the party where I hunted them down, when they lied and said they were talking about Aurora.

Not just the bartender. There was another—what had Marcella and Atena sneered at . . . *an air hostess with a baby*, or a toddler, or something. Oh god, the other card, with the goggly eyes—what was the name, a boy's name—E something? How old was he?

I tried to recall the conversation from the party with more clarity. What was the event . . . Lucomo Day. I remembered how Finn had gone still when I brought it up the next day. How he turned it into a joke, so that we'd laugh and move on. He was so deft, that man, slipping and sliding around conflict, always making sure everything went his way. *How could he have kept this from me? How could he keep so much of himself from me?* Even as I had, in my fullness, split myself open; gave all that I had to reproduce him in Jane and Henry.

Honor was a teenager. How old was the boy? *Is he older than my marriage? Is he older than my marriage?* The question a sickness, tunneling into my sternum. As I sat there losing babies, watching my belly swell and deflate, my value rise and fall, had he gone off somewhere and made another, one who lived? One that he didn't even want?

I wondered where the children resided—if they had enough money—if they were cared for. Honor said her mother had lost her job, I thought, replaying the conversation. They needed something—money probably—though it sounded like Honor wanted more than that. She wanted to know Finn, and to know me, and Jane and Henry, too. I wondered if she'd asked someone else before, whoever kept them quiet. I wondered how many people knew all these things I didn't.

Before I could stop myself I'd pulled on a robe and was sitting in the Gloria Apartment in front of my computer, looking up the dates. When I'd overheard Marcella and Atena talking, we'd been married for just about a year. Before my first pregnancy, the one who didn't make it past thirteen weeks. *He couldn't have,* I told myself. *He wouldn't have. Would he?* And then I was opening a search engine—about to type in *Finn Fieschi* and *bartender,* admittedly not a great start—when I thought of the Gardiens in the rock below, their roomful of screens, privy to my every phone call, text, and internet search. I pictured Otto watching my cursor, waiting to see what I'd type. I saw him connecting the dots, sending an email, cutting off with bureaucratic ease whatever meager financial support Honor and her mother received.

I turned off the computer.

◆ ◆ ◆

Bed was pointless. I lay awake the whole night. Why hadn't these two mothers, these two children, been acceptable? Had they squeezed their pregnant bellies into the same lineup of used dresses? Had they forced their swollen feet into those spike-heeled shoes and sat through an interview where Amelie asked if they were illiterate? Were they brought to Dr. Finney's medical bay, had their blood taken for a paternity test— followed by a check and a ride to the airport?

No. They probably never had the chance. Neither *bartender* nor *air hostess* was a synonym for *princess* even as they were jobs I would've loved to have during those fragile days in Lisbon. Funny. I'd thought my inability to find work had made me less than, but for the Talon, I now realized, it made me ideal. These other mothers were too self-reliant, too competent. Amelie wanted a bride sprung from a fountain— or better yet a locked cell—fertile and foolish.

How could Finn have two entirely separate families that he never sees? How could he live that way? I wondered for a moment, before remembering: Because—because *of course he could.* My husband was a spectacular liar, effective because he lied to himself as well as he did to others. He packed away the truth and locked it in a storeroom for his own comfort and ease, gave himself a ticket for the memory like a coat check. I bet he never allowed himself to think about it.

I tried to imagine how a conversation with Finn might play out, but no matter what opening I plotted—a frank inquiry; a hellish fight; an off-the-cuff remark—it always ended the same way, the same way our fights had always ended. Finn would say sorry, sorry he hadn't said anything, he hadn't known how, but he was glad it was out in the open now and I wasn't to worry. I'd be left holding the emotional bag of getting over it and moving on. Every possibility I could imagine ended with a door closing in my face, being told that it was being taken care of, that it wasn't my concern.

As my plots sputtered out, I plucked hairs from my head one at a time, waiting for the pluck that would hurt enough. It never came.

◆   ◆   ◆

When the sun came up, I dragged my exhausted, sleepless body to the gym, and suffered through a stern lecture from Dr. Sun over Otto's report of my midnight dash the night before. "You'll break an ankle, you'll ruin all the progress we've made, is that what you want?" *Of course not,* I assured her, *of course not, I'm sorry, I was drunk,* I lied, *it was a mistake. Of course I know it's better to be healthy than it is to feel that high.* I wasn't allowed to work out that day. Instead, they taped my eyes shut for two hours while one technician glued on a bushel of eyelashes and another attempted to repair the increasingly scabrous desert of my extensions. They sprayed me with fake tan, spackled heavy makeup over my blotchy skin, and drove me to the beach for the Yacht Classic. Amelie had refused to cancel it, even though there were half as many entrants as usual.

I was loaded onto a sailboat, part of a fleet that had recently been painted cherry red, their white sails embellished with the logo of a Chinese bank. I decided to sit astride the stern, tangled in the webbing, while we raced the fleet from one end of the country to another. When the boat crested a wave so high I thought for a second we might capsize, the press dinghy speeding alongside snapped a photo. I'm a wraith from hell, an evil grin stretched from one metal cheek to the other, the sailors behind me wide-eyed with terror.

Back at the harbor, I spotted Marcella in a leopard-print minidress, smoking restlessly at the helm of her neon-orange speedboat. Dozens of private security guards walled the parking lot behind her. Without warning Otto or Dix, I strolled over to Marcella's boat as if to greet her—then hopped into the passenger seat and told her to hit it.

She flicked her cigarette into the water and reversed out of the harbor. Dix waved his arms at her to stop. I smacked the gunnels and told her to ignore him.

Marcella sped out into the water, gaining a whole kilometer before Otto commandeered a trawler and chugged pathetically in our direction. She cut the engine somewhere toward Spain. "We have about ten minutes," she thought aloud. "I am so incredibly sorry—"

I cut her off. "I don't need an apology. It's not your fault, though I wonder, why didn't you tell me sooner?"

"I didn't think it was my place. I'll admit that I thought you should know."

I asked their ages. Honor was sixteen, she said; Edouard, the boy, was seven: one year older than my marriage. I felt my whole being washed over with relief. Sad, isn't it, that I was comforted by that small fact. I asked their hometowns, their mothers' names, what they looked like. Marcella blurted it all out, trying to make up for her transgression, a confessional sacrifice. Had she told anyone else about my conversation with Honor? *No.* Finally she asked: *What was I going to do?*

"I haven't figured it out yet." I didn't say the pathetic truth out loud, that I wanted to fix my marriage. I turned my ring around on my hand and gripped it until it cut through the skin.

But it was obvious. "You actually love him," Marcella observed. She burst into tears then, mewling like a kitten, ink drops of mascara tracing lines through her foundation. She put her hand to her forehead and bent over, trying to collect herself. It was then that I noticed she was wearing the antique mules I'd given her at Jane's baby shower. She followed my gaze. "I don't deserve these," she sniffed, slipping them off and trying to hand them back. "I'm so sorry. I got this all wrong." I put my arms around her. By the time Otto pulled up, he saw a sobbing Marcella being comforted by me. I waved him away—*Just two girls having a cry in the sea. Nothing to see here, nothing to worry about.*

Nonetheless he lingered close enough to monitor us, possibly even to hear our conversation, so I rubbed her back and said, *It's all right, everything is fine, let's go home.* Marcella shifted the boat back into gear. "I know my advice probably isn't very welcome at the moment," she whispered, the engine drowning us out, "but if I were you, and I wanted to stay, I'd never say a thing about it."

At the dock, Dix whisked me into one of his bulletproof buses and I was returned to the Talon, back to the world where everyone around me had long been able to calculate exactly what I knew and did not know. But now the balance was off: One of their secrets had become my own.

36

WHILE IT'S TRUE that I was beginning to realize my circumstances were not merely unbalanced but fundamentally adversarial, it is *also* true that I was beginning to understand the amount of power my adversaries held. The Talon had access to my phone and my computer. They controlled my body and the spaces around it; they managed my relationships and even edited the newspapers that landed on our breakfast table. I had no way to reach out to anyone, not even to try to talk through how I was feeling or gain any more information without tipping my hand.

I felt utterly unhinged. I formed the accusation in my head any time I sat or took a step or merely *breathed*. Yet I couldn't shake the belief that if I lost my composure, if I handled this badly, I might lose my husband forever. In darker moments I worried that I could lose my children and, like the women before me, be cast into exile.

Trapped in that paralyzing eddy, I moved stiffly through our life for the next few weeks. I worked hard to avoid Finn's eye in private, rare as it was, and pushed my need to confront him down to the bottom of my body. I imagined the need as a dark sludge, dripping down my veins and out through the soles of my feet. I pretended that everywhere I stepped, it soaked through my shoes and left oily footprints behind me. I told myself that with each step forward, the hurt, and the need to resolve it, lived in me a little bit less.

◆ ◆ ◆

It's not pleasant to admit what happened next. I don't relish it. But it's true.

Sally Williams pummeled Radmila Janković on the clay tennis courts of Aurora's estate in the jasmine-scented hills of Mare-Dio. I attended the match alone. In silk shorts and a matching tank, a pretend athlete, I chatted up the wealthy patrons who had paid tens of thousands to watch Sally and Radmila grunt, and me smile.

The conversations were impossible to differentiate. Any topic related to expenditure, save for politics, was explored. Should one buy into a privately owned ski resort if the nearest helipad was a full hour's drive? Was it cheating to have additional oxygen portered to the final miles of Machu Picchu? *I love your jewelry. I love your watch. I love your money. It's just like mine.*

An hour in, I got sidelined by a man from a Norwegian energy firm. Bald like a baby and as visibly enthusiastic to latch on to any breast in sight, he prattled on about his fetish for formal gardens. When he paused to demand a beer from a passing server, I excused myself and hid behind a painted screen, upon which three swans pecked a fourth to death.

The pleasure center of my brain was so completely dulled by then that only my children seemed to give me any feeling, but even so, I found myself short with them, easily irritated. I no longer slept more than four hours at a time. I kept waking up at two in the morning and wondering if life was supposed to feel this empty.

It was then that I first saw him. Hand to his earpiece, guarding my body, and making eye contact as though he was allowed.

◆ ◆ ◆

Tall, with sloping shoulders and dark curls, lips carved into an eternal pout. He stood at the open end of the screen, letting his eyes travel up and down the length of my neck. I glared, but the man didn't look away. "Get me a drink," I ordered.

He returned with a tall glass of orange juice, fresh squeezed, like the one I'd made for Christian so many years ago. I took a sip and dumped it out into the potted soil of the nearest plant. He held his hand out for the empty glass. I lifted it—and let go before his fingers could touch it, watching it shatter on the ground.

The man didn't flinch, only pushed on his earpiece, asked for a cleaner. The Gardiens never reacted—I could say anything, behave any way—as they wordlessly absorbed any evidence of my simmering rage and misery.

"Where's Otto?" I asked in the pissiest voice I possessed.

"He's been pro-*mo*-ted," the man said, his accent Lugesque, all hills and valleys. He did not introduce himself beyond that. He drove me home, held the door, followed me to the apartment, brought me a glass of water. As I went to bed that night, all I could think was that I hated this beautiful man. I hated him for appearing like this, out of the ever-thinning air.

◆ ◆ ◆

From then on, he followed me wherever I went. He watched from the doorway of the gym as I climbed the staircase to nowhere and whimpered on the massage table; he watched formal dinners where my husband and I avoided each other's eyes; he watched as I knelt to comfort my children. He watched as I lived, anticipating my every need, obliging my every demand in careful silence.

After a time, he did more than watch. He *saw* me. He witnessed my life and all the work I put into it. He knew the meaning of my every expression—every toss of my hair, every dip of my eyebrow. In exchange I refused even to ask his name.

In July of 2009, the man drove the children and me to the country house. Jane gathered flowers from the garden, Henry gurgled on the sofa. I read aloud the story of Demeter, the goddess of the harvest, and her daughter Persephone. Persephone loved to sing, I told them. But she should never have eaten that pomegranate.

Jane rolled around on the floor and asked questions. "Why does Demeter have to do what Zeus says?" "Because Zeus was the king of all the gods." "Like Mamou?" "Yes, darling, like Mamou." At this she wrinkled her nose. "Does that mean that Mamou will give me away?" "No, darling, Mamou would never give you away," I said. "You will be queen like Mamou, and the queen must live in the palace." "Will she give Henry away?" "Of course not," I lied, though I realized as she said it that it was exactly what would happen to Henry; he would be married off, live with another family, as I'd come to live here. A tear blossomed and fell before I could blink it back. "Maman, don't be sad," Jane said, patting my back with her sticky hands. She grabbed the book, scooted off the sofa, and waddled to the fireplace.

"*Jane,*" I warned her.

She proudly threw the book into the flames. "There!" As it thonked onto a log, embers flew toward her, threatening her flawless skin. I darted from the sofa, Henry in one arm, and yanked her back with the other.

"Jane!" I shouted. "You're not allowed to get so close to the fire." I held off on reprimanding her for burning a book; one correction, for a three-year-old, was enough.

"It made you sad," she said, confused. "We don't need it. That's what Daddy does when he doesn't like something. It goes *pfff,*" she said, waving at the fire. "Daddy makes sad things go *pfff.*" Her father was burning documents, she meant.

"When does Daddy do that?"

"*All the time,*" she shrieked with joy, remembering it. "Whenever he wants."

"*We* mustn't ever throw anything into the fire," I told her. "Fires are very dangerous for mamans and babies."

"I don't think so."

"Yes, Jane, they are. Can you agree with me, please?"

She frowned.

"If you don't agree, we can't have our dessert," I said sadly.

The prospect of lost banana slices was a sufficient deterrent. "We don't throw the fire," she mumbled.

Ten minutes later we were snuggled up in my bed, and after two more stories—nonsense this time, Mother Goose—they were fast asleep. I lay awake most of the night, watching their chests rise and fall, the same thoughts running through my mind again and again.

The man waited on a chair inside the door the whole time.

◆ ◆ ◆

In the morning I found him making breakfast for Jane, Henry on his hip. His green jacket hung from a peg; his shirtsleeves were rolled up, leather holster empty, the firearm hidden away. Jane sat politely at the table in her booster seat, drawing in a coloring book. "She wanted to let you sleep," the man explained, feeding Henry a spoonful of mush with his free hand. I lifted Henry into my arms protectively, the mush, too. But the man simply went back to cracking eggs for Jane as though this was normal.

He'd stuck to me from the beginning, waiting in the apartment instead of the hall. Now he even sat *in the room* whenever Finn was not there. It was the natural next step to sit together and eat our eggs and toast, drink our coffee. So we did.

When Jane and Henry went down for their naps, I sat in the garden.

The sound of his footsteps, soft on the grass. He lowered himself to the ground and took a seat beside me.

"Are you okay?"

He was the first person who'd asked me that in years.

"I'm fine," I lied. "I'm absolutely fine."

◆ ◆ ◆

We spent the evening baking a cake from the ripened pears of our garden. The pomegranates were full, ready to drop from their shrubby tree, but Jane wrinkled her nose and said she would never eat a pomegranate, never ever. Why not? I asked. Because I don't want to go live underground, she said, I want to live with you forever.

◆ ◆ ◆

After I put the children to bed, I noticed the light was still on in the kitchen. He was there, pouring us each a glass of red wine. He handed one to me, but I put it down. He smiled, as if he was beaten at some game. "So now you're drinking my wine?" I asked.

"I'm drinking Lucomo's wine," he agreed, delineating the distinction between what was *mine* from what belonged to Lucomo.

"You think that's acceptable?"

"You tell me," he said softly.

"Absolutely not. You're a disgrace."

"How to make it right?"

"Get on your knees and beg," I told him.

To my surprise, he sank to the ground. I let him remove my slippers, push up my dressing gown, rest his head against my thighs. At long last someone was trying to please me, instead of expecting me to please them.

◆ ◆ ◆

Adam. His name was Adam.

We spent the week together in the country house, taking to bed once the children were asleep. Out there, in the forest, in my green cape, the fires burning, rain sneaking through the window, I could pretend that it was a romance. I pretended Adam was my husband and that I was happy and loved, and it worked, for a time. I didn't need Adam the person, not exactly. It's more that I needed someone who wanted me to feel good, and when I was with him, the gaping hole in my heart, the spot where my marriage used to be, was papered over. Not completely, but well enough for it to beat again.

And he let me run—or I should say I ran, and Adam didn't stop me. I laced up my sneakers in the morning and paced laps around the walled garden, seeing how far I could push myself before the cramps set in. I didn't have speed anymore, and my gait was drastically different— a body changed by pregnancy and time—but I had my taped-up heart, pumping to the rhythm of my steps, filling me up with oxygen, with life itself.

We were recalled to the Talon after ten days. I packed my sneakers regretfully; back to the gym we'd go, their treads reduced to the minor task of gripping the rubber planks of the StairMaster.

Adam brushed my hand as we exited the car. My eyes skittered nervously around the courtyard: to Dix, laden with my bags; to Marie, Henry in her arms; to Lola, holding Jane. An ensign, piling the children's bags on a rolling rack. They weren't looking at me. *No one*, I told myself, *had noticed*. They were too busy working.

I took advantage. In the Talon, where Adam knew the location of every camera, we stole away to the greenhouses, naked among the flowers, invisible behind steamed panes of glass. In those moments I was lifted from the dullness of my depression, brought to heaven, tender and light. Months fueled by desire passed like days.

Finn, busy amassing capital, did not notice. One night I could hear him shouting across our living room from three rooms away. I tiptoed down the hall and lingered in the shadows. I understood enough Italian, by then, to eavesdrop. "They can't," he was bellowing. "They *cannot* pull out."

"It's time to get creative. We have to make allowances," Roland said, typing away on a laptop, one phone balanced on one ear, another open at his side.

I retreated to our bedroom. Finn's money wasn't my problem, I told myself. I undressed—remembered *being* undressed—unhooked my lace bra—remembered its *being* unhooked—and then suddenly I was back there again in the greenhouse. I took a hot bath and repinned my hair. By the time I was dressed for an "informal" family dinner in the Petit Ange, Finn's panic was forgotten.

At the silver table with its golden plates and crystal glasses, the staff swinging in and out, we politely chewed our food. Finn spent the whole meal on his BlackBerry, poking those little keys like they held the secret to eternal life. Amelie cooed over Henry and Jane.

Where was Adam now? Downstairs, in the Gardien quarters, eating his dinner. Perhaps closing his eyes. I pictured the line of his sternum rising and falling. The next time we'd be alone together was in three days. I sat listless, lost in a dream, and I don't think any of us said a single word to each other.

37

In January, I returned from a rendezvous looking downright disheveled, glowing like an ember. I stopped in the Gloria Apartment to put myself back together. As I was washing, Schätze rapped sternly on the secret door—"Paperwork," she called out.

I exited the restroom, still flushed, and took the papers nervously from her hand. I dashed off my signature again and again without reading, all the while watching Schätze out of the corner of my eye, searching for confirmation that she knew more about me than I had ever told her. As she pushed her glasses up her nose three quick times in succession, *She's on edge about something,* I thought. She seemed tenser than usual, uncomfortable. *Was she judging me for what I have wanted?*

Schätze's hand hovered over the unsigned papers, eager for their return. I glanced down at them, and as I did so, Schätze pushed up her glasses *again*—too late to cover a nervous twitch in her left eyelid. I realized then that whatever she knew or didn't know about Adam wasn't her concern. *Schätze didn't want me to read whatever was written here.*

Was I conscious, at that moment, of a genuine desire to leave? Fantasies of a different life cropped up whenever I watched other people commit acts of spontaneity, or even walk unguarded on the beach, but they were more akin to pangs of jealousy. I think that for the most part I was fired up with longing, caught in the breathless net of my affair, and I couldn't imagine living away from my children. All I could prioritize was a desire to maintain the status quo.

All the same, the reality of my situation nagged at me. It didn't matter what Finn had kept from me; I was the one who'd broken our vows. I needed to start protecting myself—and it occurred to me that these papers, which Schätze so clearly didn't want me to read, might be a useful shield, *if* I could understand what they meant. Zola's advice from long ago echoed through my mind. I opened my hand and dropped the pen.

Schätze reacted immediately. "What's wrong?"

"I'm dizzy." It was the only thing I could think of to say.

She picked up the pen, shoved it toward me. "If you could please finish these . . ."

"My vision is blurry—as if it's been ripped in half and taped back together. It's a migraine, I think." I shut my eyes. "Close the curtains," I asked, "please?"

After a moment's hesitation, Schätze pulled the orange drapes together, and the room fell dark. She reached for the paperwork, saying, "I'll bring these back another—"

I folded my arms over the stack, pinning it in place, and laid down my head. "No, no. I'll finish them in a bit. It'll pass." I sensed Schätze looking around for a place to sit. "Don't wait. I'll have them brought to you later. I need quiet."

Schätze wheezed with displeasure a little bit—she wasn't happy—but I heard her walk out. Once the door snapped shut, I fanned the papers across the table, pulled the English-Italian dictionary and the long-abandoned children's workbooks from the shelf, and started reading.

❖ ❖ ❖

It turns out that I was the owner of many little companies, ones that owned parts of other little companies. The declared assets were minuscule: one euro here, ten euro there.

This was obviously a scheme. Even at the rate of one euro, I didn't make any money. I was never directly paid for anything. I hadn't read a bank statement or zeroed out a bill in years. I read through the stack a second time, noticing that three specific companies had their upper-left-hand corners double dog-eared—Finn's unbreakable habit of marking the things he wanted to reread.

I considered not signing. But to what end? I'd signed so many of these over the past few years already. It was too late to do anything about it. Still . . . they meant something. I was sure of it. A faint clicking sounded from the hall—heels tapping. I held my breath, one hand on the dictionary, the other on the pile. The noise crescendoed—*was it at the door?*—then faded, as whoever it was kept walking.

I stood up and started searching for a solution. The Gloria Apartment received many conveniences when it became the headquarters for my initiative: a raft of filing cabinets, and a combination printer, copier, and fax machine had been plugged into my computer. I considered faxing the papers to Zola but thought better of it; the service would see the call, and probably the image of the fax. I considered saving them on the computer but knew the service would see that, too. That left paper copies. The machine wasn't very sophisticated; I didn't think it would save an impression on the network. After a few false starts, I managed to shuttle them through the copier, its beige mouth spitting out a cascade of doubles.

The noise was much louder than I would have liked—*shuzh-shz-shusz-shuz*—and I searched frantically for a place to hide them. But everything was so clean. The undersides of the cushions were vacuumed regularly, mattresses were flipped, cabinets wiped out, chimneys swept weekly. I almost gave up. I was leaning against the filing cabinets, the handles pressing into my back, when I had to clap my hands over my mouth to stop from laughing because it was so obvious.

I slid open a drawer, parted the hanging files, and stowed the copies on the bottom. To the naked eye nothing was different; they were effectively concealed at the bottom of the drawer.

I sat down at the table and signed the rest of the originals. Then I really did get a migraine, and I lay on the sofa with a pillow over my head, waiting for it to end.

38

THE DOOR OPENED. Finn, confused by the darkness. "Caro?"

I lifted the pillow, gave it a little wave. "Headache."

It's not that we didn't speak. It's just that we used very few words.

"You'll have to take a pill," Finn said. "We've got to go out tonight. Do you want the details?"

"Do I?"

"Probably not. See you later."

No more I-love-yous, by then. He closed the door.

◆ ◆ ◆

A plastic shroud waited on my side of the lacquered red closet, satin stilettos paired beneath. I unzipped it to find a leopard-print gown with a high slit and an open back. "I can't wear this," I said.

Finn settled himself against the doorjamb. He was no longer losing weight—it was already gone. His bones seemed too big. Those topaz eyes were opaque all the time now, his thoughts invisible to me. "Trust me," he said. "You don't want to stand out."

"It's sleazy. And it's too thin. One flash and you'll see my labia."

"There won't be any flashes."

"What do I get?" I was almost flirting. *Almost.*

"You get to keep living here." Finn said it so coldly. It was a hammer—and as I stood there dumbfounded, too hurt to speak, a technician let herself in, dragging a clear plastic coffin filled with be-wigged foam.

"*Signora,* your extensions are in such bad shape, and so little time, we will use hairpieces tonight, okay?" she asked rhetorically, already re-moving the lid, plunging her arms into the cornucopia of plastic scalps.

"That would be fine," Finn told her, opening a drawer, searching for a bow tie. It was always like that. The debt we owed to the people who waited on our hands, our feet, our hair, our teeth, was the most basic politeness. It always shut me up.

Twenty minutes later, I was nothing but red lips, caramel hair, leopard-print silk, and legs. Finn added one more thing—the rope of diamonds he'd given me on Coursalis's yacht—then nodded approv-ingly. The technician left. I followed him to the car.

◆ ◆ ◆

I realize now that Finn took great care to shield me from the Brevard side of his family. I'd heard about Roger very little and his father, Mar-tin, Finn's uncle, even less. I knew they were hideously, mind-bogglingly rich, with a thirty-billion-euro fortune stemming from two centuries of petroleum and textile concerns (farmer *and* baker, as Finn put it) span-ning the globe. I suppose technically, of course, they lived in Lucomo, but they were rarely *in* Lucomo; they had real estate on six continents and funded a research station on the seventh.

Roland drove us to the end of the country, to Lo Scopo, where Finn's development plans had laid the most eggs. We didn't speak. Finn was a world away, completely detached, by the time we made it to the centerpiece of his plan, the Terrazzo. What had once been just a drawing in a tourist brochure at the end of a line of sugar cubes, in those days before we were married, was now a white whale stretching to the sky. We parked in its underground garage, next to a tourist coach—*Curious*, I thought, before wondering if perhaps there was a band here—and a string of high-end cars. A private elevator lifted us to the penthouse.

A dozen thick-necked guards in rented suits and a metal detector guarded the foyer. A signal-blocking case to the side was filled with BlackBerries and iPhones, the plastic boxes jumping up and down in time with the heavy bass pummeling the crowd.

Through air thick with cigar smoke and pungent with perfume, a herd of young women and slab-bodied men writhed across the room. It was jarring, even for Lucomo, how ugly the men were, and how young the women; girls, almost.

We were greeted by Roger Brevard, nursing a fat cigar, clutching the ample bottom of a doe-eyed teenage girl staring blankly at a painting of a saddled horse. He tried to plant one of his wet kisses on my cheek; I leaned backward. "Nice dress," he yelled into my ear. "Getting into the spirit of things!"

"Roger." I failed to keep the disgust from my voice. He smiled idioti-cally as Finn shook his hand. "Congratulations, Roger," Finn said, his voice deadened, before towing me away. Disoriented, I followed Finn through a maze of breasts—*honestly, had I ever seen so many young women in one place? Had they always looked so very young?*—and when we passed an empty corner, I yanked him into it.

"I think this party is full of prostitutes," I whispered to Finn, grab-bing his jacket. Emotion finally crossed his face: surprise. "Aren't they?" I whispered again, second-guessing myself.

"You're so simple, Caro. It's what I love about you," he replied, amazed by the stupidity of his wife. He unwrapped my fingers from his lapel. "Caroline the Innocent. Look, they insisted we come. We'll only stay for an hour or so."

"Why?"

"To celebrate the Brevard triumph," he said bitterly, threads of anger pulling his brows together.

"Triumph of *what*?" I genuinely didn't get it.

"The Terrazzo. All of Lo Scopo, really." He bit back a sneer, clicked his jaw.

"Theirs? But you've been building it up for years—"

"With their money, Caroline," he said. And then suddenly his eyes got soft and I could see him again, my husband: He was disappointed.

"Oh," I started—but we were interrupted. Alexei Coursalis clapped Finn on the shoulder, put a hand around my waist. I squirmed away.

"You missed the auction," Alexei protested, a tumbler of scotch sweating in his hairy palm. He surveyed the penthouse with a satisfied leer, his piggy eyes darting from bosom to bosom. "This unit went for three hundred million. It's legally registered to a fucking *boat*." He laughed. "This country. It's a gold mine."

"You shouldn't have brought so many girls," Finn muttered, stepping between us, trying to block me from hearing anything else.

"The party favors? They're employees. They work for the boat." He snickered. "Well, temporarily, anyway. Tell you what. If you want to hire them, I'll lend you the money." He parted his mealy lips and let out an ugly laugh, his spittle flying onto my décolletage. "Fuck, I love this country," he exclaimed, putting his hand on Finn's shoulder, a sentimental shine in his eyes. "When I first borrowed your big, beautiful tunnels—" He paused, raising his drink to me. "Remember, pretty princess? You almost fucked it all up!" Finn shoved him back, but Alexei didn't seem to mind. "I never thought we'd get this far. You've come along, little Finn. You've come a long, long way."

Finn's jaw clicking, neck burning red. "I need a drink," Finn told Coursalis, cutting off any further discussion. But it was too late. I'd heard. *When I first borrowed your big, beautiful tunnels. Remember, pretty girl?* The night I'd gone down there with Jane on my misbegotten adventure—the tunnels filled with wooden crates smelling of chemicals and hot metal that disappeared—they were not the Talon's food supply. They were cargo, a test balloon, a stain on the heart of the Talon, for Coursalis to gauge precisely how elastic our boundaries could be.

As Finn led me to the bar, we passed another dozen girls. Every single one looked me in the eyes eagerly, with unvarnished admiration. Some were excited; some were nervous. They were mostly the same, a blur of eyeliner and spray tan. It was only the terrified ones who stood out.

I clung to Finn with numb desperation, shadowed him around the party. I circulated in that room full of investors and "temporary employees" until we'd met enough that we could leave. Enfolded in the living, breathing human cost of our greed, I chose not to intervene. I said nothing, I did nothing. Wealth had made me into someone who prioritized most her own comfort, her own wants and needs, above all other things.

For whatever it is worth, probably very little, I could not help becoming that person. I was particularly vulnerable. I've tried not to be dramatic about the pain, but pain can break you. In the scope of things, women are vulnerable, people in pain are vulnerable, and mothers who cannot leave their children are the weakest of all. I know that not everyone will agree with this. Nobody wants to admit that they can be rendered weak by the things they want. But I was.

◆　◆　◆

Back in the Terrazzo's submerged garage, the building's private tunnel into Italy shone bright. The travel coach, waiting to shuttle the women to wherever their term of employment would end, squatted in the darkness.

I didn't speak until we were safely cocooned behind two-inch-thick bulletproof glass with the partition up to keep Roland from hearing. "I don't understand why you would make me do something like that," I told Finn.

"I'm sure you don't," he agreed, pressing his forehead to the window. The veins in his neck pulsed with rage; his once-custom collar hung loose.

"I didn't like that. I don't like those kinds of people."

"That's too bad." He snorted, as if my dislike was a joke, then reached for the car's liquor hatch and poured himself a drink. "Debt is a social relation."

"I don't want Henry growing up and believing you can traffic busloads of women whenever you want to sell some real estate."

"That's what you're worried about?" Finn ran his finger around the edge of his glass. "I *wish* that was all I worried about."

"How can you be so remorseless? Those girls didn't even look old enough—"

"What am I supposed to be upset about, Caroline? It happens every day. *You* of all people," he spat. The drink went down in a single swallow.

I didn't hear the dig, only the cruel indifference. "I don't like how these people make their money, Finn—"

"Then you don't like money," he snapped, rolling back the sunroof a crack to let in the fresh air. "Caro—I can't talk about this. Okay? Just—just *leave it alone.*"

I tried. I really did. I sat there, leather seats sticking to my thighs. I tried to calm down, to listen to my heartbeat, to tamp down the panic, the disgust. But then I recalled his joke from Shanghai, so long ago: *What has your evil twin been up to—assorted arms, light human trafficking, but his real passion is money laundering.* Not a line, just the truth, a mad gamble for capital. I only made it a minute or two before I exploded. "You've *ruined* those women's lives. You've made such a disgusting mess—"

"Oh! You suddenly care? Now you want to give me your input?" he barked, cutting me off. "You couldn't even be bothered to *learn Italian.* You never came to a *single* meeting. You never tried to understand what I told you. You *never* cared. You don't have the right to care now."

I leaned my head back against the seat. "I didn't think it mattered."

"It mattered." His leg began to tap, his finger running around the glass edge again. I'd never seen him fidget so much.

"You don't really believe that's the reason you're in business with criminals."

"I don't think it would've made a difference," he admitted, my husband again for one short moment. He poured another drink. "There's a . . . bigger influence."

As I watched him make the same bitter expression he had when congratulating Roger Brevard, it hit me. "The Brevards are the lender," I said aloud. I should have known all along. Who else but family would keep such an investment secret?

"Bingo," he said. "Brevard and Coursalis have been buying up the leveraged assets we were using in a CDO to pay out the loan. They did it under my nose. I didn't see it," he said ruefully. I shook my head—I didn't know what that meant. He cleared his throat. "A collateralized debt obligation is a structured asset that pays out by weight. Brevard and Coursalis bought enough pieces of the CDO to bump us down several tiers. When it's a tangible asset, like the Terrazo, it's . . . unbeatable."

"Why would they do that?"

"To exert influence." He uttered these words with equal parts shame and distaste. I began to understand, at last, the position we were in. The private citizens of Lucomo—the Brevards, Coursalis, and their associates—had acquired enough pieces of Lucomo's portfolio to control its ability to repay its debt, and by default, its income. Finn stared listlessly at the floor.

"How much longer?" It was the only thing I could think of to ask. *How much longer until he repaid the debt. How much longer until we were out from under their thumbs.*

Finn loosened his tie before he answered. "A long time," he said. "In a manner of speaking, you could say that they own us."

"You'll make it work," I assured him. "You have to."

"I'm the one who ruined it all after *seven hundred years*," he said, rubbing his chest. "I honestly don't think I can bear it." Roland sped up. The streetlights strobed through the glass, illuminating us in pinwheel flashes—Finn unbuttoning his collar, me balling up my dress in my hands.

"You once told me Roger was illiterate," I reminded him, trying to lighten the mood. "You were joking but for the longest time I felt sorry for him. I really thought, *Oh, that poor man, he relies on pictograms everywhere he goes.*" We both let out a strained laugh.

"I'm sorry, Caroline," he said painfully, clutching his glass. "This is how things are now. I need you to go along."

I exhaled. "I don't want to."

"Until Lucomo can withstand the scrutiny of the new banking regulations, we're stuck with private investment. We can't withstand the scrutiny until we pay off the bond. We can't pay off the bond until the economy revives itself. There's no two ways about it. *We are trapped* with Roger, and Alexei, and the rest of them. We can't insult them, we can't ignore them, we can't avoid them."

"You can't," I agreed. "But I can." I pushed the snaps lining my hairline and removed my wig, resting the platinum curls on the seat between us. "I didn't do this, Finn. I'm not responsible for this."

He shifted, stretching out his legs. "Caroline, neither of us are perfect. I know we've spent too much time apart. You've been"—he lost his voice for a moment—"at the country house too much."

I thought he meant that he missed me.

That he loved me.

That we'd grown too far apart.

When did we last kiss? I wondered, looking at his mouth. *A year? Longer.*

"We could live there. Together." I suggested, meaning it. "I don't need all this," I told him, gesturing to the car, the skyscrapers, the diamond leash around my neck. "I only need to be loved."

And with that simple comment—what I meant as a romantic

suggestion, the gift of my self-sufficiency, the simplicity of my most basic need—I broke the chain between us.

Finn's head rotated smoothly on its axis.

First he sputtered, "I—oh—you—that—"

and then he laughed incredulously—

and then with all his might, he splintered.

"I gave . . . ," he growled. "Christ, I can't even say his name."

I stopped breathing.

Finn's anger sharpened to a point. "I *gave him to you* because you needed to be loved."

Gave him to you. Cymbals, clanging between my ears, deafening me. *Needed to be loved,* like it was a fault. He might as well have slapped me across the face; I think I would have preferred it.

"You thought it was a secret, didn't you." He ran his tongue across his teeth. "Caroline, you are so dumb."

"I know *your* secret," I couldn't stop myself from saying. "You have two other children. Honor and Edouard."

Finn grunted, eyes darting back and forth, caught in the trap of his lie. "Who told you that?"

"You did, just now," I said, my voice hoarse. "I might be dumb but I know you."

"I've *never even met them,*" he said quietly. He sounded so hurt; if he hadn't just wounded me like that I think I would have reached for him. "It was taken care of. Without my input." Finn's legs tapped tapped tapped against the carpet as he decided to reset himself. "I've gotten over it. You should, too."

I'd imagined this confrontation so many times and here it was—playing out exactly as I'd feared. The truth was not a key I could turn to bring us back together. The advantage I'd worked so hard to keep slipped away as he closed his eyes and breathed in for ten seconds, out for the same. He pulled himself up and out of his body, and now Finn was colorless, jaw still, legs no longer tapping, no more fidgeting.

In a measured voice—the one of the aggrieved spouse, the one who had been wronged—he explained to me what was going to happen. "I've let you take all the space you want. Caroline, it's time to be an equal partner, for once in our marriage," he said. Then he dropped the veil and sneered so precisely that it cut me in half. "You will do as you're asked," he said slowly. "You will not create trouble. It's not good for our children."

The bomb: *Do this because you want to live here. Do this because you want to live with our children.*

I had no recourse.

I was a paper doll. Tabs held my dress on. Hands moved me from place to place. And I owned so little that even my lover belonged to my husband.

At home, Finn stopped at his gray apartment, went inside, and locked the door.

39

LIKE SO MANY NIGHTS before, I climbed into bed alone. Except this night I understood that my husband had left me for good. He left months ago. No. Longer than that. Nearly two years, I realized. Finn first moved into the gray apartment after Henry was born. It didn't feel like leaving at the time, but I suppose I hadn't really paid attention; I was too busy trying to get Henry to stop crying.

I tried to imagine Finn's point of view: I never learned his languages. I didn't ask enough questions. I didn't try hard enough. I didn't help him steer clear of the world we now found ourselves in. He'd implied that I wasn't an equal partner, even though the terms of that equality were never made clear to me.

And, of course, I had an affair.

An affair orchestrated for his own convenience, but an affair, all the same.

I wondered if he was actually hurt by that. I didn't believe it. The Finn I know did not have time or space for intimacy, with me or with anyone; he was too consumed by the weight of his responsibilities. He would rather pay someone else to love me than love me himself.

I wish I'd been able to see it as a freedom, if that makes any sense. I

wish that I'd simply woken up and gone about my day and had my lover
and lived with it. But I loved my husband. I was shattered.

◆ ◆ ◆

The next few days were a skinless agony. I couldn't look anyone in the
eyes, not Dr. Sun, not Marie, not even the children. I ricocheted between devastated and mortified. *How complicit is Adam? Does he take
notes? Give reports? Follow instructions?*

But I wouldn't get an answer. Adam was removed from the prem-
ises. I never saw him again.

Finn avoided me with great effectiveness. I caught glimpses of him,
twenty meters down the hallway, leaving the playroom moments before I was about to arrive. I saw him doing jumping jacks in the courtyard, with the Gardiens, but by the time I got down there, he was
already gone. I smelled his cologne in our closet and found his side
empty, his suits moved.

I walked to the door of his gray apartment three times. Each time
the ensign reached for the knob to open it for me and each time I waved
them away, backed down. I didn't know what to say. I didn't even know
how to begin.

And finally, I had the full and complete thought: *Could I have a real
life somewhere else?* I imagined leaving the Talon—walking out the
front door like I'd done so many years ago before I married Finn—and
after that the fantasy persisted, appearing as I opened my eyes in the
middle of the night or the afternoon or frankly any time I pictured
Finn's face, his eyes that didn't look at me, his hands that wouldn't
touch me. I obsessed about the papers I'd copied, safe in the bottom of
the filing cabinets for the dormant initiative, and wondered if I could
get them to Zola, somehow; if there was something in them that could
be useful leverage. I wondered what kind of deals they'd made with the
bartender, the air hostess, with Adam, to stay away. I wondered how
many people knew that my husband had accidentally gambled an

entire country into the hands of his debtors. I wondered if it even mattered whether or not anyone knew.

❖   ❖   ❖

It wasn't easy to absorb this new reality, or, worse, the dawning realization that I'd gone out of my way to ignore its progression for the past *seven years,* so I took to bed like a coward.

At first I told Dr. Sun it was a spasm that wouldn't quit. Then I said I thought it was the flu. Whatever it was, I was sick. Something was wrong. I was in pain, I said, a lot of pain. I'd spent my whole life taking care of a body in pain, and now it was back. I spent days, then a week, in bed.

I knew how to fake it, but after three weeks of complete inactivity, I didn't need to. My arthritis kicked into a full-bore flare-up and I was swollen, cracking, crumbling. Dr. Sun asked Finn to stand by while she gave me a full exam. He stayed in the doorway and wouldn't make eye contact with me.

Dr. Sun said she was certain postpartum depression was the root cause. Henry was over two. *Postpartum depression this late is dangerous,* she said. It was possible I could descend into a near-vegetative state. *Watch her speech patterns,* she said to Finn, like I wasn't in the room. *Make sure she is awake at least twelve hours a day. Measure her cognitive abilities at least once a week. You don't want her to atrophy.*

I laughed when she said *atrophy* but my husband didn't even blink. Dr. Sun reiterated that there was obviously nothing wrong with me physically and then expressed her belief that the single tried-and-true curative for depression was her gym routine. *I can't move,* I told her. *Yes you can,* she said. She told Finn that I had to get up. He said that I knew my own body better than anybody on earth and he wasn't going to hurt me, and then he turned around and left.

Dr. Sun gave up on Finn and tattled to Schätze, who, after telling everyone that I had tuberculosis and was in for a long recovery, tattled to Amelie, who subsequently took it upon herself to force me out of bed as soon as it was convenient for her, which was nearly two months later, so I didn't see it coming.

I think it was the afternoon. I lay in my sweaty cocoon with the sheets over my face, diligently chewing the dirt from under my fingernails. It was very pleasant and very warm, and so it was also very shocking when the sheet was pulled away and the queen of Lucomo sat there staring daggers at me in my dirty underpants. "This. Will. Not. Do," Amelie said sternly.

"Your Serene Highness," I mumbled sarcastically. "I don't feel well."

"Get out of bed this instant or we will have you institutionalized," she said coldly. At that her little cardigan-draped shoulders turned and left.

I lay in bed for an hour debating whether or not I *ought* to be institutionalized. I thought about Scoria Vale and how they'd given me my pills and brought me coffee on the lawn, how they made my bed, how they took me apart and put me back together. *Was it any different from my life now?* Someone would make my bed, if I'd get out of it. Someone would put me back together, if I let them. All that Amelie wanted was for me to sit dumbly at the dinner table. I could do that.

I emerged for dinner wearing slacks and a blouse, which turned out to be entirely the wrong thing for a seven-course meal with Amelie, my husband, and the full court of ministers and ladies-in-waiting. I was sent back to change into a dress and heels. Everyone was told that my TB was no longer contagious, but I was still a little fuzzy, of course, in the head.

Quail came; I wrapped it in my napkin and dropped it under the chair. Trout rillettes were next. I hacked them into pieces and moved them busily around the plate. Finn watched me nervously. When our desserts materialized, small clusters of palace-grown apples, grilled soft and dipped in chocolate, he leaned over and whispered in my ear. "Caro, you really ought to eat something."

I chewed the dessert bite by bite. It wasn't dramatic, I simply ate it as everyone else did. Then I excused myself to the restroom, stuck my fingers down my throat, and forced it all back out.

◆ ◆ ◆

The children were my only joy. I was sitting in bed, pretending to read, when Jane started climbing over my chest and Henry tugged at my socks. They were both wearing foam dinosaur costumes. "Extinction is coming!" Jane squealed, giggling hysterically. "The volcano is going to explode!" Henry was worried, wrinkles around his topaz eyes.

"We'd better find shelter, then." I yawned. Henry perked up, looking so happy at the idea that I rose from bed. "Let's go somewhere to survive it." They took my hands and towed me down the hallway, cackling hysterically. When we happened upon their father's apartment, Jane screamed, "Open sesame!" at the ensign, who saluted her and snapped the doors open wide. I hesitated, lingering in the hallway, but the children won out and dragged me inside.

Finn looked up from his computer, obviously startled by my presence. Jane and Henry let go of my hands and burrowed into the safe space under his desk.

"Papa, get down," Henry begged. Finn obliged, curling up next to them. I hung a few meters back until I heard Jane demand that they "make room for Maman." I rolled Finn's chair aside and sat crosslegged beside them. Finn glanced at me—the first time he'd looked at me in months—and when our eyes connected I knew that I could never stop loving this man.

"What are we playing?" he asked our children.

"Dinosaur Extinction," Jane whispered. A curl of hair stuck to the snot on her cheek. Finn gently detached it, tucked it back under her spiny hood. "We have to survive," she explained. "It's almost time."

"Ready?" Finn asked. Henry and Jane nodded solemnly. "Five, four, three, two, one," we counted down together, until Finn shouted,

"BOOM!" and fell upon the children, tickling them mercilessly. Henry shrieked with delight and tried to squirm away. I dived for him—and smacked my head against the desk, hard. Finn reached for me instinctively. "Oh," he said, stopping his hand in midair, and I could see he wanted to take it back.

Henry and Jane took this opportunity to run free, returning to the hallway, where nanny Lola waited. *It's time for dinner,* she was telling them. *Such hungry little dinosaurs!*

Finn and I were left alone, sitting on the floor behind his desk. The space between us was so vast and I was desperate to claw him back to me. He was about to stand up but I couldn't let him. I grabbed his arm and held him down. It felt unfamiliar beneath my fingers; I wasn't used to the shape of it, not anymore. "You have to speak to me."

"I know." He brushed my hand away, tilted his head against the desk drawer.

"I can't live like this."

"We've *been* living like this," he replied. "Why change now?"

"That's not true."

"Obviously I feel differently." His was a manufactured calm.

"I would never have been with Adam—"

"Don't say his name—"

"The man you paid to be with me? I would never have been with him if you hadn't already left me," I fought back. "You kept yourself from me. You lied about having two other children. You made a thousand bad decisions without me. You stopped wanting me."

He let my list of grievances hang in the air. "I didn't *stop* wanting you," he said, after a moment. "I ran out of things to give you."

I wasn't convinced. "You hired Adam to keep me warm for you."

"No, you chose to be with him," he insisted. "*You chose him.* I merely paid him. I pay everybody, in case you haven't noticed. That's my job."

"I am *so lonely,*" I said, tears streaming down my face. "I am so lonely, all the time—"

"This is not a hard job, Caroline," he said, exasperated. "You're making it hard on yourself."

"It *is*," I told him. "It is incredibly hard. I'm an athlete who doesn't run. I'm a mother who isn't needed. I'm a wife who isn't loved."

"They need you," he replied, the only thing I'd said that he cared to rebut.

"I'm telling you, I don't think I can live like this," I said, "not anymore."

In the silence that followed was an ultimatum—that we didn't have to do this.

We don't have to live together.

We don't have to be married.

Not if this is who we have to be.

"You shouldn't say things like that." Finn's voice was low and careful, the same tone he used with that bomb in the car, *do this because you want to live here.* But I didn't believe he wanted to walk around wounded all the time. I knew he wanted to be loved. I knew he wanted to love in return.

"You don't want to be unhappy," I told him with every fiber of sincerity that I possessed. "If we're broken, then . . . why make it worse?"

"It would be worse if you left," he said.

"You won't hurt me," I insisted. "I know you. I know you won't."

"Do you remember when we met?" he asked suddenly. "At the hospital?" He paused. In an instant, the peach of his skin leached out, and he turned gray as the floor. As it happened I think I understood him at last: Finn summoned his courage by turning to stone. "The car crash was my fault," he said definitively. I raised my head to protest but he dismissed me before the breath left my lungs. "I know it was my fault because in the moments before it happened, I thought to myself, *What if I just . . . swerved? What if I just didn't have to do this anymore?*" This time he didn't click his jaw or turn red. It was a clear-eyed assessment of a real memory. "And then it happened," he continued, "I did it. My hands turned the wheel before I had time to reconsider. Lidia died. Amelie kept it quiet. We are not allowed to make mistakes."

I know that I should have seen a murderer. But I didn't. I saw my husband, hollowed out by duty. "Yes, you are," I told him. "You're allowed to make mistakes." I kept going. "We're *both* allowed."

"You think our marriage was a mistake."

"I think that I'm unhappy, and you're unhappy. I don't see what purpose there is in unhappiness."

"Our happiness is not . . . relevant," he said, still made of stone. He'd become part of this building. Whoever I married was not here.

"Your mother covered something up for you," I said, trying to break through. "I would do that," I admitted. "I'd do anything for our children."

"I don't think you understand. I *wanted* to be responsible," he said. "But they sent me to Scoria Vale, and then . . . it couldn't be unraveled. It was impossible to atone for."

"It's not impossible," I assured him, reaching for his hand. "We can find a solution."

He didn't let me touch him. "A journalist looked into it for years. Right around the time we were married, the journalist died in an accident. You heard Roland and me fighting about it, the very first day you were here. Remember? I said if he hurt her I would report it. He did it anyway. Called my bluff." Finn sniffed, impressed by his aide's ruthlessness.

The journalist who died on the coast road during our honeymoon. A car crash. I pictured Roland creeping from the shadows and into her brake lines; slithering away as she unlocked the door and stepped on the gas. Part of me was horrified. Yet we were so removed from the world of everyday people that the killing of a journalist didn't feel like a threat to my own safety; it felt more like a punishment, a tactic designed to frighten us into staying away from innocent people. The horrified Caroline wanted to get up and run. The rest of me knew there was nowhere to go, and so, desperate to make the horror disappear, she won out. "You can still fix this," I heard myself insist. "Life is not a one-way street."

"I'm not asking for your help. I'm telling you where the boundaries are."

"If that's the price of being in power, then let it go," I begged. "Brevard wants to take over? *Let him.* Let the country belong to the bankers. Let them take everything. We don't need it."

He let out a strangled laugh. "They already own it," he said. "Any one of the people in this building could trip Amelie and break her neck on a staircase. Or you. An accident," he said, circling my bony wrist with his fingers, "would be easy. They don't—because they *don't want to.* They don't *want* to get rid of us," he explained. "Don't you see? We're a living shield. Sovereignty legitimizes. *Family* legitimizes. We make the laws they tell us to make. We take responsibility. No—*I* take responsibility," he corrected himself. "You go along."

"I go along because I thought that's what you wanted," I told him.

"I did, I suppose, I . . ." He stopped for a second, let out an enormous exhale. "When we first met you were so funny and bright. And then . . . and then you were absorbed into this place like everyone else. You lost your light."

I snorted. "I gave it to you. You're going to blame me for trying to fit in?"

"No." He shook his head. "I'm . . . I'm sorry we didn't have this conversation five years ago. Maybe it doesn't matter. There's no way out."

"Why do *you* want this?"

"Because someday I'll do more good than harm," he said, and I think he believed it.

"Why do you want me here?"

"Beauty makes us special," he said, holding his hand to my face. His fingers slid down to my neck; he pressed his thumb against the space between my collarbones, where the blood pulsed. "It's evidence of God. Without beauty we're merely bureaucracy. You are necessary, Caroline. You are an ideological necessity."

"It's only a face."

"A mother's face. Children need their mother. You can't leave,

Caroline. Nobody will allow it." He was about to say something else but stopped himself. "I can't talk about this anymore. I can't be upset today. I have to get on a flight in an hour."

He pressed his lips to mine with the briefest of kisses—a kiss that meant nothing because there was no comfort in it—then stood up and walked out.

I stayed cross-legged beneath his desk. There were so many moments when I was corralled, cajoled, convinced. *It's important for you to smile, Caroline. No, Amelie didn't turn the boat around. No, it's too complicated to explain. No, you don't really want to know more, it's too hard for you, you won't like it.*

I thought Finn wanted me to go along, to get along. He did want that. Yet: All the while, conflict brewed around us. I spent most of our marriage with my eyes taped shut, pressured into anticipatory obedience, terrified of what would happen if I opened them. Ever the avoider, he waited for me to open my eyes and see—and burned with bitterness when I could not. He asked me to be a supportive wife and a loving mother, then resented who that made me into. Every cell in my body began to burn—my throat, the soles of my feet.

I saw, at last.

Roland was not his aide but his jailer.

His mother was never his mother; she was his boss.

I was never his wife. I was his useful idiot.

For all my devotion to equality, I wanted equality as a backdrop so that I could prove without a doubt that I was an exception. My belief that I was special made me believe Finn was special, that his life, our life, could be extraordinary. I believed that we could be extraordinarily good. But the truth was that people in power, people like us, almost certainly only become extraordinarily bad.

An hour later his motorcade departed. I counted the cars as they drove across the green fields toward France: one, two, three, four. Four cars meant Otto and Roland were both with him.

That's the night I saw an opportunity, to find my way to London and file for divorce. The service were drinking in the courtyard, their ties loose, playing cards between their fingers. I did not think, I merely acted, powered by the crimson fuel of rage. I went to the Gloria Apartment and took the papers from the filing cabinet. I donned my coat, dug my old passport from my duffel bag, took the keys to my maid's car, drove to the airport, and in a panic, I flew, of all places, to Saudi Arabia. Then I came home and cried with shame until they took my children away.

But that, as I have said, that is when I woke up. From all of it.

40

Now

ALL FAIRY TALES serve the same purpose. One woman's story, told to warn the others. Here is how I lost my feet; here is how I lost my voice; here is how I lost my children. Here is the moment I was given from my father to my husband. Here is where the danger lies: the man with the blue beard, the ogre in the forest, the tricky gentleman, the lying merchant, the prince in the tower. Fairy tales are not about sparkling shoes or white cats. They are about the ribbons that adorn, then sever, your neck.

After they took my children away I stood in the hallway outside the playroom, in that silly seersucker outfit. Wig loose, cheeks sunken under garish makeup. The black and white tiles of the hallway mingling with the darkened shadows of the service. *Please eat some lunch.* Finn's text, the phone buzzing in my hand.

And then: The spell broke. I felt it snap—a stabbing pain—and clutched my stomach. The seed that was planted in Shanghai, so long ago, when we locked eyes in the car, had turned sour with rot. It began to sprout, to rise through my stomach and open my throat with its bile.

I didn't want it. I pushed it back.

That's all I'm good at, silencing the part of me that second-guesses.

The seed didn't care. It wanted out.

I raced to our apartment, biting the insides of my cheeks, a stem thick as rhubarb bulging up my esophagus. Gagging, I locked the door behind me, searched for an empty room where I might hide from the staff—but the seed, empowered by the growing body of force beneath it, moved faster than I could. As I stepped into our bedroom it shot high, stretched its leaves, and pushed itself up and out.

I screamed. It ripped my throat open with the force of a fireman's hose, snapping the high strings of my vocal cords. I kept screaming, didn't stop until they were all broken, lying flat on my back, heaving in surrender.

Eventually I noticed there was silence. I'd stopped. I opened my eyes inside a sunbeam, propped myself up over the knobs of my knees, running my fingertips over the bends and sinew. *These legs that used to run. This body that used to be mine.*

Something began tugging at my throat, first a tickle, then a wet cough. Whatever it was, it was coming up. I bent over on all fours and began hacking, choking, wracking, until eventually I produced an object. I looked down and saw it: *a small green leaf.*

I peered at its waxy, flexible skin. The tiny seed clung to its roots. Yet when I tried to close my hand around it, the leaf caught the breeze and took flight, rising to the ceiling, where it stuck itself to the vines of the chandeliers before turning to glass. I noticed all the leaves, then, in the ceiling; all the plants and wildlife crawling over stone, once alive, now immortalized in crystal and painted with gold.

I reached for it. As I raised my hand, it shimmered with iridescence. I looked down—*all of me was like this*—hard and glittering, transformed into the pearlescent, filtered debris of this world. I was changed, at last. I was different. I could see.

◆   ◆   ◆

Long ago I'd told Finn, "*One of the most important lessons that I learned from running was to expect pain. I expected it. If you try to get rid of it, you'll lose your mind. When it happens, like it's happening now, you have to coexist with it.*"

With every shampoo and fancy dress, every dose of Clomid, every embryo transfer, I'd erased my greatest power: the ability to coexist with discomfort. In seeking security at the price of liberty, I lost both. The power of authority is freely given. I gave my body away. I allowed it to be turned into a national resource. I stopped running through the fields and I became one myself. It was only once my children were finally taken from me—my greatest fear—that I realized that they'd never been mine at all. They weren't his, either. They belonged to this place and I could never get them out of it unless I stopped giving my strength away.

How difficult it must have been to find Finn a wife. A woman who would perform innocence because she was innocent; who would garner sympathy because she was damaged (never mind that becoming the reproductive appendage to a man is a life sentence). Generous, kind Finn, cast as the prince who rescued her. On top of all that, a woman he loved. Tall order.

The others would have seen right through this place. The actress would have noticed when he lied. The businesswoman would have seen that it is not preferable for any nation's debt to belong to a family. The philosopher would have argued with the impassioned defense of authoritarianism he'd made during our dinner in Shanghai. The heiress had been a contender, perhaps, but she'd died in the car wreck that brought us together. Even the bartender and the air hostess had the sense to stay away. Caroline the athlete was the only fool among them. Caroline the idiot. Caroline the fool.

The idiot. The fool. It echoed in my mind until I asked myself what anyone expected of an idiot.

Nothing at all.

I pushed myself to my feet. My handbag, the one I'd taken on the airplane, with its purloined paperwork. *Was it here?*

No—it wasn't in the foyer, living room, bedroom.

Not in the dining room, not on the coatrack.

Roland took it, I thought, *he must have*—and then I went back into the red lacquered closet and laughed out loud.

Someone had placed the bag on its shelf. The paperwork was still inside, folded neatly at the bottom. In all the commotion no one had thought to look inside it. No one suspects the fool.

I had one more chance. I would not waste it.

◆ ◆ ◆

The spell broken, the seed expunged, I saw everything differently. It started with the service—as I walked through the Talon I realized they were really and truly shadows, silk stockings designed to slip between this world and the next. Gliding and creeping, stalking me from place to place. But they couldn't touch me. Not anymore. Not with my pearl skin, hot as light. I'd burn them to ash.

In the black-and-white hallway, the portraits on the walls weren't frozen anymore—they wiggled and screeched, but they didn't have words, they could only snort and oink like pigs stuffed into velvet hides. The ladies in the Gloria Apartment were phantoms raised from the deeps. Algae stuck to their bloated skin, eyeballs flopped from the sockets as they whispered my name—*Caroline, Caroline, Caroline*—it bubbled up from the water and gurgled into my ear.

When Schätze found me I had to clap my hand over my mouth to stop from laughing—*She's a mule, how did I never notice before?*—her gray fur matted with sweat, carrying our burdens around. She brayed and whinnied. I scratched her under the neck, nickered to soothe her until her eyes grew heavy. She fell asleep standing up.

I left her there in the hallway and kept going, turning left and right, down stairs and through tunnels until I reached the guardhouse in

Cap-Griffe, where the green specters of the service caught my silhouette and pinned themselves to my footsteps.

Outside the air was so bright that I had to shield my eyes. The residents of Cap-Griffe squirmed in their gardens, lapping their coffee from bowls, wet bodies glistening as they barked like seals. *Arf*, I barked back, *arf arf arf.* When I reached Marcella's burnt-orange mansion, I slipped through the gate and peered in her window.

I saw her, tail waving back and forth, paws landing gently as she leapt over a chair. Marcella was scarred and thin, like the leopards they take from the wild, but she was still vivid—still alive. I smiled and let myself back out again, turned at the next alleyway, and dodged a shower of bougainvillea as I reached for Atena's door.

I rang the bell. When Atena appeared in the threshold she became her white cat—then her white horse—and then she was her true form, the moon reflecting the light of the sun it orbits. I let myself be pulled in like the tide, and then I curled up on her sofa and asked for help.

◆ ◆ ◆

Atena believed me because she wanted to. When I told her that I was coming out of the fog—that I'd lost myself but now saw the error of my ways, that I'd followed the yarn out of the maze, that I'd do anything for my children—she told me that everyone still wanted me to be a success. *They wanted me to thrive*, she insisted. She'd help me, she promised. She'd push me back onto my feet again.

Atena fed me, watered me, and let me sleep in her guest bedroom for the night. When she thought I was asleep, I heard snippets of a conversation. I crept down the hall and listened. She was on the phone with someone, Roland, maybe, murmuring in Italian. I couldn't understand most of it, but from the tone of her voice, I hoped she was making my case. At some point she laughed, some joke. Whatever it was, it sounded positive. I could hear optimism in her goodbye.

In the morning, Atena brought coffee and eggs on a tray. As I reached for the cup I noticed that, though a faint sheen remained, my skin was no longer a hard pearl.

"Come now, Caro," Atena cooed in a voice that was dovelike but nonetheless unmistakably human.

The intensity of my new sight, I realized, was draining away. "I think I ought to see Dr. Sun," I admitted. "It's been too long."

"You see, all you needed was a good night's rest," she told me. I nodded agreeably and let myself be towed back to the Talon like a lost sheep.

◆ ◆ ◆

Dr. Sun in her white scrubs. Irritation flew off her in a shower of sparks. "This is ridiculous, what you've done to yourself," she chided, examining the pointed bones of my left ankle. "We've gone backward in these past few months. You've got the body of an eighty-year-old." She motioned for me to take off my clothes. As I stripped down to my underpants, baggy on my weakened frame, I wondered what she'd been told about my brief departure. "I'm sorry to say this, but I saw this breakdown coming from ten miles off," she snapped unkindly as she powered up her ultrasound machine. Ah: *Caroline had a nervous breakdown.* Not: *Caroline's husband is a murderer and she tried to leave him.* "Lie back. Baselines first." The paper rustled beneath me as I lay down. Dr. Sun squeezed out the clear jelly, rolled the plastic wand over my joints. At my right hip she clucked angrily. "Completely inflamed," she observed. "Scale of pain?"

"Eight," I reported.

She removed a thermometer from the drawer and handed it to me. I wanted to break it with my teeth and drink the mercury inside. I did not.

"I'll give you a week of Vicodin," Dr. Sun offered, rooting around for her pad. She dashed off the prescription and gave it to the ensign at the door. "It'll take the edge off, but overall things will likely get worse before they get better. You've got a lot to come back from."

"I can take it."

"Good." Stern, but satisfied by my obedience. "You have no other choice."

I put my hand on her shoulder. "Thank you," I said sincerely.

"You're welcome," she replied. For a flash my sight returned and I saw that Dr. Sun wasn't a person, either. She and Dr. Finney were both skunks, hurrying their furry bodies through the tunnels, spraying me with fear.

41

Finn and Amelie stayed away with Henry and Jane for the whole week. I spent my days in the gym, submerged in ice baths, having the tight-rope of my muscles rolled out, the pain dialed down to a dull ache by Dr. Sun's prescriptions. And though my head was stuffed up with the fuzzy cotton of opiates, I did not forget that I'd seen the beasts for what they were, and the world as it truly was. After six days, I'd grown stronger. I dressed, had coffee, rooted around in the closet. I pulled out one dress after another, throwing them in piles. Lola peeked in. "*Signora*, can we help you?"

"I hate everything in here," I said, sounding frustrated. "It's one of those days when it feels like there's nothing to wear."

"Oh, I know that feeling well," she clucked sympathetically. A complete lie, one of the million everyone told me every day. "Let me know if you want any help."

I kept building my pile, working until I found the leather garment bag holding my mustard coat, the one with the dyed cuffs.

The one I'd worn only once.

I patted the pockets. They were flat. I stuck my hands in anyway. The first was empty—but the second had a torn lining. There, in the bottom hem of the coat, its bulk hidden by the fur trim, were my old cell phone and charger. How funny it looked; a Nokia candy bar, an artifact from another time. Under the cover of my elaborate mess, I took out the SIM and plugged the charger in, hiding it beneath a pile of skirts. I began to clean up after myself, placing the shirts and dresses back on their satin hangers. Lola popped her head in again. "I'll do that, *signora*," she insisted.

"No, it's all right, Lola, I'm separating as I go," I said, flinging a Prada blouse with navy cuffs across the room. "Do you think, once I'm done, you might want any of it? Or Marie?"

"We could probably find homes for them," she said, her eyes drawn to the mustard coat.

"Take it," I encouraged her. "It's the perfect color for you."

She blushed and waved her hands no. I insisted. She tried it on; it needed to be let out at the waist an inch or two, that was all. I told her to go see the seamstress in the staff quarters and get it done. Lola beamed with gratitude and said she would run down there before I could change my mind.

By the end of the day, I'd given approximately 420,000 euro worth of daywear away to our nannies, and my Nokia phone was fully charged. All I needed to do was connect to a cell tower outside of Lucomo—one that the service couldn't control. The minutes were international but I'd bought them in Italy, and so, I thought, that was where it would probably work. I'd need to return to the country house; in order to do that, I'd need to get healthy again, shake free of this depression, act like everything was fine. I stuffed the Nokia phone in the bottom of a winter boot.

◆   ◆   ◆

Finn returned at last, Henry and Jane in tow. I waited for them on my knees in the hall and sobbed when they ran into my arms. They were bursting to tell me all about their vacation with Amelie, at a vine-yard in the French countryside. Finn stood to the side, watching me. Supervising. "We picked grapes, but they weren't ready," Jane explained. "Mamou gave me a doggy," Henry said, waving a stuffed animal.

"I think we should get a real doggy," I said. "Would you like that?"

"OH YES PLEASE," they shrieked.

"Go and get your doggy books and we will learn all about them," I instructed them. They ran off, their short legs scrambling to the library in the playroom.

"I've never had a dog," Finn said, his voice light. "I've always wanted one."

"I know," I said, rising to my feet and dusting myself off. "Anyway. Welcome home."

"How are you, Caro?"

"You know how I am," I responded. I walked to the sideboard and turned on the electric kettle. "Let's have a cup of tea."

❖ ❖ ❖

We drank our tea and looked at the Dorling Kindersley dog encyclopedia with the children like a normal family. Lola appeared around dinnertime and whisked Henry and Jane off for chicken fingers. Finn and I remained on the sofa as the children's voices grew distant.

Silence—but he was still here. I cranked open one of the lead-paned windows, then dragged an armchair to face it. Climbing into the seat, I sat cross-legged. When the sun emerged from behind a cloud, I bathed silently in the rays, waiting him out, the salted breeze ruffling my thinned wisps of hair.

Finn, to my surprise, lay down on the floor in front of me. "I never lie on the floor anymore," he said thoughtfully. "Not since Henry was a baby." I leaned forward, elbows on my knees, and gazed into the golden brown of his true self. "I can't do this again, Caro," Finn sighed. I waited a beat. *Can't do what?* "What if something had happened to you?"

"The service found me pretty quickly," I reminded him, fidgeting with a loose thread on the upholstery. "Nothing happened."

Finn banged one hand against the floor. "Caroline, this is not a game. You believe we had an argument that was grounds for you to walk out. But I *told you*," he said. "There is no such thing as out. *It is not possible.*" In Finn's mind, everything he'd said to me under the desk was, in essence, the outline of the rules we had to live under. He was afraid *for* me—that I'd broken the rules.

"I realize that now," I replied. "I really do."

We remained there, eyes locked, as the curtains fluttered around us, until Finn sat upright and pulled my chair close to him, in one swift movement. We were nearly nose to nose. As I wondered if he would kiss me, he reached for my hand and gripped it like he was falling. "Promise me," he whispered. "Promise me you'll *never* do that again."

"I promise," I said truthfully. "I won't leave like that again."

Flooded with relief, he laid his head in my lap. "We live under a great deal of pressure," he said, as though he was absolving us both. "I'm not always as sympathetic to you as I ought to be—"

"No," I cut him off, running my hands through his hair. "You've been tolerating it much longer. I know it's not a lack of sympathy. It's almost an *excess* of it. And you have to get up every day and keep going, no matter what, and it makes it so much harder when I don't help you."

"Exactly," he breathed. "Caro, I love you so very much."

"I love you, too," I told him, and meant it. I did love him. I loved him like a sickness, even as I hated him for lashing me to this place. Even as I looked at his broad shoulders and the courage he summoned from this building and realized he was a gargoyle.

From then on, I played the compliant wife, the understanding partner. I let him think I was sorry for not trying harder to understand the burdens of his position. I let him think that we'd found peace with each other. I let him think I was the person he married. That I hadn't changed.

I was willing to do anything for my children. That's not a lie.

That night, for the first time in years, we slept in the same bed. I dreamed about running, the feeling of it exactly as if it were happening, *as if I had run,* and woke up in the morning gasping with relief.

42

THREE WHOLE YEARS. That's how long it took to earn the country house back, three years of smiling and nodding, holding his hand, watching as they bribed my children, living my special life in this golden aquarium. The puppy, a Leonberger that grew tall as a wolf (sweetly named Big Girl Dog by the children), was helpful, especially during that first year. I'd be itching, the memory of my pearl skin burning deep below the surface, counting the minutes until I could get across the border to Italy and finally use my phone, and then Big Girl Dog, so needy and lovely, would jump in my lap and I'd find that hours had passed.

My children grew like flowers in the sun, reaching for my love and thriving on it. Henry turned out to be a rather serious little boy, preferring to read quietly by himself next to the two iguanas named Jerome, while Jane got livelier every day. She loved cartwheels and somersaults and movement. We made a gymnasium for her with bars and padded mats, and she dazzled us with her energy.

And I indulged in my husband, my desire for him an incurable sickness. I reached for his beastly scales at night, desperate for the warmth of his hellfire eyes.

In retrospect it wasn't that difficult. As long as I didn't try to reconcile anything, as long as I accepted that my husband was a bad person, my children were going to grow up to be bad people, and I was the crown jewel doing my part for the legitimacy of other bad people— well, as long as I did that, it was fine and dandy. I went out with my ladies-in-waiting, sunned on yachts, and swanned around in ball gowns, a dead woman in a beautiful dress.

It was less boring, too. When I was alone, I read constantly, taking notes not because I thought anyone would quiz me, but because I myself wanted to understand. I learned about the instruments of finance, about collateralized debt. I learned Italian, enough to sit in on the ministers' meetings with Finn, and I learned French, too, well enough to read, anyway.

During the endless hours of smiling and standing, I kept busy hiding the bitterness that had wrapped itself around all my veins. The seed was gone, but it left a trail inside me; a dirty, stinking venom. To keep it secret I had to turn at all sorts of angles, making tricks of the light and experimenting with shadows, so that my scowls appeared to be gentle smiles. I got quite skilled at it. Few could sense the poison ivy thriving below.

I know that Marcella did, though. One afternoon, on the dock.

I'd spent the afternoon shopping with Marcella and Dasha Coursalis, who, like a magpie, purchased anything emblazoned with Swarovski crystals. Dasha had insisted on buying the three of us matching pairs of clear plastic Louboutin heels, the soles bedazzled with our initials, and begged us to wear them out of the store. An hour later we were limping on sunburned, blistered feet, and Dasha was still talking. I wanted to simply walk in the other direction. I looked longingly to the nearest Lamborghini, fantasizing about demanding the keys from the sentient dentures at its helm.

Instead I asked Marcella to take me home in her boat. She sped us across the whitecaps in silence, the wind too loud for conversation. As we pulled up to the dock, the one that jutted like a shelf from the western side of the Talon cliffs, Dasha began her chatter again about how much fun she'd had, and wasn't everything so great? I smiled my fake smile, stepped backward off the boat—and promptly broke a heel. "Oh no!" Dasha cried.

"Clean break." I held it up to the light. "They can be fixed."

Marcella reversed the throttle, eager to return before sunset.

"Can I try?" Dasha pouted.

Marcella let her take the wheel. "Why not."

I waited for them to pull out. When I thought their backs were turned, I hurled the plastic slippers into the sea. As they flew into the sky, I stopped turning at angles and let myself be as I felt: ugly and rotten, boiling over with hot rage. The shoes hit the waves, flipped onto their sparkling soles, then were swallowed up, at the very moment Marcella turned around to wave goodbye, one last time.

The lightning bolt of my wrath sped across the water, too fast for me to catch it. I saw my hideous reflection shining in Marcella's eyes—and she smiled.

◆   ◆   ◆

I kept squirreling away paperwork, whenever I could. Probably a quarter of the occasions that Schätze appeared with a stack of papers and a pen, I found a way to make copies and kept stashing them in the filing cabinets. Schätze was wonderfully organized. She kept every document, no matter how minor, sorted by topic and subfoldered by its reusability. When I ran out of space on the bottom of the drawers, I tucked a few sheets here, a few sheets there, inside folders that I was certain wouldn't be reexamined. Venues that had since changed owners, flower shops that had gone out of business since the recession, unsuccessful events we wouldn't bother to replicate.

I signed the originals the same way I always had—thoughtlessly, and fast—but took extra time to read the copies. Dictionary in hand, I learned that things were being billed to me. Large bills passed through my assets and were paid by other assets. I didn't know what the bills were for—they were classified by a numerical system of Schätze's own devising—but they were outrageous: one hundred thousand, two million, the numbers collectively spiraling into the hundreds of millions.

In 2013 the economy had nearly recovered. Corporate tourism roared again, the world's self-proclaimed lions filling the hotels, the bars, the restaurants. In turn the real estate climbed. Finn, no longer scrambling so desperately for investment, carried an air of optimism wherever he went, assuring me one night after two glasses of wine that he was nearly there on the bond. *Very, very nearly there.* If the market would hit even 80 percent of its high in 2006—if it looked like fall 2007, even—he could clear it.

I did not reply that he might clear the bond, but nothing could erase the knowledge that he'd bought my lover, killed a girl, allowed the murder of a journalist, kept secret families, tethered my children to these sins forever, broken my heart. That my desire for him was the thing I hated most about myself. Instead I swallowed the bile in my throat and said, *That sounds positive.* That time I felt the acid rise back up, my body sending a message—I didn't have a lot of time. I couldn't do this for much longer. Still, I kept at it. Every morning in the gym, I let my mind wander, forming one plan, then another, until it seemed like I had something that could work.

❖   ❖   ❖

I let Finn bring up the country house. We hadn't been there together since I'd stayed with Adam—a painful knot between us, minor as it was—and so I never mentioned it. But finally, one morning in bed, Finn rolled over and asked if I thought we might redecorate it. *Give ourselves a fresh start.*

"I'd love that," I said, no need to conceal my enthusiasm. "The children need bigger beds. And all the rugs need to be cleaned. There's endless sweet potato smashed into the fibers."

"New rugs." He kissed me. "New everything."

Not that I was sent there to renovate or anything. An interior designer presented some very elaborate sketches, and I simply pointed. But it was all done by Christmas, and Finn decided that we ought to spend our tenth wedding anniversary there.

Roland drove us up in the biggest SUV, Henry and Jane, now small people, buckled in like adults. As we crossed the border to Italy, I sat on my hands to stop them from shaking. The biggest town we would pass had four restaurants and a gas station. It was Christmas Eve. I had no way of knowing whether or not any of them would be open. But the gas station was lit up, shining in the dark.

"Roland, pull over," I called. "I'll only be a moment." Roland checked the toilet, then ushered me in, clearly intending to wait right outside the door. "Roland, if you stand outside that door, I will never be able to look you in the eyes again," I said urgently. He blushed and withdrew to the car.

I locked the door, turned on my phone, and waited for it to connect.

. . .

. . .

Ping.

❖ ❖ ❖

She answered on the second ring. "Zola Mbatha."

"It's Caroline. I need you to represent me in a divorce."

"I wondered how you'd call," she said. I'd signed Zola's card this year with a longer message than usual. *Thinking about the Elephants lately,* I wrote. *Hope you can still hear through your feet.* "Where are you?"

"This is my old cell phone. I'm in an Italian toilet. I won't have another chance to contact you. *For your own safety.* I mean that very seriously. Do you understand?"

"*That's* difficult."

"I have my initiative back. I thought that if your firm can do some pro bono work for one of the charities, you could get someone into an event. I have paperwork to hand off. I think it's leverage. I hope it is, anyway."

"Good idea," she said approvingly. "Which one?"

"I think you should approach the Le Chappe Cancer Society and the Animal Rights Association. They both do work all over the EU and in England specifically. It seems possible."

"Smart, Caroline." Her voice was sharp but approving. "If they don't need pro bono hours, though, I'll have to approach someone else."

"The initiative will announce the groups on January first," I told her. "It'll be in a press release."

"That's helpful," she said quickly, and then she softened. "We're going to handle this, okay? Don't be scared."

"I'm not scared for me. I can't say that enough. Thank you," I whispered. "Merry Christmas, Zola."

"I understand. Merry Christmas, Caroline."

I hung up, turned off the phone, and flushed the toilet, heart pounding as I unlocked the door, terrified Roland would be waiting there—

But no. In the car, behind the wheel, inscrutable as always.

"You okay?" Finn asked as I climbed into the backseat.

"Better now." I smiled. And off we went.

It was the nicest Christmas we ever had.

❖   ❖   ❖

The January kickoff meetings. Binders and coffee and pitches. I pored over the paperwork while everyone talked. The development people loved it—they worked hard on their materials, they wanted them to be read.

One meeting after the next. Ten went by—and there was nothing, no clues. The Cancer Society and the Animal Rights Association had the same list of supporters as last year.

And then I saw it: In their glossy folio, inside the section listing their supporters, the EU Breast Cancer Research Foundation thanked Clarence Cast Mbatha for their generous commitment of pro bono service.

43

CONTACT CAME AT the EUBCRF benefit in the form of a slender thirtysomething man wearing a cherry-toned summer suit and matching bow tie. "Your Serene Highness," the man said in a British accent, bowing. "It's so nice to finally meet you."

"A pleasure," I agreed, as I always did, looking past him.

"I wonder if I might have a few minutes of your time," he said. "I have six brothers, and two of them have both undergone treatment for breast cancer. It's rare in men, but we have the gene. They've had a hard time talking about it. It would cheer them up tremendously if you might be able to offer a kind word." He held up his phone.

"Six brothers?" I exclaimed. "Your poor mother."

"And I'm the only clever one." He winked. "I'm Nicholas."

Clever Nick.

Next to me, with her clipboard, Atena harrumphed. I put my hand on her shoulder. "I'll be quick." Clever Nick held up the phone as if trying to find reception. I followed him out onto the terrace, where the wind whistled, and he handed me the phone. I spoke cheerily into a dead line, waving to Atena as I mouthed a greeting, then faced the sea, phone still at my ear. Nick spoke low enough to reach me and no one else. "Zola did want me to emphasize that it's very unlikely you could gain custody."

"I realize that."

"It's not advisable to move forward until there's some clarity about your financial situation."

"He's mortgaged up to the hilt. It's precarious. He won't want it to be disrupted. I think that's to our advantage."

"How long will that last?"

"This year, maybe. Watch the real estate. He said the growth of fall 2007 is the right range. We need to act before that happens."

He cleared his throat. "Does the paperwork you mentioned cover this?"

"It looks like money laundering. You'll need to confirm it."

"I suggest you document any suspected financial improprieties. Soft spots," he advised. "Make a history. Take contemporaneous notes."

"That may be hard," I said, grinning into the phone, twisting to see Atena still watching us intently.

"Find a way."

"Fine, fine. Let me walk you out." I handed him back the phone, smiled warmly, and put my arm through his, waving back to Atena, holding up the "one-minute finger." We made our way to a table covered in large white paper gift bags, filled with goodies from local sponsors. Two hours earlier, holding a leather folio with a checklist, pretending to enthusiastically inspect the chocolates and baked goods, I'd asked the ensign if . . . *oh dear . . . were we missing corsages?* "I don't believe so," she said.

"I could be wrong," I replied conspiratorially, "but—it's probably worth asking Schätze, no?"

The ensign vanished.

I slid a fat envelope of my stolen paperwork into one of the bags.

By the time the ensign returned, plain relief on her face, I'd already hidden the bag beneath the tablecloth. "Corsages are next week," she reported.

Now, as I walked Nick out, I reached beneath the table, where the extra boxes of chocolates were stored, and came up with three, placing them into a bundle of bags, pressing them on Nick and smiling. He accepted the swag gratefully, looking appropriately starstruck, and left.

"That was kind of you," Atena whispered.

"A family of men, two of them with breast cancer but ashamed to talk about it? I *had* to encourage them. Men complain more in a month than most women do in a lifetime," I said, allowing my satisfaction to show. "That man is about to raise more money than he ever intended."

Atena radiated with her moonlight. "Nicely done. Now, speed up so we can go shopping."

I smiled and did as I was told.

◆ ◆ ◆

I was fearful, for a while, after that. Had someone heard our conversation? Had someone noticed that I pretended to be on a phone, but no call came over the airwaves? Had Clever Nick been stopped on his way out? The paranoia was a hard wood, growing knotty bumps that threatened to snag and leave a mark. Jane could see them, I think. One afternoon I was in a tizzy of obsession, convinced the service would plow through the door, that Nick hadn't made it, that nothing would change. Jane meandered over to the sofa, reached for me—and touched the shoulder of a mother who was no longer there. I heard the question forming in her throat, *Where is Maman?* It was so startling the paranoia split off of its own accord, and I brought her mother back.

It was hard to manage, but not impossible. I kept on turning, turning, turning myself on the lathe, paring back the knots, and no one was the wiser. I cut it a little close, though, sometimes, and started to fade, smiles coming too late, laugh too loud, unreal. After a month, Finn reached for my hand at dinner and asked how I was feeling. "I'm a bit tired," I confessed. "It's been a busy summer."

"Maybe you ought to take Henri and Jeanne to the Villetta," he mused. "Preventative."

That weekend, I packed our bags and left.

❖   ❖   ❖

There was a small village not too far from the house, and I made a habit of walking there to buy sweets for the children. Henry was six, Jane eight, so I towed them in a wagon. The service followed, of course, doing what they could—scanning businesses before we entered, watching shopkeepers and residents—but it was not Lucomo, and it was not the house. They didn't own the cell phone towers there. They couldn't read the texts sent on my old Nokia phone as I stood behind stacks of magazines, hidden in the aisles of the newsstand. *What does the elephant hear,* I texted Zola.

It's dirty laundry, she replied. *Bond?*

Writing now. Will hide it in the village somewhere

When

Will message u

The bell rang at the newsstand door. I turned off the phone, slid it into my pocket, bought Jane a word search book, and towed my children back home.

❖   ❖   ❖

At night, when the children are sleeping, I sit down and write. I keep the television on downstairs so that it looks like I'm watching movies.

It's been interesting, writing. What a strange practice. I've written more words in the past four weeks than in all my life put together. I don't know if I'll ever get another chance like this—to be alone, here, with my thoughts. I've tried to be an honest accountant, of what I did, and why I did it. I hope that I told the truth. It's very hard to keep it in order. I don't have a linear mind. I want to excuse myself, to explain. I'm constantly fighting the urge to make myself look better than I am, the urge to make myself a victim.

❖ ❖ ❖

Eventually Finn texted me on the phone he paid for. It was time for me to come home. He said I should leave in the morning.

It was six P.M. We could still get dinner in the village, at La Cassella. I bundled the children into their wagon and hauled them into town. We ordered pasta with red sauce and with my help they smeared it everywhere; Jane got it all over her dress, giggling hysterically. We took over the restroom. When Henry and Jane were in their stalls, I slid a stack of legal pads, everything I'd written, behind the changing table.

La Casella restaurant behind the changing table, I typed to Zola.

We will pick up. I'll come to Lucomo but not sure when, she replied. *It'll be sudden.*

Ok, I sent back. But it didn't go through. The phone beeped loudly. It was out of minutes. One phone call and a handful of texts to the UK; twenty euro didn't buy what it used to.

"What's that?" Jane asked. "That was a funny noise."

The phone beeped again. "I don't know. I think someone left their phone in here." I started frantically deleting the texts, one by one.

"We should return it."

"Yes we should," I agreed. I managed to power it off before she got her hands on it.

"That's a *funny* phone," she said.

"It's not funny, it's inexpensive," I said, trying to quiet her.

"Can *I* return it?"

"Of course," I agreed, not wanting the Jane tantrum, not now, not over this.

She made a big show of handing it to the restaurant owner when we left. He looked at it curiously but was sweet and grateful, before placing it in a cardboard box marked *Lost and Found*.

We walked back to the Villetta. It was done. I'd spent all my chances.

In the morning I went back to Lucomo, swallowed alive like an oyster.

44

I WAITED. I waited through the summer. The fall. Through Christmas. Then New Year. Nothing happened.

In April there was something to do with animal welfare. I'd sweated through the morning, the hours spent with the goal of taking two millimeters off my biceps. I stared at the razor blade in the shower—then used it to cut those four stubborn hairs on my knee, the ones that wouldn't submit to the laser. I put on a dress. I clipped a leather lead onto Big Girl Dog's collar, to highlight my animal-loving side; filled my pocket with bacon; and went to the Gloria Apartment.

Schätze and Atena sat on one side of the conference table. They both looked grimmer than usual; I wondered if it was the sight of Big Girl, who, admittedly, had terrible gas and drool thicker than shoelaces. The animal rights people had their backs to me, didn't rise. I don't think they could tell I was in the room. It wasn't until I got to the head of the table and faced them that we made eye contact.

It wasn't a development officer. It was Zola. Clever Nick sat to her right.

I almost laughed. Zola and Nick each let out a tiny smile. "Schätze," I said confidently, "Atena, I'd like to introduce my attorney, Zola

Mbatha, of Clarence Cast Mbatha, and her associate Nicholas Collins."

"I see," Schätze said stiffly. "So you are not from the Elephant Preservation Committee."

Atena coughed uncomfortably. "Perhaps I ought to come back later."

"I think that's probably appropriate," I told her.

Atena swept her long black hair behind one shoulder, fitted her gloves, took Big Girl's leash, and led her out without another word. She was so very good at being obedient, Atena. I could have learned a lot from her.

Zola looked so different from how I remembered. I knew logically that it was muscular—our expressions build us from the inside out—but nevertheless it was peculiar. The girl whom I ran alongside, forty miles a week for six years—she'd logged another twelve thousand miles in a new life. I noticed the age on her hands, the new weight behind her eyes. She couldn't help scrutinizing me, either. I touched my left cheek, the dimpled shadow of my shatter; I was different, too.

I pulled out the chair to her left, at the head of the table. We wore nearly matching pointed-toe pumps. I had a sudden vision of the sneakers she wore in the Comrades, a beaten-up pair of trail runners with those goddamn green laces. I tapped the toes of my pumps together and glanced at her with the memory. Zola shook her head ever so slightly; I wasn't to speak. I replied with a nod and took my seat. Then it went off.

❖   ❖   ❖

"I don't think you want to do this," Schätze said calmly.

"We're asking for shared custody and a settlement of one hundred million," Zola declared.

"That's a lot."

"Euro, not pounds, of which she's laundered hundreds of millions for you." Zola slid a stack of documents—half were the ones I'd copied, the others bank records and tax statements that she'd spent the last year digging up—across the table.

"Has she?" Schätze asked, fanning through the paperwork. She adjusted her eyeglasses. "Oh. No." Shaking her head, Schätze let out a little giggle. "Oh. No. Not at all." She stood. "The answer is no. It's time for you to leave."

Zola refused to budge. "You can keep those, of course. We have other copies."

Schätze sat back down, sipped from her coffee cup, and calculated something. I wasn't sure what she was doing until she reached for the first stack of paperwork and shuffled it in her hand. "It's not laundry," she finally said, almost apologetically. "It's legitimate accounting."

"Of what?" I asked. Zola narrowed her eyes, urging me to shut up, but I was so taken aback by Schätze's claim that I couldn't stop myself. "I don't make any money."

"No, but you have expenses." Schätze shrugged. "Your hair, your teeth. Dr. Sun, of course. The MRI machine was *very* expensive. Your clothes, your security. It was advantageous with regards to our tax laws to create independent liabilities for each case of requirement. These companies are your commissions of the services. We've paid these bills on your behalf, but . . . *you* have taken ownership of them. If you wish to be divested of your responsibility in these matters, then I'm afraid we will be entitled to repayment."

Zola sat up straighter as Clever Nick fell back in his chair. They were shocked.

I didn't understand.

"You've been . . . billing her," Zola said, astonished.

I choked on my water. I'd spent hundreds, no, thousands of hours, been sick to my stomach *for years* trying to get copies of these records out of here. And they were . . . *bills*? They'd forced me to spend over a decade getting my hair done and smiling, and now I was supposed *to pay for it*?

"Yes, exactly," Schätze agreed. "It's quite substantial, as you have discovered. Some charges, like Adam, your guard, were *very* high. He was a specialist."

They billed me for Adam. I wanted to climb across the table and smack Schätze's head down into it. *This was all for nothing? They've actually* indebted *me to this place?*

Zola, the heavyweight world champion of conference table pugilism, digested the fact and rapidly turned it to her advantage. "It is unequivocal that Caroline's labor made a significant contribution to the economic growth of this country. It would certainly be possible to have an actuary calculate the cost benefit against this set of charges. We'd come out ahead."

"Caroline's departure would cause an equal amount of strain." Schätze was no amateur, either. "She is an attraction. A national landmark."

"That's a precise observation, Ms. Eselin," Zola complimented her. "As a national figure, Caroline is passionate about her adopted country. Naturally she is also willing and very able to advocate for the eradication of corruption within its borders." This time, Zola let her pen rest, just for a moment, against her second stack of papers.

"Is she?" Schätze squinted at me curiously. *Was I still Caroline the Fool?* "Challenging corruption in a security state would be unusual for a devoted mother like Caroline. For anyone with two minor children in such a vulnerable position."

"She's not committed to it. Not yet." Zola's neat backhand. "Confidentiality and nondisparagement in perpetuity are a given for any settlement, which we would accept in the form of an irrevocable trust with Henry and Jane as the sole testamentary beneficiaries."

"Hmm." Schätze pushed her glasses up. "That's not exactly what I meant."

"I know what you meant," I snapped. Zola nudged me under the table, but on this subject I couldn't be managed. "You won't hurt them. You need them."

"I need them *to exist*. I don't need them to be happy or well-adjusted. Your husband is a perfect example," she said, her tone cutting, "of how much is just enough to build a king."

It was a thuggish miscalculation. "Henry and Jane have already had more love than Finn had in his whole life," I told her. "They can live on it for a long time." Zola, unbowed, put her hand on my arm to silence me. I gently pulled away. "You have no idea what the future holds," I promised Schätze. "Everything. Changes. It's inevitable. Something will change this place. It could be me. It could be one of them. It could even be you, Schätze. You never know. You could be honorable, too."

There was a long silence as the Giant of Flensburg refused to take her eyes off me—and I refused to take mine off hers. I stared Schätze down, unblinking, that poison ugliness coming to the fore, twisting me into its malice, until finally she looked away. I don't think she was afraid of me; I don't know what made her back off, I didn't know if it was shame or what, but whatever it was, it was a weakness, and Zola saw it, too. She slid the second stack of paper across the table. "These are records of a private loan made fifty years ago," Zola told her. "The repayment on this loan has come from hundreds of companies, many of which are owned by Ferdinand Fieschi. But not *all* of them. Some returns have come directly from entities whose majority shareholders can easily be nominated for investigation by Interpol for the trafficking of human beings."

"That won't affect us," Schätze responded overconfidently.

"Maybe not in the long term. But in the short term, it would likely— and we would *ensure this likelihood*—trigger an oversight investigation from the European Commission. Your bond rating *will* be downgraded, automatically; your national bank will have its assets placed in escrow. I'm certain this particular set of creditors could find a benefit in that circumstance."

We waited several minutes while Schätze examined the papers. At last she spoke: "It's certainly possible," she admitted. Then she switched her focus to me. "Caroline, where do you intend to go?"

"The country house is the most practical solution I've come up with. The children know it; the security is in place. I don't mind staying there until they're of age," I promised. "As long as I don't have to come back here."

Schätze blew out a long sigh, then placed her fingertip to one of the papers. "I may keep these, yes?" Zola pushed them toward her affirmatively. "I'm not authorized to make any decisions now. We must regroup." Schätze stood; Zola and Nick stood, too. They shook hands. It was so civilized. "Goodbye," Schätze said politely. "Caroline will show you out." She left the paperwork on the table and disappeared.

◆　◆　◆

"You didn't bring up Honor or Edouard. *Or* Lidia. *Or* the journalist."

"I was never going to. I'm sorry we didn't get a chance to prep you. Interpersonal dramas, even murder, aren't . . . of relevance here. They're far more concerned by a credit downgrade. We're very confident that this is the right approach." She was still standing politely at the table and I realized that I was waiting for her to shed this tactical demeanor, to smile or hug me—to be my friend. But she didn't.

"You're saving my life," I entreated.

"I hope . . ." Zola's voice wavered. "You *do* something with it this time around." She reached for her briefcase, closing the locks with a practiced motion.

My jaw dropped. That hurt.

Clever Nick exhaled awkwardly. "I'll go and get the car," he said. I pointed to the door. He turned to leave—but not before I threw my arms around him. He looked mortified to be the recipient of such a display, but nevertheless I squeezed him like he was my son.

Once he was out the door, Zola adjusted her cuffs and slid on her jacket. She wouldn't look at me.

"That can't be everything you wanted to say," I said pointedly.

"It's not important." Zola never did like being pushed.

"Say it," I begged. "I've known you for twenty-five years. Please say it."

"I told you so," she said, without looking at me.

"You did. That's not what you want to say."

"I'm—" She stared at the ceiling, teeming with its bejeweled flowers and birds, and scoffed. "They'll buy you off and nothing will change."

"You negotiated that."

"I'm well aware of the strategy." She sounded so tired. "Silent ex-wife."

"You'll get twenty percent. That's twenty million euro. Can't you turn that into something good?"

"That's the thing," Zola said, blowing out a lungful of anger. She put one hand on the wall, then stepped out of her high heels. "I'm sick of being uncomfortable all the time," she said, bending one foot over her knee and rubbing the callus. "Aren't you . . . just . . . *sick* of it?"

"Of course I am." I took off my shoes, too, mirroring her body language, and then we were barefoot teenagers again.

"It's all we ever do. It's laundry," she started, and then she couldn't stop. "It's what you did when you set that record—you legitimized South Africa. It's what I did when I left my home to live in London, the seat of colonial power; by *default* I conceded the necessity of that power. Because I didn't want to live in the place . . ." Zola held back her memories with a swallow. She was unwilling to allow them, even now, to take up space in her life. "I know why you wanted to live in a palace. But every time we tell ourselves that it's better to make change from the inside instead of tearing down the building . . . it feels like such a profound failure of imagination."

"I can't lose my children," I told her. "I can't burn down the house while they're still in it."

"I know that!" she said, throwing up her hands. "I know."

"It's disappointing," I said, and I meant it. "I know it is tremendously disappointing." As I put my left hand over my heart, the sunset-colored diamond on my finger cast a shower of tangerine sparks over the floor.

Zola motioned to it. "*That.* That's a perfect example. The person who dug it out of the ground wasn't free. When you put it on, you weren't free anymore, either." She bowed her head. "It never ends."

I held my hand out to the light. "I thought it was a prize."

"That's the thing that gets me. When we were young, we worked so hard to win. We thought prizes would make us safe. I could never have predicted that we'd be standing here, having this conversation."

"See? You don't know what's going to happen in the future, either."

"Hmph," she snorted. Her phone started to buzz. She silenced it.

"Is Schätze's last name really Eselin?" I asked.

"No." Zola grinned. "*Eselin* is German for donkey." That brilliant, toothy smile was the only thing about Zola that was exactly the same. Her phone resumed buzzing, in a slightly more hostile pattern. "I'm sorry. I have to go. On that note, I'm leaving this place barefoot."

"I'll walk you out."

We crossed the hallways of cold stones in the same companionable silence that had soundtracked all those miles. In the fourth courtyard, her car was running; Clever Nick was already behind the wheel. I realized as I saw him that I'd been afraid they wouldn't be allowed to leave. "Thank you, Zola."

"You're welcome, Caroline. It was good to see you." She put out her hand. I hugged her instead, and she didn't notice when I slipped my sunset-colored ring into the pocket of her jacket. I knew she didn't want it. But it was the only asset I had.

I watched her drive away, and then I returned to the Gloria Apartment. That's where I am now, finishing up these pages. Marcella promised to mail them for me. I think I can trust her to do as I ask. You see, other people have been writing my history this whole time. Everybody speaks for me. I want to speak for myself.

The only other thing I have to do is go upstairs and tell Finn that we're getting a divorce.

CAROLINE FIESCHI, PRINCESSE OF LUCOMO, DEAD AT 35

Giovanni Domi, AP
May 14, 2015

Caroline Harriet Muller Fieschi, Princesse of Lucomo, died this afternoon in a tragic accident. Talon medical staff confirmed that she had a stroke while snorkeling, and that it was not immediately clear to the gathered party, which included her husband and several courtiers, that anything was wrong. According to her physician, she had experienced several small strokes throughout the previous decade and was suffering from a variety of cognitive challenges. She was pronounced dead at the scene. She is survived by husband Ferdinand, Crown Prince of Lucomo, 44; daughter Jeanne, 8; and son Henri-Louis, 7. A complete obituary is forthcoming.

MONUMENT TO CAROLINE FIESCHI UNVEILED

Giovanni Domi, AP
May 14, 2016

One year after the tragic death of Caroline Harriet Muller Fieschi, Princesse of Lucomo, her daughter, Jeanne, unveiled a marble Greek Revival sculpture of Caroline, with winged sandals signifying her achievement as the onetime world record holder for the women's marathon. The sculpture is at the center of a brand-new park on the eastern edge of Lucomo, in the town of Lo Scopo, where it was said she enjoyed sitting peacefully and reading. The Caroline Fieschi Foundation, an environmental initiative endowed in her honor, will open its doors there next year with the sole purpose of reducing harm to the ecosystems of the Mediterranean.

Epilogue

February 2, 2022

Dear Jane and Henry,

I believe most of this was written in the Villetta in October of 2014. I asked for information on the bond and this is what I got in return. At the time I remember thinking it was as though she'd never expressed herself before. The last few pages arrived in the mail several weeks after my visit to Lucomo, along with the instruction that I was to put the entire document into this safety deposit box, and that after Jane's fifteenth birthday, the age of majority in Lucomo, I was to arrange for its publication. I have done so, as evidenced by the galley copy included herein, and the advance has been deposited to a trust in your names; all additional monies will remit to that account, less UK tax and a 15 percent fee to my firm, assigned in exchange for my time. Your mother also passed on a very valuable diamond ring to me; I believe she intended it to function as payment in the event that no other resources were available. However, the fees from your publication monies have proved sufficient, and as such, I have donated it to the Special Olympics, who will be putting it up for auction shortly.

I'm sure you would have preferred to read this sooner. I hope you can understand that by the time I received the final pages, she was already dead. I've not been able to bring myself to betray her wishes.

I've tried to put it in order as best I could. During the time I knew her well, 1990–2000, your mother had a very good memory. In my view there is no indication that her cognitive abilities degraded over the following fifteen years, despite what has been claimed publicly. I can attest that our conversations in 2003, 2014, and 2015 were faithfully transcribed. As to the accuracy of the rest, I would urge you to give her the benefit of the doubt and conduct yourselves accordingly.

I hope it helps you to know her. If you would care to be placed in touch with your half siblings, it is likely I would be able to arrange that, but I will not reach out without your express instruction. Please do let me know if there is anything else you might need; Clarence Cast Mbatha has effectively negotiated many Fortune 50 mergers and acquisitions—and, perhaps more important, a wide variety of divestitures. Should either of you wish to be extricated from your current circumstances and responsibilities, we as a firm feel strongly that we would represent you faithfully and with great benefit. And personally, I would be delighted to help you take it all apart.

    Sincerely
    Zola Mbatha

Zola Mbatha, Solicitor
Partner, Mergers and Acquisitions
Clarence Cast Mbatha
4 Old Broad Street, Suite 400
London EC2N
England

Author's Note

For many little girls, our first imaginative prompt is a baby doll. Plastic clones laid next to us in the crib are both companion and instruction: Nurture this. We obey without hesitation; carry our dolls around, tuck them into their tiny beds, acting like mothers before we can even walk.

Next come the dollhouses, miniature scenes of domestic life we learn to manage like a cartoon wife. Some girls lord over plastic kitchens; others are armed with tiny brooms.

All the while, streaming through the ether, on televisions and in picture books, a series of neutered corporate fairy tales teach us that a woman's greatest goal in life is to be chosen by the most important and eligible man in the land. Fantasies of castles and ribbons and gold and silver—monsters and heroes and beautiful dresses—hatch tiara-shaped worms in our brains. It is no wonder that at some point we have all playacted life as a princess; it is no wonder that we watch real-life princesses with a mixture of envy, respect, and not a little bit of schadenfreude.

For real-life princesses seem, upon examination, extremely miserable. Charlene Wittstock allegedly made at least two failed escape attempts before her wedding to Prince Albert of Monaco, after which it was widely reported in the press that his entourage confiscated her passport. (Wittstock spent the lavish ceremony sobbing openly.) Kate Middleton was foisted onto the steps of St. Mary's Hospital seven hours after giving birth, clad in a blue dress with white polka dots, likely still bleeding into a hospital-issue diaper while she smiled for the cameras. Diana Spencer stuck her fingers down her throat at every chance, a perversely rational response to the stiff-upper-lip culture that required a nineteen-year-old girl to swallow the whole world's slings and arrows and smile as they burned in her throat. Princesses walk two steps behind their husbands; they do not eat until their husbands eat; they do not express opinions of their own choosing. They are as limited in expression as the plastic baby dolls that littered their childhood playrooms. Megxit, in retrospect, was inevitable: A college-educated millennial American, descended from enslaved ancestors, could not, in the end, find happiness as a prop of the largest colonial empire in history. Or, perhaps more obviously, an actor best known for playing an attorney was unlikely to feel fulfilled in the balconied purgatory of what is essentially the world's longest commercial for expensive hats.

But not obvious, of course, to Meghan Markle—at least not before she walked down the aisle. Monarchies are sales pitches for a political tale as old as time: that women can feel secure if, and only if, we're able to make ourselves valuable to a valuable man. The narrative alternative—some less-strategic Cinderella married to her trash can as she hags her way toward death—is not exactly the stuff of Halloween costumes. The prevailing global view of motherhood—that mothers are best protected by the family, and the family, in turn, is best protected by the state—gives most women, in most countries, very little in terms of direct support. For a real-life woman sitting across from a prince, the princess story skips the middleman and marries you directly to the state itself. It's logical. It's rational. It's the desire for a better life. And what could be more human than that?

There will always be princesses.

Yet—what must it take to spend each day two steps behind your partner, always in shadow? What must it take from you to discard yourself—modernity, even—in exchange for the illusion of safety?

In the case of this book's narrator, Caroline Muller, it takes everything. I've been possessed by Caroline, and by the desire to find genuine beauty in the life of a princess—something that gets to the utter tragedy of *believing* in any of it, at all.

Acknowledgments

Writing this book was not a brief or uncomplicated process, and I'm indebted to the following people for their aid in the development of this manuscript over the past four years:

My editor, Lindsey Rose, for your clarity of thought, attention to detail, never-flagging love for this project, patience, consistency, and focus; you're one of a kind. My agent, Victoria Sanders, and her right-hand woman, Bernadette Baker-Baughman, for their belief in this book. Julia Langbein—I am so grateful for the many hours you gave to reading early drafts. At Dutton, special thanks to Stephanie Kelly, Christine Ball, Stephanie Cooper, Amanda Walker, and John Parsley for their care and advice.

To the members of the epic Principalities road trip of 2018: Jane Orvis in France, Italy, Monaco, San Marino, and our side quest to Lisbon—the look on your face in that castle in Tuscany as I read those first pages kept me going this whole time—thank you for believing in me. Julia Clark for breaking away from Tunisia and accompanying me to Andorra, the happy accident of Llívia, and the dozen castles I insisted we hit up in Spain, sorry I am so stubborn, sorry about that horrible restaurant. Zan and Djelal for indulging further castle-mania in Lisbon and Sintra.

Thanks to Civitella Ranieri for hosting us in February 2020, and Diego and Ilaria for their warmth and hospitality.

To my extended Brussels family: Ben and Diana for hosting me in Les Issambres in 2018 and in 2020. David and Muffy for giving me a home away from home during the early days of the pandemic. Julia P. for connecting me with an insider.

To my mom and dad, who we were lucky enough to spend quarantine with; and my mom especially, for your huge gasp at the end.

To Ian—I love you and the life we build.

The Force of Such Beauty

⟹ ◆ ⟸

BARBARA BOURLAND

———

Discussion Questions

———

DUTTON

Discussion Questions

Note: These discussion questions contain spoilers! We suggest you finish the book before you read through them.

1. Caroline's body undergoes major transformations, from elite athlete to badly injured to recovering to pregnancy and postpartum. Her facial reconstruction turns her into a woman so beautiful it's "both terrifying and edifying." When do you think she feels most at home in her body? When does she feel most powerful? How does her self-perception mirror or refute society's expectations of women?

2. Caroline also endures many physical stressors and therapies. Some, like physical therapy to manage her pain, she welcomes. Others, like advanced fertility treatment and uncomfortable clothing, she resists. How does Caroline's sense of agency influence her feelings about these restrictions and interventions?

3. Much of Caroline's identity at the beginning of the novel rests on being "the fastest woman on earth." When her record is broken, her spirit also takes a huge blow—even though, at that point, she is now one of the wealthiest, most well-known women on earth. How can people move forward when they lose part of their selfhood?

4. When Caroline first meets Finn, she insists running is "not about being better than other people," but, later, her life as a princess elevates her to a higher social position than nearly everyone in Lucomo. When Caroline becomes royalty, which ideals does she abandon and which remain steadfast?

5. When reflecting on her time in Lisbon, Caroline notes, "It may seem small and inconsequential . . . but now I realize it was the only time in my life that ever truly belonged to me. Even though, or precisely because, I wasn't anyone important." Do you see any roads not taken for Caroline to create a different life for herself?

6. Do you believe Finn loves Caroline, or is she merely a pawn in his game? Could both be true?

7. Caroline always has a circle of friends—fellow runners, pals in Lisbon, ladies-in-waiting in Lucomo—but she is close to very few people. Is there anyone you think she should have trusted more? Which friends disappointed her and how?

8. Caroline feels responsible for failing to educate herself on the Lugesque economy and the nature of Finn's dealings, and therefore remaining in the dark about them for so long. Do you agree with her assessment or do you see her as a victim?

9. How is the extreme opulence of Lucomo's royalty contrasted with the general public's much more difficult financial situations, especially as the story inches closer and closer to the financial crash of 2008? Were you, like Caroline, blinded by the "force of such beauty" that the royal family constantly displays, or did you see some of the darker consequences coming?

10. Near the end of the novel, Caroline muses, "As long as I didn't try to reconcile anything, as long as I accepted that my husband was a bad person, my children were going to grow up to be bad people, and I was the crown jewel for doing my part for the legitimacy of other bad people . . . it was fine and dandy." Do you have hope for Jane/Jeanne and Henry/Henri in the aftermath of the story, or

are they doomed to continue the practices of the Lugesque monarchy?

11. Does this story make you reconsider the "happily ever after" princess fairy tale that so many young girls are told? Do you think any real-life royals go through the ordeals and loss of autonomy that Caro experienced?